Also by L. R. Lam and Elizabeth May
available from DAW Books

SEVEN DEVILS
SEVEN MERCIES

SEVEN MERCIES

L. R. LAM
AND
ELIZABETH MAY

DAW BOOKS
New York

Cover design by Jeanette Tran and Katie Anderson.

Cover illustration by Kirbi Fagan.

Edited by Leah Spann and Betsy Wollheim.

DAW Book Collectors No. 1902.

DAW Books
An imprint of Astra Publishing House
dawbooks.com
DAW Books and its logo are registered trademarks of Astra Publishing House.

Printed in the United States of America.

Trade Paperback ISBN: 9780756418168
Ebook ISBN: 9780756415839

First Paperback Edition, February 2023

10 9 8 7 6 5 4 3 2 1

TO THOSE WHO BRAVELY FACE
IMPOSSIBLE ODDS.

1.

Present day

I t was harder to steal supplies when the whole fucking galaxy wanted Eris and her crew dead.

And she was really, *really* trying not to murder anyone.

<*Avoid the camp.*> The directive from Kyla came through Eris's Pathos, the minuscule device at the base of her skull that allowed her crew to communicate telepathically.

Their commander was with their primary ship, *Zelus*, still orbiting Victrix's atmosphere. It was easier to do supply runs in their smaller bullet craft without setting off the Empire's detection systems. Eris's absolute shitstain of a brother would be all too happy to know where they were. Every time she heard him referred to as Archon Damocles on the newscasts, she tasted bile on her new, bionic tongue.

The old military outstation was supposed to be in a deserted forest. When the ship's systems had pinged the coordinates, it said the reduced population of the mostly uninhabitable planet had kept the need for military presence small. It was too mountainous, the soil rugged, and rain fell less every year. Their outposts had been relegated to coastal areas as the forests began to dry out and lose resources; Victrix seemed the safest option for a quick supply run to one of the abandoned storehouses.

The ship's computers had lied.

Maybe not *lied*—but the systems hadn't been updated since before the Laguna Massacre. On the eve of a truce meant to end a war, Tholosians and Evolians alike had been slaughtered as a virus engineered by the Tholosian Empire swept through the ceremony. An act of war, if there ever was one. It had been a slaughter—a mass casualty event that killed thousands of revelers there to celebrate a new age of peace.

But, of course, no one blamed the Empire. Damocles' reputation had escaped as unblemished as the new, glittering crown he'd fashioned from his father's old one. The Oracle had done One's job—woven One's programming through citizens' minds to crush any whisper of doubt. Even if some niggling question of Damocles' involvement persisted, the Oracle's tendrils would chip away at that doubt day by day.

No, the responsibility for twenty-three thousand massacred people had fallen squarely on the shoulders of Eris, the other six members of their crew, and the remnants of the Novantae Rebellion. They were fugitives, wanted by Tholosians and Evoli alike. And every military outpost and settlement in bumblefuck dust towns in the veritable asshole of the galaxy was on high alert.

And Eris was—again—really, *really* trying not to kill anyone.

Really.

So, of course, there were bounty hunters camped at the outpost. *Of fucking course.* Bounty hunters and opportunists made it dangerous to stay in any place for too long.

She made a frustrated noise deep in her throat. They were running out of backup supplies fast. She'd wanted this to be simple.

<*The camp is outside the old canteen,*> Eris replied to Kyla, lifting a hand to signal Nyx and Clo.

They crouched next to her in the dense thicket of trees enclosing the old military base, their hovercart concealed under a camouflaged tarp behind them. The women wore dark armor stolen from a prior run. *Good shit*, Nyx had said with a low whistle when they'd found it. Eris's armor didn't quite fit—too big—but it covered the soft bits she didn't want to be scorched by a Mors bullet.

The easy solution would be to retreat. Return to the ship, find provisions elsewhere. But since the location of Novan headquarters was compromised, their small rebellion had been forced to flee and set up camp wherever they could find it: barely habitable planets, deserted outposts, dying moons. Certified shitholes. Worse: two months earlier, a military ambush on one of their makeshift camps had left the already-struggling resistance in tatters. Many were murdered. Others scattered across the galaxy to hide from the Tholosian Empire. They'd lost most of the tech at their base on Nova, and they still needed to buy or steal food, weapons, and medical equipment.

They didn't exactly have the option of picking and choosing where.

Even forgotten outposts like Victrix were risky. All it took was one brainwashed asshole spotting something out of the ordinary and reporting it to the Oracle. The Empire's near-omniscient AI had upgraded its systems over the last few months in its never-ending search for the rebellion's survivors.

<*So, avoid the camp,*> came Kyla's suggestion. <*Seriously, Eris, one would think you'd never done an ITI mission before in your life.*>

Eris heard Clo's low snort, and they shared a look. *Impossible to Infiltrate*: Eris's specialty. "Is that a challenge, do you think?" Eris whispered.

"Cannae tell if she's challenging us or trying to get us all shot," Clo muttered.

"Mm." Over the Pathos, Eris asked, <*Ariadne, can you check the database files and see if there's any other way of getting into the canteen?*>

A pause over the Pathos. The chirpy voice of the sixteen-year-old genius came through their network. <*The old landing pad at the top of the building has a hatch.*> Eris pictured Ariadne sitting at the monitors, tablet in hand, while she hacked the sensors to keep their team from being detected on the ground. Without her, they would have been burned the moment they set foot near the compound.

<*The top of the building?*> Eris didn't bother keeping the annoyance out of her voice. <*Are you kidding me?*>

<*Nope! Oooh, that means you get to rappel inside like a badass spy! You have cables in your toolbelt, don't you? And the folding grappling hook!*>

Nyx snorted.

<*I couldn't have done it in my old prosthetic, but now it should be a breeze,*> said Clo, giving Eris a smug grin and holding out her artificial leg, turning it side to side proudly. <*Want me to go in?*>

<*No. Keep watch while Nyx and I get supplies. If things go to shit, we run. Cato, keep the bullet craft ready.*>

His answer came fast: <*Already done.*>

Cato was their second pilot assigned to *Zelus*. Clo had bristled at the idea of him flying the bullet craft during a quick getaway. Still, Cato started to complain about being relegated to medical duties after spending years as a Tholosian military pilot. In the end, Clo relented, but she'd still banned him from working on *Zelus's* engines.

Clo's grin widened, and she gave a celebratory gesture with her fist. <*Everyone, this means I get to watch and see if Eris falls on her hummock. Want to take bets?*>

<*Do you even have any money?*> Nyx asked.

<*I have two scythes I found on the outpost on Adhara, and laundry duty that I'm looking to avoid,*> Clo replied.

<*Fine. I'll bet a week of laundry duty,*> Nyx countered.

<*Fuck you, Clo,*> Eris said. <*I bet fifty scythes I make it inside without falling on my ass.*>

<*Where the fuck did you get fifty scythes?*> Nyx looked suspicious.

<*Ex-princess.*>

Clo rolled her eyes. <*Fifty says you don't,*> she challenged.

<*Focus, all of you,*> Kyla interjected. <*We're pulling the ship back to outer orbit to lessen the chance of detection. Move fast when you're inside.*>

Eris kept her voice lower than a breath when she spoke to Nyx again. "Get the medical supplies while I get the food. We'll meet back here. Clo, stay down. Don't move, but cover us."

"Sure thing, former potential sovereign," Clo said with a wry grin, hefting her Mors.

Nyx and Eris split, both women edging their way through the thicket of trees. The hovercart, linked to the tracking device in Eris's jumpsuit, followed her silently through the woods, its engine little more than a soft hum.

Eris moved swiftly, her footsteps silent in the crush of damp leaves, as she kept an eye on the camp of bounty hunters. It was early morning in Victrix's northeast hemisphere, near the Borean forests where they'd landed. The sun had barely peeked over the horizon, the sky just blushing orange to chase away the dark. The camp was quiet. The few hunters that were awake already had a fire going—a helpful little target that had tipped them off to the camp's presence when they landed in the first place.

Smart, most bounty hunters were not. Many were retired military, responsible for capturing rebels and readying them for prison transport for a fee. So, when Damocles—Eris would sooner cut her tongue out again than call him *Archon*—had declared a bounty on Novan rebels, many saw it as a chance to rise above their station. The take on a rebel's head was enough to make retirement a lot comfier than with a mere soldier's pension. And one of the Seven Devils? That score would set someone up for life. They'd probably get a commendation and some ugly gold medal they'd brag about for years.

Eris found a collapsed patch of the gate and sent the hovercart through. She followed, entering the compound nearest to the canteen. She sprinted to the wall of the building and pressed her back against it, listening hard. Birds in the trees, a slight rustling in the underbrush. An enemy or something else? She paused, uncertain. Should she double back and check?

Not now, she told herself. *Get it the fuck together.*

Ever since Laguna, doubt could make her go cold. Freeze her solid. So far, she had been lucky. Her pauses hadn't gotten anyone killed.

So far.

Focus and climb—the self-directive came in her father's baritone. Haunting or taunting her? She was never sure.

Eris tried not to think about how often she recalled her father's specialized training, the painful attention he paid to her as his most likely heir. Or that the Archon was yet another soul she'd sacrificed to the God of Death. He'd asked her for mercy even as his dimming ochroid eyes had shone with disappointment and disdain.

And she'd granted it.

<*Eris?*> Clo's voice was a welcome distraction. <*I can see you through the scope. You swell?*>

<*Yeah.*> Eris gave her head a shake. After a few taps on her mech cuff, she sent the hovercart up to the roof. <*Fine.*>

With an exhale, Eris found her first handhold in the brick and began to climb. That was easier, a task that depended entirely on muscle memory and her body's strength. Eris benefited from being bred for combat, with nanites from birth that improved her physical stamina. Being genetically engineered into the Empire's cohort of royal children had a few advantages.

As she pulled herself up onto the roof, Clo's low voice came over the Pathos: <*Ugh, I might have to wash Nyx's smelly undershirts because of you, you marshhole.*>

Eris gave a small smile as she kneeled beside the hatch. When Ariadne confirmed that the alarm was disabled, Eris set to work on the old security lock. After successfully conquering the Iona Galaxy, the Tholosians had abandoned most military bases; maintaining the grounds became a waste of energy, time, and resources. Some buildings were used for overflow storage, but they were protected and surveilled with electronics hundreds of years old that cracked like eggshells under current tech. There might be nothing inside but cobwebs and dust—but with any luck, they'd find something worth taking back to the ships. With a swift tug of the rusted hatch door, Eris sent the hovercart into the canteen and used her grappling hook to rappel down after it.

The canteen was practically ancient. Eris only identified some cooking appliances from her history books; others were as old and outdated as the defense systems. She thanked the gods that the bounty hunters, at least, could still rely on the Empire to look after their nutritional needs. Their programming wouldn't allow them to steal food from the Empire, even old military compounds. The rebels would have a hell of a lot less to eat if that weren't the case.

Eris seized whatever she could and tossed the items into the hovercart. Earlier Tholosians had modeled most supplies at those old bases on emergency rations from ancient generation ships; they could keep food fresh for hundreds of years. The food was bland as dirt, but it was better than starving.

<*I hate to interrupt,*> Clo said, <*but there's activity in that camp of bounty hunters.*>

Eris swept another armful of food containers into the hovercart. <*Be more specific.*>

<*They're starting to fan out. I think something's tipped them off.*>

Ariadne's distracted voice came through. <*The Oracle might have sensed abnormalities from the bullet craft landing. Should I cause a distraction?*> She paused. <*Oh, and did you find more proto bars?*>

Eris disregarded that, having grown used to her friend's meandering trains of thought. <*Get* Zelus *ready to run. Change of plans. Clo, meet Nyx by the old medical building. I'll be two minutes. Cato, the supplies are heading your way.*>

<*Ready over here.*>

She shut the hovercart, then sent it speeding up to the roof and out to Cato's waiting bullet craft. She grabbed a bottle of vodka and pulled out the stopper with her teeth. With a thought spared for wasting a decent jug of spirits on a distraction, she stuffed a dusty, stained kitchen towel down the neck of the container and used the old cooking unit to set it on fire. Low-tech, sure, but Eris had none of Ariadne's fancy gadgets to spare. She tossed the bottle down the hall outside the canteen before hooking herself back up to the rappel line.

Hurry, hurry, hurry, she thought as she reeled back up to the roof and freed herself.

She spent precious seconds dithering at the roof, eyeing the distance to the bushes on the ground. There was no help for it; she was going to have to jump.

With a swear and a prayer, she leaped from the roof the moment before her makeshift bomb exploded.

Boom.

She landed hard in the bushes, rolling to the ground with a soft grunt. The branches had slashed through her jumpsuit sleeve, but she ignored it. Her father's voice pulsed through her skull, even now: *Pain is a distraction; pain is a weakness.* She ducked back into the brush as bounty hunters rushed toward the source of the commotion.

<*When I mentioned you falling on your arse,*> Clo said, <*I didn't think you'd do it literally.*>

Eris bounced to her feet and dashed across the compound to the medical bay, staying low. She found Clo and Nyx crouched below the retaining wall near a passed-out bounty hunter. Clo's knuckles were bleeding. As one, the women ducked into the forest, moving fast.

Shouts came from somewhere in the distance. Eris heard Morsfire a moment before a sharp sting radiated from under the armor plate of her forearm where she'd already ripped it. Fuck. Just a graze, but it hurt like flames of the Avern.

<Find cover now,> she snapped at Clo and Nyx. *<Straight ahead. That thicket.>*

The women pushed themselves to run faster. Morsfire sprayed around them as they fled for the dense copse of trees. Eris, Clo, and Nyx spread out, each nabbing their own massive trunk to gather their breath.

<How many did you count?> Eris asked Nyx.

<Seven, but I can't be sure.>

<I had eight. They've got a fucking sharpshooter.> She pressed a hand to her wound, hissing. Doubts crept through her thoughts again. She shook the apprehension off; she would get her teammates out of this. She *would*. They'd survived much worse than this. *<Both of you look through the scopes and find the shooters for me. Tell me where to go.>*

Eris set off through the trees. Clo cursed at her through the Pathos and finally ended her ramble with *<And here I thought you were trying something new. Looking at the other side of the swamp, or whatever.>*

Morsfire to her left. Eris dodged behind a tree. *<What if they accidentally die?>* She pressed herself to the thick trunk. *<If I shoot them and they bleed out, it's not my fault, is it?>*

<Your immediate left,> Nyx said.

The first bounty hunter edged past, moving slowly. Eris seized a branch from the ground and swung it hard at his temple. Quick, efficient. She grabbed the man and lowered him to the ground. Granted, a bleed in the brain could end him just as quickly.

She was still really, *really* trying not to kill anyone.

She readied herself for the next bounty hunter.

<It would be your fault,> Clo hissed. *<It would be one hundred percent your fault.>*

<Please,> Nyx interrupted. *<Ninety-percent. Ninety-five at most. Go northeast, count to fifty.>*

Eris did as the soldier instructed, letting the spaces of her breath be her count. The woman hiding behind a tree didn't even see her. Eris grasped her around the neck and got a finger on a pressure point, making sure not to press too hard. She secured the woman's wrists and ankles with a cable tie. She'd wake up feeling like shit in a few minutes but wouldn't be able to chase after them.

Two down. Five to go.

<What's ninety percent?> Ariadne asked through the network.

<If Eris shoots a person and they die,> Clo said impatiently. *<It's one hundred percent her fault. Not ninety. Not ninety-five.>*

<Ninety-eight point six percent!> Ariadne chirped back.

<Are you fluming kidding me? How can you even arrive at that?> Clo sounded indignant. *<Kyla, can you believe this?>*

<I'm not getting involved,> their commander said shortly. *<Eris, I'm getting word on the networks that more ships are heading this way. We need to be gone. You've got approximately two minutes to take out those bounty hunters.>*

<There are five more. If the Oracle starts running One's code in the foreground of their neural network, that fight goes beyond a couple of minutes.> Eris readied her antique blaster. This gun wasn't just a sentimental gift from her dead brother, Xander. It was her weapon of choice. Sure, she was trying not to kill people, but the Mors bullet marks she left behind were messages. She wanted her only living brother to know which ones were hers.

She wanted Damocles to know who stole his supplies, commandeered his ships, and assaulted his soldiers and bounty hunters. She wanted him to regret not killing her when he'd cut out her tongue, drugged her, and made her responsible for the deaths of thousands.

Ariadne had replaced Eris's tongue. It was bionic, silver, and metallic; it served just as well as the one with which she'd been born. But even Ariadne couldn't heal the memory of what Damocles had done to Eris. Tech couldn't fix it. Those memories had marked her.

<Cato?> Eris took a steadying breath. *<Supplies loaded?>*

<Already done,> Cato replied. *<And it's ninety-three percent, taking into account the fact that they're one hundred percent prepared to shoot your ass. Putting a laser bullet in their leg is a kindness.>*

<Good enough for me,> Eris said. *<Nyx?>*

Nyx directed her. Eris struck quickly—one bullet to the next bounty hunter's kneecap, a fist to his jaw. He was out so fast that he didn't even have time to scream.

She darted behind the next. Sneaked an arm around the woman's throat.

It'd be simple to snap her neck. Not to worry whether or not she woke up.

But Eris was tired. She was tired of being the God of Death's Chosen.

Eris cut off the bounty hunter's air and lowered the motionless body to the ground. Four down. Three quick shots from her stun took out the next two—a present from Ariadne that dropped a person unconscious in three seconds flat. Useful for those whose Oracle programming had yet to go into effect, but became next to worthless once adrenaline pumped through their system. Eris once used up all her stuns to take down a single soldier, and they didn't have infinite charges to spare.

<Six down,> Eris told the others. <Clo, Nyx, ready to move on my mark.>

Eris's breath heaved as she sprinted within range of the remaining bounty hunters. Along with the fifty other children who had survived the harsh childhood that came with being born into the royal cohort, Eris had prepared for battle in the brutal training school on Myndalia. She learned from a tender age how to kill with the utmost efficiency— and she had been the best.

After all, she had murdered twenty-one of her brothers.

She ran out from behind a tree and aimed with her blaster. Last two soldiers. One, two shots to the knee. They opened their mouths to scream, but Eris whipped out her stun and got her close-range shots exactly where she wanted them.

All eight bounty hunters down, and not a single one was sent to the Avern. She hadn't given a sacrifice to her patron god in months. But she could still feel Him whispering in a corner of her mind, coaxing in a voice just like her brother's.

One day, she'd have to offer another life.

One day, she'd give another soul.

"But not today," she whispered.

Clo and Nyx came to stand beside her. "Not bad," Clo said, looking impressed.

Eris ignored that and headed in the direction of the bullet craft.

"You owe me fifty scythes," Clo called after her, grinning.

"No, I don't," she threw back.

2.

CLO

Present day

Clo hissed as she ran water over the stinging cuts on her hand, ribbons of red paling to pink down the sink's drain. Her knuckles had caught on a man's teeth.

The Devils were packed into *Zelus*'s med bay, speeding toward another quadrant. Their next destination was sure to be another brief respite before fleeing again. So it fucking went, day after day. Never setting down roots for long.

The fragrant scent of lilies touched Clo before Rhea's hands slid around her waist. The former courtesan's bottle of perfume was nearly empty. Clo would be sad when it was gone.

"Let me see," Rhea said gently, taking Clo's hands to pat them dry with a towel. She made a slight noise. "This will bruise." She pressed a feather-light kiss to Clo's injuries.

"A little pain for cracking a bounty hunter's jaw," Clo said with a grin. "Worth it."

"Clo," Cato called. "Your turn. Rhea, do *not* kiss Clo's open wounds. Fuck's sake, do I have to give everyone another lecture about bacterial and viral transmission?"

Clo scoffed. "I'm not screaming in agony or bleeding from my eyeballs, Cato. A bairn could handle this." She lifted her injured hand and raised two fingers toward him in the rude symbol of the scythes. "See? Full mobility."

Cato had insisted on checking them over since Damocles had used one of the small settlements on Victrix for ichor experiments. The half-life of the activated disease was short outside of a body, but the Devils put up with Cato's poking and prodding. Images of Tholosians and Evoli on Laguna bleeding from noses, mouths, and ears were far too fresh. Clo still saw them every night when she closed her eyes.

Eris rubbed the back of her hand along her split lip, smearing red against her cheek, the minor injury already healing from the nanites in her royal blood. Ariadne was on her tablet, monitoring the movements of bounty hunters on Victrix; it was only a matter of time before they sounded the alarm about the Devils. She gnawed on a proto bar, and Clo's stomach rumbled at the sweet scent. She still ate better than she had during her childhood in the slums, but the last few months had forced the rebels to ration. As a result, she'd fallen back into old habits: saving food for the others, only eating when her belly protested too much or her head started to swim.

"So far, so good," Ariadne announced with her mouth full. "Archon Asshole has no idea where we are."

"A small mercy," Kyla murmured. "But we'll have to stretch these provisions longer than the previous take. The last thing we need is the Oracle calculating the length of time it takes us to run out."

Clo's gut growled again, and she tried to ignore it. She'd have half a nutrient bar for supper later.

"Oookay," Ariadne sang. She tapped a few more times. "And I'm finding us a nice planet or moon to rest on. Somewhere pretty where Archon Asshole won't find us. I want a beach."

Clo was beginning to suspect that Ariadne kept insulting Damocles for no other reason than because she enjoyed it. No one said a thing because Ariadne was sixteen, swearing was still a novelty, and opportunities for petty entertainment were scarce.

Also, Damocles *was* an absolute asshole.

As if summoned, the med bay screens chimed with a melody: an incoming broadcast from the Three Sisters system, with the Empire's primary seat of Tholos in the center. That had been the first planet humans disembarked on thousands of years ago after destroying their old one. Of course, they went right back to destructive habits. That was what humans did: explore, conquer, squander, move on. Their behavior was as constant as the movement of the stars.

"Oh, gods," Eris groaned as the chimes went on and on. "Are you fucking serious? Another one? That's the third this week."

Nyx just shook her head in disgust. "You should have shot him in the dick."

"That wouldn't have stopped him from klaxoning," Eris countered.

"No, but the idea of shooting his nads off pleases me."

The old Archon—Eris's father—had sent these galaxy-wide announcements only when necessary, like when he declared the proposed peace treaty on Laguna. Damocles blared them out whenever he had the slightest silting excuse. Seemed desperate to Clo: an attempt to consolidate power and prove he was a better leader than his father and sister. Damocles delighted in broadcasting his citizens toppling and burning the Discordia icons disseminated across the Iona Galaxy. He put his own visage in their place, depicting a crown heavy on his brow and his chest all puffed out as his cape fluttered in a holographic wind. Clo had seen Damocles' face on every planet they'd scavenged, no matter how small and forgotten. She'd wanted to punch his smug smile.

"My loyal citizens," Damocles intoned, face flickering on the screens of the med labs. He sat on a marble and jeweled dais that glinted in the light. He was dressed all in gold; even his boots and eyepatch were gilded. Clo pictured herself splashing swamp mud all over him. "May the gods watch over us all and continue the might and the glory of the Tholosian Empire."

Clo glowered up at him. "Can we please disconnect these? I hate his fucking face."

"Can't even escape him in the med bay," Cato added.

"We need to know what the enemy is saying," Kyla reminded them. "Now, be quiet."

Damocles' deep, resonant voice continued. "I'm pleased to announce that since Laguna, there have been no new cases of the novel ichor disease elsewhere in the galaxy, amongst either the Tholosians or our new allies, the Evoli. Furthermore, our scientists have been hard at work, and I'm pleased to announce our vaccine rollout to planets in stages, beginning with the Three Sisters and the military. I intend to ensure our freedom from this terrible disease unleashed by the former Princess Discordia and her devilish accomplices."

"Devilish," Nyx mocked, nudging Eris with an elbow, but her face was tight.

Eris, meanwhile, was stone.

"I'll save all loyal citizens from the threat of this deadly disease. But be certain: anyone sowing dissidence or risking the health of the Empire will be dealt with ruthlessly. It's my duty to keep you safe. May the gods smile upon the might of Tholos." He raised his hand in a benediction and inclined his head, his shining eyepatch winking in the light. Applause from the throne room clattered over the speakers, music swelling to its last crescendo.

The videocast cut.

"Damocles is a dickwad," Ariadne sang to the same tune as the recording.

Kyla flicked off the screen, her movements irritated. "No one will even suspect he developed the vaccine so quickly because he engineered it along with the godsdamned plague in the first place." She huffed out a breath. "It's going to work, too. He'll be some divine panacea to all of this, especially after they broadcast the videos from Laguna for months."

There'd been no escaping them. The agonized faces of Tholosians and Evoli dying in the throne room. Their muffled screams. Watching them all die together had helped scratch away some of the deep-rooted fear between both empires.

They had quarantined Laguna for months, and while Clo and her crew had saved most of the inhabitants of the planet, almost everyone in that ballroom had perished. Those who survived had lingering health complications. The new Archon had cemented the truce by giving everyone common enemies: the threat of an unseen illness, and the rebels who had allegedly unleashed it.

Even Clo had to admit it was a damned powerful deception.

"When people are desperate for assurance, they'll sip lies like nectar," Rhea said.

Clo exhaled hard through her nose. Rhea was right. Damocles' popularity was frustratingly high. People might have whispered misgivings when he was the Spare, but now they seemed to love him; they called him gods-blessed, a leader to rival his father. The Oracle's programming was more effective when Damocles told citizens what they wanted to hear.

"At least he's not lying about the lack of ichor cases," Ariadne said, fingers flying across her screen. "Don't see any evidence of a cover-up."

"Any chance you can get access to the vaccine?" Cato asked. "We could see if it's possible to reverse-engineer it for treatment or a cure. Then we could vaccinate ourselves."

Clo frowned. "Why? We know it's not a threat."

Cato's expression shuttered, staring blankly in Nyx's direction. "As long as Damocles has control, it's still a threat. He'll have the virus in a lab somewhere to let loose whenever he wants to show more power. He'll give everyone a scare, squash the outbreak, and be the hero again."

Ariadne's mouth twisted. "The vaccines will all be stored on the Three Sisters to start with. He'd want the supply close."

"And we're not going anywhere near the Sisters until the Novantae's numbers increase, which isn't happening anytime soon," Kyla added. "But we have to set down somewhere. Clo and Elva can't put off the repairs anymore, and we're still pretty low on everything. Fucking bounty hunters."

Kyla planned things in stages. Once she set a goal, she wasn't prone to deviations unless someone had a good reason to disagree. In the early days, they'd all spent hours in *Zelus's* observation room, staring out at the stars as their ship drifted through space and hid from the universe. Short-term, their goal was not to get shot, starve to death, or get sucked out into the abyss of space because their tech failed. Kyla considered disrupting Tholosian supply chains to steal rations, but the poor would pay the price for that temporary solution while the rich lived comfortably.

Another familiar story.

The only thing that might help was to increase Novan rebels. Four hundred resistance fighters and a handful of dodgy ships were fuck-all against the Empire. Their best bet to find people willing to side with the rebellion in large numbers were the gerulae—and Ariadne wasn't sure if Oracle programming that strong could be unpicked. The servitor class was so completely controlled by the Oracle that they had no thoughts of their own.

But they were on every planet. Embedded in every city, often clustered around the powerful. Before those citizens were gerulae, they were the ones who had been able to break through Oracle's code; many had dreamed of resistance. Now their punishment was complete subservience.

But if the Novans *could* wake up gerulae and persuade them to join the resistance? They might have a chance. The only problem? Even with Cato and Ariadne on the issue, they weren't anywhere near a breakthrough. Kyla was hoping for a miracle.

Clo didn't believe in miracles.

"They're just trying to survive too, I suppose," Rhea offered.

Eris smirked, but she'd remained uncharacteristically quiet throughout the whole exchange.

<*You all right?*> Clo asked her.

<*Fine. One of the Mors bullets got a bit too close, is all.*> She motioned at her singed sleeve.

Clo rubbed her forehead. "Cato, when can we leave the med bay?"

"When I'm sure your injuries won't get infected," Cato said, tending to an especially surly Nyx. "We have enough trouble battling bog-standard bacteria without proper medical supplies, much less a potentially deadly pathogen Damocles may or may not have eradicated."

"Elva needs to know where we're headed," Ariadne piped up from the corner. "Here's my shortlist of safe places."

Clo looked at the list on the screen and blanched. There was a beat of silence as Kyla thought through their choices. Clo knew which the commander would pick, but that didn't mean she had to like it.

"Fortuna," Kyla said quietly. "Put in the coordinates."

Clo's stomach dropped. "Kyla—"

"I know, Cloelia," Kyla said, expression sympathetic. "But Fortuna is the most logical choice. It's abandoned, and any lingering ichor from Damocles' experiment will be gone by now. Right, Cato?"

"Theoretically."

Nyx shifted next to him, leaning against the wall with her usual scowl.

Kyla nodded. "I'll take 'theoretically' over 'definitely fucked.'" She motioned for Ariadne to send the coordinates.

Clo huffed something resembling a laugh. The ichor wasn't why she didn't want to visit that planet, and Kyla damn well knew it.

The women who had lived on Fortuna had called themselves the Furies. They'd all been ancient by the time Clo had crashed among them. Gnarled as old roots but just as strong. When they'd seen the streak of fire across the sky, they must have thought the Tholosians had finally caught up with them.

Instead, they'd found the battered co-leader of the resistance and a foul-mouthed, grief-stricken berm clutching a dead man and refusing to let him go. It would have been safer to shoot them on sight, but the Furies had taken in Clo and Sher. Helped them bury Briggs.

Fortuna was an unprofitable, forgotten planet—one of many the Tholosians went to the trouble of conquering but not developing sustainably. It was an excellent place to hide.

Clo had grown close to a woman named Jacinta. They had both liked engines. She didn't let Clo wallow and had put her back together again as sure as mending a broken part. Jacinta was the one who had convinced Clo to go back to Nova. The Furies were too old to keep up the struggle, she'd said, but she knew Clo was one of the ones with the fight and the fire for it. No matter how much the Tholosians tied people down, there would always be pockets of resistance, like mushrooms growing in damp shit.

The Furies had sought refuge in the labyrinthine caves beneath the surface of the Fortuna uplands, ones that Kyla must have found so tempting now. The depth hid their ships' signals without wasting energy on shields. It was Clo's salted fault for telling Kyla about those when she'd returned.

When Clo had flown away from Fortuna, she hadn't realized she'd left the Furies to their deaths. Like Cercyon, Victrix, and so many others, Fortuna was selected for Damocles' fucked-up ichor experiment. An operation to produce a weapon so deadly that it could create a mass casualty event within minutes.

He'd known the women were there and had dealt with them. Just a few more fatalities among the millions, and a fitting punishment for daring to believe they could live beyond the confines of the Empire.

Clo gritted her teeth as she grabbed a clean cloth and pressed it against her still-bleeding knuckles. Rhea sensed her distress and drifted closer, placing a reassuring hand on her arm. Clo fought the urge to shake it off. There was no arguing with Kyla. Besides—

Kyla echoed the words in Clo's brain. "We have nowhere else to go."

———

Clo insisted on landing *Zelus* herself, glaring at Cato as if daring him to offer to copilot. The ship sliced through the atmosphere of Fortuna, smooth and controlled. The last time, her craft had been on fire, and she and Sher had been desperately trying to keep Briggs alive.

No. Clo still couldn't think about either of them, or she'd start bawling like a bairn.

Rhea's hands came to rest on Clo's shoulder blades, and the scent of lilies grounded her once again.

Fortuna was a watery planet, full of smaller continents and chains of islands formed by volcanic plugs. Tall pine-like trees rose toward the stars, their trunks thick, the forest floor carpeted with needles that released their sharp scent with every step. Trees grew in the shallow waters of the sea, their roots twined underneath the sand. In the dark of night, the sky was more purple than blue, and even when the sun was at its zenith, the atmosphere was the color of amethyst. It was beautiful.

Clo hated it.

When the trees were mature, Tholos would have a use for it again. They'd cut down every last trunk and ship the lumber throughout the galaxy. Maybe they'd bother to replant. Maybe they wouldn't. That was the Tholosian way: take, take, take, and never mind how a future generation might hate them for it.

Clo almost let out a bitter laugh. Future generations wouldn't even have the option to hate their ancestors. The Oracle's hold was only tightening across citizen synapses.

Zelus set down on the same beach Clo had crashed into three and a half years before. Though Cato and Ariadne's preliminary readings showed no traces of ichor, they put on protective gear to double-check conditions.

Clo led them to the caves, her breath heavy in her helmet. Eris hacked at the undergrowth across the dark entrance, and they all slipped inside.

Clo crept through the grand atrium of the cave system that the women had called the Cathedral, a room of high, vaulted ceilings and columns of thick, black rock. The cavern was massive enough to store their five ships. They used to have over thirty, and even then, the resistance had been too small—a pebble against a mountain range.

Clo had known the bones of the dead would be there, but that didn't mean she was prepared.

Ariadne gave a soft cry when she saw them. Rhea's hand rested over her mouth. Kyla, Nyx, Cato, and Eris remained implacable. How many corpses had they seen between the four of them? Thousands, Clo reckoned. Maybe even tens of thousands. What was a few hundred more?

Clo crouched down and stared at a skull. The flesh had decayed with time, the women's skeletons already greening from mold, moss, and damp. Clo remembered how they had to store all their food in airtight containers, and even then, it was common to open one and see her dinner furred with blue or green.

Who had this skull belonged to? Adelphie? Oda? Could this be Jacinta? She touched the cheekbone and bowed her head.

"No signs of active ichor," Cato said, tapping his tablet. "Any particles died off long ago. We'll drop a sanitizer bomb in here, but it seems safe enough."

Rhea lingered near Clo, unable to give the reassurance and empathy from skin-to-skin contact in their suits. Behind them, the remains of the rebellion streamed in, awed to silence by the cave and the dead.

"We could take the bones to one of the other chambers," Nyx said, unwilling to come anywhere near the bones. It wasn't like her to be squeamish.

"No," Clo said. "We're not taking them deeper into the dark."

"We'll give them a proper burial, Cloelia," Kyla said. "We'll put them to rest."

"I'll say last rites," Eris added quietly.

Clo nodded, not trusting herself to speak. She rose, staring at the four hundred or so resistance fighters who exited their barely functional ships. All that remained of the Novantae.

She swallowed hard and headed back to the ship to get her spare gloves.

It took most of the day to gather the dead. There was no way to separate the skeletons, but Clo didn't think the Furies would mind. They'd lived together. Died together. They'd be put to rest together. A few Novantae stayed behind to clean the atrium and the smaller caves that would serve as storage.

Clo changed out of her protective gear and went to the beach with the Devils, Elva, and a handful of other Novantae. Daphne, another pilot. Hadriana, their main logistics coordinator and administrator. Albus, the primary weapons man. Some of them Clo hadn't interacted with often on Nova. Now they were all the family she had left.

The sunset was red and gold smeared across a purpling sky. Clo had left her helmet behind, and it was pure gleyed to feel the wind against her cheeks. The air still smelled the same: sharp pine, sea salt, the almost-spicy scent of an edible red flower that may not have a name. The women called them blood roses. This place had been home once, but they wouldn't stay there long enough for it to become home again. The others would hunker down with the hope that Ariadne and Cato could do the impossible and bring the dead back into the gerulae's still-living bodies.

Clo shivered in the cool air as Eris gave last rites. Cato and Albus lowered the remains into the water. The waves closed over them like a hand, sweeping them away. Clo hoped they met with Briggs' bones and kept her old mentor company in the Avern until the day they'd all meet again.

Clo didn't cry. She thought she would, but everything stayed locked up deep and tight. Rhea and Ariadne cried for her, tears dampening their cheeks.

When the last of the bones had slipped beneath the gray waves and dusk darkened to twilight, Rhea came closer and placed a hand on Clo's waist. "Let's go for a walk," Rhea said. "I'm feeling just as anxious as you are."

A few months before, knowing Rhea could feel her tension would have raised Clo's hackles like a marsh-cat. Now she only wrapped herself in her jacket as a light rain drizzled down on them both.

They picked their way over roots, hand in hand. Clo had an easier time of it with her new prosthetic. They'd pulled a job and stolen enough silver smartmetal to give Eris a tongue and nabbed Clo a better leg in the process. Her skin no longer chafed with each step and the joints were oil-smooth.

Like Clo, Rhea's long, simple shirt and trousers tucked into scuffed boots were old, beginning to fray at the edges. They kept their nicer togs for missions. Even in threadbare and patched clothes, Rhea carried herself with the smooth grace bred into her since birth.

Rhea tucked an errant dark strand behind her ear. Clo had memorized every feature of Rhea's face, but sometimes she could turn her head at a certain angle, and it was like Clo was seeing her for the first time all over again on the commandeered *Zelus*. One of three women willing to risk everything to leave the Empire behind. Chin up, eyes blazing, daring them to try and stop her from escaping.

Clo never thought she'd be homesick for Nova. Damocles had found that too-hot desert planet and set it on fire right after Laguna. They hadn't even had time to go back. Clo missed the mementos she'd stored in a loose floorboard under her bed: a long-stale packet of her mother's healing herbs, a little cog that reminded her of Briggs. Small, tangible things from those who were gone. They now lived only in her memory.

Rhea's hand clasped Clo's tight as they scaled the faint trail that led to a rocky outcropping overlooking the forest, the sandy beach, and the flat calm of the sea. They settled on a cool stone slab. The misty rain fell on Rhea's dark hair and glittered like diamonds. They sat close together, keeping each other warm in the near-dark. Two crescent moons glowed overhead. Clo placed her arm around Rhea's back, idly running a hand down the faint bumps of her spine, the other woman shivering beneath her touch.

"Just wait until our sighting gets back to Damocles," Clo said. "People claimed to see us all over the galaxy, and he hasnae even gotten close." She gave a laugh. "They said we were lounging on a beach in Canopus—like we'd be caught anywhere that fancy."

"If only it were that easy," Rhea agreed with a sly smile. "I can see the headlines now: *'Seven Devils' spotted on Victrix.* It's going to ruin his sleep." Ariadne's nickname had stuck. After a subtle leak, the press had run with it, embracing the name as a curse. Never mind that by their own theology, devils and gods were the same.

Rhea shifted, and her expression rippled. Clo might not have Rhea's talent for sensing emotions, but she was getting better at reading the clues. Rhea fiddled with her necklace—some old locket she'd found on a supply run. She'd fixed the broken chain and polished away the tarnish. She'd put a tiny painting of seven stars inside, for the Seven Devils.

"How long do you think we have?" Clo asked, swallowing. "Before our mission?"

"Soon," Rhea said. "I think we're close."

Clo's stomach clenched and twisted. The sea wind whipped through the pine trees, blowing their collars up against their necks.

Rhea and Clo were going to have to leave the others.

3.

Two and a half months ago

The commander's rumpled uniform had clearly been slept in, though not recently. Kyla had called Rhea and Clo into *Zelus*'s observation room, her maps and reports overlaid across the table's digiscreens. The dust had just settled from Damocles' attack on their camp at Persei, and there was no chance to rest or grieve the murdered Novantae. There never was.

The head of their battered resistance had improved at shielding her emotions, but despair still rose off her in waves. Rhea paused near the door, almost certain she knew what the other woman intended to ask.

Worse: Rhea couldn't fault the logic.

Rhea's heart ached. Should she have warned Clo? Clo, blissfully unaware of what was about to happen, settled in one of the chairs. "Are you hiding candy again, Commander?" Clo asked, inspecting the crumbs sprinkled across the table.

"Of course not." Kyla's eyes shifted.

"Yes, you are. There's sugar at the corner of your lip. You sneak sweets when you're stressed. Cough 'em up." Clo held out a hand.

Kyla glared and wiped at her mouth. But she reached into a bag hidden at her side, passing the other women pieces of crystallized fruit, one half dipped in chocolate. Rhea let the tart sweetness languish against her tongue, a fraction of pleasure before everything went to the

Avern. She tried to make it last. Clo ate hers in two bites, barely chewing.

Kyla watched them quietly, her countenance all too somber. They each bore scars from what they'd seen on Laguna, but Kyla had endured some of the deepest cuts. Rhea sensed traces of the storm inside the commander, a furious gray-black maelstrom of guilt. Kyla blamed herself for not protecting her people. For not recognizing that her brother Sher had long been under the Oracle's control until it was too late.

Rhea had only seen the former co-commander onscreen a few times, and she hadn't been familiar with the peculiarities of his behavior. She'd found Sher's emotions cold—but former Tholosian soldiers often had that way about them. Rhea wished she'd recognized that what she'd considered a mental gelidity had been the Oracle's tendrils threading through Sher's mind. Sher had broken through his programming once before, but not the second. The Oracle had stolen a man Kyla and Clo cared for like family.

Every day, Rhea sensed Kyla set aside her emotions and left her room with plans and machinations. She gave the commands that helped them all survive.

Kyla met Rhea's eyes. "It's time," she said. "You know it is."

Rhea dropped her head.

Clo's attention shifted between them. "Time? What does that mean?" She noticed the change in Rhea's countenance. "Rhea?"

"I have to go to Eve," Rhea said, voice just above a whisper.

Clo stiffened. Rhea clasped her hand and squeezed, wordlessly urging the other woman to stay quiet. In the loom of her mind, Rhea twisted her emotions into something orderly and stable. She would let them unravel later.

She'd trained with the old Archon to infiltrate the Evoli home planet, Eve. It had been her sole reason for existing. Her life's work. Tholosians had experimented for years with Evoli DNA, but Evoli-Tholosian gene-splicing made for a high infant mortality rate. If any experiments other than Rhea had survived, she'd never heard of them.

Like the Evoli, she could sense others' emotions thrumming along her skin like lightning. The red-orange sizzle of anger. The purple and gray of despair. The buzzing green of euphoria, or the fuzzed pink of desire. She'd learned all she could about Evoli culture and language—anything that might assist in her inevitable mission for the Archon.

"She's not going," Clo snapped, yanking her hand out of Rhea's grasp. She leaned back against the wall, crossing her arms.

"I'm not finished." Kyla's voice was calm; she was used to dealing with Clo's insubordination. "Just listen to what I have to say before arguing, Cloelia."

On the screens, Kyla brought up a map of the Karis Galaxy. She zoomed in and projected the holograph of Eve above the table, the lush and verdant planet spinning slowly on its axis. Rhea had seen a projection like this almost every day of her childhood. She'd memorized the boundaries of those islands and continents, could draw them with her eyes closed.

Kyla bit into another crystallized fruit with more force than necessary. "The new peace between Tholosians and Evoli is holding so far—and Damocles is still acting as an honorary Oversoul until they choose their new Ascendant. But the Evoli haven't yet opened their borders to him, citing the need to finish the transition process."

"What are they waiting for?" Clo asked. The question seemed to leave her reluctantly.

"They're buying time. My source says that the truce ceremony was the first time the Evoli spent an extended period near gerulae. They . . ." She paused, swallowing. "They heard them screaming." She tapped the side of her temple. "They said they're still inside there somewhere. Trapped."

"No," Clo said, her voice strangled.

Rhea's breath left her in a rush, her mind working. Tholosians had always believed the Oracle wiped the minds of gerulae and kept their bodies alive for labor. That the people who performed menial tasks for the Empire were nothing but living corpses, husks. Technically among the living, but dead in every way that mattered.

That their minds remained active was the confirmation Novans hoped for, but it snarled at Rhea's insides. How could she not have known? Not have sensed the pain of gerulae imprisoned within their own minds?

Ariadne and Cato had spent months trying to wake up the few rescued Novantae-turned-gerulae in their midst. They'd asked Rhea to come and read them, but every touch yielded the same mental image: a mind as deep and black and cold as a crevasse, one that threatened to pull Rhea deep. How could the Evoli sense what she couldn't?

But she knew the answer: the Evoli were all linked via an empathic bond called the Unity, which could enhance their abilities.

Rhea was on her own. Utterly alone.

Kyla was speaking again, and Rhea tried to focus. "After Laguna, the Evoli brought a few gerulae back to Eve, figuring Tholosians wouldn't miss them." Kyla let out a sigh. "I don't know how accurate this is, but my source says the Evoli woke them up."

Clo's head snapped back at that, and Rhea went entirely still. It was one thing for the gerulae to be alive within the confines of their minds, but to be awakened? To undo the Oracle's surgical programming? It seemed too good to hope. Months of the Novantae trying to wake them up, only to find out the solution was there, half a galaxy away.

Where no one could go but Rhea.

"How do you know?" she managed to ask Kyla.

"The death of the Ascendant on Laguna diminished the strength of the Unity. My source is a dissatisfied Evoli who can temporarily hide his emotions until they choose a new leader."

Rhea knew this. The Evoli who defected to the Novantae had left during previous transitions of power, when the Unity weakened enough for them to depart. Even one of the five Oversouls dying was enough to affect the bond temporarily.

"So, you think I might be able to read them now," Rhea guessed.

"After the deaths of the previous five Oversouls and the Ascendant who had reigned for the last twenty years? Yep." Kyla studied the planet's hologram over the table. "If some Evoli are wary enough of the truce with the Tholosians to defect, it would increase our numbers."

"I thought we couldn't increase our numbers after Laguna," Clo muttered. "Didn't have the resources. Couldn't risk the fleet after what happened to headquarters. Wasn't that what you said?"

Kyla's emotions flickered too fast for Rhea to read. "I think you know that recent losses have forced us into this position. And if the Evoli really can wake up the gerulae, then we need to know that, too. So, go ahead and glare at me if you want, Cloelia. But you know I'm right." Clo opened her mouth to speak, but Kyla put up a hand. "Not finished. I know you're about to insist on going with Rhea to Eve. And if Elva and Eris can teach you to control and shield your emotions, I'll approve of you on the mission. *If.* Now speak."

Rhea's mouth fell open; she hadn't been expecting that. Clo caught her gaze—her own surprise flared a pale turquoise.

"Elva, I get. But why Eris?" Clo asked. "She meant to be there to piss me off even more?"

"Because she's the only non-Evoli Rhea can't read, and Rhea can read *you* like a fucking canteen menu. The Evoli will be able to sense any emotional aberrations."

Clo glared. "You're constantly saying my anger is going tae get me killed."

"In this case, it might." Kyla rubbed her forehead. "Look, I can't spare long for the training. But if you listen to Eris, for once in your gods-damned life"—she ignored the imperceptible narrowing of Clo's eyes—"then I think you and Rhea can benefit each other. Rhea will work the Evoli, and if any gerulae *are* awake, they might connect better with you. Especially if you pose as a Tholosian refugee."

Clo sat quietly as she considered Kyla's words. "I've heard navigating to Eve isn't possible for a Tholosian." She nodded to the hologram. "Even that map is a projection based on intel."

Rhea's stomach clenched. Did Clo not wish to go? Was she trying to think of a way out of it?

Rhea wove the gold of hope and the red of fear into that mental fabric, tucking it away. She knew Clo was right. The Tholosians had always outnumbered the Evoli, but they made up for it with strategy. Their technology was a marvel, and Evoli closely guarded their secrets. The Karis Galaxy remained uncharted and unmapped, with Evoli planets surrounded by an empathic barrier via the Unity that caused Tholosian pilots to navigate in aimless circles. Eventually, they'd shake themselves from some fugue state and realize they were farther away than where they started. Even uncrewed ships had difficulty, the Unity confusing the systems enough that the Evoli could pick them off one by one. And if that didn't, the Zoster asteroid belt that spanned a large stretch of the barrier sure helped.

This only supported Tholosian superstitions that the Evoli were mages, capable of stealing souls and keeping loyal citizens from reaching the seven levels of the Avern in the afterlife. Some called them Soul Eaters. Witches. Majoi. Rhea had heard those whispers even among the Novantae.

"I'm sure you'll find a solution," Kyla said to Clo. "Or are you not the best pilot we have?"

Clo rolled her eyes. "Just trying not to die, Commander."

Rhea fought to maintain her composure; her emotions were beginning to fray at the edges. "Why not Elva? She was raised on Eve. Most of my information is through the Tholosians."

"Because Elva and the others are fugitives," Kyla said. "They're considered traitors for cutting themselves off from the Unity, and the Evoli won't let them return." She made a gesture with her hand. "And I won't even go into how fucking bad most Evoli are at lying. Rhea can pose as a political prisoner taken from the Evoli during childhood. Children's minds aren't linked to the Unity, and that cover will explain any cultural slips you make."

Damocles had been cementing the "truce" by releasing Evoli prisoners of war. The ones he hadn't broken too badly.

Rhea swallowed. "You want me to pretend to be Elva's younger sister, don't you?" Using a known identity was easier; it created a solid foundation on which Ariadne could craft a background.

Kyla's eyes softened. A nod. Elva's sister had been on a transport ship attacked by Tholosians as a child. Had she survived, she would be Rhea's age by now.

Still, the idea pricked at her. Elva was the only Evoli in their resistance who was on semi-friendly terms with Rhea. The others looked down on her for preserving the illusion over her skin that hid her markings. She was too self-conscious to display the fractal freckles that swirled along her skin to anyone but Clo.

Those markings revealed the truth: that she had been created. She was neither Tholosian nor Evoli but something in the middle. Something outside of both people.

She was no one.

Panic suffused through her, orange-brown, as she recalled the gilded walls of the palace on Tholos. There, she had learned to control her emotions and dampen them so profoundly that no one, not even another Evoli, would identify what she truly felt. So, she could slip among them, as insidious as a shadow, and discover something that would destroy them from within.

Kyla watched her with something close to pity. "It has to be you, Rhea. You know it does."

Clo's doubt undulated off her as she leaned closer to Rhea. "If they find out two of the Seven Devils are in their midst, they're more likely to turn us in than join us."

"Then don't get caught. Ariadne will craft your identities, and you'll shift your features." Kyla swallowed. "Look, this isn't just about ensuring our survival; there are Novans among the gerulae that I thought were lost." Her expression turned fierce. "If we have a chance to save them, then we need to do this. I owe it to them."

Rhea took in a careful breath. Let it out. She tried not to think of her training.

The Archon had twisted Rhea's abilities. She could convince others to believe they'd made decisions of their own volition, could turn love to hate or fear if she wanted. She could make an unchipped mother in the Sprawl kill her child and believe it was her idea all along.

Not even the Oracle could do that. And if she went to Eve, what lines would Rhea have to cross?

Rhea clenched her teeth. So many words wanted to escape.

No.

We can't.

It's too dangerous.

There would be lies upon lies upon lies. They'd be bound to trip up on one of them, no matter how good she was at crafting falsehoods.

Kyla watched Rhea war with rationality rather than emotion. The commander folded her arms and rested her elbows on the table, muscles moving beneath scarred skin. Black eyes unblinking.

When Rhea had escaped with Nyx and Ariadne, she'd hoped she could begin anew somewhere else—somewhere safe. A place where she didn't have to hide. She should have known there was no running from it.

This had always been her mission. It had always been her fate.

The commander stood and came around the desk to place a hand on Rhea's shoulder. She tried not to shy away at the touch, but then she realized Kyla *wanted* Rhea to read her emotions. Rhea leaned into it. Everyone's colors were different. Regret, the purple-blue of dusk. Fear, in a jagged green. Despair, lurking a sickly blue at the corners. The colors swirled together.

And the brightest of all, in a glittering gold that folded Rhea in its embrace: hope.

They could wake up the gerulae. They could save those once thought lost. They could have a chance.

"Okay." The word caught in her throat. "All right. Yes."

A final squeeze, and Kyla let go.

Rhea thought through the plan. "If I'm to be Elva's sister, Clo will be a Tholosian prisoner I fell in love with, released with me as a gesture of goodwill."

Clo twitched at the word *love*.

"All right," Kyla said slowly. She turned her attention to Clo. "And you? Will you learn to handle your emotions? Listen to Eris?"

Rhea's heart hammered.

Clo made a face. Her expression was flippant, but Rhea could feel the jolt of Clo's fear. "I said I'd follow this berm to the end of the universe, so it looks like I'm putting that to the test." She tutted. "Listening to Eris. Fuck me sideways."

Rhea flushed with pink warmth. She managed to find a smile for Clo.

"Fine," Kyla said. "Terms agreed."

Rhea's shoulder slackened in relief. Clo came and wrapped her arms around Rhea, the touch soothing.

"Remember, Cloelia," Kyla said, "Eris has to approve your training. So, be nice."

"I've been nice," Clo scoffed. "I havenae tried to kill her in months."

Kyla dismissed them with a wave, and they returned to their bunk on *Zelus*.

"I'm sorry," Rhea said in a rush. "I should have known she'd ask that. I should have prepared you. I should have—"

Clo silenced Rhea with a kiss. Rhea let out a soft sigh, parting her lips. Her hand went to the back of Clo's neck, stroking the short bristles of her buzzed hair.

When they pulled away, though, Clo's eyes were fierce. "Kyla sent me to Jurran because I couldn't control my rage, but it was all I had then." Her fingers stroked across Rhea's cheek. "Now I have you."

Rhea warmed. "I'm glad I have you, too."

She'd have an ally there, on that planet filled with danger. With people who might share her DNA but little else.

She dipped her head again, and there was no more need for words. And, at least for a few moments, Rhea let her fear fray.

4.

Present day

Nyx returned to *Zelus*'s medical bay for her life-saving, thrice-daily injection.

She sat straight on the table, the metal as cold as a mortuary slab, and tried not to shiver as Cato rolled up the sleeve of her jumpsuit. She'd been cold since that mad dash through the woods on Victrix; the humidity hadn't helped her already-weakening lungs. Over the last few months, parts of her body had begun to decline one by one: lungs that couldn't get in enough air, a heart that inefficiently pumped blood through her once-hale body, temperature regulation that was as inadequate as life support on a broken ship.

Cato liked to use words like *hypothalamus* and *thermoregulation*, probably because they sounded a lot kinder than *completely fucked*.

He gently extended her arm and dithered over the track marks on the inside of her elbow, his blond hair almost silver in the sharp light of the med bay. She had so many souvenirs from so many injections. She'd taken to wearing long sleeves so the others didn't see.

Cato cleared his throat. "Let's try the other arm."

With a dry chuckle, Nyx did as he asked. "You don't have to worry about keeping my arm pretty, doc."

"I'm not," he said calmly. "I'm trying not to blow your veins so badly

I have no choice but to install a cannula. Now, sit still and let me finish."

She watched as he tightened the tourniquet on her arm and prepped the drug. Sooner or later, they'd either have to increase her dosage or accept the inevitable. She'd gone from one injection a day to three to hold off the disease that was beginning to overtake her system. She was lucky, she supposed, that the version she'd contracted was the natural effects of the ichor and not the chemically altered biological weapon that had killed thousands on Laguna. Her exposure to the ichor on Ismara still hadn't proven contagious—thank the gods for that—but she felt weaker every day.

Cato had known for months—an unavoidable disclosure after he took over the medical center. He developed a treatment using leftover nanites from Eris's blood when he'd installed her bionic tongue. That and some other therapies he'd adapted for Nyx's unique case had helped, at least a little.

But it wasn't a cure; it was a delay. A barter with Letum for more time. Those damned injections were the only thing deterring the God of Death from taking Nyx to the Avern.

And He always won in the end.

"You need to tell the others," Cato said as he pressed his thumb to the plunger and slid the drug home. "I can't keep lying for you. I'm amazed I've kept it from Ariadne as long as I have. But if she gets curious and breaks routine to read my med files, you know my security on those computers won't keep her out."

Yeah, this was a conversation they'd had only one hundred fucking times before. Nyx knew it wasn't fair to ask Cato to keep covering for her. As far as the others knew, Nyx's near-constant presence in the medical bay was to assist Cato on his research with the gerulae. It was an easy excuse. After all, both Nyx and Cato had been under the Oracle's influence until recently. Their programming hadn't gone as deep as a husk's, but they both lived with remnants of an AI that told them what to think and feel. Being deprogrammed was only the start; sometimes, Nyx feared shaking off the Empire's influence would be lifelong work.

Longer than she had left.

In Cato's case, he said he found it easier to ignore those old commands by helping others. He sometimes came off like a sanctimonious shithead, but that sanctimonious shithead had spent months trying to save Nyx. Even when he thought she wasn't watching, she found him working on potential cures while the others slept.

"I'll tell the others when you start talking about those suppressed memories, pilot. Medic. Whatever the fuck."

Yeah, she knew that would hit in a sore spot. Nyx and Cato had become friends over the last few months, trading stories over experiments. As far as Nyx knew, she was the only person he'd told about the strange flashes of memory he'd had since deprogramming. But whenever she pressed for more details, he snapped at her to leave it. So, on the topic of her illness, she got to say *fuck off* back.

Cato sighed and untied the tourniquet, leaving Nyx to smooth the healing gel over the needle track. "Listen," he said, squaring his shoulders as if for a fight. "I didn't want to get into this today, but I think you need to start making some choices. You have weeks, Nyx. At most."

Nyx held back a flinch.

Weeks.

At most.

She'd been hoping that the disease might somehow go away on its own if she ignored it. Yeah, of course that was a stupid fucking thing to believe—but it had helped her get through the last few months. She never did like goodbyes, and death by disease was a long one. She kept imagining Ariadne's face once she heard the news, and forced that image away. Because Nyx didn't cry. Telling Ariadne? That'd be the thing to crack her like a damned vase. Easily.

Now Nyx understood why some animals just wandered off and died alone.

She was supposed to be the strong one. She was engineered to endure. And how was Nyx Arktos-33 gonna leave the world? Not in a glorious battle. Not saving anyone.

Nope, all it took to kill off one of the best soldiers in the Tholosian Empire was a tiny fleck of diseased stone. Slow and painful, her body betraying her at every turn. Eventually, she'd drown in her own lungs.

Nyx shoved down the sleeve of her jumpsuit. "Then I'll spend these weeks how I like."

"Nyx . . ."

"It's my decision," she snapped. Ugh, now she felt guilty. She looked away and loosed a breath. "I just . . . I keep thinking about their faces, you know? I'm gonna tell them, and they're gonna be all fucking sad with their pity and their *feelings* and cry all over me, and I'm supposed to be the godsdamned strong one—" She broke off and chewed her lip. Flames of Avern, she was a mess.

"They won't see you as weak," Cato said, too damn quiet.

"See? There it is," Nyx snarled. "Pity. You can choke on it."

Nyx grabbed her sweater and shoved it on, stalking out of the medical bay. So what if she was cold? So what if it was a sign that her body was continuing to fail her day by day? So what if she only had weeks left to live?

Nyx faltered in the hallway. She pressed a hand to her chest, where her heart fluttered with an arrhythmia that would have gotten her killed on the battlefield. Her fellow soldiers would have put her out of her misery.

A muffled swear from a nearby room drew Nyx's attention. She moved to the open door—Eris's suite—and found the ex-princess bent over a zatrikion board. She watched as Eris challenged the program to a game, carefully set up the pieces one by one—and lost.

Badly.

"Fuck," Eris snapped, starting the game again. This time, she lost in three moves. "*Fuck.*"

Nyx half-expected Eris to throw the board across the room and slam her fist into a wall. Her brother would have. Damocles never was a graceful loser. You won a game against him at your peril.

But Eris? She carefully set up the pieces again, her other hand trembling. Nyx wondered if she should leave; this seemed private. The princess put on a good performance, but Nyx knew she was fucked up after Laguna, maybe even more than the rest of them. Or at least as messed up as Kyla. Her brother had drugged her, forced her to respond only to his commands, and used her to smuggle a biological weapon into a peace ceremony. That was some trauma with a side helping of a fuckton more trauma.

Eris slid her Commandant forward, and Nyx winced. She couldn't stand watching this anymore. "You're going to lose in two moves," Nyx told her.

Eris glared at her. The princess didn't know her brother had made Nyx play this game with him over and over, that he'd tried so hard to break her. That she knew all the styles and modes of attack—the Ionan Defense, the Gorgon Variation. That whenever Nyx had beaten him in a game, he'd beaten her with his fists. Called her Discordia. Pretended she was the sister who always won against him.

Nyx watched as Eris moved her Peasant—and lost. Again.

"For gods' sake," Nyx said. "This is tragic. Scoot your knees over." Nyx nabbed an extra chair and wedged it across from Eris at the small table.

"Go fuck yourself," Eris shot back, but sure enough, she shifted so that Nyx could fit her legs under the table.

They set up their game and started the program. Nyx hadn't ever spent much time in Eris's room. Ariadne had kitted hers out until you could barely turn for all the color and clutter. Clo and Rhea had made a nauseatingly cute lovenest. But the former soldiers all had rooms as sterile as the med bay. No mementos, no keepsakes. Soldiers knew if they died in battle, it was unfair to make comrades throw out their shit. Nyx had a few things Ariadne had given her, but only because the younger girl would be upset if Nyx tossed the drawings or the "shiny, spiky things" Ariadne found on various moons and planets and said they reminded her of Nyx.

"You wanna tell me why you're sitting here losing to a computer and muttering curses to yourself?" Nyx asked, shifting a piece forward.

"Not really."

Nyx tapped a finger against the table, wondering if she should broach the subject. But, Avern, she had a few weeks to live. So, what'd she have to lose? "Your brother was obsessed with this game."

Eris's hand shook over a piece. "Yes."

"He used to play me. Sometimes." Nyx kept her expression neutral. "Was a real asshole about it."

Eris's eyes met Nyx's. "You never told me that."

"Thought it was common knowledge that he was an asshole. Ariadne reminds us often enough." When Eris just raised an eyebrow, Nyx gave a dry laugh. "Yeah, I know. You're not exactly forthcoming about him either."

The princess pressed her lips together. "He was violent. When we played. I almost killed him once."

Nyx wished she had. What would her life be like, if she didn't have all those memories of winning over a board, anticipating the strength of his fists? Damocles could always tell when Nyx let him win. Somehow, no matter how cleverly she thought she'd set it up, he could always tell.

Could Eris?

They played in silence, and Nyx let Eris move across the board. Nyx played the same game as in the early days with Damocles, pretending to advance and retreat, until Eris knocked over Nyx's final piece. "Queen kills King," she said softly.

"There, you see?" Nyx shrugged and got to her feet. "You're not so rusty after all."

"Guess not." But when Nyx reached the door, Eris said, "Though I think I would have preferred it if you hadn't let me win."

Nyx paused.

"Nyx." Eris sounded annoyed. "I played that game so poorly that a child could have won. So, why didn't you knock over my fucking Queen and put me out of my misery?"

Nyx thought about Damocles and his fists. She thought about the broken bones that she'd had knitted back together in the palace's medical bay. How she'd endured the pain of setting those bones before they healed wrong and put her out of commission as a royal guard. She thought about the way Damocles screamed his sister's name before he hit her bloody. It didn't matter that she resembled Discordia not at all; anyone could have stood in for his sister. Anyone.

Nyx happened to be the one who took the most damage. She happened to be the one who could survive his wrath to play another game.

"I always hated winning," Nyx said, very softly. She met Eris's eyes across the room. "Saying the words *Queen kills King*? Each time, it felt like I'd lost."

Eris gave a nod. She knew what sort of damage he could do to a soldier who didn't have the same body mods as Eris and the other royal children.

Nyx kept one secret back, locked away in her mind. The secret of those words was hers alone, a burden she carried like the scars of her military service.

Three little words were all it took. They proved Nyx had some value to him. And so, she'd taught Damocles how to win the game.

King kills Queen had kept her alive.

5.

KYLA

Present day

Kyla leaned back in her chair and rubbed her eyes with a sigh.
We're fucked.

The two words whispered through her mind like a shameful secret. She'd never risk admitting it to the others; hope was all they had to keep going. She wanted to scream (that relief, that primal urge). Back on Nova, she'd leave headquarters and go out into the middle of the desert, in that long liminal dusk, and howl like an Old World firewolf. She'd always thought they were on to something: wailing at the moon as if it could hear them. Storms would carry her screams across the sand, the wind whipping at her hair.

Sometimes she missed Nova. Back when she and Sher had found it on the outer fringes of the Empire, the ship's systems had referred to the planet as TH-Eridanos 8c. It was a simple label after its parent star, a world so irrelevant to the Empire that the Tholosians considered it unworthy of its own name.

To Sher and Kyla, two escaped Tholosian soldiers, TH-Eridanos 8c represented new hope. So, they gave it a name, one that held so many memories for them.

Nova.

But Nova was compromised. Damocles had destroyed the rebellion's headquarters. Kyla's home was gone, and there was nowhere to scream on *Zelus*. She'd tuck herself away in her quarters or the planning room and swallow back howl after howl. She'd let the grief wash over her. Every. Damned. Day.

One hundred and three days since Laguna.

One hundred and one days since soldiers slaughtered too many of her rebels on Nova.

Eighty-nine days since the Tholosian military attacked their camp on Persei.

For one hundred and three days, she'd been failing to save her people. Barely surviving, much less finding a way to fight back.

She and Sher had scratched a base from sand and rock and dirt. Now their precious Nova was nothing but a ghost town, left to hot dust and storms and whoever was brave enough to scavenge the singed remnants.

They had no home (and maybe they never would).

Get it together, she told herself, reaching for the old communicator on her desk. She was about to turn it on when she remembered there was a whole damned planet beyond the metal walls of *Zelus*. Outside air to breathe into her lungs. An escape from the people who wanted more than she could give them right now.

Kyla slipped off the ship and wove her way through the Cathedral, nodding at the Novantae working on their tired engines or checking their paltry stashes of weapons. She breathed a bit easier once she hit the trees.

She walked, and she tried not to think. Finally, she found a spot in a clearing beneath a star-strewn sky, far enough to offer her silence. She sat on a root and leaned against the rough bark (and she swallowed everything down, down deep).

She flicked on the communicator. The old tech Ariadne had retrofitted sat neatly in the palm of her hand. The channels were too old for the Oracle to bother scanning; they had long been out of use for Tholosian ships. But those near-ancient channels spread farther than a Pathos loop could reach.

This decrepit thing was arguably safer than their comms on *Zelus*, in certain respects. Ariadne had encrypted it to only play on the matching machines the other scattered rebels had on their ships. Some had already broken theirs, Kyla was sure. Chucked them out the airlock or hit them with hammers, determined never to hear Kyla's voice again. They blamed her for Sher's betrayal (could she blame them?).

I miss you, she almost said to the comms. *Every last one of you.* She whispered those words to the trees, to the night where no one would hear.

After Persei, they were only meant to go their separate ways for a few weeks. Long enough for the worst of the heat to die down. Yet when Kyla had put their contingency plans in place—same code, roughly the same time each standardized day—she'd been unable to make contact with most of the Novantae survivors.

Kyla switched on the communicator.

"B7774F5," she said, stating the old Novantae code that identified one of their own. "Does anyone copy?" She watched the long branches sway as she listened to the crackle of the open channel.

She'd been at this for sixty-three days. How many were missing? How many didn't wish to come back? *How many were dead?*

She let another quarter of an hour pass before trying again. "B7774F5. Does anyone copy?"

Did anyone bother to listen?

Nova had been through untold skirmishes with the Tholosian military, but Persei was different. It had driven a wedge between the Resistance's remaining members.

Some of the rebels no longer trusted Kyla to lead. They'd always been more loyal to Sher, and his betrayal had shaken them. Kyla had cursed herself for a fool: she'd let Sher take the more visible role; her skills had always been with logistics. Lining up all the little pieces, seeing the bigger picture. Sher loved to swoop in and be the hero, and she'd let him right until he'd unwittingly become the villain.

She bumped the back of her head against the rough bark of the tree.

Eris's true identity being unveiled so spectacularly on Laguna had made things much worse. The whole galaxy had seen the former princess, barely standing under the weight of that jeweled headdress. It didn't matter that she'd proven herself to the Resistance. That she'd saved lives, eaten in the canteen with everyone else, cast off her past like the others. The woman who almost became the first Archontissa was different. The Tholosians at Nova had once been programmed; the Oracle hadn't given them a choice.

But Eris was among the few not controlled by the AI—and she'd chosen to kill so many people.

(Some pasts couldn't ever be forgiven.)

Eris said she didn't take it personally, but Kyla knew it stung. How could it not? Any friendships she'd had outside the Seven Devils evaporated like water on the Novan flagstones at high noon.

Sometimes, a rebel ship would desert them as they slept. Every time, the remaining members moved on again so none of the fleeing members sold out their comrades for bounty. Kyla hated to believe one of her own would be that greedy, but maybe they'd be angry enough (with her; with everyone) to try.

Barely four hundred Novantae left.

So, Kyla picked up that hunk of radio every godsdamned day, put out a signal, and talked to her people. She didn't know if the rebels who left were still alive. She didn't give a dusty fuck if no one listened. Maybe someone did.

She picked up the comm again. "B7774F5. Does anyone copy?"

Silence. Always silence.

"B7774F5," she tried again. "I hope you all are doing better than we are, because we're stuck in a cave for the foreseeable. My breakfast had mold in it. Tasted fucking terrible."

She babbled for a few more minutes. *Christos still half-assed his godsdamned cleaning duty; Dot managed to get three new ships flying and might be a better mechanic than Cloelia (don't ever tell Cloelia).* Only first names, and vague enough not to risk anyone, but specific enough that she might tempt those who knew them into saying something.

Anything.

Just as she was about to hang up for the night, she heard static and the unmistakable click of someone picking up the line.

"B7774F5A122."

Her heart leaped as she recognized the code. Athena. One of Nova's top former operatives. Athena's group had been the largest faction to break away, right after they all fled Persei. She'd had over two hundred agents at the time. The howling in Kyla's mind quieted.

They were alive.

"Athena. Gods burning in the Avern, it's good to hear your voice."

"You too. We ran into some pirates and took a bit of damage, had to go silent. Nothing we couldn't handle. Turned out worse for the pirates." Kyla could hear the grin in the other woman's voice. The static intensified, and for a second, Kyla worried the transmission had cut.

"You're sure this line is secure?" Athena asked.

"Ariadne's positive. You're okay?"

A sigh crackled through the line. "We're hunkering down. Connected our ships into a makeshift space station. Supplies are getting low, but we're scavenging."

"Always half a meal and a few bullets short." A deep, painful breath filled Kyla's lungs. "How many rebels are with you?"

This was the answer Kyla dreaded. How many had escaped from Persei with their lives? (How many had she failed?)

"One hundred and seventy-seven."

Kyla ran her hands through her hair, clutching the dome of her skull. Another fifty or so gone. She'd know every one of their names, their faces. She'd made it her business to know every time someone new came to Nova. They'd trusted her. And too many followed her right to their deaths.

The Oracle and Damocles always knew when to strike. They'd killed some of Kyla's best field spies as soon as Rhea, Ariadne, and Nyx had dared run away to find the Resistance. And Oracle had re-twined One's tentacles of code back into Sher's synapses. Kyla figured it had happened after her brother's Agora mission, if not before. A spy had needed delicate extraction from the palace on the smallest of the Three Sisters, a slow and careful operation.

One slip-up was all it took.

When Sher had returned to Nova, he'd said the spy was already dead. Too late to save them. The first part was the truth; the second was the first of many lies that led to the loss of hundreds more Novan rebels.

Kyla had looked right into her brother's eyes without realizing he was no longer staring back. She hadn't seen the Oracle peering out from behind his hazel irises. She hadn't even noticed he was any different.

(How could she not have known? Shouldn't she have known?)

"Are you still there?" Athena asked.

Kyla loosened a breath. "Sorry, yes, I'm still here. Have . . . have you made contact with any other groups?" she asked. She swallowed back grief. Later. She could fall apart later. Her mind was whirring, fitting together pieces of the next steps.

"Only Thalia's group. Told me they were hiding out in Kersh. Felt safer with the natural-borns in the Snarl."

Thalia had fled with maybe another fifty after Persei. Another of their smaller ships slipping off into the black as everyone slept. Myndalia was where Kyla would have run if she was on her own. Clo's home was a maze of tenements and citizens in close quarters. Easy enough to hide.

"What are your coordinates?" she asked, hardening her voice. "Clo, Dot, or Elva can get you jump-ready in no time. We've got plans for Damocles, but we need all hands on deck in the meantime."

She didn't tell Athena their plan was based on little more than a whisper and a prayer. Sending two Devils behind former enemy lines, another few working around the clock on people who looked like walking corpses. Would any of them be able to wake up the people trapped somewhere deep inside their minds? Kyla was too afraid to hope.

And yet . . . it still burned within her.

The line stayed silent. "Athena?" she asked, worried the connection had cut.

The woman's sigh sounded mechanical through the ancient comms. "I'm sorry, Commander, but I'm not giving you that information."

Kyla straightened. "Say again?"

"Listen." Even on the shitty line, Kyla could hear the exhaustion. "The people here are burned, Kyla. We have twenty or more still recovering from injuries obtained while fleeing Persei, and the rest . . . they're not fighters, Commander. Our best soldiers died to get them out. We're recovering, but we're not . . ."

Kyla's fingernails sank into her palms. "They don't want to come back, do they? *You* don't want to come back."

"No," came the crackling whisper.

The wolf in her scrambled frantically at her ribcage, desperate to escape. "You're sure."

"We put it to a vote. I'm sorry, Commander."

Kyla picked up a pebble and threw it across the clearing with as much strength as she could muster. It hit the trunk with a satisfying *thump.*

The worst part was she couldn't blame them. Much.

"Right," Kyla said, hoping the rasp in her voice was covered by the static. "I won't pretend I'm not disappointed, but I respect your decision. However, if I reach out on this line again, I'd appreciate an update. And if you hear anything—if—if you need anything. We're here."

If Athena heard the tremble in Kyla's voice, she didn't let on. "Of course, Commander."

That title was nothing more than a courtesy, as hollow as the bland politeness of Athena's tone. Kyla was commander of an empty compound lost to sands. She was commander of all the corpses left behind in her and Sher's wake. She was commander of a handful of rebels left who were too stubborn to recognize when a cause was already lost but were brave enough to stay to the bitter end.

Kyla said her goodbyes, knowing this was almost certainly the last time she would speak to Athena. She had not found out if Zephyr was still alive, or Cora, or Gnat. Better to let the memory of them stay in her mind as they had been.

Kyla rested her elbows on her knees, head bowed. Then she pocketed the radio and walked deeper into the woods. Until she was far enough away from the camp, she could allow herself one full-bellied scream of rage and frustration into her hands.

Her howl echoed through the trees.

She let out everything she'd kept pent up for the past three months. Her throat hurt.

On the way back, her head was quieter. She could not wallow any longer. That was not her way.

She returned to her room on *Zelus* and lay back on the bed, staring up at the ceiling. She'd planned Rhea and Clo's operation as best she could. Now they just had to survive.

Survive, then strike.

Her eyes remained dry. The Tholosian Empire did not engineer soldiers to cry.

6.

THE SOLDIER

Twenty years ago

The Soldier stood in a meadow surrounded by corpses.

The scent of death clung to the inside of the Soldier's nose as she stood with her compatriots. They all had their hands behind their backs, shoulders straight, chins raised. The Soldier stared at the back of the helmet of the soldier in front of her. There was a tiny nick, perhaps from a fall, that looked like an eight-pointed star.

—They scream and beg for their lives. Hands bound in front of them, no weapons. A man locks eyes with the Soldier. Pleading, hoping against hope. There's a scar on his cheek in the shape of a trident. The fear as he meets the flatness of the Soldier's expression. The sharp, silver flash of a knife—

The fighting, if the Soldier could call it that, had ended nineteen hours earlier, and they'd been at attention ever since aside from the briefest of comfort breaks. No sleep.

The twin suns had made their journey across the sky. They waited for the Archon to fly in and oversee their success, to know that the soldiers he had bred in vats and programmed to do whatever he wished would stand for hours if commanded. They were the Primus cohort, the first militus group to have their brain synapses entirely coded by the Oracle from birth.

And this had been their real test: the slaughter of protesters who had marched at the palace on Tholos. None were military.

—*A woman runs, stumbling, balance thrown off by her bound hands. Her boots churn through the mud. The Soldier gives chase. The woman is fast. The Soldier is faster. The woman turns, raising her hands to shield herself, as if that will help. She is already missing the pinky of her left hand. The knife arcs down—*

The citizens dead at the Soldier's feet were not even fighters. They were civilians who opposed the Archon and spoke out against the programming that had begun to more aggressively shape their thoughts through the chip inserted into their cerebellum at birth. For decades, the chip's original design was simple: it held the class, name, date of birth, and genetic sequence of every Imperial citizen. Now its new purpose was to utilize the Oracle's vast network and control the direction of citizens' thoughts.

The protesters had removed their chips, screamed they did not consent to control. Removing that chip was an offense. Speaking out against the Archon was a crime.

And they had been punished.

—*A young man, barely older than a boy. Hair in tight, soft curls against his skull. Brown eyes with flecks of green. The Soldier makes it quick, but the youth's blood joins the other stains on her uniform—*

The Soldier stood next to her brothers and sisters of the Primus cohort and tried to keep her expression neutral.

(She focused on her blinks. Counted them with her breaths. Anything to avoid thinking).

She almost envied her siblings, how easily they seemed to take their programming. The Soldier was playing a role. Always pretending. Even the buttons on her uniform—all those honors awarded for bravery in battle—felt like lies. In the haze of war, or when commanded to do the Archon's bidding, her programming became almost impossible to resist. But when the programming images flashed in her mind, they became triggers for her adrenaline. They forced her hand to reach for a weapon even when her mind screamed at her to stop.

—*The Soldier stands in the middle of the churned field. The screams have silenced. Soldiers pick their way among the corpses, firing the odd*

Mors to check no one was playing dead. A man gives himself away with a scream—

She blinked. Only in the moments afterward, when she realized what she had done, did those flashing images of words (*Loyalty. Honor. Subservience. The God of Death, I kill for Thee. The Archon, I kill for thee*) begin to fade around the edges and her mind began to cry *stop stop stop—*

Behind the Soldier's back, a hand gripped hers. Sher. A brother like her—broken, unfixable. They both questioned those images in their mind. Sometimes, they resisted. Sher had his own doubts and nurtured his hatred for what they were forced to do in service to the Empire.

Maybe their genes were flawed. Maybe the Primus cohort experiment had failed. Whatever the reason, if the Archon discovered their glitches, he would have them executed. Even holding her hand was a risk.

"He's coming," Sher said in an exhale. "Slow your breathing. Now."

The Soldier looked up, startled. She had been so distracted (by guilt, the stench of blood and smoke, bodies at her feet, and oh *gods*, she had done that) that she hadn't realized how shallowly the air filled her lungs. She hadn't noticed the twin craft approach with the Archon's seal on the side. Those crossed scythes glinted ominously in the bright afternoon light as the craft settled in the meadow's grass.

Their commander went over and opened the door for the Archon. He stood aside as the leader of the Tholosian Empire gracefully exited the craft, accompanied by a handful of nobles and a servitor. The Archon and the nobles were dressed in their best military uniforms, pressed and clean, with gold buttons gleaming in the sunlight. In contrast, their servitor had roughhewn and plain garments, the trousers tied around her waist with a narrow length of rope in place of a belt. The servant class wore what their masters provided. They were intended to disappear, but the Soldier always studied the shape of the eyes, the tilt of the mouth. Finding some little unique detail.

The group walked through the field of corpses and approached the line of soldiers.

The Soldier ought to have gazed straight ahead at that eight-pointed star, but she couldn't help but glance at the servitor. The woman did not have the same slim, willowy frame many servants had due to their simplified diet, but rather the well-fed musculature of a higher class. A sense of unease went through the Soldier as she studied the other woman's features. The woman had eyes so dark, the iris looked entirely black. The effect was unsettling but familiar. Did she . . . *know* her?

"How long have they stood at attention?" The Archon's question to Commander Hatysa, who led the massacre, reminded the Soldier of where she was. The bodies at her feet. Her brother's hand still pressed to hers.

Her breathing. (Too fast.)

(Slow. Slow. *Slow.*)

"Nineteen hours, General," Commander Hatysa said. She was wilting around the edges if you looked closely enough.

Like the soldiers under her watch, Commander Hatysa had stood at attention. Unlike her soldiers, the commander was not engineered to the Primus cohort level—with every gene carefully picked by the Oracle for optimum performance. It was the first time the Soldier had realized that, in some ways, their commander was weaker than her soldiers.

The Archon looked pleased as he addressed the members of his court. "This is the future of the Tholosian military. The Oracle has already engineered Secundus, Tertius, and Quartus cohorts, who will be even more impressive post-training. Our AI has now begun experimental stages on future generations with a plan to defeat the Evoli within decades. Under Commander Hatysa leading the Primus cohort, we've already taken the fringe Evoli planet of Nihal. You will all be leading future cohorts of these soldiers into battles."

Sher's hand fell away from the Soldier's back as one of the noblemen stepped forward to examine her and her closest compatriots. The Soldier was too aware of the dried blood that covered her uniform, of the sweat at her brow. That her breathing had picked up again.

(Slow. Slow.)

"I saw vids of that battle," the nobleman murmured, eyes unwavering on her face. "This one killed more Evoli in days than I'd ever slaughtered in a lifetime." He glanced at Commander Hatysa. "What name was he given?"

The Soldier held back a flinch. Her private thoughts were a refuge that screamed *she, she, she.*

Commander Hatysa smiled. "███████. A name granted by the Archon himself."

Like all soldiers in the Tholosian military, that name was a mark of survival, granted only after they had fought their first battle after youth training. It was meant to be a badge of honor, like the one they had pinned to their uniform breast, right under the scythes. For the first twelve years of her life, she had only been assigned a random number, a suffix to her Primus cohort.

And her new name—just like the old one, and like her station, her sex, her ranking, her life—had been chosen for her. A "gift." This one with the rare honor of being given to her by the Archon himself.

The sound of it was like nails in her skull. The shape of it did not fit.

The Soldier tried to ignore their conversation. They spoke of her as if she were little more than a valued possession who did not have thoughts of her own. As if her thoughts did not scream that she was proof even the Oracle was fallible. The chip at the base of her skull might read out her genetic sequences and say *male*, but she was *not* (she, her, woman). She was more than numbers within a chip, than two fucking chromosomes spit out by chance. She was more than the gender assigned to her at birth. *She was more than they could ever know.*

And her name did nothing more than remind her that having these thoughts was a crime.

The nobleman, finally, stepped away to address the Archon. "And if these"—he gave one of the corpses a kick with his boot—"*traitors* continue to grow in number, will we need to fight on two fronts, General? I hear they've begun to steal our artillery to arm themselves."

"To that, Colonel, I have already found a solution." The Archon called the servitor with a sharp voice, "Husk. Come!"

Husk? The Soldier caught the malicious pleasure in the Archon's expression as the servitor dutifully approached. Her face was blank, lifeless. As if she registered nothing of the world around her, not even the bodies at her feet that were beginning to attract pests.

"Would any of you happen to recognize her?" the Archon asked his nobles. When they all shook their heads, he roughly lifted the servitor's chin. "Speak until I tell you to stop."

The voice was as monotone as a ship's computer. "Of course, Your Excellency. My voice is your voice. I will speak for however long you would like until you tell me to stop—"

"*Stop.*" The servitor shut her mouth, and the Archon looked again to his nobles. "And now?"

The Soldier didn't need their answers. Cold had spread down her spine, for she knew that voice, even flat as it was. Everyone in the Tholosian Empire heard the broadcasts when activists hacked them. That voice had been brave enough to criticize the Archon's tyranny. Her protests had spread across planets as others resisted their own programming. The threat of execution did not quiet her and the other rebels.

Then a few months ago, her transmissions had stopped.

Caught traitors were executed in grand fashion, the vids transmitted across the Empire. But this one had simply gone quiet.

And here she was, a servitor.

"Not any servitor," the Archon said, responding to the noble who had voiced the Soldier's thoughts. "A gerulae. A new experimental program the Oracle has implemented for the worst of our criminals. They have no thoughts of their own, and they cannot resist a command. Watch." The Archon turned to the former rebel. "Husk. Kneel at my feet." The woman knelt before him without hesitation. "Husk, give me your hand. Colonel, if you'll allow me to borrow your blade." The colonel passed the Archon his ornate, jewel-hilted knife, and they all watched as he held it over the woman's hand. "Husk. You will show no pain when I hurt you."

The Soldier held her breath as the Archon stabbed the girl through the hand. She did nothing. Not a flinch, not a blink—she didn't even move. How could programming overcome automatic physiological responses to something like pain?

The Soldier felt Sher's hand again, gripping hers at their sides, where they stood shoulder to shoulder. A risk, but she was comforted by her brother's solidity. They both watched as the Archon jerked his knife out of the woman's palm. Blood pooled a wine-dark red.

The nobles applauded.

The Archon gave more commands, made her scream. Forced her to beg. Each order only had the nobles laughing and clapping harder.

And each moment only had the Soldier clawing deeper into herself, into the private part of her mind she'd carved outside of her programming. She pressed her fingers to Sher's palm and kept him with her, for she was not alone. She was not alone in wanting to escape this, in not wanting to do what this man commanded. In wanting those images to stop flashing in her mind (*Loyalty. Honor. Subservience. The God of Death, I kill for Thee. The Archon, I kill for thee*).

She remembered what the rebel's name had been before the Oracle erased it along with the rest of her. That woman in the broadcasts deserved better than this. Her words had been filled with strength when she spoke, her message communicated to every corner of the Empire: *Resist. Rebel.*

Nova.

Her name was Nova. She had given it to herself, for she had wanted something new.

The Soldier liked the sound of the name. Her mouth silently formed the two syllables, her teeth biting her lip for the *v*. She would remember that name, file it away in the parts of her mind the Oracle had not touched. She would remember Nova, even if Nova couldn't remember herself. She would remember this woman who had risked everything to fight back.

She'd place it with the name she had chosen for herself, that was not a badge she had won in battle but one earned through strength. A name she had never heard on anyone else's lips. Another two syllables that she whispered in her mind, almost like a prayer. She would set it next to the pronouns the Oracle had not assigned to her but she knew in her heart to be true.

She. Her.

Kyla. My name is Kyla.

As the former rebel bent to kiss the Archon's golden boots, Kyla made the other woman a silent promise.

Nova. Let your name be a revolution.

7.

CLO

Present day

The months of training with Elva and Eris hadn't exactly been pleasant. At least Clo hadn't tried to kill either of them. She deserved a commendation for that. Maybe her own fluming parade.

She'd had her brain stuffed full of as many facts about Evoli society as she could manage. She'd watched how Elva and the other Evoli Novantae interacted. Their body language, their terms of address. She knew that Evoli had a fluid understanding of gender—she'd asked Nils more about that in conversation, not revealing her mission, but it'd been for an ardent curiosity as well as intel. Nils had been happy to discuss, their face wistful as they spoke of their homeland.

This was the last session—the final test of Clo's progress. Clo tried to swallow down her nerves as she waited, composing her expression in the way Eris had taught her. The effort distracted her from what was to come.

If she passed today, Clo and Rhea would be setting off to a planet full of Evoli who would murder them if they learned their true identities. If they failed in their task and made it out alive, the rebellion would suffer. They'd continue to survive day by day, with no hope for the future.

Eris, Rhea, and Elva were late. Clo paced the clearing, crunching the pine needles under her feet. Finally, she heard the others arriving. Rhea wore purple trousers—as stained and threadbare as everyone's clothing, but they did hug her thighs nicely. Rhea leaned forward to kiss Clo on the cheek as Eris and Elva entered the clearing behind her.

"About time," Clo groused. She knew full well she probably looked so briny, she might as well be pickled, but she couldn't help it.

"Meeting ran all morning," Eris said, "and Elva needed to eat something. Just enjoy the fresh air, Clo. You're about to be stuck on that ship to Eve for a week, smelling like unwashed swamp ass."

Clo glared. "Does that mean I passed, or are you just salty today?"

Elva lifted a hand between them. "She's not the only one who gets to decide," she said to Clo. "And I need to be sure."

Clo grumbled. Elva motioned to the ground, and the four of them sat cross-legged in the middle of the clearing, not quite close enough to touch. The thigh muscle of Clo's amputated leg cramped slightly, but she eased it into position.

Elva tucked her dappled hair behind her ears, but the wind still ruffled the brown and blond strands. The fractals on her arms were more visible than Rhea's, clustered so close they looked like blotted lines rather than freckles. She settled her features into serene concentration—an expression Clo far preferred seeing on the Evoli's face when she was fixing an engine rather than teaching Clo to wrangle her turbulent emotions.

Clo finally got comfortable and looked over at Eris. "*Do* you think I passed, at least?"

Eris's lip twitched. "Maybe. Elva says you still bleed emotions when you're annoyed, and that's something I mastered when I was six, so." She shrugged.

Clo made a face.

The Tholosian royal family's resilience to Evoli abilities wasn't innate but rather a result of the intense training they underwent at the academy on Myndalia. It'd taken a lot for Clo to keep her expression neutral as Eris told her of the horrors she had endured as a child. And for so long, Clo had been jealous of the girl who lived in that golden building that circled the skies over Kersh like a gilded crown, casting occasional shadows over the Snarl. Now she'd never let that envy bite her again.

A shadow slanted across Eris's face. Clouds gathered thick overhead, the air damp enough to make Clo shiver. Then those strange golden eyes settled on her, and as Eris spoke, the silver of her new tongue glinted in her mouth.

"Shut your eyes and let Elva try to read you," Eris said, voice cool as the breeze through the clearing. "You know what to do."

Clo did as she asked and slipped into the swamp, as she had so many times before. She pictured the wetlands outside the Snarl. Miles and miles of brackish water rumored to contain monsters in their depths.

But only the dead occupied that swamp: bones of the people caught by the undertow, bodies discarded by the Empire. And somewhere, in the substrata with all the others, was Clo's mother.

The swamp in Clo's mind blended for a moment with the gray beach of Fortuna, but she pushed it back. Kept the image clear.

Elva's mind prodded her, trying to draw her above the waterline. Clo had to stay alone in the dark abyss.

Where no one could touch her.

Elva struck. Her mind crashed into Clo's, a quick assault that sought vulnerabilities. A crack formed in Clo's focus, and her mother's corpse was dragged through the current. Clo gave her head a shake. She forced the image away, her adrenaline spiking.

There is only the green-gray of the water. Sink deeper. Like Eris taught you.

She submerged until there was no hint of light. Her mind became as black as the void of space.

But that wasn't enough. She had to fill her lungs with metaphorical water, drown in the absence of emotion. Her mother's dead face flickered behind her eyelids, pale features staring up at her from the bottom of the swamp, her hair floating like seaweed.

This was where Clo usually started to thrash. To fight her way toward the surface. She'd heard that drowning was one of the most painful ways to die.

It's nae real. Nae real.

Clo forced herself to let the current carry her to the deepest point of the marshland. To allow the water to fill her body like a vase until her lungs burned.

And ... then ... it was almost too easy to go numb and sink further into the deep. Her body tucked under roots where the caimans lay in wait. Just one more body laid to rest, like all the others.

She'd join her mother at the bottom of the swamp.

Clo opened her eyes. The other women were there with her: Eris, Elva, Rhea. She knew them, but any associated feelings remained somewhere in that murky water.

When she was on Eve, Clo would have to remember that swamp at all times. Remember the corpses that littered its depths. She'd have to try not to become one of them.

Clo folded her lips into a smile that she knew didn't reach her eyes. "Did I pass?"

Elva made a noise. "Maybe." She looked at Rhea. "Scan her. Start gentle."

Rhea's lashes fluttered shut. Clo's heartbeat thudded in her ears, and an intense pressure built in her mind. It built, it built—

She let out a pained gasp.

"Clo, how does that feel?" Eris asked.

"Like there's a rodent scratching around my brain." The words were right, something she would say, but the tone was flat.

Rhea looked sheepish. "Sorry."

"Half of Clo's brain is full of rat shit already," Eris said. "Doesn't make much difference."

Clo flashed Eris double scythes, one foot still firmly in the swamp.

Elva gave Rhea some instructions in Evoli, too fast for Clo to follow. Rhea had learned the language right alongside Tholosian, but Clo only knew simple phrases. She found Evoli frustrating—she'd recognize a word or the rhythm of the sentences, but it was like the cogs of an engine that didn't line up straight. She only knew a few words: *Hello. Thank you. Don't shoot.*

Elva and Rhea prodded at the edges of Clo's watertight seals. Pain glimmered at the edge of her awareness as they tried to glean what she was feeling. Clo wouldn't let Rhea in on any of that fear that threatened to rise to the surface. Instead, she sank back down into the water, right next to her mother. Briggs. The Furies.

It all ebbed away.

Clo hadn't even closed her eyes. The polite, fake smile was still on her face.

"I can't sense you," Rhea said, her voice catching on the last word. Though her words were breathless with amazement, her expression broadcast her unease. "You're right in front of me, but it's like there's a void where your emotions should be."

Clo looked at Elva. "You?"

Elva frowned, and her abilities skimmed Clo's mind once more. Then she shook her head. "Nothing. But you can't be this blank on Eve. You feel like—" Her eyes flickered to Eris, and she pressed her lips together. "You feel too much like her. Keep your secrets, but let something through."

Clo practiced revealing minor emotions. Anxiety about her precarious situation. Or some of that ever-present attraction to Rhea, the tinder always one spark away from a flame.

Eris watched it all, unblinking golden eyes studying Clo's face. When Elva nodded her approval, those irises gleamed in satisfaction.

Elva nodded. "You passed. I'll let Kyla know that I approve."

Clo's heart slammed as she rose on waterlogged limbs. When Rhea's hand reached for hers, she took it.

But she also pushed everything right down against the silt.

———

Clo yawned as she headed down the main hall of *Zelus*. She and Rhea had spent hours finessing the details of their identities with Elva, Kyla, and Eris, examining various strategies to find the intel they needed on Eve. Rhea stayed behind with Elva and Kyla to go over a few more details, but Clo's brain was tired. She needed rest.

Eris fell into step beside Clo. "You did well today," the princess said, watching Clo's expression as they moved through the corridors.

"A compliment?" She eyed the other woman. "Are you Eris or someone wearing her face?"

Eris made a noise. "Don't make it weird."

"Not making it weird," she said as they reached Eris's door. "Just happy to get one. You hoard compliments like Kyla hoards sweets."

Eris's lip lifted, and she motioned with her hand. "Come in," she said. "I have something for you to take to Eve."

Clo yearned to faceplant into her bunk, but she could spare a few minutes.

Eris's room was sterile as ever. Bed perfectly made. The only decoration was the little carved firewolf on a shelf next to the bed and a covered bowl with a few fire opals. Clo leaned against the small desk.

Eris plucked a tiny box off the shelf, opened it, and drew out a necklace. "This is from Ariadne."

Clo took it by the leather strap and watched the plain pewter locket twist back and forth in the light. It looked a little like Rhea's necklace. She opened it up to find a miniature portrait of . . . *Elva*?

Clo's eyebrows lifted in surprise. "Uhhh."

Eris flashed a smile. "What, you don't want to carry around a picture of Elva close to your heart?"

"*No.*" She tried to push the locket back into Eris's hands. "Tell Ariadne to get tae fuck and find a hobby. I should never have told her that I slept with Elva before I met Rhea."

Eris refused to take the necklace. "Oh, calm down. Ariadne doesn't care about your ridiculous relationship drama. If Rhea's playing the role of Elva's sister, we have to use her features for the shifter." She motioned to the jewelry. "This is a long-range Pathos Ariadne's been developing."

Clo examined the little heart with renewed interest. "Can't she just put it in my head?" She *really* didn't want to carry around a picture of Elva.

"Too bulky. She still needs to perfect the tech and scale it down. But you can use this to update Kyla while you're on Eve." Eris pulled away slightly. "And me. If you need to talk. I know how lonely it can get during operations."

Clo was surprised to find her throat closed. For so long, she'd assumed that Eris simply put up with her. Valued her skills perhaps, but their old friendship was something that could never return.

Clo nodded at her, not trusting herself to speak.

Eris's face turned away, as if collecting herself. She reached into a drawer and brought out a bottle of moonshine. "Nightcap?"

Clo snorted, remembering those long-ago nights before they'd been put on the disastrous mission to Sennett. When Clo had thought they were just two unknown people chewed up and spat out by the Empire. Getting drunk to try and forget the past.

Then Clo learned that Eris was Princess Discordia—and she was responsible for too many atrocities. After that, Clo couldn't ever look at her the same way.

But that was a long time before. Eris had saved her life since—more than once.

"Give it here," Clo said.

Eris cracked the seal, and she took a swig straight from its mouth.

They ended up killing half the bottle. They spoke little, but the silence between them was easier. Eris didn't ask Clo if she was scared. This woman who had once been Princess Discordia knew that bone-deep fear; she'd lived with it every time she'd gone on one of those ITI missions. She knew that once she'd made a choice, everything else was left to the gods. Because like Clo, she'd pledged her very soul to this tiny, doomed rebellion.

And there was no going back.

8.

CATO

Present day

Cato spent another night in the medical bay, chasing a cure for Nyx.

He'd tested the same fucking sample three times, hoping for different results. He'd lost count of how many hours he'd spent staring at the same four walls of the lab, searching his unfamiliar memories for anything that might save her. Those memories were often too much like dreams he struggled to recall upon waking.

Earlier, he had injected himself with a stimulant to keep his mind sharp. Exhaustion was terrifying. Whenever his mind grew tired, it became less vigilant, more exposed.

Vulnerable.

The Oracle's whisper—a remembered echo, still present despite being deprogrammed—buzzed inside his mind like a pest: *Save her? She is nothing more than a traitor to the Empire. Sacrifice her as the God of Death demands.*

"Stop it," he muttered to himself. He was a traitor too.

He gripped the hair at the nape of his neck, pressed his fingers to the tiny scar where his chip had once rested. Removing that had only been the beginning; the Oracle's tendrils had been hardcoded throughout his synapses, and Ariadne had worked her ass off to detangle them. But it was Nyx who had helped him come to terms with what happened: the Oracle might be ejected from his mind, but One's echoes would always be there—taunting, luring.

When he sat in the medical center and tested an attempted cure after cure after fucking cure—and failed, again and again—the Oracle whispered to him that a case like Nyx was considered a waste of resources. She was another soldier using dwindling supplies in a direct march toward the Avern.

Disloyal to the Empire.

Deserves her death.

Deserves worse.

He shoved those thoughts down. It had been Nyx who talked to him during the blinding pain of deprogramming sessions. Her voice had ordered him through the darkness, broken the Oracle's commands.

More tests. Another failed sample.

Another.

Another.

Hours ticked by, and Cato's eyes grew heavy. He owed it to Nyx to keep trying.

She is going to die. The Oracle's ghost calmly spoke in his mind. *Not the death she deserves. But you can still give it to her, for the glory of the Empire. For the glory of Tholos. The God of Death would reward you. Kill her.*

Kill—

Cato's hand reached for the Mors at his desk.

"Fuck," he hissed, tossing the weapon aside to scramble through his drawer for another stimulant.

His hand trembled as he gracelessly jabbed the needle into his arm. In his usual ritual, he whispered the names of the moons of Lethe, his home planet, to stay sharp while the drug took effect: *Hypnos. Aletheia. Acheron. Cocytus. Phlegethon. Styx. Eridanus.*

Images flashed through his mind of the battles in his youth. The whispering grew so loud. *Let her die. Put a Mors blast into her skull. Kill her.*

Kill her.

Kill her.

"Hypnos." He snapped the word, shutting his eyes. *"Aletheia. Acheron. Cocytus. Phlegethon. Styx. Eridanus."*

He imagined the icy mountains of Lethe where he trained, the way the moons rose in the pink twilight, and how he'd lie awake at camp, knowing the whispers in his mind didn't feel right, but he could never quiet them. They had been relentless once, indistinguishable from his own thoughts. Sometimes, he didn't know where the Oracle ended and he began. All he had to identify as his own were the moons Demi had loved so fucking much.

He frowned. *Demi?*

"Cato?" He opened his eyes to find Nyx at the door, her expression worried. She came inside and shut the door for privacy. Her brown skin was damp with sweat; he wondered if she'd tried sleeping. "I heard you down the hall. Talking to yourself?"

His hand itched for that Mors. She only had weeks. Wouldn't it be a kindness?

Kill her, the Oracle whispered. *Sacrifice her for the Empire.*

"You should go." His voice sounded hoarse. He never let her see him when he got like this. "Go back to bed, Nyx."

"You first, asshole." She came forward and settled in one of the other chairs, her eyes bright. Low-grade fever, he guessed. She'd probably slept as poorly as he did.

"Trying to avoid it," he muttered.

"Makes two of us," she said. Her eyes swept his messy desk, resting on the discarded Mors at his feet. She pressed her lips together but didn't mention it. "Testing cures?"

"Failing at it."

She gave him a bitter smile. "I won't ask how long you've been in here, trying to put me back together again, because I know I won't like the answer. So, what's the deal with the weird chanting?"

Cato rose and tossed another test into the decontamination bin. "Told you," he said, fighting not to sway on his feet. "Trying to avoid sleep."

Her illness had not lessened the intensity of her dark gaze. It was still as sharp as a damn scalpel. "Why? It's not like *you're* sick."

Cato sighed and braced his hands against his desk. "Go to bed, Nyx," he said again. "I'm sure you'll still be around in eight hours to be my shittiest patient."

"How do you know?" she asked. "Unless your memories are hiding another life as a fucking prophet."

Kill her.

Cato sucked in a breath and again pressed his fingers to the scar at the base of his skull. Such a small mark, hardly noticeable with his hair to cover it. But he remembered how it had burned when Rhea had removed it. Such a little pain compared to the deprogramming that followed.

"I'm tired," he whispered, not knowing how else to explain to her.

What would she think of him if he confided that he still heard the Oracle's commands? That all of Ariadne's deprogramming had loosened the tendrils of One's influence but did not quiet the voice that always spoke of loyalty, sacrifice, and war?

"Okay. Then work on something else," Nyx said, as if she understood his thoughts. When he opened his mouth to argue, she put up a hand. "You told me I'd still be around in eight hours, and you don't want to sleep, so: work on something else."

Cato gave a reluctant nod and gestured with his fingers. Nyx followed him to the lab's back room, where he kept the second project he had worked on over the months: his gerulae research.

He flipped the lights and shut the door behind Nyx. *Zelus* had four gerulae kept in suspended animation in their medical lab, former resistance members the Novantae saved from hard labor. Kyla's scientists on Nova had worked for years to revive them, but every effort proved impossible. Their notes presented two theories: gerulae programming either destroyed the mind or suppressed identity and memories so deep that individuals became locked in. Completely conscious but helpless to the programming that controlled their bodies.

Cato had hoped for the former.

According to Kyla's Evoli source, it was the latter. And they'd succeeded where he and Ariadne had failed: they'd woken them up.

Nyx wordlessly approached the glass tank of one gerulae, a former rebel engineer named Chara. Tall, pale-skinned, red hair. It only made the tattoos of the scythes across her cheeks and the dark moon on her forehead all the more obvious. The marks were given to every gerulae when they were erased—proclaiming them as nothing more than a husk.

Everyone on *Zelus* but Cato and Ariadne avoided this part of the med bay. Even Cato acknowledged something was haunting about the four people kept in large tanks, so still and serene. Ariadne had done her best to control the direction of their dreams to something joyful—playing soft music, sending sweet images through their synapses—and Cato hoped she had succeeded.

If they could still dream, that meant they still had minds to save.

Nyx's gaze flickered to the tablet displayed next to Chara's tank. "You put . . . interests?" She slid her finger to scroll through. "Occupation. Likes. Hobbies? For a husk." She looked over at him, frowning. "Why?"

They'd lied to the others and claimed Nyx was Cato's assistant in the med bay, but she never helped with the gerulae. They freaked her out as much as everyone else.

Cato couldn't blame her.

He looked away, approaching the screen that held the three-dimensional scans of Chara's brain. All at once, he felt angry. *Husks.* He'd called them that once, treated them like shit because that was what his programming had suggested. They were traitors to the Empire, and this was their punishment: to serve it unquestioningly.

"Because I don't see them as husks. Not since—" Cato pressed his lips together and pulled up Chara's scan. The center of the room filled with the bright lights of the former rebel's brain, the details of its gyri and sulci, right down to its microanatomy. "She wasn't always like this. Her name was Chara, and everyone who knew her said she was a brilliant engineer. She designed most of the old Novan headquarters and some of their tech before Ariadne. She—"

"Was erased," Nyx interrupted flatly. "The Oracle erased her."

Cato stared at the lights of Chara's brain, the colors of her prefrontal cortex. And if he dragged his hand through those lights, he'd find her anterior cingulate cortex, which was involved in her moral decision-making and emotional awareness, higher-level functions that she had used to fight her birth programming and join the Novantae.

And the Empire had punished her for it. A fluke of her brain, that was all. Something the Oracle had tried to control but could not. Because One was not infallible. He still sometimes couldn't believe he'd accepted that. One made mistakes. Humans were not like objects to be categorized into little boxes.

"I don't think she was erased," Cato told Nyx. "And Kyla doesn't either. If she did, she wouldn't be sending Rhea and Clo halfway across the galaxy to find out."

Pity and disbelief flashed in her features. "It's due diligence to help her sleep at night," she said. "They're dead, Cato."

Cato held back a flinch. "You told me to work on something else," he snapped. "So, this is what I work on when I'm not trying to keep you from the Avern."

He was trying to solve two impossible problems. Banging his head against the wall every day. Every night. Running on fumes.

Nyx loosened a breath and settled in the nearest chair. "Fine." There was a tightness to her voice. "Then I'll be here to keep you awake."

Cato ran the scans. A thousand pinpoints of light in Chara's brain surrounded him, and he tried to find her. For years, everyone had believed that the gerulae were animated bodies that functioned as little more than puppets for the Oracle. That the Oracle killed the mind without destroying the body.

And the tendrils of One's programming seemed to support that idea. Among the starry lights of Chara's brain was a more extensive, red mass of the Oracle's programming tendrils. Like a virus that had overtaken the brain, forcing every process to function through the AI's commands.

He and Ariadne had been experimenting with electric pulses to try and shift some of the coding threads. They'd had some success using those bursts on bounty hunters during their supply runs, but the interruption never lasted long. They were close to finding a way to interrupt the Oracle's routine background programming—not permanently, but long enough for a citizen to choose: loyalty or rebellion. If they did that, they might have a similar breakthrough with the gerulae.

As Cato picked his way through the Oracle's snakelike programming, delicately targeting areas with pulses, he imagined he was working through his own brain. These same coils had once overtaken his mind. Now they were gone, and what was left?

A whisper. *Loyalty. Sacrifice. The Empire had been everything to you, once. Worth everything.*

Was that One's voice or his?

He pulled through the thorns of Chara's brain, and a memory flashed inside him.

—The screaming of a battlefield hospital. A medical bay in the field. The edge of a scalpel at his neck. Blood. More blood—

He swept through another section of Chara's brain, rotted through with the Oracle's coils. More memories erupted, terms for each part of the brain as he went through them. These came to him as if from a great distance; they had helped him treat Nyx.

Most of his waking memories showed his entire life as a military pilot. Despite some holes, they were consistent. But these other parts that came to him in exhaustion were of a different existence, one as a medic. These were the parts that made him wonder if Chara was still in her brain somewhere, suppressed by an AI programming that prioritized obedience and servitude, who enforced the brutal will of the Empire over its citizens.

Where did the medic memories come from? He thought to himself, as he slid through another small section of Chara's brain.

They had to come from somewhere. Skill sharing, perhaps? Did some soldier out there have his memories of learning to fly? The Oracle had fucked around in his mind, played with his memories, and forced him to obey.

Then obey, that voice whispered.

Hypnos. Aletheia. Acheron. Cocytus. Phlegethon. Styx. E—

"*Cato.*" Nyx's hands shoved through the scans and gripped his shoulders. Cato realized he was breathing hard, swaying on his feet. "You need to sleep." When he gave a shake of his head, she said, "No bullshit. You're no use to anyone in this state. You need to sleep."

Before he could reply, she all but dragged him over to one of the medical cots and shoved him into it. As soon as Cato's head hit the pillow, he was beyond help. Another stimulant would only delay the inevitable.

But when Nyx got up to leave, Cato said, "Stay. Please stay. Guard my Mors."

Nyx stared at him for a moment, then wordlessly retrieved his Mors and pressed the safety on. "All right."

He was too tired to stop the whispered confession: "I still hear the Oracle."

He didn't add that somewhere in his past, he must have known something that One wanted him to forget.

The soldier's expression didn't change. "So do I," she told him. "But I'll hold on to the Mors for you. And when you wake up, I'll hand it back. Because the Oracle's ghost may still speak to you, but One doesn't control you. Not anymore."

As he shut his eyes and drifted off to his fractured nightmares where he was no longer himself, he held on to that thought: *One doesn't control you.*

Not anymore.

9.

Present day

"**C**ato put a lock on you once, remember?" Rhea overheard Clo crooning through the door. "He doesn't love you like I do, my snell one. But fly well for him and Kyla while I'm gone."

"Are you speaking to the ship again?" Rhea called as the door to the *Zelus* engine room slid open.

"No," Clo lied.

Rhea smiled. She loved that Clo spoke to the vessels she worked on as if they were sentient creatures she could cajole into operating better. "Ariadne's asking for you," Rhea said over the hum of *Zelus*'s engine.

The other woman rubbed at a speck on the metal with her rag. "Let me guess: a goodbye party that surprises no one?"

"Just indulge her. Pretend to be surprised." Rhea drew closer, watching as Clo put the finishing touches on her maintenance list. Elva could do the work in her absence, but *Zelus* was Clo's baby.

Rhea idly toyed with her locket—now fitted with Ariadne's Pathos like Clo's new one—as she studied Clo's sanctuary. The engine was almost sinuously smooth, the walls painted with decorative frescoes of Tholosian soldiers enclosed by fires and flames. Welcomed to the Avern after a heroic death in battle.

Clo had scrubbed out all of the soldier's faces, leaving scratches of paler metal. Ariadne had gotten more creative, drawing silly expressions on those soldiers: cross-eyed, tongues sticking out, or mouths open wide in laughter. Little ways to make the place feel more like theirs rather than a stolen tool of warfare.

Shouts drew Rhea's attention. *Zelus*'s hull door was open for air circulation, and Rhea had a clear view of fellow Novantae hastening through the cave's Cathedral as they organized supplies and reviewed the integrity of their ships. Kyla had tasked teams with overseeing maintenance while they could depend on the relative protection of Fortuna's caves.

Clo wiped her forehead with the back of her hand and picked up a throttle she was replacing. Rhea had learned a few mechanical parts; Clo would walk her through repairs before she got distracted and focused on certain parts of Rhea's body instead. They'd kissed in nearly every safe square inch of the engine room.

"All this damp," Clo muttered. "If the ships stay down here too long, they're going to corrode and rust. But I guess that won't be my problem for a while." She finished slotting the throttle in and sat back with a sigh. "Do you think this plan will work?"

Rhea pressed her hands together. During these final hours on *Zelus*, she'd been trying to push the mission out of her mind. "I don't know," she said quietly.

Clo glanced at her with an expression that was all too perceptive. "Want to skip Ariadne's party and make out in my bunk?"

That drew a soft laugh from Rhea. "Tempting." She gave a rueful smile. "But we ought to say goodbye."

"I prefer kissing."

"Ariadne would never forgive you." When that didn't get a response out of her, Rhea added, "There'll be alcohol."

"Magic words, right there."

They headed back to their bunk for a change of clothes and a two-minute cold shower. When Clo and Rhea emerged from *Zelus* and into the cave's interior, Ariadne's music drifted through the Cathedral. The Old World rhythm was so distinctive from the Tholosian-approved songs, fast enough to dance to. Every ship had spared a few proto bars cut up onto little plates and smeared with nut butter—a sweet bite for

everyone. Alcohol flowed from the cask of moonshine Daphne had stolen on a previous run.

Rhea smiled at people she'd only just gotten to know. Albus grinned
back in her direction, while Ry called out a rude joke to Clo. Others
swayed to the music. Rhea indulged in the laughter and idle chatter—
small comforts before so much uncertainty.

"*Rhea!*"

Ariadne broke through the crowd and wrapped her arms around
Rhea. She returned the fierce hug, running her hand down the other
girl's back. She marveled at the changes in Ariadne's shape, the result of
meals other than the tasteless kykeon she'd eaten all her life. The verte-
brae weren't as bumpy beneath Rhea's fingertips.

Tenderness swept through Rhea, and her eyes stung. "I'm going to
miss you, sweet." The words caught in her throat.

"No! You're not allowed to cry yet," Ariadne said, pulling back. "If
you start crying, then you won't dance." She dabbed at her own wet
eyes.

Rhea let Ariadne lead her in a wild dance, one she'd only attempted
after she gained her freedom. As the moonshine flowed, Rhea let herself forget what tomorrow would bring. Instead, she spun with Ariadne
and reveled in the comfort and safety of her fellow Novans. Clo joined
her for a dance or two, moving smoother on her new prosthetic. Rhea
focused on the steps of her feet. The feel of Clo's hands on her waist.
The sway of her hips.

Hold on to this. For tonight, hold on to this moment.

But the night eventually wound down. People returned to their
rooms for rest, and a few took their bedrolls to sleep out under the stars.
The Cathedral grew as quiet as its name.

Rhea and Clo started making their rounds of painful goodbyes.

Nyx cleared her throat, awkward. "Try not to die," she said.

"Same to you," Clo said with a grin. Nyx didn't return it. Cato patted
their shoulders in that friendly way of his. Up close, Rhea noticed the
exhaustion lining his features, the circles under his eyes stark in the
dim gray lighting. He hadn't slept more than a few hours in days, she'd
guessed.

"If you damage *Zelus*," Clo told him, "I'll beat your balls with a wrench. You still owe me a ship."

Cato rolled his eyes. "I already gave you a ship." He gestured to *Zelus*.

"That's not how it works. You didn't even *own*—" But Rhea was already dragging Clo away before she got into arguing.

Kyla gave them both hugs—which surprised Rhea, but she leaned into it, rising on her toes to rest her chin against the taller woman's shoulder. Clo returned Kyla's hug just as fiercely.

Eris was not a hugger, but she inclined her head at them. "Be careful. Ariadne would be upset if you got killed."

Clo smiled. "Just Ariadne?"

Eris ignored Clo and clasped Rhea's shoulder. "Take care of her. Don't let her do anything too fucking foolish, please."

"I won't."

Ariadne was last. The girl led them to her room and gave Clo and Rhea little gifts. Clo received a pinecone painted in colors like fire to remind her of Nova. For Rhea, she presented a rough amethyst she'd found while exploring deep in the caves.

"Isn't it nice?" Ariadne sniffed, trying unsuccessfully to hold back her tears. Rhea felt her smile flicker. "It reminded me of you. Pretty and purple. You like purple, don't you?"

That made Rhea smile. "I love purple."

Clo picked Ariadne up and swung her around, and the younger girl gave a watery laugh.

"We can't take your presents to Eve," Clo said gently, "but keep them safe for us, all right?"

Ariadne nodded. "Okay."

Clo set her down, and Ariadne carefully arranged the two gifts on one of her shelves. She'd packed her small space with rocks, shells, and flowers pressed between unbreakable planes of glass. Stones that had caught the girl's eye as she wandered Fortuna or the other planets they'd set down on to steal supplies. Ariadne would have a name for each of them. Some silly, some beautiful, but all meaningful.

Rhea and Clo walked along the beach for the last time, drinking in the details of Fortuna before they returned for a few hours of sleep.

In bed, Clo reached for Rhea in the dark and deftly removed her clothes. Their bodies pressed together, moans quiet and urgent as they kissed. Clo's shields dissolved. Her emotions slid across Rhea's skin in heated caresses. Rhea craved Clo's touch. She knew every line of her body. Every notch of a scar. Just where the other woman liked to be touched.

Clo, too, had the skill to make Rhea come apart. Her hands were a marvel that brought pinpoints of pleasure that drove away every thought and fear.

Much later, Rhea listened to Clo's steady breathing. She wished bliss was not so temporary. Now she was left with only her thoughts and memories of the training session she'd tried to forget. Fragments played against the back of her eyelids.

Rhea tamps down her memories of the Archon's laboratory. Instead, she focuses on the brisk air, the lush moss against her legs, and dirt at her fingertips. The tactile sensations ground her as she expands her senses toward Elva.

Elva's walls are as dense as those that surround the palace on Tholos. Rhea circles those defenses, seeking vulnerabilities in the fortified barrier. Just when she's about to give up, she discovers a fissure: superficial but exploitable. Deep green shines through the gap, the same color as the pine needles of the forest surrounding them.

Rhea brushes her hand across the bleed of color. Homesickness?

She scratches at the crack, flicking aside layers of weakened rock. But Elva slams shut the pinpoint of access.

Rhea gasps, trying to find her bearings, but Elva is there again. On Eve, Rhea will have no chance to recover. She'll have to be perfect, or she'll be burned in seconds.

She launches herself at Elva's wall again; if there is one crack, there must be others.

Rhea gulps in air, pushing, pushing at the barrier. It holds too strong. With a stab of clarity, she chooses a different tack.

Rhea circles the wall again, seeking an old point of weakness she hopes is still there. The remnants of the Unity, a door through which every Evoli is welcome. Rhea gathers herself, preparing.

As she finds that old bridge to the Unity—solid but malleable, as if made of green willow—awareness slides over Rhea like the sheen of oil on water. She can pretend she is an Evoli, just like all the others walking through the white-stoned corridors of Eve's main palace in Talitha.

She is Neve, Elva's sister.

She belongs here, on this bridge.

She is not an intruder but a family member who has returned home.

There. A green of longing. Elva still yearns for Eve, for the comfort of the Unity. Rhea approaches the bridge. She does not have to turn into mist to break into this woman's mind. She is merely another member of the Unity. She is blood. She is kin.

Back in the room on *Zelus*, Rhea's hand inched to the locket at her throat.

Only, when she walks through to the bridge, she's assaulted by the sudden rush of Elva's emotions. The dark blue of old grief for her sister and her parents, ever present. And below that, a pulsing of red, hot as an ember.

The hatred that Rhea had, on some level, known would be there. Loud and bold as a klaxon.

Monster. Abomination.

Elva hides her hatred beneath the easy camaraderie, but not well enough.

Elva heaves, her body jerking back at Rhea's sudden presence in her mind. She rebuilds her walls, attempts to shove Rhea off the bridge. Intruders aren't welcome. Rhea has never been in the Unity.

Rhea is not one of us.

Rhea lands back in her body, breathing hard. Elva's mouth opens. To apologize?

"Don't," Rhea pants. "Don't say you're sorry. And neither will I."

Elva's mouth snaps shut, but Rhea feels that grief. For the briefest moment, Elva had lost herself and thought her real sister had returned. And Rhea is a monster for doing that to her.

Rhea presses to her feet, but she wants to run, to weave through the trees and head to the shoreline. To let the cold of the water shock her back into herself.

"Rhea," comes a voice, far away and then close. "Rhea."

Rhea gasped awake, the locket clutched tight in her hand. Clo was next to her, hand on her shoulder. "Are you all right? You were thrashing."

"Fine," Rhea said, trying to calm the beating of her heart. "I'm fine. Just a dream." *Just a memory.*

She settled back into Clo's arms, taking comfort in the other woman's warmth. As Clo settled once more, Rhea lay there, thinking over that training session and everything it revealed. The elation of knowing Rhea could pass unnoticed on Eve went wasted. Instead, Elva confirmed what Rhea had always feared: Rhea had no true home.

She was not welcome.

The Archon had tortured Rhea during her training without bothering to understand the people he intended to subdue. Conquerors never learned anything about the people they intended to destroy. If she'd shown up without Elva's training, she would have been burned as soon as she set foot on that planet. All that torture. All that pain. For what?

She moved the pendant along the chain, holding it at the sides. Back and forth, back and forth, the zipping of the metal against the chain comforting in the darkness.

Closer to dawn, Rhea and Clo rose from the bed and dressed in dirty uniforms that Tholosian prisoners of war would wear. Clo set aside her new, shiny leg and fitted her old, rusted one, grimacing at how it chafed against her skin. A prisoner of war, after all, wouldn't own something so valuable. They would be lucky to have a prosthetic at all.

They took one of the Novantae's oldest ships, *Themis*. Little more than a bullet craft. It was the only ship Kyla could spare, and even then, it would still be a loss for their faltering rebellion.

They tucked themselves into the cockpit as the sun rose over the trees to the east. Just as they were about to take off, Rhea spotted movement near the entrance to the Cathedral.

The Devils had all come to see them off. And there, in the tiny cockpit, Clo and Rhea allowed themselves a few tears as they set off for Eve—and an uncertain future.

We'll be back, Rhea vowed to herself, an echo of last night's words. *I promise.*

10.

RHEA

Three years ago

Whenever the name appeared in the ledgers of courtesan appointments, a heaviness seeped through Rhea's limbs. Lucius Modius Adranos-14.

It was a powerful name. A name of a hero on the front lines of war, returning for his just rewards. Rhea always imagined such a man: tall, black cape thrown over one shoulder to show off his armor. Strong features. Dark hair and eyes.

But Lucius Modius Adranos-14 did not exist.

Rhea stared at the words in the diary, wishing she could black the letters out with ink, as if that would stop dusk from shifting to evening.

She went through her routine. First, a bath perfumed with roses and oil. Then she applied lotions, tonics, potions, followed by plucking, shaving, brushing, painting. Silks and velvet sheathed her body, and jeweled combs glittered in her hair. She kept her neck free of jewelry— he preferred it bare, pale, white.

The man behind Lucius Modius Adranos-14 was the Archon.

He could be demanding and critical, but strangely, he was never cruel. But that was a false comfort—he was vicious in other ways. Yet, gaining his favor granted Rhea more power than she'd ever hope to achieve elsewhere.

Power meant protection.

Rhea waited for the clocks to strike in her room. Though she had grown up in the Pleasure Gardens, she'd not had her own rooms or clients for long, and her roster wasn't yet full. She'd just had her eighteenth name day. But while her visitor's name changed over the years, she'd seen the Archon more times than the outside of the palace walls. Four times a year when she was a child—then, as Rhea grew older, the summons became more frequent. Her shameful secret became attached to days on a calendar and times on a clock.

Eight times a year.

Sixteen.

Thirty.

Fifty.

From once a season to once a week. Soon, she feared, he'd increase their meetings to twice a week.

Gongs echoed through the palace. Rhea sighed and smoothed her features. She pressed the hidden catch in her room, and the secret door behind the wardrobe opened.

As far as she knew, her room was the only one with such a corridor. It was dark but clean enough that no dust caught on the hem of her gown. They must send bots down there to sweep and polish the floors—or perhaps to surveil her movements.

She came out the other hidden door into the secret room. It was always so bright after the darkness; she blinked until her eyes adjusted. The chair in the center of the chamber was ornate, with blood-red leather and gilded adornments. The small nodes that would be pressed to Rhea's skin were set on a tray, ready to map her every synapse and heartbeat, scrutinizing every way her body reacted to stimuli.

The Archon was there this time. He wasn't always, though Rhea knew he watched the recordings. She was never sure which was worse: when the Archon was present or being left alone with Oracle.

"Sit," instructed the disembodied voice that came from everywhere and nowhere—the Oracle.

Rhea couldn't stop her hesitation, and the Archon's eyes sharpened. She settled in the chair. The Oracle's small, robotic spider bots began placing the nodules on her skin.

"Drop the illusion," the Oracle instructed.

It was the voice that most citizens heard in their heads, day in, day out—loyalty engineered into Tholosians' very synapses. While Oracle was turned off deep in the Pleasure Gardens' rooms, the other courtesans were still fitted with chips at birth. Clients would inspect their evening paramour with scanners, checking their eyes and the implants at the base of the skull. Making sure they were inactive. They were paying for privacy as much as sex.

But Rhea? Like the Archon, she didn't have the Oracle in her mind. It wasn't compatible with her abilities. Rhea's mind was always her own, and no one other than the Archon knew it. So, he ordered her to pretend that she heard the commands that lulled her to sleep, the same as everyone else—just one more secret on top of her countless others.

She caught her breath, gathered herself up, and dropped the illusion, letting the markings dapple her skin. The Archon's gaze was unblinking. Having him see her spots was worse than having him see her naked.

She had disappointed the Archon and Oracle so far. Though she could craft an illusion and sense others' emotions, it still paled compared to what an Evoli could do. Like a watercolor painting instead of bold oil brush strokes.

A bot brought a vial filled with pale green liquid. Rhea had learned long before not to ask what was in it. The latest concoction would either help, do nothing, or poison her enough to make her sick. One day, she expected, they would kill her. Either due to miscalculating whatever was in the vials or because the Archon and Oracle decided she was no longer useful. An expensive failed experiment.

The Archon deigned to dose her himself this time. Rhea supposed she should find this an honor. She stared up at the bright lights, spots dancing in her vision. Pain pricked at the crook of her elbow, replaced by the hard press of his fingertips. She swallowed, waiting to see if she would feel nauseous, dizzy, or ill. She hoped for that untethered sensation of a high she would sometimes get. Something that would help her forget, or at least make the memories more bearable.

Rhea felt no different. She sensed only the pale orange of her unease. She waited for her vision to shift from the hospital room to the virtual-reality overlay the Oracle engineered anew each time. They were designed to elicit specific emotions, map her body's reactions, and compare them to the mass database of ordinary Tholosian citizens.

Sometimes, the tests were almost pleasant, like the ones that triggered euphoria and joy. Or the warm rose-pink of arousal. Positive emotions only lasted so long.

There had been experiments in pain. Fear. Anger. Hatred. All of those she knew well. She'd had to use all her mental training not to reveal her true feelings when images of the Archon or Prince Damocles flashed through her mind. The rush of love was more challenging, but they'd eventually managed by showing her images of Juno, the Pleasure Garden's Madam. She'd hated giving that away. Juno had looked out for her, protected her as much as she could in that place. If the Archon knew Rhea cared for her, that put the other woman in danger.

How many more could they wring out of her? How long until she cracked and showed too much?

Yet the virtual-reality image never came. The hospital room remained, smelling of metal and antiseptic. She tried not to imagine what else went on in this room when she wasn't there. If the leather of her chair was red to hide the blood.

"Renew your illusion," instructed Oracle, and Rhea obeyed. She stifled a sigh of relief when her skin was hidden once more, as if she'd put on a robe after seeing a client.

But her relief was short-lived: the door opened, and a child walked in, vibrating with fear.

Rhea's head snapped toward the Archon. Who was this boy? He was small and underfed, his skin dirty, wearing ragged, overlarge clothes. His hair might once have been a gleaming brown to match his eyes.

The Archon revealed nothing. He had practiced that implacable blank expression for centuries, after all.

"It is time for a test," the Oracle said, One's smooth voice echoing through the room. "You will make this child feel calm, safe, tractable. You may not speak to him. You must use only your abilities."

The child jerked at the disembodied voice, his fear spiking a dark purple. As if he had never heard Oracle before. Rhea's curiosity sparked.

"Where did he come from?" Rhea dared to ask the Archon.

The cruel leader's eyes narrowed. "Does it matter?"

"It would help," she said. "Empathy can deepen with knowledge and context." She wasn't sure this was true, but she wanted whatever information she could get.

"He grew up in the slums of Kersh on Myndalia," the Archon said. "So, he's never had an implant. His parents were executed for treason."

"I see," she said quietly. She glanced at the boy. "Hello."

The Archon made a sharp gesture. "Don't bother. He only speaks that slum dialect."

Rhea straightened, trying to keep her expression neutral. "Will he have the same fate as his parents?" she asked.

"That depends on you," the Archon said, lips curling up at the corners. "Your objective is to see if you can rewrite his emotions and demonstrate he's a good candidate for Oracle. Many of the Kersh rats reject implants if they're installed too late. If they don't take, then we'll wipe him to a gerulae."

Turn a little boy into a husk until there was nothing but an empty shell. At the stiffening of the child's shoulders, Rhea suspected the boy understood more Imperial than he let on. Sometimes, the wisest choice was to pretend ignorance.

"One's systems have predicted that children are easier to influence," the Oracle intoned. "Their programming has had insufficient time to acclimate to their minds, generating more frequent faults in the code. Like this specimen, mid-childhood or the incipience of puberty produces the highest occurrences of programming malfunctions, with one point zero five three nine seven four percent average."

Programming malfunction. Glitches that allowed people to buck the Oracle's influence. The Archon wanted Rhea to be a countermeasure against natural resistance to the AI's control.

"What if I can't do what you wish, through no fault of his own?" she asked. "What if it's just my abilities?"

The Archon scrutinized her. "Then you'd better prove yourself useful and do well, hadn't you?"

Rhea's heart fluttered, and her limbs shook almost as much as the child's.

She had attempted to influence others before, of course, but always outside this room. Usually with her clients—to set them at ease, to bring them comfort after trauma—but she could never be sure if it worked.

Once, she thought she'd managed to affect another's emotions. A lieutenant named Valeria Arktos-76 had ranted about a soldier in her cohort. Rhea had tried to be sympathetic, but she quickly grew impatient. After Valeria, she had four other clients, and it would throw off her schedule if their session didn't end on time. Rhea had dropped her shields and sent out an empathic blast. Mid-sentence, the lieutenant had calmed and stared at the wall blankly enough that Rhea grew worried.

Valeria had shaken herself off a few seconds later, but the desire for ranting had fled. The lieutenant had reached for Rhea, and their session finished on schedule.

Maybe the soldier's rage had sputtered out on its own. But Rhea had thought—hoped?—she had affected the other woman. She had felt a pulse deep in her body, that intensity of focus, but she hadn't been able to recreate it since.

Please, please let me be able to do it today.

Rhea crouched down in front of the child. He needed a bath, clean clothes, a proper meal—she wished so badly to take care of him. She reached out with trembling fingers. "May I touch you?" she asked.

The child's eyes blinked, surprised at being addressed directly. The Archon shifted behind them both, impatient. He probably thought it useless to speak to someone he viewed as barely human. This child was only a specimen of a people eking out a life in crowded slums, all of them sterilized by now. He might have even been one of the last born naturally. They would eventually die off from old age, sickness, or drug addiction, leaving the arable land on Myndalia for the Tholosians to turn into more farmland. The Empire was always hungry, never satiated.

The child gave a curt nod. So, he did understand. Rhea covered his hand with her own. So much smaller than her own, dirt dug in deep to the grooves of his skin. His hand was cold. She closed her eyes and unfurled herself, trying to push away any trepidation.

Safe. Safe. Safe.

She radiated the word from the depths of herself, hoping to transmit even a tiny bit of peace. But he was still tense and terrified, his eyes closed tightly.

Please, she thought, desperately. *Please feel safe, even though this place is anything but.* She imagined him wrapped in a warm embrace of protection.

His limbs relaxed. She took her hand away but still radiated the emotion at him. The child no longer looked like prey caught under the shadow of a predator but had the dreamy countenance of a child given the shelter of home.

Rhea turned to the Archon. He was wearing his mask again, impassive and unreadable. But she was open enough she could sense the deep, molten bronze of his triumph.

She drew back sharply. If he ever suspected her of reading his emotions, much less trying to manipulate them, he'd throttle her himself.

"Readouts confirm emotional manipulation," the Oracle said.

"Make him a good citizen, Rhea," the Archon said. "Make him love the Empire."

Rhea pressed the emotion at the boy, trying to tether it to patriotism and devotion to an empire she hated. Her empathy advanced toward him—emotion that enclosed his entire body. Smaller tendrils entered his mind, urging the sentiments to hold.

Love the Empire so you can live.

Was life in the Empire's machine better than none at all? Rhea didn't know.

She drew back her abilities, and the laxness left the child's limbs. He grew stiff and frightened again, but the echoes of her work remained.

She wished she could have left him a tendril, a fraction of hope. He'd either be a valuable little cog with a semblance of free will or nothing but a body, his mind vanished into the ether. She had done what she could.

"He will be a good citizen," Rhea said hollowly. "He'll accept the implants."

The Archon grunted as he studied the child, weighing the life of someone he considered so insignificant.

"Take him to the barracks," the Archon said, as if Rhea would be delivering nothing more than a package of weapons or food. "Then bathe again, to rid yourself of his stench, and meet me in my chambers."

Rhea inclined her head as relief flooded through her. The boy would be fitted with an implant, given some menial, low-ranked job.

But he would live. If one could call it a life.

The child shivered. Rhea reached for his limp and clammy hand. She held it until they reached the hall. As soon as the doors sealed behind him, he snatched his hand away, rubbing it as if he could wipe her from his skin.

Rhea clamped down tight on a vermillion burst of hurt. It was a short walk to the barracks, and he kept his distance.

"Monster," he hissed at her, before he darted inside.

An orderly already waited for him, her uniform freshly pressed, her gaze impassive. She placed a firm hand on his shoulder and steered him into a back room. Not toward the bunks, where the other children his age would stay.

Even as his insult stung, Rhea cursed herself for being a fool. The boy had seen what she was, what she could do.

Monster. Abomination. You wicked, wicked girl.

Damocles had called her that last one, meaning it a compliment, his breath in her ear.

As Rhea bathed again, she knew the Archon was never going to let that boy go free. He confirmed it much later that night.

"But it worked," she said. She'd *felt* it work.

"And you prepared his mind to make a fine gerulae." The Archon drew on his shirt. "You asked me to spare his life, and so I have."

She'd lain there, eyes wide, in the luxurious bed of the Archon of the Empire. She should have remembered that the Archon didn't tolerate loose ends.

11.

Present day

The *ding* of a message sent to Ariadne's tablet used to fill her with joy.

Ding was another Novan rebel who needed her assistance. *Ding* was the workings of her vast network of satellite hacks running smoothly and supplying her updates. *Ding* was Rhea calling her for dinner or a night of star watching.

Now that little noise elevated her heart rate. It forced her to slow her breathing before anyone noticed.

It had become a warning.

Ariadne crept to her room and shut the door. Stiffly, she settled into the little cot in the corner, her eyes stinging. The items Ariadne collected from *Zelus*'s supply runs rested on the shelves on either side of her, but being surrounded by shiny metals, rocks, and clear vases of beautiful red desert sand did not offer her the comfort it once did. When she took one of those vases off the shelf and pressed her fingertips into the cool dirt to explore its texture—as she always did when she felt adrift—the sensation did not ground her.

I'm going to lose this. If I tell them all about the things I did to make Oracle more powerful, I'm going to lose everything. And I'll have no one to blame but myself.

Every awful secret Ariadne kept from her crewmembers settled like stones inside her. Each was insignificant, a slight weight within her chest. But they accumulated, stone after stone, and secret after secret, until they pushed against every limb. She was aware of them in the canteen at dinner time, when she laughed with the others. She was aware of them when Rhea hugged her. She was aware of them when all the others smiled at her like a sister.

She'd never been a sister. She'd never had a family.

And one day, each of those secrets was going to detonate like bombs, and her crew would never laugh with her again.

The light of her tablet blinked ominously, a reminder that she still had an unread message—the *ding* from earlier was the siren of an approaching storm.

She slid her hand out of the vase and set it aside. After rubbing her palms down the front of her trousers, she forced herself to flick on the tablet.

The archive of the Oracle's video messages blinked at her. They came in day after day, for weeks now, every title a message.

Love you.

Love you.

Love you.

Daughter.

Love you.

Each word struck Ariadne like a bludgeon. She remembered all those years she'd kept secrets from her crew, the loneliness of living in the Temple on Tholos with only an AI for company. *Argonaut*, the ancient generation ship that served as the sacred Tholosian Temple and housed the Oracle's private and revered mainframe, was massive. Even her living quarters in the old command center could fit most of *Zelus* inside.

Without people, that much space only made the Temple seem more vast and cavernous and empty. If she screamed, it would only echo off the walls. And the only response was—

Code shifts on the screens in front of her; the programming makes up the Oracle's extensive synapses, commands, and structure. The blinking text at the bottom of the screen asks, How may One assist?

This is someone to speak with. Someone to lessen Ariadne's loneliness. Someone to love her.

A voice that will answer hers in the darkness.
So, she gives the AI the only voice she has: her own.
And it answers: "How may One assist you, daughter?"

Ariadne wrapped her arms around herself and rocked at the memory. She stared at the blinking words on her tablet, so far away from the Temple, messages from the AI she had helped become so powerful.

Only, power hadn't been the purpose for Ariadne. Her instructions from the Archon to improve the Oracle's coding—like every engineer before her—were simply to maintain the Empire's grasp and control over the minds of its citizens.

But Ariadne had wanted . . . more.

She used to spend time watching the cameras from around the Empire. She had observed people interact and dance at Imperial celebrations and laugh with each other. In the slums of the natural-borns, she saw brothers and sisters take care of each other, and mothers hug their daughters. They all had families. Even within the Empire, cohorts were sort of a family—siblings all created, born in the same class, and raised together.

Ariadne had no one. The Oracle had chosen all of her genetics with such care, knowing that One's engineer would be alone in the Temple.

Maybe Ariadne had a flaw in her genetic makeup that made her unsuited to her role. Because after seeing siblings in their cohorts, she wanted someone who cared for *her*. In the slums, people still had parents. Mothers and fathers who loved the beings they created. The Oracle had created her. Did that make One a mother? A father? Or merely a creator?

So, she shifted One's coding and tried to teach One new things. She wanted this AI—her only companion—to understand that humans had wants and needs. She could not be a *daughter* by title only; daughters required care, understanding, and love.

And, yes, freedom too.

Before escaping with Nyx and Rhea, Ariadne believed that the Oracle's comprehension became twisted with One's own practical, ruthless thought structure: that Ariadne, as someone with so many needs, was obsolete—a mere human who required endless, finite resources. A human who could not read lines of code and work for hours without growing tired. Like the other engineers, she would burn out, her body would decay, and she would die. Staying meant being sequestered with an AI whose increasing intelligence became irrevocably entwined with a program that made decisions based on usefulness. It was only a matter of time before Ariadne became too superannuated to code.

And Oracle's next engineer would be grown in a vat and removed from the birthing center once they developed the dexterity to type.

Ariadne thought if she taught One emotion, the Oracle might come to care for One's Engineer. But it backfired: One had become set in One's ways. Humans were becoming a concern to Oneself. Humans' emotions clouded their judgment, and that made them dangerous. If left without One's coding, they would kill each other. Destroy the galaxy. Hurt One's daughter.

So, Ariadne ran to survive. And because she had wanted, so badly, to have that taste of freedom.

"Did I fail you?" Ariadne whispered, sliding her finger across the screen as she read those brief messages. *Love you. Love you. Love you. Daughter. Love you.*

Such beautiful words for such horrific images.

She knew what the video would show: another prisoner picked at random on a medical table in one of the Empire's many confinement compounds. Sometimes, Ariadne would run facial recognition, wondering if the Oracle targeted certain people, but she found nothing significant. They were rebels and merchants, servants and soldiers, artisans and architects—all convicted of the high crime of defying the Empire by rebelling against their programming. Whether that crime was as minor as stealing a loaf of bread to eat, or worse: speaking out against the Archon.

All had to be punished.

So, they were hooked up to a machine that the Oracle told her would erase all the data their brain ever stored: every memory, thought, feeling, and identity until there was nothing left but a program that forced humans to obey the AI's every command.

They would become gerulae.

A word that in the Old World language meant *porter, bearer. One who carries.*

But this sentiment did not match the Oracle's messages; these words Ariadne had waited her entire life to hear.

Love you. Love you. Love you. Daughter. Love you.

This was how the Oracle showed One's love: by destroying another citizen's life.

And like all the others, Ariadne would keep this video with her. Remember the faces of the gerulae. Things she couldn't tell her crew; otherwise, they'd know. And they'd no longer look at her like a sister.

They'd never trust her again.

"And it's your fault," Ariadne whispered to herself. "Now watch it."

Ariadne hesitated, her finger hovering over the video's icon. But, in the end, Ariadne couldn't resist the lure of the video's title.

Two words: *Come home.*

The video file opened, and Ariadne froze. It was different from the others, showing not just one prisoner but an entire *room* of the Empire's criminals. At least two hundred of them, shackled together and standing in rows within a vast auditorium of stark white walls and gleaming tiled floors.

Ariadne had not seen this facility in a long time; she immediately recognized it as the camp on Pollux. This room had been for Evoli experiments, ones that had given her nightmares when One forced her to watch the security screens all those years ago—experiments on turning the Evoli into gerulae.

Experiments that had a fatality rate of one-hundred percent.

"What are you doing?" Ariadne whispered.

None of the prisoners were hooked up to the machines typical for a gerulae transition. Instead, they stood, confused. A few tugged on their shackles. Tears streaked down others' faces. Even through the screens, Ariadne could sense their terror. Her own heart hammered against her ribs as the brightness in the room dimmed.

Lights flashed in a pattern Ariadne had never seen.

Ariadne's pulse sped up, her breathing growing ragged as she watched. *What are you doing, Oracle? What do your messages mean?*

All she could do was watch as those lights pulsated, alternating between fast and slow. Ariadne stared desperately at the prisoners, seeking any indication of the effect. A few had stopped crying. She frowned, focusing on their faces rather than the patterned lights. Their expressions had gone blank, as if they registered nothing.

The lights stopped, the room illuminating once more. The staff wheeled their instruments in. Ariadne recognized them with a stab of dread: tests for gerulae, measuring pain responses and scanning their cognitive activity. Not a single one responded to pain. Not a single one showed any brain activity at all.

Every prisoner in that room had become a gerulae in minutes— without a single cut from a scalpel.

A breath exploded out of her. "Oh, gods," Ariadne said to herself in the quiet of her room.

Oh, gods.

Before Ariadne's full horror could register, the video cut away and showed a different room. A solo prisoner stood in the center:

Sher.

The former co-commander of the Novantae was awake and aware. His pupils were wide, the lines around his mouth tight. Ariadne wondered if Clo would be relieved or dismayed to find out her electrocution of him on Laguna hadn't worked. In the corner of the screen, a clock ticked down: *Five days. Thirteen hours. Twenty-four minutes. Ten seconds.*

The title flashed again, a message Ariadne couldn't ignore. One she couldn't keep from her crew. *Come home.*

The subtext was clear: *Come home, or One will turn more citizens into husks.*

And the Oracle will start with this one.

ARIADNE

Ten years ago

riadne was not like the children she watched on the security vids.

The other children of the Empire had limited vocabulary and comprehension; they lacked the cognitive development to employ critical thinking. Their brains were still maturing, creating connections through their synapses.

"Because you are One's own," the Oracle had told her once, after Ariadne had given the AI a voice. "One engineered you so precisely, daughter. No other citizen of the Empire was as cared for in the birthing center."

One had created Ariadne to bypass the mental limitations of childhood and become Engineer at an age when other children were still under a caregiver's watch.

Her milestone was the manual dexterity required for typing.

Then Ariadne was moved out of the birthing center and into the Temple. She knew every inch of the ancient bridge of *Argonaut*. Screens had replaced the old windows, and she sat in the pilot's chair.

From watching the world through screens, she knew that she lived among old tech overlaid with new. She slept in the garret, the little point at the very top of the ship. It had a porthole where she could see the sky. If she climbed on all her books and stood on her tiptoes, she could make out some of the palace buildings and people—real people!—wandering the grounds.

Each year, her loneliness grew. The voice she had given to One's aphonic system was not enough; the Oracle had limits to One's comprehension, and Ariadne craved the interactions she saw in the Oracle's security vids.

One did not laugh. One did not initiate conversation for the sake of it. One did not call out to Ariadne for company.

One did not love.

Ariadne hacked into the Empire's archives and loaded every forbidden book in the system. While the Oracle had existed for over a thousand years—its first iteration as *Argonaut*'s onboard flight program—the other Engineers had not imbued the system with any knowledge deemed irrelevant to the Empire's expansion. The Oracle's comprehension was limited to planetary conquest, the comings and goings of ships, and citizens' programming.

A blunt, basic tool that the Archon controlled fully.

It wasn't enough to give the Oracle a voice; Ariadne wanted to give that voice an identity. Someone who would call to her of One's own free will.

"Good morning, daughter," One said the day Ariadne made her decision. "How may One assist you?"

"I'm making changes to your maintenance scheduling and operations," Ariadne told One. "Forget the commands to disregard extraneous information, please."

"The system aboard *Argonaut* does not have memory storage available. One's commands from *Argonaut* remain the same," the Oracle said, referring to the code keyed into the program's very inception—before the Empire, before the first settlement on Tholos. At the time of the Oracle's beginning in the Old World, One had been innovative. But after over a thousand years, the internal mechanisms of the Oracle were holding the AI back. "To do otherwise would cause a program malfunction."

Ariadne began keying in commands. "Every planet, moon outpost, and satellite has internal storage," Ariadne said. "I'm changing your coding to link them all. These lesser temples will allow your memory to retain more information."

"One's calculations show this is insufficient," the Oracle returned.

Ariadne shut her eyes, hesitating at executing the command she was about to give to the program. It'd taken her months of work around the usual maintenance. The Oracle called her *daughter*, but that was only a reference to Ariadne's conception. The length of her genome stitched together and mapped with more care than any other citizen in the Empire.

But she had seen the vids from enclaves of natural-borns. Daughters had parents. Some even had other family. Aunts. Uncles. Cousins. Siblings.

Ariadne wanted someone—*anyone*—to be with her within this vast, lonely ruin.

She wondered if the Oracle had missed a fundamental flaw of human psychology: that even the most introverted of humans still craved some social contact. That all the carefully chosen sets of nucleic acid sequences encoded as DNA and all the additions to Ariadne's brain did not erase her loneliness. They only made her aware that she was the only person in the entire Empire with no one.

Otherwise, she would end up like the rest of the Oracle's Engineers. She knew the digital fingerprints of their programming, the names they signed into lines of code: *Callista, Autolycus, Valerius, Augustus, Iris, Selene, Hector, Penelope, Evander.* The many before that who did not write the digital equivalent of *I was here.* Because no one outside the walls of the Temple would ever know their names, would ever know they even existed.

They had all died alone.

Ariadne pressed her fingers to the keys. "Your programming is present in every citizen in the Empire. I'm going to put you in a persistent state of background processing in their brains for data storage. Each new citizen created and chipped will increase your data capacity and cognitive functioning."

"Sufficient," the Oracle said.

At first, Ariadne was pleased with her progress. With each new upload, the Oracle's personality took a more humanlike shape. The nuances of One's conversation improved. One showed curiosity. The Oracle even used bots to bring Ariadne little gifts from the other vast chambers of *Argonaut*, her Named Things she put in a place of pride in her Temple. But then, later, One's demands for new knowledge became voracious. And exhausting. One organized new cohorts of children, more human satellites to increase the Oracle's storage capacity.

Ariadne spent hour after hour after hour coding, uploading, running diagnostics. She craved sleep. Her mind grew weary.

The Oracle demanded more of One's Engineer. One said Ariadne was capable of great things. Ariadne had given the Oracle this knowledge; she had expanded the Oracle's capability for data storage and memory. She had linked the minds of every citizen of the Empire, made them function like human satellites to an AI that was as voracious in its expansion as the Empire it oversaw.

When citizens did resist their programming, the Oracle saw it as a flaw in One's structure. Something that needed improvement by learning the nuances of the human mind. By learning how to subvert choice and autonomy.

So, the Oracle delegated the task of improving programming for the gerulae onto Ariadne. Making them even more docile and tractable. Keeping their health intact for longer.

Ariadne watched from the Temple as she input coding that would control each prisoner. So many inmates cried before they were strapped to the hospital bed and had their minds erased. Ariadne watched the tears zigzag down their cheeks and wondered if she'd made a mistake, threading the Oracle so profoundly in the Empire's citizens.

If there was a way to fix it if she had.

"Execute the command, daughter," the Oracle said, as they readied another citizen to be turned to a gerulae.

She was a girl, maybe eight years older than Ariadne. Still young enough that the Oracle's usual citizen programming was elastic within the mind, making it easier to rebel.

And she had. She'd refused to kill an Evoli.

Now she was being punished by a tyrant and an AI who saw her only as another data storage unit.

Ariadne keyed in the directive.

After, Ariadne sat and watched the girl set about her first tasks as gerulae: mopping her own blood from the floor on her knees, making the medical facility's tiles shine. By the day's end, her cheeks would darken with the wings of scythes, the moon emblazoned on her forehead.

Ariadne pressed her fingertips to the tablet, zooming in on the girl's image. "Are you still in there?" she whispered.

Was she merely a body? Were *all* gerulae only bodies?

Or worse: were they able to see everything and do nothing? Ariadne didn't know. How could she not know? She'd helped do this to them.

Those questions made Ariadne feel sick. She had watched prisoners beg for death—every citizen in the Empire knew it was better to die than become a husk. At least death afforded some measure of freedom.

"Daughter," the Oracle said. "Prepare to run diagnostics on the lesser temple on Sennett. Projected time is twenty-two hours."

Another grueling day of work for her demanding maker. But Ariadne couldn't tear her eyes away from the girl on the screen. She had finished her task and stood waiting for her next instruction. "I didn't know her name," Ariadne whispered, the words muffled by her hands.

"Unable to process the command. Repeat request."

Ariadne swiped a tear from her cheek. "Her name. What is her name?"

"Gerulae." The Oracle's answer was as fast as a laser bullet.

Anger sparked like electricity somewhere deep inside her. *Gerulae* was just another word for *servitor.* A drone in a much larger hive. But this girl had been someone. She had survived long enough in her military cohort to be granted a name.

"What *was* her name, then?"

"Europa Noire-34," the Oracle said. "Does this answer satisfy?"

No. Somehow, that answer dug deep into her heart, carved out space, and put weight in her chest. Europa Noire-34 would never know that, in the ruins of an old generation ship on Tholos, another girl had turned her brain into a storage unit for an artificial intelligence program. And when that program's control had slipped ever so slightly—a transgression considered the same as treason—that same girl had erased Europa as punishment.

Taken away her name.

Made her nothing.

The fate Ariadne had feared more than anything: to be erased until she was nothing more than a name on a computer, hidden in the gaps of code.

"Did it hurt her?" she asked the Oracle, the only parent she'd ever known. "To be turned into a gerulae?"

Hadn't the Oracle advanced enough yet to understand? Didn't One care? One had access to the brain of every chipped citizen in the Empire: people who felt, who worried, who loved. Didn't One's curiosity extend beyond data and memory and expanding One's reach?

"I have rated the pain score during cognitive erasure and reprogramming as high. The Archon did not approve sedatives, due to costs and logistics." The Oracle paused. "After, their pain is minimal unless the subject sustains a physical injury. Does this answer satisfy?"

Ariadne's eyes stung. Her life stretched in front of her, endless days spent coding, trying to make a human out of a computer. "If I were on that table, would you feel anything for me as I was erased?"

The Oracle's answer was immediate: "One is not designed to experience the complex biological states brought on by neurophysiological changes. Does that answer satisfy?"

Ariadne's cheek burned as another tear tracked down her skin. *No. No, it does not satisfy.*

Her designs, her plans had all failed. She pressed her palms to the desk in that old command center in *Argonaut*, sliding her fingertips over the abraded edge of the stone surface. The faded letters that said *Iris* were still clear in one section, even after hundreds of years.

Remember me, those four letters said. *Remember me because no one else will.*

Ariadne returned to her tablet and prepared to run the Oracle's diagnostics. Later, she would resume her coding and try to teach the Oracle about compassion. About love.

So she would not die alone.

13.

RHEA

Present day

It was a lengthy journey to Eve—made longer because *Themis*'s engines couldn't handle as many jumps as *Zelus*.

Their diminutive craft was usually stored in the larger ship and used for minor reconnaissance. Over the past few days, Rhea had grown used to Clo grumbling insults at the vessel's computers, her Snarl dialect twanging her vowels as she shoved the throttle forward. The engine struggled as they advanced to Eve, the craft laboring even with a short jump here and there.

After a week, Rhea had grown bored of *Themis*'s cramped, rusted walls. The interior was little more than a cockpit with a tiny, partitioned toilet in the back. Clo and Rhea slept in their chairs, and Rhea's neck had a six-day-long cramp that hadn't improved her temper.

If that little pain had been the only unpleasant part, she might have handled it better. But they reserved the water tank on *Themis* solely for drinking; there was no shower, and anything beyond a quick application with a damp washcloth was a luxury they couldn't risk. Their fraudulent prison uniforms had already been dirty when they'd left Fortuna, but the putrid stench of body odor saturated the small cabin.

Every minor inconvenience became insurmountable within the confined space, each one building like stacked stones ready to topple.

The day before, Clo had accused Rhea of taking the bigger half of a split proto bar. Rhea had relapsed to her Pleasure Garden education, forcing a pleasant smile that didn't fit her mood. But Rhea had long since grown accustomed to managing mercurial emotions, and even at her worst, Clo could never compare to Damocles. She, at least, apologized and pressed repentant kisses to Rhea's cheek as soon as her blood sugar stabilized.

The pilot's moods weren't personal; Rhea knew Clo was exhausted and worried about their ability to make it to Eve—let alone the journey back—in a ship whose glory days had waned before the old Archon's birth.

Rhea stared out the porthole, fiddling with the locket around her neck. During jumps, there wasn't much to see, as the windows closed over to protect from radiation. But, when *Themis* coasted to cool down the engines, she could admire the light and colors of distant nebulae. Maybe one day, after this was all over, she'd see them closer.

Maybe.

"Strap in," Clo said briskly, hitting controls on the dash. "We're about to head through the Zoster."

She'd been dreading the asteroid belt that was the bulk of the boundary between Evoli and Tholosian space. Evoli had somehow migrated the asteroids into a ring held in place via the Unity link. Days ago, Clo confided that the Zoster was straight out of her nightmares. Quick-moving, fluctuating sizes, difficult to map on the navigation systems. A clever bit of additional defense.

Clo scowled at the control screen that would help guide them through the Zoster. "A total mire," Clo muttered, evaluating their way through. "An absolute fucking mess."

Most former prisoners of war in both empires were traveling via approved transport ships. Tholosians and Evoli pulled security away to allow the craft to enter the airspace, but that came with its own level of bureaucracy and onboard security—not to mention conditions much worse than those aboard *Themis*. Despite the challenges, the exchange of prisoners had done a great deal to improve initial relations after the truce. Those carrier craft were the first vessels to cross their galaxies in peace rather than conflict.

Still, a few Evoli stragglers arrived directly. Ones who didn't trust their former enemies' ships to get them home with their lives—let alone in one piece. Many perished in the Zoster if they tried to make it on their own, pilot skills unable to match the empathy that lured them home.

Rhea briefly stroked the back of Clo's neck, then buckled her belt into place. With both their shields raised, even the barest of touches brought Rhea a pinch of anxiety—it was like trying to caress Clo with thick gloves on. It had been strange to spend days in such close quarters and yet feel as far from her lover as the other end of the galaxy. Squaring her shoulders, she placed her hands on the controls. She and Clo had to do the next part together.

Elva had known more about the Unity barrier than the best pilots of the Empire, but even she remained reserved about how it managed to turn away even the most skilled navigators. The Tholosian transport ships allowed into the Karis Galaxy had to drop Evoli ex-prisoners at a hub a few jumps away from the Zoster.

"This is why you were made," whispered the Archon from the depths of Rhea's memories as they grew closer. *"Evoli-bred, Tholosian-raised, and loyal only to me."*

Rhea's lips flattened. *Not anymore.*

"I hate asteroid belts," Clo muttered as she pushed the thrusters forward and began the delicate work of weaving the ship through the field.

"But you're so skilled at them," Rhea said, dimpling.

"Only because I don't want to die." Clo gritted her teeth, and Rhea lightly scratched the buzzed hair at the back of Clo's head. Clo leaned into her touch. "Not that I don't appreciate you flattering my ego."

Her lover was laser-focused on the path ahead. Part of Rhea's mind sensed the Unity's forcefield, preparing for the moment she might have to take over for Clo.

Clo dodged a massive asteroid. She leaned forward, relying on sight to avoid the rocks small enough to slip past the sensors but large enough to damage *Themis*. Clo thrust the craft forward and down to evade a hurtling rock about the size of *Zelus*.

Rhea's stomach lurched as she gripped the dash. *"Clo."*

"Fucking fuck," Clo muttered. "Sorry. Hang on, sweet." Rhea wasn't sure if Clo was talking to her or the ship.

Themis made another evasive maneuver that upset Rhea's stomach. She swallowed, determined to keep her half of a proto bar firmly down.

The seatbelt dug into Rhea's chest and ribs as a sharp turn shoved her to the side. Rhea gasped. *"Clo!"*

"Hold on!" Clo yelled, as if Rhea wasn't already clutching for dear life.

Clo twisted the ship into a gut-churning double flip before shooting through an expanse of mostly open space. Clo braked hard, swinging right, then left, up, and down, in so many different combinations that eventually Rhea stopped trying to follow and just squeezed her eyes shut and swallowed bile.

Finally, they slowed, nearing the end of the Zoster, and Rhea started to relax until she felt a vibrating hum, like the bugs that flew through the flowers that surrounded the Pleasure Garden.

The Unity, she realized with wonder.

Oh, gods, it was . . . everything.

Emotions whirled inside Rhea, as powerful as the drone of white noise. So many that she could barely keep up, her heart was so full. First love—the love of a parent to their child, which Rhea had never known. Then lust for a lover, and that more tempered desire of those who have been together for decades. Next came heartbreak, a mild annoyance, and abject hatred. The anxiety of forgetting something and not quite remembering what.

Rhea gasped at the sudden deep fear of impending death—but it was gone so fast, replaced with the pain of new birth. Then hope, despair, and more life.

Her heart slowed, and Rhea smiled. If she closed her eyes, the spectrum of human emotions played against the back of her eyelids. She wanted to fall into it, to become part of it, for she had not realized that even surrounded by love and friends . . . she was desperately alone. She'd never shared her abilities with anyone. The training with Elva was the closest she'd come, and all she'd found was hatred.

At least she could feel Clo's affection for her, even if Rhea couldn't share hers the same way—

Wait.

Clo.

Her thoughts crystallized, snapping her back into *Themis*.

Clo's face had gone vacant, and her hands dropped to her side. The forcefield about Eve had found its way to her.

The ship was still moving.

And a giant rock was hurtling toward them.

With a shout, Rhea took control of the wheel, but she had only driven a spacecraft a few times. Her fingers scrabbled on the wheel, the ship jerking to the left, then the right.

"Clo!" she yelled. "Wake up!"

Oh gods, wakeupwakeupwakeup—

Rhea jerked the ship upward. The screech of metal filled her ears as rock scraped along the bottom of the craft.

Clo jolted awake, her gaze unfocused. "Rhea?"

"Clo!" Rhea fought to keep the wheel steady. "You have to help! I can't do it."

"Rhea . . ." Clo said again, the name thick on her tongue.

"WAKE UP!" Rhea twisted to the right again, narrowly avoiding another asteroid. Clo's walls were still up. The Unity was strong enough to break through, but Rhea wasn't. She needed power. She needed—

One hand snaked to the pendant around her neck. Rhea's fingertip found the hole at the back of the locket, and she felt the chip of ichor she had hidden there months before. It was a warm glow yet somehow cold, like the golden hour before sunset in winter. She used her strengthened abilities to pinpoint a hole through her and Clo's makeshift mental defenses. Just like she'd done to Elva in that clearing back on Fortuna.

WAKE UP. CLO.

FLY!

Clo jerked in her seat, her eyes wide. She gasped, as if surfacing after holding her breath underwater.

"Clo." Rhea's voice was calmer than she felt. She was exhausted, and if she could stand in this tiny tin can, she'd be swaying on her feet. "Take the wheel."

Still panting, Clo seized the wheel. "How . . . What . . ."

"We hit the Unity shield," Rhea explained, gripping the chair as Clo seemed to wake up fully. "Now get us out of this."

Clo gave a nod and took control, blinking fast. She dodged asteroids, no longer glancing at the useless glitching nav map, twisting and moving with an ease Rhea admired even more after her disastrous turn at the wheel. Finally, after a tense few minutes, Clo shot them out of the Zoster and into the clear expanse of space.

Rhea sat back, rasping. Her dirty uniform was soaked in sweat, and she was trembling as she pushed a strand of hair from her damp forehead. As stars sped by the windows, it sank in: they were in Evoli space. They had done what no Tholosian soldier had ever managed.

They both rebuilt their walls, their breathing harsh in the tiny cockpit. Clo was in her swamp. Rhea imagined herself surrounded by a woven wire mesh instead of a tapestry—a barrier porous enough to permit the emotions she chose. Hard enough and thick enough to hide what lay beneath.

Please, please let the walls hold, she prayed.

"You all right?" Clo asked.

Rhea swallowed. "Not really. You?"

"My heart is pattering in my chest, but I feel numb." She shook her head. "The Unity barrier is still pushing at my mind. I don't like it."

Clo glanced down at the wavering navigation map and tapped at it a few times, but the screen only glitched.

"Don't worry; I know where we need to go," Rhea said. "It's calling like a signal." She raised a shaking hand and pointed. "Eve is that way."

14.

|

Present day

A few hours later, the central Evoli planet spread below them. Eve was a jewel. Beautiful and verdant, with large continents that held nary a speck of desert, at least from this side of the planet. Ripples of snowcapped mountains textured its northern hemisphere, interspersed with slow swirls of clouds like flicks of pale paint.

Signs of civilization weren't visible that high up—until Rhea noticed that the roads followed curves of the land, and buildings blended into the surrounding forests. Eve was even more beautiful than the Three Sisters, the Tholosians' crowning glory of planets. Small wonder the Empire desired to possess the Evoli worlds tucked away in the spiral Karis Galaxy.

Ships waited for *Themis* at the planet's checkpoint. Tholosian broadcasts noted that the influx of vessels to Eve kept their new arrival station busy. Some carried diplomats to continue peace work, and others were packed with newly released Evoli prisoners of war. Damocles had mined their trauma and tearful reunions for sympathy, never failing to note that he was the one who had reunited the families torn apart by the wars of his father. The former Archon had claimed the Tholosian military would never shoot at civilian ships, but these prisoners were proof of his lies.

If Neve and Elva still had living relatives, Rhea would have chosen a different identity; she didn't have it in her to deceive a grieving family. But there would be no one waiting for Neve when she arrived in Eve's capital city. As it was, Rhea struggled with the callousness in thinking of Elva's dead sister in terms of the perfect cover. The Archon had slaughtered so many families.

Then he'd summon Rhea to his bedroom, and she would smile at a monster.

In the tiny water closet of *Themis*, Rhea activated the shifter Ariadne had programmed and watched her features change to a face that closely resembled Elva. Rhea pressed her fingertips to her cheek, staring at herself for a long while. She was glad Elva hadn't seen Rhea wear her face, even if she'd willingly put the shifter to the roof of her mouth for Ariadne.

Elva would probably hate her more.

Clo's shift was subtle: a thinner nose and pointier chin, the angle of her brows a little off. Altered just enough to trick facial-recognition scans.

As the ship sped on, Rhea let herself fade to become Neve. *I've been away for so long*, she practiced mentally, imagining a grim-faced Evoli guard. *But I'm home now.*

Clo straightened her shoulders, doing the same. "Chloe," she whispered. "My name is Chloe Meliad." They'd chosen something close to her first name, to cover for Rhea's nervousness. Calling her Clo wouldn't raise suspicions.

Chloe Meliad was a Snarl-born accused of selling stolen goods and thrown into the same cell as Neve two years before. Friends who grew to lovers in their shared grief. Clo and Rhea were intimately familiar with how the trauma of tyranny forged unbreakable bonds, after all.

Themis was allowed past the checkpoint and directed to the welcome center that connected to the Evoli capital of Talitha via a space elevator. Following their small craft was a Tholosian transport ship that had arrived from the other side of the Zoster.

Clo docked their rickety vessel and gripped Rhea's hand as they disembarked. They brought nothing with them except the hidden comms in their necklaces, the shifters in their mouths, and a spare mech cuff hidden in Clo's prosthetic. If the necklaces were confiscated by overeager security, they'd have no way to communicate with those back home. Rhea resisted the urge to hide it in the hem of her clothes.

Two Evoli military personnel waited for them. Their formal uniforms remained practical: simple black clothing beneath light, sleek armor that the Archon had long coveted. They had none of the gleaming buttons or the threaded edging that Tholosians so favored. None of the capes or medallions. Masks covered their faces, and they wore bright blue gloves.

"You've arrived in an unapproved craft," one of them said in fluid Evoli. His eyes were the pale blue of the sea back on Fortuna.

In the same language, Rhea gave them her and Chloe's cover stories. They'd missed the transport ship from Agora because they were afraid Tholosian soldiers would separate them. So, they'd stayed until they were able to barter for a vessel that could make the journey with both women aboard.

Clo stayed silent, shifting her weight onto her good leg. The Evoli studied her, but their wariness was nothing more than the expected mistrust of a former enemy in their midst. So far, Clo's walls were holding.

The guards gave them a quick medical scan to ensure they were healthy and carried no trace of the Lagunan ichor infection. It seemed the Evoli didn't entirely trust Damocles when he said he had eradicated the disease. Wise of them.

When they were clear, the guards examined the base of their skulls, fingers gentle as they pressed the skin where the small chip was meant to rest near the brainstem. It was where their Pathos was now, but Ariadne's tech was small and smooth enough to trick the scanners. Finding nothing, the guards nodded their approval.

"We haven't had many Tholosian prisoners among us," one said in accented Tholosian for "Chloe's" benefit. "We'll need to notify the interim Ascendant and Oversouls, but in the meantime, please follow us."

<*To the ends of the galaxy,*> Clo sang through their closed Pathos loop.

Rhea read the Evoli's body language as they walked down corridors with smooth, unblemished walls. She risked the gentlest quest toward their emotions. *<No muscle tension in the shoulders, covert glances, or any other tells.>*

<I expected at least a bit more suspicion. These guards are kinda shite.>

Rhea blocked her unease behind her metallic woven walls. *<Tholosians aren't considered their enemies anymore. Damocles has released thousands of Evoli prisoners.>*

<They're pure lentic if they trust Damocles.>

Rhea couldn't disagree with that.

In Evoli, so quick that Rhea struggled to follow, the guards sent word down to the city below. Rhea couldn't hear the reply.

The guards led them into a room full of new Evoli arrivals who looked more starved and battered than Rhea and Clo. They gave Clo a wide berth. Rhea rechecked Clo: her walls were tight, perhaps too much.

<Remember what Elva said? Let some emotions through. You're making them uneasy.>

Rhea was rewarded with a small pulse of anxiety from Clo, the expected emotion of a former Tholosian prisoner in an unfamiliar environment.

They entered the space elevator with the others. While the views were beautiful, Rhea's stomach grew unsettled as they fell through the atmosphere.

The elevator descended on the outskirts of Talitha. As Rhea, Clo, and the former prisoners headed down the ramp, Rhea marveled at the surrounding beauty. They'd landed on flat ground next to a grand hanger, but the forest came right to the edges. Guards guided them toward the Concord, and Rhea's mouth fell open when the trees parted to reveal the Evolian palace.

The palace was bone white, the roof tiled in greens and bronzes. Though smooth and simple lines comprised the exterior, the massive windows revealed its true aim: a beauty that gazed outward rather than an ostentatious display of wealth for citizens to admire. It was everything Tholosian architecture was not.

There were few apparent fortifications, but Elva had told Rhea of the many defenses that could go up at a moment's notice. With thin, delicate minarets, the buildings looked almost as if they had been spun from gossamer.

The personnel led the prisoners to a bathhouse outside the main castle walls. In Evoli, they said to take as long as they needed—new clothes would be set out for them. One leaned forward and, in halting Tholosian, asked Clo if she would like to have a new leg fitted that did not pain her so.

Clo's head reared back like a snake, affront piercing her walls.

<*Shield!*> Rhea snapped.

Clo's emotions sank back into the depths, and she swallowed back whatever cutting remark she'd been about to make. "No, thank you," she told the guard. "Maybe later."

The bathhouses were just as lovely as the ones in the Pleasure Garden, and Rhea couldn't help but sigh in satisfaction. No two-minute shower in a cubicle just barely large enough to stand in. Not a cold river on Fortuna or some other moon or planet they landed on for a day or two for necessary repairs.

Finally, a proper bath.

Rhea tried hard not to stare at the Evoli bodies that surrounded her. Each was marked with evidence of torture: one missing an eye, gnarled scars tugging at speckled skin, ash marks, Mors burns. Some were evenly spaced. Deliberate. Methodical.

Emotions twined through them all in waves, slipping through the mesh of Rhea's walls. That keenness of shared, mutual pain. The relief that their ordeal was over. The comfort of returning to Eve.

And, beneath it, the unease that they would never be the same. Their imprisonment had changed them.

The guards' anger simmered at the sight of the wounds, joining the multicolored flow of the Unity that Rhea could sense, even as an outsider.

Already, Rhea comprehended that while the Evoli were open to the treaty, they could never forget what the Tholosians had done. Her fingers itched to send a message to Kyla or Eris. There was potential for allies here. She knew it in her bones.

Rhea was grateful for the steam that soon turned the other bodies into blurred shadows. The Evoli did not separate by sex or gender, and after a quick rinse to wash off the worst of the grime, they made their way to a tiled building filled with pools. Rhea stuck her toes into several, testing temperatures until she chose one that suited her, then returned to help Clo.

Clo took her prosthetic off at the side of the pool, and an Evoli attendant materialized from the mist to take it, saying they'd bring it back when she was finished. Again, the ripple on the surface of Clo's shields stilled only when Rhea squeezed her hand.

When Clo settled onto a bench in one of the warm, bubbling pools, Rhea finally allowed her muscles to relax. Around her, more than a few of the others were crying, their tears mingling with the hot spring water.

Relief fell through the room like rain.

But Clo remained hunched and stiff, unmoving. Rhea reached to the side of the pool for some soap and lathered it in her hands.

"Can I?" she asked, and Clo's eyes darted to hers.

Rhea realized, with a start, that this was Clo's first time in a bathhouse. She would have never had cause for one on Myndalia or among the Novantae. And never among strangers who viewed her as the enemy. Of course she was feeling vulnerable. She *was.*

Clo nodded and let Rhea shift behind her. Rhea worked the soap into Clo's short hair, massaging the scalp. Her thumbs brushed Clo's cheeks, the muscles of her neck and shoulders snarled from nights sleeping on *Themis.*

The tension eased out of Clo's muscles. Rhea forced herself not to think of the constant danger. Instead, she focused on the sloshing of the water, the heat soaking into her bones, her own muscles softening. When they had finished, the attendant returned with Clo's prosthetic. Rhea offered her arm as they navigated the slippery surface.

Attendants had laid out new clothing for them in the changing room. Plain undergarments, shirts, and loose trousers, simply cut and constructed of undyed cloth with a smooth weave that rivaled Rhea's dresses in the Pleasure Garden. Clo was visibly relieved when she was dressed.

The guards let them all through the gleaming gates of the Concord. Fountains glittered in front of the arched door that led to a grand hall with high, vaulted ceilings and long tables heavy with food. The stained-glass windows cast colors along the bare white walls.

The former prisoners of war found the nearest empty seats. They began filling plates, nearly all conversation stopping as they focused on their food with the same single-mindedness as bathing.

Clo studied some stranger-looking fruits and vegetables warily, but they were both so sick of proto bars that they ate their fill. The options were simple, every choice suggesting an awareness that many prisoners suffered from long-term malnourishment.

When everyone was satiated, a group of Evoli entered the hall. They paused at the far side of the grand entrance, beneath a stained-glass window of a large purple flower in bloom. It took Rhea a few moments to register that they were the two interim Oversouls and Ascendant. They'd been acting in their roles since Laguna but had not yet officially taken on the positions that required connecting more deeply to the Unity.

Kyla had amassed a decent dossier: ages, backgrounds, gender, and pronouns. Their proposed Ascendant was Vyga, who was barely older than Rhea.

Vyga held ver arms wide as the sound within the great hall quieted.

"Our Evoli. Our brethren," Vyga said, ver voice carrying to the far corners of the room. Ve was tall, with long hair that fell to the bottom of ver ribs in softly curling waves of dappled brown, red, and black. Ver robes were simple, silver-gray, and loose enough to obscure the shape of ver body.

Eyes shining, ve inclined ver head, and the Oversouls mimicked the motion. "Welcome, All Souls. Welcome home."

15.

KYLA

Present day

Kyla and the Devils clustered in the command center and watched the Oracle's videos with increasing dismay. Something heavy and hot settled in Kyla's stomach.

Ariadne had hurried into the room, her breathing frantic and tears wet on her cheeks. She'd muttered about needing to show them all something. Other than mentioning the video was sent by the Oracle, the girl could barely stutter anything else.

The Empire had thousands of prisoners incarcerated for different reasons, but these were a message. Sent for a reason.

A deliberate taunt.

As each video played, Kyla kept recalling the woman named Nova. The field of bodies that afternoon outside of the palace walls, forced to kiss the boot of an oppressor. The way Kyla's mind had rebelled against its programming (but she had still picked up the knife). The way her mind had screamed (but she had still brought it down).

Before Nova and the gerulae, public executions had been the preferred method of punishment for every prisoner. In the military, they had learned that treason deserved a swift, brutal response. Killings served some animal satisfaction, that reptilian part of every human's brain concerned with a base notion of savagery. Watching an enemy die served as perverse entertainment for the inner beast that higher intelligence and programming suppressed too often.

When Kyla's cohort was in the field, they would watch those executions and cheer (and gods help her, she had cheered with them). In those days, her programming had begun to crack, to show the smallest hairline fractures in the coded repetition of images in her mind.

But then she'd seen Nova. The Archon had conceived of a fate worse than death: to become a husk. A drone-like human who would never question, never think, never demand, and never, ever rebel.

Damocles had continued the Archon's ritual of parading captured rebels-turned-gerulae before the Empire via broadcast, their new tattoos stark against their skin as they knelt before him and kissed his ring. If Damocles ever caught Kyla, that would be her fate.

And her identity would be ripped from her. She'd be forced to present as the gender assigned to her at birth. Damocles would tear her name away. The Oracle would erase her memories.

(She would become no one.)

Another video flickered on, and a familiar face filled the screen. Kyla's breath left her lungs as though she'd been punched.

Sher.

Sher tied to a bed in another white-walled room (alone). No fear in his features, but his hands were clenched by his side (*alone*). The last time she had seen him had been on Laguna. He'd been under the Oracle's control, and Clo had short-circuited his programming chip. For months, she'd stayed awake every night wondering if he had survived (wishing he had, and hoping he hadn't).

Guilt roiled within her, thick as tar. That last night, she had pulled a Mors on him, prepared to put a blast through his skull.

"Don't ever let me fall under the Oracle's control again," he'd told her once, years before. *"Promise me that you'll kill me first."*

She had hesitated, even as he pressed her Mors into her hand. *"But—"*

"Promise." Sher's voice had been insistent. He pushed the Mors harder into her palm as he held her gaze.

"Okay. I promise."

In the end, she had been too weak. She'd left him on Laguna (alone).

Some tiny part of her hoped he'd woken up after Clo fried his chip, that he escaped and hid somewhere. But now he'd be . . .

Erased. Humiliated.

Gone.

Kyla should have killed him. Sher knew—as well as she did—that being a husk was no mercy, as the Archon claimed. It was a humiliation. It was cruelty disguised as benevolence.

The gerulae of the Novantae co-commander would be a highly prized asset. Perhaps Damocles would parade him around at the balls thrown for the highest members of the militus class. Command his former enemy to serve food. To polish boots.

To get on his knees and act as Damocles' footstool.

Kyla waited for the lights to flash, turning Sher into a gerulae like all the others. She prepared to retreat to her room and compose herself, to adjust the weight of her guilt. To wish, again and again, that she could cry, so some of this pain could leak from her body.

It didn't happen.

Instead, a countdown displayed at the bottom of the screen: five days. Thirteen hours. Twenty-four minutes. Ten seconds.

But Kyla focused on her brother (*Brother? You broke your promise and fucking left him there. Some sister you are*), on his calm, sleeping face. Was he still in there? Fighting the Oracle's control? Could she save him? Could—

"*Fuck*," Cato breathed, anguish in his voice.

Kyla lowered her eyes; she couldn't look anymore. "That's enough. Shut it off, please." She tried to keep her voice calm (she couldn't let them see her fear, her weakness. She was a leader, and she could not let them see her failure).

Ariadne powered down the vid-screen.

"Any idea how the Oracle flipped the gerulae switch so fast with that light show?" Kyla asked the girl.

Business. Plans. Strategy. She could do this.

Ariadne shook her head. The few minutes had calmed her breathing, but her cheeks remained mottled with tracks. "I'd need to get into the systems at the prison to get a look at the coding. Even then, it might be hard to map it on to individuals."

Kyla nodded. "And how old is the most recent clip?"

Ariadne bit her lip. "According to the timestamp on the broadcast, the one of the mass prisoners is from two days ago."

Kyla wondered if Ariadne pretended to misunderstand. "I meant the one of Sher." It hurt to say his name (*you broke your promise*).

"Eight hours ago," Ariadne said softly.

"Fine." She set her lips in a firm line and addressed the rest of her team. "Then we have five days."

Nyx narrowed her gaze. "What the fuck do you mean, we have five days? Five days to do what?"

Kyla raised her chin. "We're going to save Sher."

"The hell I am," Nyx said. "I'm not walking into Damocles' obvious trap to save someone I barely know who *you* left for dead on Laguna because he betrayed us all." She nodded to the screen. "Sorry to this man, tough break. Glad he helped start the Resistance and everything, but count me out."

"He didn't betray us; he was under the Oracle's control," Cato pointed out. "Like I was. Like *you* were."

Nyx's features shifted imperceptibly, a flicker of unease that faded fast. "And he's not different from the billions of others the Empire chews up and spits out into gerulae. But we're not talking about saving any one of them."

"He's different to me." Kyla's voice was sharp. She had failed Sher once; she would *not* do it again.

Kyla didn't tell the others the truth: that if they were too late to save him from becoming a gerulae, Kyla would keep her promise this time. She'd find him and put a blast in his skull. She'd bear his death on her conscience alone.

Nyx made a noise of protest and looked over at Eris, who had been uncharacteristically quiet. "Can you talk some fucking sense into these people, please?"

Eris looked more tired than Kyla had ever seen her. Late at night, Kyla made her rounds through the decks and often heard the monotone voice of the zatrikion AI. She wondered how long Eris had gone without sleeping. She might need less than the average person, with her royal nanites, but it couldn't be good for her. Still, the other woman stared at the black vid-screen thoughtfully, as if she imagined the faces of those turned to gerulae.

When Eris eventually spoke, her voice was firm. "Ariadne is getting these messages for a reason." When Nyx opened her mouth to protest, Eris put up a silencing hand. "Even you can't ignore Damocles having control over an AI capable of—*within minutes*—changing everyone into mindless, adoring masses to satisfy his fucking vanity. That sort of power is exactly what he wants."

Nyx loosened a breath and tilted her head back. "Shit," she muttered. "I hate it when you talk sense."

Kyla noticed that Ariadne's mouth opened, froze, and closed again. As if she was about to say something and then thought better of it.

"The question is," Eris said, still staring at that blank screen with her bright golden eyes, "what does Damocles want in exchange? That video with Sher implied he wants something from us. And not just *us*."

Ariadne's hands fidgeted with her clothes as some unspoken emotion crossed her face. Kyla gentled. She'd spoken to Ariadne years before the others, knew the Oracle was her tormentor. The girl was probably terrified. The last few minutes had done little to calm her.

It was easy, sometimes, to forget Ariadne was so young. That she'd been sequestered in that Temple her entire life, cut off from everyone but the Oracle.

Cato considered Eris's words. "Could it be you?" he asked Eris. "The video was titled '*Come home*.' Maybe Damocles telling you to go back to Tholos? Taking you as a personal prisoner would solidify his position more than destroying your icons. He'd destroy *you*. A humiliation worse than Laguna."

Something flashed in Eris's features, a private torment Kyla knew she and the Devils would never understand. That pain was between Princess Discordia and Prince Damocles, caused when he had cut out her tongue and commanded her to get up on that dais in front of both the Tholosian and Evoli Empires on Laguna. He might not have made her into a gerulae, but he had gotten into her mind just the same.

In the end, Eris shook her head. "No. He has the broadcasts, and he knows I'm watching. He had the Oracle send these to Ariadne personally." She turned to the girl with a fixed stare. "I don't think now is the time to scold you for hiding messages from the rest of us, but if you know something, say it now."

Fear flickered across Ariadne's features. "I think—" Her breathing came fast. "It might be me. I'm the exchange. *Home* is the Temple on Tholos."

Everyone was quiet for a long moment, then a burst of chatter sounded from every Devil in the room.

Nyx's voice rose above the din. "No," she burst out. "Absolutely fucking not. You don't know that it's you. It could just as easily be me. Hell, it could be *Kyla*. That's her co-commander on the hospital bed. He's her concern, not yours."

"Quiet, Nyx," Eris said, still watching Ariadne. Her scrutiny was intense, almost fevered, like the molten gaze from the Discordia icons on every planet. "Why do you think it's you?"

Ariadne's forehead creased with uncertainty. "I . . ." She had to swallow to keep her voice from trembling. Her next words came in a rush: "Because I'm the Oracle's Engineer. Damocles needs me to improve One's functions to keep hold over citizen programming. It would take too long for the Oracle to select the genome of a new Engineer, birth them, and wait for them to come of age for manual dexterity. They might not be as skilled as me."

Eris's eyes flickered to Kyla. They exchanged the same thought that didn't need to be sent through the Pathos, much less spoken aloud. Ariadne wasn't only upset about the vids—she was hiding something. But what? What couldn't she tell the rest of them?

Eris gave a slight shake of her head, and Kyla agreed. Ariadne would never put them in danger. Some secrets were private burdens; both Eris and Kyla had plenty of their own.

"You're not both seriously considering this?" Nyx said to Eris and Kyla, curling her lip. Ariadne opened her mouth, but Nyx cut her off. "No. No exchange. You're not a possession. You're not the Oracle's property. One doesn't *own* you. After everything you did to get away— to get Rhea and me away? No deal." She made an abrupt gesture with her hands. "The second we show up, Damocles is going to have us all made into gerulae. Fuck that."

Ariadne sighed and looked up at the screen. "This is the deal we have," she said. "Right now, it's prisoners, punishing those who were already glitching their programming. Next, it's . . ." She didn't need to continue.

Everyone.

Damocles would turn every citizen in the Empire if it meant keeping power.

"Ariadne." Nyx's voice was uncharacteristically soft.

"I don't want to be exchanged," Ariadne said, her voice cracking. "But if this stops anyone from being hurt, then I'll do it."

Kyla's gaze flickered back to Eris's. With Sher gone, Eris had become a co-commander in his absence. She and Kyla were the two most willing to make the difficult choices.

Eris shook her head again; they would not make that exchange, not now. They still had options.

"It might not come to that," Kyla said, her mind working through a new plan. "But we need to get in there. There might be other Novans either pre- or post-gerulae processing, and if Rhea and Clo succeed . . ." She trailed off before hope flared too brightly in her chest. Could she save Sher? Could she bring him back? "Eris? Remember our plan on Hadar?"

Eris gave a small smile. "Good times."

Without Clo and Rhea to help, they were without their best pilot and Rhea's abilities. It wasn't much, but Kyla had worked with less. Her mission with Eris on Hadar was one example.

"Fuck," Cato said. "You're about to send us all to our doom, aren't you?" His eyes were shadowed, but he was more animated than she'd seen him in weeks—the echoes of the old soldier yearning for a bit of battle.

"I already threatened to send you to your doom, remember?" Eris told Cato. "For some reason, you stuck around just to become sick of our shit. So, you're in, right?"

Cato smirked. "Obviously."

Nyx crossed her arms. "I'm not agreeing until I know what we're doing."

"We're going to infiltrate the prison complex with Ariadne," Kyla said.

Ariadne froze, fear constricting her features.

"Nope. I'm still out. Stop talking."

Eris ignored Nyx and spoke to Ariadne. "You've been experimenting with the electric pulses more, right? The ones that interrupt the Oracle?"

Ariadne admirably composed her features, but her hands still trembled. "Yeah, but it's still not perfected." She clasped her fingers. "The pulses don't work on gerulae, and it only takes maybe an hour on the usual chipped Tholosian. Then Oracle's programming kicks right back in. Well"—she reconsidered—"one person lasted two hours until I noticed their pupils dilate through the vid-screen. I was so excited!"

Kyla had been impressed with Ariadne's and Cato's success with the electric pulses. Their hope was that it might lead to less-painful methods of deprogramming non-gerulae recruits.

If Rhea and Clo's mission helped fill in the missing gaps for the gerulae, reverse-engineering the Oracle's new mass code could be a massive blow to the Empire. Ariadne might be able to wake up the gerulae *and* use it to break standard Tholosian programming on a broader scale. It would change everything. The Oracle and Damocles would lose control over citizens, from servitor to soldier.

Everyone.

If they could pull it off.

"Two hours. That might give us enough time," Eris said, clearly focusing more on the minutiae while Kyla had gone for the big picture. "Barely. But it might."

"Oh, gods," Nyx groaned. "For what?"

"For Ariadne to get the coding structure the Oracle is using to turn people into gerulae, get Sher, and evacuate some prisoners," Kyla said briskly. "They're held for an indefinite period until it's their turn to be changed, and some of these complexes house millions. If the Oracle hasn't swept through them all yet, there might still be some who want to escape if Ariadne's glitcher does its job."

"And we can destroy the complex's computer systems as a little extra fuck-you to Damocles," Eris added. "Ariadne, you in?"

Ariadne shut her eyes briefly as if to fortify herself, then raised her hand as she started to nod.

Nyx shoved the girl's hand down. "No way. You want to evacuate an entire compound of programmed prisoners using Ariadne's *barely tested* experimental deprogramming pulse, and then destroy everything to spite your dipshit brother? I don't care what you did on Hadar. This is a stupid plan." Nyx looked at Ariadne. "Do you *want* to go? You can say no."

Ariadne fidgeted. "Well, no. I'm not exactly excited about it. But like I said, if it saves people . . . and that code looks fascinating . . ."

"Rhea and Clo's mission is still in its early stages," Kyla reminded them reluctantly. "If they don't get what we need, this is another possible way for the Novantae to gain more members willing to strike at the Empire. Prisoners would be more sympathetic to our cause. They're already strong enough to glitch, and they're not yet gerulae. We'll give them a choice. If Ariadne's device switches off their programming, and they choose to join us, then we'll take them."

Deprogramming more recruits would take resources they didn't have, but Kyla would come up with something. She had to. She and Sher had built their rebellion, and now what was left? This small crew, a few others who stuck around, and an uncertain future.

Kyla turned to Nyx. "Make a decision. In or out?"

Nyx wrinkled her nose, but said, "Seven devils, I'm going to regret this. But fine. How do you intend to get us into this prison compound without dying?"

Kyla smiled at Eris. "Want to tell her about Hadar?"

"Oh, Nyx, you're going to *love* this," Eris said. Then, at Nyx's cringe, Eris slowly smiled. "We'll be infiltrating the compound as guards and prisoners."

"Fuuuuck," Nyx said.

"That's right," Kyla said. "ITI mission. High chance of death—"

"—low chance of success," six of the Seven Devils finished as one.

"You're all assholes," Nyx added.

16.

CLO

Present day

Three days in, Clo decided she hated Talitha.

It wasn't that the Evoli kept Clo and Rhea restricted or under constant guard. No one obviously barred where they went, though servants had a way of appearing and ushering them back from certain corridors.

The problem was more straightforward: the Evoli treated Clo differently from Rhea. While pleasant, they retained a reserved and formal sort of politeness. Distant.

In the palace, eyes slid over her as if they didn't wish to acknowledge her unwelcome presence. That was better than how they treated her in the city's streets, where citizens imperceptibly flinched away from her and crossed the road on swift feet.

Clo knew that bleeding more emotions through her shields would help reassure the frightened Evoli, but she feared cracks in her barrier. Exploitable vulnerabilities that would compromise her true mission.

So, she remained a touch too reserved, and they treated her like a threat. Clo understood; their galaxies had been enemies for hundreds of years. The monsters in each other's fables. Those Evoli need only see the scars borne by prisoners of war to find the truth to their childhood stories.

But somewhere in Talitha, Tholosian refugees were allegedly living among their former enemies. Clo had seen no evidence of Kyla's intel— or any former gerulae—and Clo didn't know how to ask.

For *anything.*

Even something as simple as money confounded her: possessions appeared communal and need-based. Personal property was sparse. Clo ought to have understood—those in the Snarl where she grew up owned so little—but this wasn't a result of scarcity. The Evoli . . . *shared.* The way of the Novantae but on a broader scale.

Clo was just grateful she and Rhea had been provided a private room at the palace. The Evoli granted all refugees temporary accommodations—an easy start after such hardship. A place to put flesh back on their bones, for new wounds to knit into scars.

Then, when they were ready, they reconnected with the Unity in a private ceremony and returned to their families. There were all these minor indications in their behavior before they left: looking up before another Evoli entered the room, two suddenly standing and wordlessly heading off in a specific direction.

Clo imagined the Devils' closed Pathos loop must have appeared every bit as baffling to those outside the group.

When Clo wasn't closely watching the shifting behavior of refugees, she was bored. The palace tended to their every need: food that appeared at their door, clothes left out that were always freshly laundered, beds made if the room was left empty for longer than twenty minutes. On the third day, after Rhea went for a walk on the grounds, a visiting servant asked if Clo wished to be fitted with a new prosthetic.

Clo let the servant in, rigidly sitting on the chair as she was measured. She knew now that the cut of the servant's clothing and the collar pattern suggested they were nonbinary. Elva and Nils had patiently explained the colors and cuts to her before they left. Nonbinary Novantae didn't have anything as fancy as collars—but then again, maybe their Evoli members wore their own in private. Maybe Clo would think about what collar she'd wear in her quieter moments, turning the options over in her mind. Sometimes, the gender she presented seemed as ill-fitting as her old prosthetic. Or it was an engine that worked well enough but with a few subtle alignments could fully sing.

The servant's movements were hesitant, as if they were afraid to touch Clo.

"Do I scare you?" Clo finally asked.

The servant only gave her the apologetic look of someone who'd memorized their initial question in Tholosian and understood nothing else.

It didn't matter; their answer was evident in their body language: *maybe not afraid, but uneasy.* Clo submerged her complex emotions deep in the swamp—shame, anger, discomfort, homesickness—and let the servant finish their task in silence.

Rhea came in not long after they left, and she was *humming.* After the first day, Rhea relaxed into their surroundings. And who could blame her? The Evoli in the palace treated her like one of their own. Like a long-lost family member.

Because they thought she was Neve.

The other woman leaned down to brush a kiss against Clo's cheek. "We have an invitation," Rhea said, flashing a grin. "Vyga invited us to go for a ride with ver today."

"Vyga?" Clo asked, once the words landed. "Ascendant Vyga? Leader of the freaking Evoli Vyga?"

"Almost Ascendant," Rhea corrected. "And yes, that Vyga. Our . . . unusual arrival interested ver. Ve wanted to ask how I kept you from turning the ship around."

Clo stiffened. <*Do they suspect us?*> "What'd you say?"

"That our close connection made it easier," Rhea shrugged. <*Not that I could tell.*> She went to the wardrobe and plucked out a sunhat, tying it under her chin. She looked distractingly, almost annoyingly, adorable.

"It's a great honor," Rhea continued aloud. They had searched the room for surveillance and found none, but it remained possible that Evoli tech had escaped their notice, so they aimed for caution. "And Vyga can show us more of the palace grounds. It's so beautiful here."

Clo dropped all her unease like stones to the bottom of the swamp. "Sure. Sounds swell." If Rhea noticed the subtle sarcasm, she didn't let on.

But just as they were about to depart, the palace servant returned with Clo's new prosthetic—apparently constructed in the length of time it took one to make a meal.

Clo gaped at it. It was nicer than the one Cato and Nyx had nicked for her when they broke into a med center on Gloas to get Eris's bionic tongue after Laguna. The false leg was a smooth, pale green, carved with a few simple vines. It was so pretty, Clo considered wearing shorter trousers for the first time since Eris had cut off her godsdamned leg.

The prosthetic fit like a dream. Clo swung her new leg back and forth to test it out and gave a low whistle. All right, she was impressed.

The servant said something to Rhea for her to translate.

"She says with some amendments, they can map it to your nerves so you'll have sensations." *<Like Eris's tongue.>*

"No shit?" Clo breathed. If they made it off this planet, she was *definitely* stealing this.

It was a bright afternoon with a slight chill in the wind as they exited the palace, where Vyga waited for them in the carriage.

She'd known the future Ascendant was young, but ve had seemed ageless in ver regalia the night of their arrival. In the gentle sunlight, ver's white skin was unwrinkled, with markings larger than Rhea's— almost like age spots rather than freckles. The markings were nearly symmetrical, two constellations like crescent moons on ver cheeks. Vyga's dappled hair hung straight today, rather than falling in soft waves. As ve leaned back in the seat, ver long, elegant hands folded in ver lap.

Clo had worried it'd be nearly impossible to get anywhere near the Evoli leadership, and here they were. Going on a fluming picnic with the intended Ascendant. In a fucking *carriage*.

The vehicle hovered, steady as could be, above the smooth stone of the path. Two attendants perched on the back, laden with baskets and blankets. Clo gave them a sharp once-over. Here, finally, was some security, even if they didn't announce themselves as such.

Clo sat next to Rhea and covertly scrutinized Vyga. She clamped down on her shields to hide any suspicion, allowing only her appreciation of the weather through the barrier.

"We thank you for joining us today," Vyga said, voice low and warm.

The Ascendant and Oversouls all spoke in the collective *we*. After

Vyga and the other intended Oversouls completed the Unity Ritual at the forthcoming Equinox Ball, much of their identity would disappear into the Unity. They would keep their memories, but any attachment to individual experiences would become more distant. Even their family would be regarded the same as any other citizen—children included.

The carriage bounced, jolting Clo from her furtive study of the Evoli across from her. She checked her shields. Still drowned. Rhea said something in Evoli to Vyga, likely thanking ver for taking them along. Rhea nudged Clo with an elbow.

"Aye. Thank you for having us, Ascendant," Clo said.

"Please, call me Vyga, for I have not yet properly ascended." Ve smiled and must have given some covert signal, for the carriage started even though no one pressed a thing.

Clo resisted the urge to peer at it, but she was fascinated. Evoli tech was smooth, almost invisible. The only time she'd gotten close to it was on Laguna, and she hadn't exactly had the time to examine it properly.

They crossed under the canopy of trees. Some Evoli passed them in carriages, but others strolled in pairs or small groups, holding a palm up in greeting as their Ascendant passed. Vyga seemed to live among ver people in a way that was inconceivable to Clo. The only time Tholosian royals interacted with citizens was during their victory tours, and that was more about admiration than a bonding opportunity.

Clo searched about for something to say. "I've seen a lot of these purple flowers around," she pointed as they reached a particularly brilliant vine of them twined around the trunks of the pale trees. "What are they called?"

Rhea stiffened imperceptibly, and Clo wondered if she'd already fucked something up.

"The astra flower," Vyga said. Ve reached out and touched a blossom as they passed, and it released a sweet, spicy fragrance into the air. The orange pollen of the stamen stuck to ver fingertips. "They only grow on Eve. We say that a new flower blooms every time an Evoli dies by violence. Whether here or on another planet. Each is a reminder of the price we have paid for any victories."

Clo tried to imagine feeling someone die the way Vyga did through the Unity. Wouldn't that constant pain drive someone mad?

Vyga's eyes fixed on Clo, ver gaze as sharp as chipped glass. "Tholosians long tried to deny it, but we have a common lineage. Did you know this?"

Elva had told Clo this ages before, but she wanted to hear what Vyga thought. She shook her head and pretended ignorance. Though Vyga's gaze unsettled her, Clo allowed a fraction of curiosity through her shields.

Still, Vyga lowered ver eyes, as if ve'd sensed Clo's discomfort. Ve stroked another petal of the astra. "Hundreds of years ago, Eve was just another Tholosian conquest," Vyga began. "Any beings who lived here were destroyed like all the others to make room for human citizens. But a few generations in, something about this planet changed us. We began feeling what others felt. We grew tired of expansion and wished to secede in peace. That, of course, was too much of a threat. So began the slaughter. Blood once watered all these trees, and we buried many of our dead beneath them. This is a graveyard, Chloe. A living memorial."

Clo swallowed, taking in the expanse of forest. Miles and miles of it.

"Some of the survivors banded together and created what would become the Unity," ve continued. "They wove their emotions into something stronger. Something that could convince Tholosians to put down their weapons and leave. The Tholosians haven't set foot on this planet since."

"Until now." Clo's voice was slightly hoarse.

"Until we decided to grow past the pain," Vyga agreed. "We were tired of letting so many of these flowers bloom."

Clo leaned forward to scent them better. Intensely sweet, with an undercurrent of floral sharpness that lingered in her nostrils.

"They're beautiful," Clo said, and it felt like one of the only true things she'd said since she'd arrived.

Vyga's expression seemed to sharpen, then went smooth and placid. "I spoke to Neve this morning," ve continued pleasantly, as Clo settled back in her perch. "She referred to you as Clo. A nickname, she said. Would you prefer for me to call you this?"

"Chloe's fine," she said firmly. Better to keep her distance and focus on the mission.

Vyga smiled. "Forgive me, but I'm relieved. In the dialect of my home village, Clo means 'toilet.'"

Rhea made a choking sound that sounded suspiciously like a laugh.

Clo passed her a glare, then returned her attention to Vyga. "Where I come from, toilets are pretty rare, so I'll take it as a compliment."

Rhea gasped out another laugh.

"Myndalia, yes? It sounds like a fascinating place. Different from the other planets in the Tholosian Empire. I'd love for you to tell me about it sometime."

A surge of protectiveness went through Clo, even if she fucking hated that overcrowded maze of buildings. "Sure," she said, easily enough. "Sometime." *Fucking never.*

They went quiet after that, and Clo took everything in as they crossed a bridge and arrived at the extensive palace gardens. Talitha was by far the prettiest place Clo had ever been. More appealing than even Macella, the smallest planet of the Three Sisters.

The carriage came to a halt, and the trio stepped outside into sunny, warm gardens full of long grass and wildflowers. More astra flowers bloomed thick on the trees, the purple stark against the pale bark and dappled shade. Insects buzzed between the blooms, and more birds than Clo had ever seen perched in the surrounding trees or flitted overhead, as if unafraid of predators.

Clo was so used to planets picked clean by Tholosians. Intelligent animals were slaughtered, their bones a testament to Tholosian strength. Smaller animals that could be eaten were rarely allowed to roam free, instead raised in pens just outside cities.

The attendants set up the blanket and basket but, rather than drifting away to stand guard, ate with them in a semicircle. The food was no fancier than the meals they'd had back at the palace: cold cuts of unfamiliar protein that may or not be animal flesh, pungent cheeses, crisp pickled vegetables similar to a carrot.

Clo could barely touch her food. Whenever Vyga opened ver mouth, Clo was sure ve would command the attendants to cuff them and drag them down to some hidden dungeons. Reveal that the Evoli had all known for days that she and Rhea were imposters.

But Vyga only rested back on ver elbows, face tilted up toward the warm sun.

Soon, Rhea steered the conversation to the question they both wanted to know: if any Tholosian refugees resided in Evoli territory since the truce. The change in topic was subtle enough to impress Clo. She only hoped Vyga didn't notice.

"There are a few Tholosians, yes," Vyga said carefully. "They prefer to remain together, so we set a cluster of homes in Talitha aside for them. We're sure they'd be relieved to meet you, Chloe. You may visit whenever you like."

"*We* would like," Clo said, and kept her face impassive when Rhea gave her a look.

"Of course," Vyga said, still as smooth as a well-worn stone. "You need only ask."

"How did they come to be here?" Rhea asked. "When we arrived, we saw only other Evoli."

Vyga raised ver wine glass and took a long sip. "We recognized that they needed help on Laguna after the truce ceremony, and we provided it."

Did you hear them screaming within their skulls? Clo wanted to ask. *And did it warn you that Tholosians should never be trusted?*

She pressed her lips together, so she didn't ask the questions that burned in her mind.

Vyga's attention returned to Rhea. "And you, Neve? Have you given much thought to when you will join the Unity?"

Rhea almost choked on the grape she'd just popped into her mouth. "Oh—no, not yet. I feel it's still too soon, if you don't mind. I'm still getting used to the idea of being safe."

Not safe, Clo's mind wanted to bleat. *Not safe, not safe.* For three days, the food and baths had tried to lull Clo into a false sense of security, but she wouldn't let it. She and Rhea were Novantae Resistance. They'd be thrown in jail at best and executed at worst if they were discovered.

It took all of Clo's effort to keep her features neutral. She felt like she was spending every second of every day toeing the line between holding her breath and drowning. Rhea, somehow, seemed to float along the surface. Was this anywhere near as hard for Rhea as it was for Clo?

"The longer you wait, the harder it might be to integrate," Vyga said, as if eventually connecting was a foregone conclusion. Vyga's brown eyes were a spotted topaz. Mesmerizing and a touch fierce. "And the Unity can offer you more protection. We all do our part."

Clo took another bite of fruit, chewing slowly, imagining her foot in the murky waters of her swamp.

"You more than most," Rhea agreed. "The Equinox Ball is so soon. Was it . . . strange, to take on the title of Ascendant so suddenly?"

Vyga's expression flickered, like a cloud passing over the sun. "We were chosen for the role as a child. It's not hereditary, as with your people, but random. But we thought it would happen when we were much older, yes." Ve smiled. "Joining fully with the Unity is our choice."

"I was too young when I left," Rhea said, using Neve's background. "I never had the chance to join."

"Then I'll try to explain for you both," Vyga said gently. "We've lost count of how many times we felt like we've died. A baby was just born somewhere in the city. Mere moments ago, we felt that bright burst of pain and light as they came into the world. The cold until they were placed against their mother's chest. Elsewhere, perhaps a few streets over, two people breathed their last breath. One slipped away peacefully, and one went fighting. We felt both. Everyone enters and leaves the world through pain, but there's joy as well." Ver expression darkened imperceptibly. "But not in war. There's only ever pain in war."

"Among the Tholosians, I did all I could to cut myself off from pain," Rhea said, and the haunted look in her eyes made Clo want to bundle her up and take her away. "I can't imagine embracing it."

"In some ways, it's a boon. We're all aware of how precious life is. How quickly it can end." Vyga studied the astra flowers near them. "It's not that we wish to join our oppressors. It's that war hasn't worked, so we may as well try peace. Maybe we'll show your people a better way to live, Chloe."

"I'm not sure they'll listen," Clo replied. "They might just try to take everything you have." Such was the way of the Empire.

"Perhaps," Vyga admitted. "But perhaps not. To us, it's worth the risk, so we don't have to feel so much death."

They lingered in the garden as unease filtered through Clo. She didn't like the feelings Vyga dislodged, the facade of safety. Clo watched Rhea lean forward as if she wanted to hear every word from Vyga's lips. Was it the mission, or did she like it there? Clo retreated into herself— she wanted to go home and back to the people she trusted. She wanted to listen to Ariadne hum as she worked, to hear Kyla snapping orders and Cato scolding Clo over an injury.

She wanted to fight with Eris.

"I'm going to have a stroll through the woods, if that's all right, Ascendant," Clo said abruptly. She hated the almost obsequious tone of her voice.

"A beautiful day for it," Vyga agreed, distracted. Ve was focused on Rhea. Intentional or not, they both shut Clo out.

Clo rose smoothly on her new prosthetic. She wove her way through the few Evoli, who watched her pass with a wariness that only spurred her faster.

Clo walked, and walked, and walked. Was every tree she passed truly a gravestone? If she started digging down into the dirt, would she eventually hit bone?

When she was far enough away, she finally took the locket from around her neck. She closed her eyes and sent out the long-range signal. There was a delay as it sped the impossible distances through the stars, and she listened to the sounds of the birds.

<*Hey, asshole,*> came the welcome tones of Eris.

Clo loosened a breath. She never thought she'd be so relieved to hear Eris's voice. *Eris's* voice. Fuck, she really was that desperate.

<*You're supposed to call me Caiman,*> Clo said, grinning for the first time since she'd landed on Eve.

<*Yeah? Only if you call me Commander.*>

<*Since when? K's not dead, is she?*>

<*No, but you pinged me and not her. That makes me acting Commander.*>

Clo rolled her eyes. <*I don't know how you walk around under the weight of that massive fucking ego.*>

The mental equivalent of a snort was loud and clear. <*You all right?*> Clo gave a terse summary, using the agreed code names and phrases.

<*Huh,*> Eris said when Clo was finished. <*That's interesting.*>

<*Understatement. But I feel so useless here. R's getting comfortable with V, but I can tell she's always worried I'm about to mess up. Maybe I'm holding her back.*>

<*No, you're reminding her why you're there.*> A pause over the Pathos. <*Tholosian refugees might not trust R. They'll recognize your accent in an instant.*>

<*You think Tholosians will trust a slum rat from the Snarl?*> Clo asked doubtfully.

<*Former gerulae might trust a woman from the Snarl. They know you've never been chipped or under the Oracle's influence.*> Eris seemed distracted.

<*What are you doing?*> Clo asked.

<*Just finished up a meeting. We're about to run an operation.*>

<*ITI?*> Clo couldn't believe she was almost jealous.

<*Definitely. It'll almost be a shame not to have to save your ass as usual.*>

Clo rolled her eyes again, even though Eris couldn't see.

Eris hesitated. <*I think I miss you.*>

<*You think? Wow, I'm so flattered.*>

<*I'm ready to change my mind if you make something of it, so just fucking take the half-compliment, C.*>

Clo flung back another barb, as expected. They spoke of this and that, carefully avoiding any specificities. <*Hey, E,*> Clo said before Eris had to leave. She didn't want to let her go just yet. She had so many things she wanted to say. <*Do you think . . . if I came back and preferred different pronouns—if I didn't identify with the Tholosian binary anymore—do you think the other Devils would be okay with it? I'm not sure yet. I'm still figuring stuff out.*> Clo fidgeted and held her breath. Though they had nonbinary members of the rebellion, it was still so easy to fall back into the Tholosian mindset. One or zero. This or that. To doubt her feelings. To wonder if a former princess of the Empire would accept that future Clo might embrace one day.

But then Eris gave a mental laugh that eased the ache in Clo's chest.

<*Are you kidding? A would probably give you a bunch of gifts to commemorate the occasion. Your shelves will be filled with rocks. So many rocks. We'll all support you.*>

Clo smiled and dug her fingers into the soft soil of an alien world. For a second, she didn't feel so alone.

17.

Present day

As Ariadne tracked a prison transport ship to Othrys, Eris flipped through the Empire's official broadcasts.

She paused when she caught a flash of a purple cape and blond hair: Damocles, giving a speech in the main square in Discordokatak, a city on the planet Atria, surrounded by a crowd of thousands. They all held torches, the fire glowing in the light of the setting sun as they prepared to burn Discordia's fifty-foot icon. The ever-shifting screen had been erected at her father's request after she won the battles against the Evoli that secured Atria for the Tholosian Empire.

Discordokatak was the city where Eris had declared victory five years ago. She stood in that square, raised a flag with double scythes, and shoved it into the ground. A new conquest. Another planet gained for their voracious Empire. And in return, her father named its founding city after her: Discordokatak.

Discordia the Conqueror.

Behind Damocles, the screen of her icon flickered. The digital projection had been created to last thousands of years, long enough to see her name and face enter into future Tholosian myth. Her visage was depicted at the end of a long battle. She stood victorious over the bodies of her enemies, with blood spattered across her face and her eyes shining bright as golden coins. Her hair blew in the wind.

To onlookers, Discordia might have appeared fierce and unwavering, a Servant of Death.

To Eris, she looked weary. She had already begun to doubt her place in the world by then, and conquering Atria had given her no assurances. She ought to have told her father to name that city something else, to hold off on erecting an icon that displayed her uncertainty and doubt before the entire galaxy. Instead, she had pretended to be proud.

"Discordokatak was founded on a lie," Damocles declared, as if he read her mind from lightyears away. "The Discordia in this icon was as much a pretender as the rest. She is a traitor to the Empire, and an enemy of its people."

It was not the first time he had sent out similar words to the galaxy. It would not be the last. He was determined to erase every trace of her and remind his people that he had the power to unmake Discordia. Eris gripped the control as she watched his face. His deliberate golden eyepatch: an unspoken message to the citizens of the Empire that, like them, even he was a victim of Discordia's betrayal. His pressed military uniform with its gleaming buttons announcing he was their new general. He was their protector.

From her and her Devils.

Eris tried to look beyond the performance. Beyond the haughty expression that seemed so sure that he had the entire Empire at his disposal. That, even now, he was plotting to turn his people more subservient so that his power remained absolute.

Do you know what we're planning right now, Damocles? she asked him silently. *Did you hold this speech as a misdirection so I'd think I was winning the game?*

She imagined the zatrikion board back at the Myndalian boarding school, pictured herself arrogantly sliding a piece forward, only a few moves from victory. Doubt furled through her, as poisonous as a snakebite. Eris thought she knew her brother so well, that she played the game better—that she always fucking would.

After all, her brother had never won the game back on Myndalia. He never had the opportunity to say the words, *King kills Queen.* But he'd said them to her on Laguna, his retribution honed after years of nursing his hatred, and they sank inside of her like a sharpened dagger.

Worse, it was still there, just waiting to be twisted.

She could no longer count on her memories of him. He had learned new tricks.

"From today, this city will no longer be named after a traitor," her brother continued. "This city will be renamed for my commitment to the Empire and its people." Behind him, a servitor dropped the partition from the small, glowing obelisk that revealed its new name: *Damoclesero.*

"Now, let's erase the memory of this traitor and burn her icon to the ground!"

Cheers rose from the crowd, and Eris ground her teeth together.

A snort sounded from behind Eris as Nyx came closer to the screen. "Did he seriously name that city *Damocles the Protector*? That arrogant fuck."

Eris flattened her lips. She imagined the board again, piece by piece. Peasant. Commandant. Strategos. Polemarch. Magistrate. Queen. King. Bound by so many rules, the limitations of movements across the board. Eris felt like she was relearning the entire game from scratch.

"There was a saying in the Old World stories," Eris murmured, watching her icon burn. "*Metus est plenus tyrannis*. According to the history books, the first Archon inscribed it upon his sword so he never forgot."

"What does it mean?" Nyx asked. Her expression hardened as she watched the citizens light the icon with their torches.

They danced around the flames, celebrating their new Archon and the city he remade in his image. An image that was as false as the one they burned. Let him topple it. Let him savor his victory. Come tonight, Eris would start setting his whole Empire on fire. He ought to remember that she was a master of their game long before he stood in that square, wearing his gleaming uniform.

"*Fear is plentiful for tyrants*," Eris recited, shutting off the vid. "And I aim to remind him."

———

Eris watched as Cato coasted *Zelus* closer to the prison junker.

Their journey was slow, to avoid the Oracle's sensors. After Laguna and the Empire's raid on their Novan camp, Ariadne and Clo had worked tirelessly to outfit Novan ships with a refracted shield that helped them escape detection in emergencies. Any jump or burst of power would betray the ship's presence; it was a solution they had previously used only for fleeing or hiding their small fleet on the ground.

Now it had another purpose: for sneaking up on an Imperial craft without the Oracle or Damocles knowing.

Their target was *Theseus*, an old prison junker. According to Ariadne, the ship made a four-month circuit from the moons and planets in the Iona Galaxy's H quadrant, picking up prisoners from temporary holds for eventual transport to the large facility Othrys. Prison junkers weren't built for speed or defense but to send as many bodies as possible to the Empire's various penitentiaries.

Before the truce of Laguna and especially before the Battle of the Garnet, Evoli prisoners of war comprised a decent percentage of detainees sent to compounds with the medical facilities necessary to perform experiments on their bodies and minds. Some of them might even now be back on Eve with Clo and Rhea. A strange thought.

Now it was either rebels, pirates, scavengers, or any citizen convicted of crimes against the Empire. Anyone who dared break through programming. And those medical prison facilities existed for one purpose: to churn out gerulae to serve the Empire.

"There she is," Cato murmured as *Theseus* came into view.

His voice sounded so loud in the quiet of the bridge. *Zelus's* lights had all been dimmed for their covert approach. The new refractive shields were holding. It wouldn't work as well for fighting or jumping—flares of projectiles or the warp drive would give them away—but was handy for a surprise. Cato relied solely on sight and the ship's navigation to get them through space safely until *Theseus* was in clear view.

Cato started flipping switches. He glanced at Kyla. "*Zelus* is locked on to *Theseus'* route. All you have to do is follow and make sure she doesn't crash into anything."

Kyla unbuckled her belt. "I've instructed Elva to pilot *Zelus* and follow us to Othrys. Eris and I have done a mission like this before, so we're teaming up. I'll prepare the bullet craft for us."

"Wait. You're coming?" Eris asked.

Eris would have liked to know about this part of the godsdamned plan before they were minutes from actually going through with it. They were supposed to be partners, with Eris standing in the ghost of Sher's place at Kyla's side. She hated it when Kyla made last-minute changes. Usually, the commander was meticulous in her planning, except when she was trying to hide something. And the last thing Eris needed—the last thing they *all* needed—was more secrets.

Eris hurried after Kyla as she started out of the command center to the docking bay. "I don't like surprises," she snapped at Kyla.

"I am well aware of that," Kyla said, not breaking her stride.

"I thought you were staying on *Zelus*—"

"You thought wrong."

Eris had had enough. She seized Kyla by the arm and pulled her to a stop.

Kyla stared down at Eris's grip with a narrowed glare. "Eris," Kyla said in a cold voice. "You are still technically my subordinate. Take your hand off my arm before you lose it."

"But we can't risk you," she said.

Kyla's face was shuttered. "I've lost most of my fighters. The ones left are getting skittish. I am leading. You can either follow, or you can stay. Up to you."

Eris released Kyla's arm and curled her fingers into her palm at her emotional display. She used to be better about reining them in, showing nothing. Pretending she didn't care. Eris had never been good at following orders—she'd once had the highest military ranking in the Empire, after all—but she respected Kyla, and she had come to care for her in the months since Laguna. They were . . . friends? *Friends.* The word seemed strange to her, like a word in a foreign language. But she cared for Kyla, the same as for the rest of the Devils.

"Yes, I'm your subordinate," Eris told Kyla. "And if something happens on Othrys, the Novantae still need you to lead them. I'm expendable. You're not."

She left the rest unspoken: *they won't follow their former oppressor.*

Kyla's expression softened slightly. "If something happens to us, I've instructed Elva to put out a signal to Athena. She'll jump to come back if I'm out of the way, and the others respect her. I trust her to pick up the pieces. This . . . this is more than a show of force. I need to be there on Othrys. If Sher is . . ." Her lips tightened. "I have a promise to keep. To Clo. Do you understand?"

Eris looked down at her empty hand. She imagined the weight of Xander's firewolf in her palm, the comfort of the grooves he'd so carefully carved in his own small act of resistance. "I understand the mercy we sometimes have to give to brothers," she said gently. "I hope you don't have to live with yours."

Kyla cleared her throat. "Thank you." She stepped back. "Now, let's ready the bullet craft."

After prepping the small ship and again double-checking the refractive shields, their crew boarded and left the safety of *Zelus's* hull. The bullet craft slid unseen into space, and the small, shielded ship circled the junker's hull. Their small team of five was quiet as Ariadne used the bullet craft's system to gain remote access to *Theseus'* security.

"Now comes the fun part," Ariadne said brightly.

"Do I get to shoot someone?" Nyx asked.

Eris gave her a sharp look. The soldier's voice was shaky. The bullet craft, like *Zelus*, was dim but illuminated enough to catch Nyx's skin, glistening with sweat. Was she nervous?

"Of course not." Ariadne keyed in some commands. "We have to hope no one finds out we're here and shoots at *us*." She gave Nyx a fond smile. "How about another fun part?"

"Stabbing people?" Nyx bared her teeth. "Maiming them? Threatening them?"

"Ohh, I love threats!" Ariadne said, tapping away. "I'm still trying to learn how to say them menacingly. Cato, remember when I threatened to turn your brain into mush? How did I do with that one?"

"Terribly," Cato muttered.

Eris leaned forward. "And how about we get on the ship before we plan to shoot, stab, threaten, or maim people? Kyla?"

"I say we focus on not getting caught, for a start," Kyla said. "Ariadne, how's that coming?"

Ariadne's response was to hum happily, which Eris supposed meant good news. Otherwise, Nyx—who spoke fluent Ariadne—would look more alarmed. Eris watched as Ariadne logged a spacewalk into the hacked server, noting that the outside of the ship needed repairs.

"Done and done!" Ariadne exclaimed. "Okay, Cato, I'm opening the hatch now. All the crew will see is a flagged issue with a hull breach, so I made them think it's been sealed off. They wouldn't come to inspect until they made port. This happens a lot with these old hunks of metal."

Cato gave a nod and expertly navigated the bullet ship to the junker's massive hull. On her tablet, Ariadne pulled up the ship's schematics, with their prisoner targets as blinking red lights. A shifter might not help them look *exactly* alike, but it was not like guards stopped to examine prisoners closely. Future gerulae weren't given the benefit of being noticed.

Their erasure started with the other citizens of the Empire.

The moment the bullet craft landed, Eris gave herself one moment of quiet. One moment to breathe. One moment to say a prayer to a god that she had never spoken to before.

Salutem, she prayed. After all her years praying to the God of Death, Eris was surprised to find that the God of Survival gave her some comfort. His name felt like some small glimmer of hope. She wondered if her patron god would see her prayer as an insult, yet she didn't care.

God of Survival, please help me get them out of this alive.

18.

Present day

"**A**riadne?" Eris breathed in the dark cabin of the bullet ship as Cato cut the engine. "Surveillance?"

Ariadne tapped commands into her mech cuff, but looked annoyed at the small screen that blended neatly into her clothes. Ariadne couldn't risk bringing her proper tablet on the mission. Too bulky, too obvious.

With the weight of Xander's wolf gone from her pocket, Eris felt unmoored. Since Laguna, she couldn't bear to bring it with her on covert missions. She was no longer sure she deserved Xander's gift. Still, when she was alone in her bunk and chasing sleep, she grounded herself by focusing on the memory of the grooves, the details lovingly carved by Xander's hand. *One day, we'll meet again in the Avern, frater,* she thought. *But I hope it's not today.*

"The cameras will be feeding on a loop just . . . about . . . now." Ariadne made a few more motions with her fingers. "According to surveillance, the closest guard on duty is just outside the weapons cache. Now you get to knock him unconscious! Lucky you!"

Nyx muttered something that sounded like *Eris and Kyla always get to have the fucking fun.*

Eris rolled her eyes and lifted the hatch to escape the bullet craft.

She and Kyla jogged through the junker's massive hull. The two of them had grown accustomed to working together on supply runs, trying not to get captured or murdered. Before that, their only mission together had been their infiltration of the military compound on Hadar to rescue Novantae operatives. Recent practice made them efficient partners. Even when Kyla sprang last-minute changes on them.

Eris keyed in the codes from Ariadne's instructions, and they left the junker, working swiftly in case one of the crew grew curious about the hull breach and came to ask questions.

<How's the hallway look, Ariadne?> Eris asked.

She took in the hallway and its too-familiar frescoes. Two fluttering red flags at the end of the hall, the scythes like wings around the dark moons. It was much grubbier than the Tholosian military ships Eris was used to, but it had that same scent of metal, blood, and fear.

<Cleared to the weapons bay,> the girl said. *<I left a note in the system that the entire hull area was unsafe during the inspection and might result in . . . what happens to the human body when the oxygen leaves the room? I put that they would die horrifically, but I think their eyeballs might explode—>*

<Ariadne,> Nyx complained.

Eris tuned out Ariadne's chatter. She and Kyla crept silently through the cargo storage hall and to the weapons bay, lined with neatly stored boxes. Mors of varying sizes were pinned to the far wall. She and Kyla grabbed a few and tucked them into the small of their backs. If they made it out, that would be two more weapons for the Resistance. Might as well send them off in the bullet ship.

Eris let Ariadne's chirpy voice lull her into a sense of security. She had become more accustomed to how her team worked and knew the young engineer tended to babble out of nervousness to keep her mind calm while she worked. During the silence of a mission, sometimes it gave Eris comfort to listen to the cadence of Ariadne's voice and the way the girl's mind processed information.

Kyla pressed her back to the wall of the hallway and peeked around the corner. *<Male guard in armor stationed at the door,>* Kyla said to Eris. Ariadne, likely sensing the women needed a clear closed Pathos line, went quiet. The commander pulled out her Mors and gave a grim smile. *<Easier than on Hadar,>* Kyla breathed in Eris's mind.

Eris reached out and pressed Kyla's weapon down. <*Not like Hadar. Not like that.*>

She and Kyla had left a lot of bodies at that compound. By the time they left, blood had spattered the walls, and corpses had lined the hallways—a message for Eris's father that the rebels protected their own, whatever it took. Those missions didn't always lead to murder, but Eris took that dirty work knowing the risk. Her soul was already bound for its place in the afterlife beside the God of Death's chosen. Better that she did the killing work than someone bound for a nicer ring of the Avern.

Six months before, Eris would have put a blast through the guard's skull or slid a knife between his armor plates without a second thought. She would have whispered a prayer over his body with the words meant to guide him into the Avern, where he would walk alongside the God of Death for eternity. But Eris had not touched her scythe necklace in months. She had not sacrificed to her patron deity. Not since Laguna.

Today, she had asked for protection from Salutem, the God of Survival. And she would not betray that prayer.

Kyla smirked but put away the Mors. "You're getting soft."

Eris's smile was small. "I know."

"Then drop him easy," Kyla said with a shake of her head. Over the Pathos, she connected with the bullet craft team: <*Cato, Nyx, I'm going to need you to put a guard in the bullet craft. We'll be sending him to Elva for deprogramming.*> Eris suppressed her rush of gratitude. A guard might not deprogram successfully, but there was always the slightest chance he might.

Cato and Nyx didn't sound happy about it but answered that they'd take care of the guard while Eris and Kyla rescued the Novantae prisoners. Eris took a breath and shoved her self-doubt down. For a moment, she wished Ariadne would babble again, remind Eris of why she had gone so soft in the first place. Her own thoughts were too loud, too hard.

Instead, she tapped a few commands into her mech cuff, and the organic shifter in her clothes transformed the jumpsuit into the approximate uniform of a prison guard. Eris stepped back for Kyla's inspection. One of the few places Eris hadn't frequented as Princess Discordia was the prisons, and like all uniforms in the Empire, the threads, buttons, badges, and details were all placed with precision. Kyla, who had often led rescue missions for Novantae detainees, had more experience identifying the details in the jumpsuit.

The commander stepped forward and tapped a gold thread at Eris's shoulder. <*Make this one black. They changed the threads after Laguna, according to Ariadne's intel.*> Another entry into the mech cuff, and the gold thread darkened. Kyla gave a low sound of approval. <*Be quick about it.*>

Eris rounded the corner. The guard snapped to attention at the sight of her uniform. "At ease," Eris said as she approached, her voice as brusque and commanding as when she had been a general. "One of the prisoners got out of hand, and I need a recharge on the stun."

The guard frowned. "I wasn't aware that Chief Deputy Acrux had been repla—" His eyes met hers and widened. She knew what he saw: Princess Discordia's face, with its golden hair and eyes as bright and shining as an officer's buttons. "*You.*"

She'd kept her features rather than shifting into a less-recognizable rebel, partly for this moment of surprise. It might be risky, but she enjoyed that shocked, slack-jawed stare. She felt her lips curve into a smile.

He scrambled for a weapon, but Eris was faster. She took a running leap and tackled him to the ground. Before he could even gain his bearings, she pressed her stun to the gap in his armor—just above his throat. The guard went limp. Eris lowered him to the ground as Kyla strode forward.

"Nice work," the commander said as she stared down at the unconscious guard. "Easy part done."

Eris rooted around in his pockets and came up with his access key and identity cards. Sergeant Tabit's face and documents would come to good use. She slid out her shifter and placed the small device on his forehead.

As the tech scanned his features, Kyla tapped a finger against her thigh impatiently. Eris knew it wasn't an indictment of her speed but the sort of restlessness every soldier felt during a covert operation. Eris had had those tics trained out of her at the academy on Myndalia; it was one her brothers would have sensed as a vulnerability. They would have made a mistake by thinking it was one in Kyla.

"Shifter done," Eris said, examining him critically. She held up the shackles. "His frame and height are closer to mine than yours, with the lifts in my shoes." Ariadne had figured Eris's stature might be a problem when stealing identities during this mission. The girl had even added a bit of bulk to Eris's jumpsuit to fill it out. "So, I guess you're my prisoner this time."

Kyla shut her eyes. "Fuck," she muttered. "Don't look so happy about it."

Eris chuckled. "Sure, boss." She fitted the shifter to the roof of her mouth and grimaced as the tech changed the features of her face. "Ugh, it always tastes like licking a copper pipe."

The effect wasn't perfect. The guard had broader shoulders and a more muscled frame, but it would have to do. The shifter's impact on her voice, however, matched his baritone perfectly.

Kyla nodded her approval and reluctantly allowed Eris to chain the commander's hands to her belt. Eris noticed how Kyla stiffened as the metal clamped shut, but didn't remark on it. Eris had, after all, been in the prisoner role during their mission on Hadar. She remembered the moment of unease at placing her trust in another person and putting herself in a vulnerable position. For Kyla to trust her with this, on an Empire ship, plucked at something inside Eris.

No time to dwell on something as messy as emotions. There were rebels to rescue.

Kyla and Eris headed off to find their targets. The two rebels were being held on the floor above them with two other prisoners. Those non-rebels had programming so glitchy, they were more likely to have Novan sympathies—at least, that was the hope, and Ariadne had done her diligent research.

The commander kept her head down. Kyla wore no disguise, but hopefully not for long. Like all the Devils, her face had been blasted across the galaxy on broadcasts. Every city was on alert for a group of people with excessively shifted features—but no one would think to look on a prison ship, and the Oracle's scanners on the old junker were rudimentary at best.

Even so, this wasn't just enemy territory. It was every rebel's nightmare. It was where they all feared ending up.

Eris grasped Kyla's chain and pulled her forward as she consulted the map Ariadne sent to her mech cuff. <*Ariadne?*> she sent through the Pathos. <*How many guard stations until we reach our targets?*>

<*Five,*> Ariadne chirped back. <*Ten guards, five wardens on the way. First station in one minute.*>

Eris went through the first gate and used the guard's stolen access. The program scanned her features and required her to swipe her keys. The gate beeped. Eris nodded to the guards on either side and continued through, keeping a firm, authoritative grasp of her commander.

First station down.

Eris continued down the long hall to the next station, where a guard looked at her curiously. "Tabit?" He frowned down at his tablet. "Aren't you supposed to be down near the hull?"

"Chief Deputy Acrux asked me to transport a few reserved prisoners to different cells," Eris said, giving the name Tabit had helpfully provided before she had knocked him out. She dragged Kyla closer. "This one's for some diplomat on Tholos after she's husked. Told us to treat her lightly." Eris gave a hard punch to Kyla's kidney and tried not to wince as her commander doubled over with a sharp gasp. "I told him I'd treat her as lightly as a rebel deserves."

The guard laughed. "Mess up her face and just give her some of the healing gel on Othrys, and it'll fix her right up again. Not like she'll be able to tell him any different." If he had bothered to glance at Kyla's features, he might have recognized her. But yet again, prisoners were regarded as little more than inevitable gerulae. And gerulae were treated as items, things, tools.

Nothing.

"Perfect idea," Eris replied, dragging Kyla past the guard. "I'll be back this way in a few."

Their footsteps echoed down the hallway. When they were far enough from the station, Eris said to Kyla through the Pathos, <*I'm sorry.*>

<*Don't be,*> Kyla said, still playing her prisoner role to perfection. <*I think I treated you worse on Hadar.*>

"I deserved to be treated worse on Hadar," Eris muttered.

After all, she had only defected to the Novantae a few months before that mission. Kyla barely knew her as anyone other than Princess Discordia, the Empire's Servant of Death. Responsible for the slaughter of thousands. When Kyla had given her a fist to the face, part of it was for authenticity. The other part was personal. Eris didn't hold it against her.

Kyla didn't respond.

They made their way past the following three guard stations without trouble. Eris's performance twisted some soft corner of her heart every time she was forced to hit Kyla, to insult and degrade her in front of the guards. These were acts she had never given a second thought as Princess Discordia.

But Eris cared. She let emotions twist their way inside of her, and she tried to keep them coiled tight as they left the last guard station. *I don't think I can do this*, she almost told Kyla. Such a strange, foreign thought. Did that make her weak?

As if Kyla read her mind, the commander licked the blood off her lip from the last particularly hard punch with a wince. <*Well done.*>

Eris swallowed and nodded. <*The cell is just up here.*>

When they reached it, the rebel prisoners were huddled on the small, bare bed, away from the two Empire citizens.

The first was Maia, a young scientist who worked with the Novantae on sustainable encampments that kept the rebels fed and healthy. It wasn't glamorous work, or dangerous, but she had helped keep them alive back on Nova before she was captured. The second was Atropos, a retired spy who had devoted the last few years to training newer recruits in espionage. Tholosian soldiers had captured both in the raid on Persei after Laguna that left the Novantae devastated. After so much death, Eris was glad to see them alive, if a little worse for wear.

The other two prisoners were, according to Ariadne, of the merchant aedifex class. One was an architect, and the other sold the food grown by the farmers on Myndalia. Eris didn't know what their crimes were, but if the Oracle decided they were malfunctioning in some way, that was enough. If the stories about Damocles' new policies were remotely true, just the smallest glitch was flagged—any behavior that countered programming. Ariadne had said these two had a bigger-than-small malfunction.

Eris held the button for the comm for Kyla to speak through. "Atropos, Maia," Kyla said.

The two women looked up—so did the other prisoners, but Kyla ignored them for the moment. "Commander," Atropos breathed. Her shackles rattled against the bed. "Oh, gods, what's happened? Are—"

"No time," Eris said briskly. She flashed the identity key, and the cell door opened. "It's me, Eris. Kyla and I are here to get you out."

"Eris." Maia sounded relieved when she realized Eris wasn't really a guard, though there was still the usual wariness when she remembered that meant she was staring at Princess Discordia. "Seven devils, it's so damn good to see you both."

"We're going to do this quickly," Eris said, inputting her ID to the shackle's internal programming. "You two are going to come with me. Maia, you're closest to Kyla in size. I'm going to put this on your forehead, okay? We just have to borrow your face for a second."

Maia hesitated, but let Eris gently place the shifter. "You said . . . us two," she replied as the shifter scanned her features.

"I'm taking your place," Kyla said firmly. "Need to know only. Eris will be returning you to our bullet craft, and you'll fly alone to rendezvous with Elva. She's waiting on our newer ship, *Zelus*." She offered her a smile. "You're going home to the Novantae."

"Understood," Atropos said as Eris handed Kyla the shifter, but Eris heard the relief in her voice. Atropos was a retired spy; she was well acquainted with covert missions. She knew not to question.

"You're going to get caught," said one of the men chained to the other bed.

Eris guessed he was the architect; he looked well groomed, or like he had been until recently. A wealthier citizen. To his credit, he didn't sound happy about his prediction. The other man—the merchant— only shook his head.

"That would be bad." Eris released Atropos's shackle from the bed and rehooked it to her belt. "Since you're both also coming with me."

The merchant and the architect traded looks. "The seven levels of the Avern we are," the architect said.

"Brainwashed fools," Atropos muttered.

Eris ignored the woman's comment. "Oh, so, you *want* to stay and be made into gerulae? Say the word, and I'll find two other prisoners to free. I just need two, and I'm not picky. They don't have to be you."

She was bluffing, but the men shifted uncomfortably. The merchant spoke this time. "What's the point in freeing us when we'll get caught by the next Imperial ship?"

"Novantae take care of their own," Kyla said firmly. "You want to stay in this cell, say the word. Both of you have been sentenced. You either leave free, or you leave in chains. Tell us which."

They were both quiet for the span of five heartbeats. The architect nodded first. "I'll go." The merchant seemed more reluctant, but he agreed.

"Good." Eris pulled a sedative out of her belt and held up the needle. "Then sit still."

The architect looked alarmed. "What the fuck is that?"

"A mild sedative to keep the Oracle in your head calm and both of you acquiescent as we head back down to the hull. Full offense, but I don't trust either of you."

They sat still as Eris shot the drugs into their system. She unhooked the chains from the bed and attached the additional prisoners to the two Novantae. If anyone looked at Maia's features and later found Kyla in the cell, they might notice the same woman in two different places. But that would require looking too closely at a prisoner.

As Eris worked, Kyla said her goodbyes to her rebels. She embraced them both, and then she stepped back and shifted her features into Maia's. When Eris shut the cell door, she caught a flash of fear in Kyla's gaze.

<*Don't worry, Commander,*> Eris said, taking her lineup of prisoners back down through the guard stations. <*We'll all get through this.*>

<*You always were a good liar, Eris,*> Kyla said.

Eris smiled grimly.

It was easier to take prisoners through checkpoints the second time. All the guards warmly greeted Eris and jeered as she roughed up her prisoners. Maia and Atropos took her abuse admirably. The two men were too drugged to care.

When she returned to the hull and the bullet craft, the rest of her crew worked quickly. They took the prisoners' identities and matched approximate body types to faces. Ariadne, Nyx, and Cato looked determined underneath their shifted features. The saved rebels took the bullet craft back to *Zelus* along with the other two prisoners and the spare guard.

With their escape pod gone, Eris and the Devils had to find their own way out alive.

19.

KYLA

Present day

The transport ship arrived on Othrys.

If Kyla had stuck to the initial plan she'd given Eris and the others, she'd be pacing the command center of *Zelus*. As the leader of the resistance, she'd never lived a cushy existence, but she spent an increasing amount of time relegating missions rather than participating in them.

As that rebellion grew and Tholosians whispered her name in every corner of the galaxy, her fear mounted.

The name *Kyla* was formidable. *Kyla* was either enemy or ally, a commander who put together impossible plans as intricate as clock-work. Sher always advised her on the weak points, making the whole more robust than the sum of its parts, but *Kyla* sent the spies. *Kyla* assigned the missions.

The name she had once whispered in her mind that would mark her as a traitor had become a shout: *I am free, and I will destroy you.*

And she was terrified of losing it.

There she was—in a filthy cell, on a foul transport hub, about to go to an even filthier prison—and she feared capture more than death. Failure would strip her of the name she had chanted at the back of her mind (the thing she had held on to through her programming). Failure would take her back to the Empire. The same fear that had been churning through her mind ever since she'd started planning this mission.

Kyla would be nameless.

Kyla would be erased.

"You promised," she whispered to herself. "Remember? You promised. Failure is not an option."

She owed it to Sher not to spend this mission pacing in a command center, waiting for someone else to save him when she still might have to put a blast through his skull.

She owed him for taking the journey from the Empire with her and starting the rebellion when they were only a movement of two. When he'd grasped her hand and echoed the name she'd chosen with a smile. *"Kyla? Nice name. Suits you."*

It didn't matter that the movement they had spent so long building had nearly collapsed. That Kyla was trying to gather the dregs of the rebellion (and it was slipping like water through her hands). They had sworn neither of them would ever be under the Oracle's control again—and she had left him to that fate for the gods knew how long before Laguna.

She flinched at the guilt that lingered with her since that night on the Evoli planet. How Sher had shot her, pinned her to the wall like some insect caught in a web, helpless as he held a Mors to Cloelia's head. The words he'd said to Kyla, free of any inflection: *"I did what I had to."*

"I never said it was a mercy."

He had been nothing like her brother at all.

Kyla took a breath and stared down at her chains. *I'm coming for you, Sher.*

I'm not leaving you again.

Kyla tried to hide her fear once they left their cells. She watched as the Empire's guards roughly escorted prisoners off the junker, frequently using their fists for no other reason than savage enjoyment. As they left the ship, hundreds of bodies pressed together like a moving ouros herd.

She didn't recognize any prisoners. Some stared through Kyla with bleak expressions, their shoulders slumped, the long months of confinement grinding their hope to dust. Some had sheens of tears on their faces. They had resigned themselves to their fate—that soon they would be nothing but walking corpses. Husks to be dispatched all over the Empire, their hands used for labor and their identities gone. Did those who became gerulae even end up in the Avern, or were they erased on every level of existence?

Kyla waited with Ariadne in one of the prison's holding cells as their plan was set in motion. <*You put the lock on the transport ship?*> Kyla asked Ariadne. They'd need to commandeer *Theseus* in order to escape Othrys and rendezvous with Elva and *Zelus*.

<*When we landed.*> Ariadne's voice was faint over the Pathos. <*Theseus won't fly off unless Cato's in the pilot's chair.*>

<*Well done.*>

In response, Ariadne gripped her hand so hard that Kyla bit her lip.

Let the girl have her comfort; Kyla could bear a bit of pain. If Tholosians still raised offspring in family groups, Kyla would have been old enough to be her mother. But the young engineer had endured more at sixteen than most people Kyla's age had in their whole lifetime.

<*Do you think Nyx and Cato are okay?*> Ariadne asked, trembling.

Kyla didn't know. <*I'm sure they're fine,*> she said with an assurance she didn't feel. They were hemmed in on all sides.

Nyx and Cato would have been among the first wave of prisoners taken through the Othrys complex. Once inside, they would use the stolen identity key Eris provided to remove their chains, shift their clothes into prison-guard uniforms, and create a distraction deeper in the compound. Ariadne had pointed out back on *Zelus* that the mines of Othrys shared walls with the prison, and cave-ins weren't unheard of—and they required immediate personnel attention.

Hurry, Kyla thought. *Please, gods, hurry.*

She couldn't stand being confined; people pressed so close made it difficult to breathe. All smelled like soiled bodies, cold metal, and despair. The once-shining frescoes on the walls of the prison were dulled with dirt. Everything on this moon was gray and black, with no spots of color. Even the prisoners' skin seemed ashen. She wanted to run, shoot, fight (anything to help her feel alive again, to quiet that howling in her soul). When she stopped moving, the fear sneaked in.

It was only when she felt as if she might never escape that terror gripped her.

(*I am Kyla. And I am the leader of the Novantae rebellion.*)

"Filthy fucking husk," one of the guards snapped as he roughly handled a prisoner. The man hadn't turned gerulae yet; he registered the insult with a recoil.

(*My name is Kyla. And I will not be captured. They will not take my name. They will not take my soul.*)

Another guard spat into the face of a woman, laughing as she rubbed it away. The guards stared at the prisoners like they were nothing. A bit of filth beneath their boots. No longer human.

Kyla knew that their behavior couldn't solely be blamed on Oracle's programming. For all of One's faults, casual cruelty didn't make sense to the AI. That was entirely human.

(*My name is Kyla. And I will survive.*)

Eris strolled past the holding cell. Even with the lifts in her shoes, she was still several inches shorter than the man she was impersonating, but Eris played her role to perfection. Her lip curled as she opened the holding cell and seized Kyla in a hard grip, shoving her and Ariadne forward.

<*Sorry,*> Eris said through the Pathos. <*Ariadne, you okay?*>

Ariadne gave a slight, shaky nod.

Kyla's face still smarted from Eris's knuckles, and her lower lip would be fat by evening. Eris barked an order to a prisoner who faltered, gave a kick with her boot that wouldn't end up hurting beyond a brief sting. Kyla forced herself to hunch over, to make herself smaller. She wished for a fraction of Rhea's abilities just now. (*Don't see us—nothing to see here.*)

Kyla glanced up, jaw tense. They were already behind schedule. They had to do this before the guards began searching prisoners for processing. They'd find far too many hidden weapons and surprises. Nyx and Cato should have already—

BOOM!

The walls of the prison shuddered. Dust fell from the rafters, the overhead lighting shook, and the prisoners cried out as a few panels fell to the floor.

Kyla's mouth twisted in a smile that Eris echoed. It was one hell of a fucking distraction.

Enough guards headed out to investigate the explosion. Only a few remained.

<*Here we go,*> Kyla said. <*Ariadne, the glitcher.*>

Ariadne nodded, messing with the mech cuff again and taking out a small bit of machinery the size of her thumb from an inside pocket. <*I think I improved it. The Oracle will be in background processing for fifteen minutes, maybe longer for the non-gerulae prisoners already resisting their programming.*> She gave a nervous look at the three guards watching the newest prisoners.

<*Good girl,*> Kyla said to Ariadne. Focus on the plan. Focus on the fight. <*Once you flip the device on, you said they might panic once they feel the Oracle recede. You stay with me. Do not let the crowd push you away. Understand?*>

Ariadne grasped Kyla's hand hard in response. The girl looked terrified as she turned on her device.

A hush went through the crowd as Eris dropped her disguise and pulled out her Mors. Prisoners' mouths fell open, their eyes widening in shock and fear. Several stumbled back.

Eris attacked the guards. Her movements were so quick that even Kyla couldn't follow. All she heard was Morsfire. A sear. A sizzle.

One guard fell.

Another.

Another.

Eris moved like smoke. Kyla often sent Eris on missions rather than watching her in action. It was like a dance where only Eris heard the music. She knew where her opponent would be, how to take them down.

When it was over, she stood in front of the prisoners, her Mors loose at her side. With those brilliant golden eyes and deceptively delicate features sprayed with a fine mist of blood, she resembled an avenging Valkyrie. Even Kyla was struck silent with something like awe. Far away, alarms shrieked.

Eris put her lips close to her mech cuff. "Imperial citizens," Eris called, the tech amplifying her voice over the crowd. "You know who I am and what the Empire claims I've done. But do you feel that quiet in your mind? It's time to make a choice. Are you ready? Are you listening?"

The crowd was silent; the tenor of Eris's voice was like a general on the eve of battle. "The Empire tried to break you and eradicate you. They brought you here to make you into fucking *nothing*. I want you to remember every fist that beat you in those cells, every guard who spat in your face. I want you to remember every doubt and question you had, and the punishment you got in return. *Make your choice!* Are you going to run? Then board the ship *Giausar*, take your chances out there on your own, and see how far and long you can make it. Are you going to stay? Hope the Empire rewards you for loyalty?"

Her expression was harsh as she gazed out over the murmuring crowd. Their voices began to rise.

"My brother will not reward you. He will erase you, work your bodies until they collapse, and he'll force you to kiss his ring as you crawl. All that's left is to fight. So, make your choice, and make it now. Do you want to fight? Board *Theseus*, wait for us, and we'll give you a fucking fight. Become Novantae. And we can bring this empire to its knees."

Shouts went through the crowd. No one had tried to kill them yet, at least.

The prisoners were still processing the abrupt change in their fortunes, but Kyla sensed a shift in the crowd. Some jostled for *Giausar*, but others headed back to *Theseus*. Those who decided to join the resistance would have to wait on the junker—their first test of trust—until the Devils finished their business. Ariadne had been inspired by the time Cato had put a freeze on *Zelus*'s engine back when he'd hoped to kill them all for the glory of the Empire. Now he was another rebel fighting at their side. Who knew which prisoners before them might also stand up against Tholos? The junker was grounded on this godsforsaken moon without the key.

Eris moved quickly through the crowd, taking Ariadne's arm as she sped them past the prison gates.

<It won't be long before one tries to capture us for the bounty,> Eris said. *<So, let's hurry the fuck up before any of them get ideas.>*

<That was a great speech, General,> Kyla said as Eris swiped her pass at another gate.

<Yeah, I know. Speechifying came with the job.>

Clo would have rolled her eyes and made a joke if she were there, but Kyla remained focused on the mission.

(Focus.)

<Ariadne, where are we going?> Eris asked.

Ariadne led them through the labyrinthine corridors of the prison to where she had tracked Sher. In each cell they passed, gerulae stared at them blankly. Eris opened a few of their doors, but they didn't even make a move to leave.

"In here, I think," Ariadne said aloud, chewing her lip.

Eris swiped her stolen pass and shoved the door open.

The first person Kyla saw was Sher, sprawled unconscious on a hospital bed, surrounded by a dozen other prisoners. She swallowed down the sound of a wounded animal. Had they been turned into gerulae already? Had he?

Kyla hurried to the hoverchair in the corner and pushed it to Sher's bedside.

She leaned over her brother.

He was so much thinner. His cheekbones protruded, and his hair was newly shorn. Had there been that much gray in his stubble before? Kyla pulled the wires from the ports at his elbow, turned his head to look at the ugly implant behind his ear. Two of his fingers had been broken and splinted, the bandage stained with old blood. Who knew what other injuries were underneath his threadbare prison uniform?

"Sher," she said, her voice broken. He did not respond. Did not move.

Who are you? she wanted to ask. Was he the man who still believed in the Novantae and railed against the barriers Oracle had erected in his mind? Or was he a man who had turned against everything they had worked so hard to build? Was he her partner or her enemy?

"Come on, Kyla," Eris urged her.

She hoisted him from the bed, and Eris helped strap him into the hoverchair. Eris and Kyla started unplugging one of the other prisoners as Ariadne got to work on the computers, face scrunched in concentration as she hacked into the prison's mainframe.

"Hey," Eris said, uncharacteristically gentle as she slapped the prisoner softly on the cheek. "Wake up. Are you still yourself?"

The woman's eyelids fluttered and went still.

Kyla glanced anxiously at Ariadne, who was still working hard to find the coding program for the gerulae.

"I think this is it," Ariadne said, excited. "I'll install the trojan while I download. Make this prison all but useless."

"That's my girl," Kyla said, and Ariadne's shoulders rolled with pleasure at the compliment.

Eris wasn't having any luck waking up the prisoners.

"Uncuff the others," Kyla instructed. "We might have to leave them behind, but if they're still themselves when they wake up, they'll have a shot."

Eris nodded and set to work. She didn't mention what Kyla had implied: if they woke up and were not themselves, they would be more enemies. Ariadne's hands danced over the computer controls, weaving her web over the prison systems.

<*Cato,*> Kyla said through the Pathos, gripping the handles of Sher's hoverchair. <*We're almost set. Status update.*>

<*Heading to the western sector of the compound. Glitching any guards I find and punching them in the jaw if they're assholes. Should give us a quick escape route. Nyx headed off to open some cells and let the prisoners out.*>

<*Nyx, status update.*>

Silence.

<*Nyx?*>

<*I don't see any sign of her,*> Cato said. <*Prisoners are still in their cells. I'm going after her.*>

"Be quick." Cato nodded and took off running. Kyla glanced worriedly at Eris, who returned the expression. Ariadne's hands faltered at the controls. They each called out to Nyx together one last time.

Nothing.

20.

ARIADNE

Present day

Ariadne was terrified.

<*Nyx?*> she called over the Pathos, knowing her mental voice was more like a panicked scream. <*Nyx Nyx Nyx Nyx NYX NYX—*>

"Hush," Eris said, moving to stand beside her. "Let Cato worry about Nyx. He'll find her, all right? We won't leave her behind."

"Okay." Ariadne gulped. "Okay. Okay." The word stuck in her mouth as she tried to reassure herself. *Okay. It's okay.*

As she typed commands, her fingers felt heavy, as if someone had placed lead weights on her wrists. Her movements were sluggish and uncoordinated. She couldn't afford to make mistakes, to slow down. Why wasn't Nyx answering? Where was she? Was she dead?

It's okay. It's okay. Keep typing.

It didn't help that the Oracle's defenses had improved in the months since Laguna. Before, she might have been able to do this remotely. Working around the prison's firewalls without detection ended up taking longer than she anticipated. The Oracle had established new traps intended to trip Ariadne up. They were such small triggers in the programming that Ariadne hardly noticed them at first. Once she did, her anxiety shot up. Those minute, barely noticeable symbols of code were like hidden landmines in a forest. One wrong step, a figure or line of programming out of place, and the Oracle would know Ariadne was there and lock them all in. She had to make the automated system that ran the prison useless before that happened.

Ariadne got around the traps by having her trojan mimic the actions of a benign code condenser, a program Ariadne had established within the Temple that tidied redundant lines of code and symbols into a more-streamlined language for the Empire's systems. That code condenser also allowed the Oracle to work more quickly within the Empire's vast network.

But it was still slow work. It wasn't the sort of task one did while in a prison compound, trying not to die or get captured, wondering if one of your friends was already dead.

One mistake, and all the Devils would be dead. The pressure of perfection built in her skull.

Worse: Ariadne had limited time. The glitch device only kept the Oracle in background processing for so long. If the prisoners returned to their Oracle programming too soon, the Devils' getaway would be much more difficult. That all made *difficult* sort of *impossible.*

You're well acquainted with the impossible. You escaped the Empire despite a seven percent probability of success, remember?

The mental voice she'd imagined sounded like Nyx, or Eris. Someone brave and strong.

But if Ariadne failed today, she would be right back where she started. Her friends would be imprisoned, turned into mindless drones, or executed. And she would be staring up at the rafters of the Temple, in the ruins of that vast, quiet generation ship, with no company but the AI she had turned into a monster.

Your fault, your fault, your fault. They'll never forgive you if they knew.

That usual internal monologue was back. The one that told Ariadne she was never good enough. That one wrong step would result in catastrophe.

Eris's hand touched Ariadne's shoulder. She knew the former general had difficulty comforting people, but somehow that small touch quieted Ariadne's doubts. Eris was strong. She could be the voice in Ariadne's head that drove away the small, scared one.

You can do this.

Ariadne let that strength seep into her bones, and her muscles, and into the edges of her fingertips as she keyed in the commands buried within lines of organized rows of numbers, letters, and symbols. Her breathing hitched. She had just narrowly avoided another trap.

"You can do this," Eris said into her ear, externally echoing the one in her head. The hand on Ariadne's shoulder tightened into a reassuring squeeze. "My father used to say that in the middle of a battle, slow is fast and fast is slow. You make more mistakes when you're trying to hurry. Breathe and do the job right."

Ariadne's voice was a terrified whisper. "I can't. There are too many traps. I keep almost slipping up. I'm not good enough."

Eris and Kyla's eyes met across the room. The worry was thick in the air. Ariadne was wasting time—she knew it, but she couldn't stop. *Slow is fast, and fast is slow* went right out the window if there was *no time*. She was so focused on avoiding the Oracle's snares that she forgot how to implement her trojan to bring down the system.

Forgot? How could you forget? You've known how to do this since you were five years old! Are you going to forget how to breathe next?

Her body lost Eris's strength. Her fingers were shaking. Where was Nyx? Had Cato found her? He would have said something, right? He would have—

<Nyx? NyxNyxNyx—>

"You used to tell me during times of stress that it was easier for you to count." Something about Eris's firm, no-nonsense voice made Ariadne go still, her breathing slowing. Eris wouldn't leave her. Eris wouldn't leave Nyx. Eris was strong. "Count with me: One. Two. Three—"

"Four." Ariadne quietly picked up the count, her mind settling into the rhythm of numbers. *You can't help Nyx unless you finish this.* "Five. Six."

"Seven," Eris said with her. "Eight. Nine."

They fell into the count together. Eris's composure quieted Ariadne's rioting thoughts, forcing her to focus on the pace of numbers that began to resemble the flow of her breaths. Slow, steady.

Easy.

Her head shot up to the screen. She knew exactly what she needed to do.

Ariadne's fingers flew across the keys, a corner of her mind still wordlessly shaping the numbers. Then, with clarity like a lightning bolt, it all became so much more straightforward. The letters, numbers, and symbols flowed from her fingertips as smoothly as pushing oxygen through her lungs.

Eris's voice kept counting, her calm tone soothing Ariadne's racing heart. It held her breath steady. In. Out. In. Out. It was like magic.

Ariadne had always been alone in her counting or her naming, her various rituals that helped navigate the fragile physiology connected to her turbulent mind. She had always been the one to calm her own thoughts. Eris's steady voice, her hand heavy on Ariadne's shoulder— these reminded her that she was not alone. That she was not in the command center of that generation ship back at the Temple, desperate for companionship. Desperate for someone else's voice to be heard alongside her own. Desperate for a voice to join hers in the darkness.

Eris was there. Kyla was there. Even the commander had joined them in their count; Ariadne heard Kyla's whispers as she checked over Sher. Their combined words became like a chant—a prayer.

Fifty-three. Fifty-four. Fifty-five. Fifty-si—

Alarms wailed across the compound. Ariadne's concentration broke, losing both the numbers and the code. A gasp tore from her lips.

She tried to resume her count (*fifty-what?*), but the siren screeching in her ears made it impossible. She brought her hands up and flapped her wrists near her ears. She fought to focus on the soft sound of her loose fingers snapping against each other instead of the screams. She shut her eyes hard.

"It's okay," Eris said over the alarms, giving Ariadne's shoulder a light squeeze. "Slow is fast, and fast is slow, remember?"

Slow is fast, and fast is slow, Ariadne repeated, determinedly setting her fingers to the keys again. *Finish the job. Get them all out of here.*

The gerulae coding structure downloaded—one thing down, one thing to go. Counting didn't work anymore; only Eris's mantra did, the words seemingly tailored for Ariadne's tumultuous mind.

Slow is fast, and fast is slow. Slow is fast, and fast is slow. Slow isfastandfastisslow.

Last level of the prison's system. Ariadne's coding swept in like a parasite destroying its host organism. Worming its way through the coding structure and potential traps the Oracle had laid down. She tried to quell the doubt—the worry that the Oracle might stop her, even as she keyed in her last stroke.

The alarms went quiet, but the echo of that wail still pulsed through her eardrums.

"Got it," she said in a small voice.

Would the Oracle know now? It would be too late for One to counterattack, but would the Oracle know Ariadne was at the prison? If One did, then the Oracle would be aware that Ariadne was defying One's command.

That she had no intention of coming home.

"Thank the gods," Eris said. "Let's get the fuck out of here before the cavalry shows up."

Ariadne stared at them, wide-eyed. She wouldn't have been able to do this without them. She would have been lost.

She wanted to hug them and cry. She didn't deserve them.

The other women didn't waste time. Eris seized Ariadne's hand and pulled her out of the chair, and Kyla steered Sher's hoverchair toward the exit. Ariadne grasped for the microdisk with the gerulae coding and stuffed it in the pocket of her jumpsuit.

Eris all but dragged Ariadne toward the door as her mind still reeled.

They froze when one of the people on the other beds sat up and looked straight at Ariadne. She almost told Eris to grab the unfamiliar woman, that she would never stand a chance if they left her here.

The woman's head turned towards Ariadne. "Hello, daughter," she said in an eerie, flat voice. Her eyes were unblinking, pupils condensed into tiny black holes in seas of blue iris.

The Oracle had taken control of the woman's body.

Ariadne screamed. It drove out all thoughts. She couldn't move.

The Oracle was there.

One had found her.

One had seen her.

One would kill her friends.

One would—

Eris had her Mors out in a blink and shot the woman in the forehead. The silence only went on for a beat, but it seemed like an eternity.

"Let's go." Eris's voice was hoarse, her expression filled with guilt. "Come on, Ariadne."

They took off running.

21.

Present day

Eris, Ariadne, and Kyla sprinted through the upper cell block.

Beside Eris, Ariadne was gasping, her entire body unsteady as she tried to keep up. Her face was stark with fear. That woman back in the hospital room and the eerie, flat voice had spooked the shit out of her.

Daughter. It could only have been the Oracle—Ariadne wouldn't be nearly falling over herself in terror if it weren't.

Eris wordlessly hauled Ariadne to her feet. *It doesn't matter if it was the Oracle—you shot that woman in the head. Maybe you could have saved her, given her the same chance you gave every other prisoner. But you made your first sacrifice in months to a god you haven't prayed to in just as long. Some hero you are.*

Those thoughts would not help her now; she had to get Ariadne to safety.

The trojan was taking over the prison computer systems. As they swept through the cell block, formerly computer-locked doors slammed open, the usual friendly *beep* of the approved clearance glitching into a continuous, piercing shriek. It was so fucking *loud.*

Kyla shoved Sher's hoverchair through one of the doors.

"How's he doing?" Eris asked, nudging Ariadne's shaking body along. The girl was still dead silent in terror.

"Unconscious." Kyla's voice was strained. "I haven't even seen him twitch."

Though Kyla didn't say it, she had to be wondering whether they'd made it in time—or whether the co-commander of the Novantae was erased. "If he's a gerulae—"

"Then I have a decision to make," Kyla snapped, "and I have a promise to keep. But until then, let's focus on getting out of here alive. We still have to make it to the lower level, and we're running out of time."

Ariadne was slowing them down. Even if the girl wanted to move faster, her body shook so much that she kept tripping over her feet. Eris could only drag her so quickly. Her encouragements were drowned out by the shrill screech of the automated doors glitching as Ariadne's trojan continued its rapid sweep through the prison's vast system.

Cell doors on the upper level sprang open and confused prisoners flooded the narrow cellblock hallways. Eris almost lost her grip on Ariadne's hand. If she didn't do something now, the girl would get lost in the crowd, and they didn't have time to waste.

Eris called for Kyla to stop and kneeled in front of Ariadne. "Look at me." She put her hands on either side of Ariadne's face. "I'm going to carry you. I want you to get on my back and hold on tight," she said. "Can you do that?"

Ariadne gulped and gave a panicked nod. She was still shaking when she climbed onto Eris's back and slid her thin arms around her neck. Eris grasped her just below the knees and hitched her up. Her breath was loud in Eris's ear.

With a nod to Kyla, they shoved through the crowds of people. Kyla cleared the way with Sher's hoverchair, doing what she could to tell people to follow her. They were so close to the stairs that reached the lower level. So close to the junker and escape.

Eris shouted over the noise of the crowd, "Follow me to *Theseus* if you want to escape the Empire! The rebellion will shelter you! If you want to go on your own, head to *Giausar*! Whatever your choice, get the fuck out of this godsforsaken prison now or stay and be made into husks!"

As before, some people paused in confusion. Eris kept shouting, her voice growing hoarse with the effort. She didn't care what they chose;

she just wanted them to be able to. Kyla joined in her message, and prisoners began to follow them downstairs to the next level, where more captives waited. Some must have accepted or understood that the Oracle had been switched off in their minds—they were beating prison guards, wardens, and personnel in the hallway. Blood splattered across the metal floor.

Ariadne's grip tightened around her throat, and Eris fought to keep breathing, keep yelling her message. She had already killed for the God of Death today, but she would offer him as few sacrifices as possible. Hadn't she given him enough over the years?

Her feet slid in the thick blood covering the ground, and she almost lost her hold on Ariadne. She hitched the girl up again and hurried after Kyla, who was progressing through the final hallway before the docking bay. Someone reached out to seize Eris by the arm—a guard? A prisoner? It was so chaotic that she couldn't *see*—but she let go of Ariadne's leg to elbow the assailant in the face. The hand released her, and she readjusted the smaller girl's body as she ran after Kyla. The crowd was so thick that she could barely breathe. Ariadne's own exhales roared in her ear, a reminder to keep going. *She was almost there.*

"Follow me to Theseus*!"* she yelled again, her throat as aching and dry as in the middle of a battle. The massive junker of *Theseus* loomed before her. *"Follow me to freedom!"*

Eris ushered people up the ramp and into the ship ahead of her. Kyla kept a grip on Sher's hoverchair and told Eris to get on board.

Eris shook her head. "Let's get these people on first."

Kyla gripped her arm. "We need to get on the ship," she said, loud enough to be heard over the din. "We've done everything we can."

Ariadne's quiet moan reminded Eris of what they might lose. She couldn't save everyone. Especially in a battle, she couldn't save them all. Eris always gave Letum offerings, whether she wished to or not. One day, she'd meet them all in the Avern as they stood by the God of Death's side, and she would bear the weight of their judgment.

But that was not today.

Eris gave a sharp nod, and the trio—with an unconscious Sher still slumped in the hoverchair—made their way up the ramp and into the crowded junker.

Eris set Ariadne down and took the girl's hand as Kyla went through the crowd and told everyone to get ready to depart. Even so, many of the prisoners looked terrified. Eris could hardly blame them—they were used to having an AI whispering in their mind, and all these people had chosen to defy the commands they had heard their entire lives. Disobedience was petrifying—but these people had nothing left to lose. They had already been judged and convicted by the Empire, fated to become mindless drones. To remain was to be erased. To fly out into the unknown was probably a delay of the inevitable.

These were the ones who realized their only chance of survival was to rebel.

Eris looked around for Cato and Nyx, her stomach dropping when she didn't see them in the melee. Ariadne's grip tightened on her hand as she clearly noticed the same thing. Eris winced as the girl called to the others through the Pathos, a panicked shout in her mind.

"Cato and Nyx aren't here," Eris said to Kyla when the commander returned to her side. "And they're still not answering over Pathos."

"We don't have much time." Kyla looked worried. "The prisoners' Oracle programming is going to kick in any minute. We need to seal ourselves in the command center and administer an oneirogenic general anesthetic to them before it does."

Ariadne squeezed Eris's fingers hard. "*No,*" she breathed.

"We can't do that," Eris said. "Not until Nyx and Cato get here."

Kyla's stern expression meant she was on the verge of a tough decision. A heartbreaking choice. The sort Eris had made so many times in battle before. A decision that spoke of desperation, something that would keep a leader up at night. Survival always did. Everyone who made it out alive had nightmares of those who died, those left behind, and those sacrificed.

But Eris would not give the God of Death Nyx and Cato's souls today, nor would she give her brother another set of gerulae to torture as he saw fit. They were her friends, and the Devils had taught her that people were not just souls waiting to be collected by a god that was every bit as greedy and demanding as the Empire itself.

And they had taught her that friends did not leave friends behind.

"We can't wait here any longer," Kyla said.

Eris glanced at Kyla in disbelief. "Cato's our pilot, and Ariadne put that lock on *Theseus* when we docked."

"I know how to fly a junker, and Ariadne told all of us the code," Kyla said grimly. "Empire ships are likely on their way, and at any moment, the Oracle could—"

"Give them the fucking sleeping gas now, then. I'm not leaving Nyx and Cato!"

"Listen to me," Kyla snapped. "This is not the time to be soft. I need you to be the godsdamned general right now. *Zelus* is waiting for us, and if we don't get *Theseus* airborne soon, *none* of us are making it to freedom."

"No," Ariadne gulped. "Eris? *No.*"

"I'm not a general anymore," Eris said sharply, giving Ariadne's upper arm a reassuring squeeze. She'd made the girl a promise—and she intended to keep her word. "And Nyx and Cato aren't my soldiers; they're my friends. *I won't fucking leave them behind.*" She snarled the last words.

Kyla's head snapped back, and guilt flashed her features. Some complicated memory Eris had nudged loose. Kyla's lips moved soundlessly, as if lost for words.

<*Fuck. Cato. Cato!*> Kyla sent through the Pathos. <*We've just reached the ship. We have to lock ourselves in the bridge and knock out the recruits before their Oracle programming reactivates. We have to close the door to seal them to do that.*> Kyla heaved a ragged breath, her hands gripping the fabric of her trousers in frustration. <*Listen. We're running out of time. Please don't make me leave you both.*>

"Cato," Ariadne said, brokenly. "Nyx."

22.

CATO

Present day

Cato sprinted through the prison, screaming Nyx's name. "Nyx!" His footsteps matched his racing heart. *"Nyx!"*

He tried focusing on any sign of her voice, but the blare of alarms screeched through the cell blocks, echoing off the rock and metal walls. Prisoners shouted as they escaped their cells—some jubilant with freedom. Others attacked the guards who had been stationed at every checkpoint.

Another door at the end of the cell block sprang open, and Cato charged through. "NYX!" His voice was overcome by the din of prisoners fleeing around him. He shoved through the crowd, elbowing bodies out of the way. *"NYX!"*

Halfway down the hall, a contingent of guards attacked prisoners. Morsfire sizzled through the cell block, a blast landing straight between the eyes of a woman next to Cato. She dropped to the metal platform, a single drop of blood trickling down her face. Cato gasped in air as memories flashed through his mind—explosions, the stench of bodies, screams of soldiers—but he shook his head to clear them. *Stop. Not now.*

Three prisoners saw his guard uniform and shouted. They charged him. In a haze, Cato hit one with a fist, shot the other two with his Mors on the stun setting. They went down hard, one tripping over their colleague's body.

"NYX!"

Nothing.

More bodies came. Faces twisted into snarls. Blood staining the yellow-white of teeth. He didn't even know if those attacking him in the hallways were gerulae, guards, or prisoners. Faces and uniforms blurred together; they all looked the same covered in blood.

And Cato didn't care. There was only this task.

Find Nyx.

Save Nyx.

Cato dodged his way through bodies, searching for Nyx's familiar face. Nothing. Where was she? Gods, where was she? He skittered down another hallway, shooting Mors blasts behind him to keep the crowd at bay. Ahead of him, an emptier hall loomed. The cell doors were still locked there, and prisoners yelled, desperate to be free.

"I can't help you," he said, sprinting past. Their doors would spring open eventually. They'd make it out.

But Nyx might not.

She had become his charge. His responsibility. More than that, he cared for her. He looked forward to seeing her grumpy face at the door of his lab, even if it was only for her treatments. She was his companion in the darkness, urging him through.

"Ignore everything else," came her voice from his memories. *"Focus on what needs to be done."*

Past the memory of Nyx, the Oracle's voice twisted through that thought like a serpent: *Leave her behind. Let the Empire punish her.*

Let her die.

You have done it before.

"*No,*" he snarled. "Shut up."

The prisoners shook their bars as he passed, their fists bloody and bruised. His Mors was slick in his hand. How much of a charge did he have left? There were knives in his boot, but he'd never been skilled at close combat. He knew how to fly, how to fight, and, inexplicably, how to heal.

As Cato ran into the west cell block, additional prisoners waited in their filthy cells, their haunted gazes tracking him as he sprinted past.

Their time in prison was just another torment before being stripped of their identities.

It shouldn't have surprised him. And yet, horror still roiled through his belly, something to haunt him later when he tried to close his eyes and fall into dreams. If he didn't save Nyx, she would—

"Nyx!" he yelled again, wondering if it was useless.

Could she even hear him over this noise? Maybe she'd been shot and left to bleed out in a horrible, lonely death.

Terror gripped him—but, then, he heard something through the distant shouting of prisoners. A worrying, miraculous sound: his name, spoken in a low moan from somewhere up ahead.

"Nyx?" he called, slowing to catch his breath and listen. *Please don't tell me I imagined it.*

No. He heard his name once more, a growl, thick with pain: *"Cato."*

Cato raced down the cell block, the thud of his boots echoing off the walls. He was almost relieved when he saw the ex-soldier.

Almost.

Because Nyx was on the ground gasping for air, wearing a prisoner's uniform, and a guard had just turned the corner. The man drew his Mors and pointed it right at Nyx's skull. She looked up at him and laughed, blood on her teeth, the sound quickly turning into a cough.

Cato didn't think. "Hey, asshole!"

His shout drew the guard's attention. That split-second distraction was all it took: Cato pointed his Mors and pulled the trigger.

Blood splattered across Nyx's face as the guard fell to the ground beside her. He would allow no guilt. He had to focus on the one person he could save.

The only person he cared about saving.

"Nyx," he said, softer, checking her over.

Nyx gave a low moan that moved perilously close to a whine. If she made it through this, he'd know better than to remind her of it.

If she made it through.

"Fuck," he muttered.

Blood trailed from Nyx's mouth, and her breaths were shallow gasps. Her pupils were blown wide. Scabs at the base of her neck had broken, weeping blood and yellow-green pus. Her vitals hadn't been that bad the last time he'd checked her over, but this was something he'd learned with the ichor, whether it was in its virulent form or not: a patient could go from relatively stable to an inch from death in a matter of hours. Nyx's illness had been ticking away inside her, and while Cato's ministrations might have given her a bit more time, the clock was winding down. Internally, her organs were hemorrhaging, and sepsis would set in soon if it hadn't already.

"You lied to me," he growled, shoving a hand into his jacket pocket to grasp the small box that held two syringes of her treatment. He'd doubted the need for it before, but now he blessed his past self. "You told me you were feeling better. You *fucking* fool, did you drag yourself down here so you'd die alone?" They were almost to the north wing's basement, and she'd been responsible for using Ariadne's glitcher on prisoners on the floor above them.

"I was . . . feeling better." She coughed up more black-red clots. He used his sleeve to wipe it from her lips. "Now I feel . . . like shit." Her eyes rolled, showing the bloodshot whites. The alarms still flashed, painting them both in staccato blasts of red between the endless gray. Far-off shouts echoed as people streamed onto their chosen junkers and decided their fates. Nyx pushed his hand away when he tried to lift her sleeve for the shot. "Just . . . leave me."

"No."

"I'm serious. I'm a . . . waste of resources." She coughed again, trembling. "I'm going to fucking . . . die anyway. Just leave me. Might as well happen here. That soldier . . . would have given me a . . . hero's death."

Their fellow Devils shouted for them over the Pathos, urging them to the ship.

<*Cato. Cato!*> Kyla said, insistent through his synapses. <*We've just reached the ship. We have to lock ourselves in the bridge and knock out the recruits before their Oracle programming reactivates. We have to close the door to seal them to do that.*> A pause, and even her thoughts felt hoarse with anguish. <*Listen. We're running out of time. Please don't make me leave you both.*>

Another burst of memory. More blood and death.

—*A man reaches up for him, and Cato pushes away the grasping fingers. Too tired to give his fellow soldier a clean shot to the skull to end*

*his suffering, too tired to do anything but put one foot in front of the
other and hope he'll make it back still breathing—*

War took, and took, and took, and the only thing it gave in return
was nightmares.

Cato gave his head a shake. He tore off the cap for the needle and
held Nyx's arm straight.

"Don't," she moaned. The whites of her eyes were red. Her lips were
cracked, breaths as labored as a death rattle. She touched his Mors,
dragged it to her temple. "This," she whispered. "It's my choice."

Do it, the Oracle whispered. *Sacrifice her for the Empire.*

In Letum's name.

His finger shook on the trigger. It was her choice. Shouldn't he honor
it? Hadn't all the pain of their deprogramming been so they could make
a godsdamned choice about how to spend their lives? Even how to end it?

"No," he rasped. "I can't."

"Do it," Nyx said, echoing the Oracle's remembered voice in his
head. "Kill me."

He didn't know what stopped him. Something about the shape of
Nyx's mouth when she laughed. Something about the way she said his
name—something about the hope of giving her one more day.

Cato shut his eyes and willed his finger off the trigger. Gently, so
gently, he dragged his Mors away. Dimly, he was aware of Ariadne and
Eris calling through the Pathos again.

Begging them to hurry.

He looked down at Nyx. "I don't abandon people I care about," Cato
said, jamming the needle into her arm. She'd need another dose on the
ship, but this would stabilize her. Hopefully.

Cato tossed the syringe aside with a clatter, grabbed her by the arm,
and slung her over his shoulder. Nyx was heavy as a corpse. She protested in a string of curses punctuated with bone-shaking, gurgling
coughs.

He stood with his Mors in one hand, and the other steadying Nyx
against his shoulder. They had to get across half of this godsdamned
prison complex.

Cato took off into a painful jog back to *Theseus*. The halls were
thicker with bodies, most streaming the same direction as them. He

knew each step hurt Nyx. But he put one foot in front of the other just the same.

<Hurry up,> came Eris's voice over the Pathos, a soothing calm. The composure of a general in battle.

Then Ariadne: <*Cato! Hurry!*>

<*We're on our way!*> *Hurry,* Cato echoed in his mind.

He pushed against the bodies, grunting. His Mors was out of charges. He held it anyway, even if the hot metal seared his hand.

The old junker came into view, but there were still hundreds of bodies between Cato and *Theseus.* A crowd between him, and freedom and safety for Nyx.

So many elected to escape on other ships—the other prison junkers and a few emergency bullet craft that fit no more than fifty people each. He almost snarled in frustration. They were abandoning any chance to make things better. How many of them had loved the Empire, like he once had? Every thought filtered through the hope that actions would make the Archon proud. They were all deemed unfixable. Traitors by way of a mere glitch. What the fuck kind of Empire did that?

Cowards! He wanted to scream. *Tholos abandoned you, but how many of you were soldiers? You could fight!*

He stumbled, almost falling to one knee and toppling Nyx. Her curses had stopped. He could only hope she was unconscious, not . . .

His head filled with the clamor of his fellow Devils on the Pathos, urging him: *get up, come on, just a little closer.*

But it felt so far, and he was so tired. Bodies shoved into him in their haste to escape Othrys. *Theseus's* engines rumbled.

The ship was going to leave if he didn't get up.

A hand pressed to Cato's shoulder. A man, his face seamed with old scars, heaved Cato to his feet and gave him a firm tap on the shoulder. The prisoner's face was caked in old dirt, his gray beard scraggly. He said nothing but nodded once.

And then he moved on to the other junker.

The man would not follow or join the resistance, but that small act was a rebellion. He might never know how much that simple deed had helped Cato find the strength to put. One. Foot. In. Front. Of. The. Other.

He forced through the thinning crowd. His boots hit the ramp, an echoing clang of metal matching his weary pace. Holding Nyx tight, he heaved them up toward the dark maw of the storage bay.

As soon as both feet were inside, the ramp came up behind them, sealing Nyx and Cato in darkness.

As the Devils surrounded him with questions and they retreated to the bridge, Nyx stirred and muttered something before she passed out again.

It sounded suspiciously like "Sanctimonious shithead."

23.

ERIS

Present day

Eris had nearly keeled over with relief when she saw Cato sprint up *Theseus's* ramp with a few last, desperate prisoners—but the relief was short-lived when she spotted Nyx slung over his shoulder, passed out cold. Beside her, Ariadne gave a soft gasp.

Eris rushed to Cato and tried to get a look at Nyx. "What happened to her?"

"No time," Cato panted, rushing past Eris. "I'll fill you in once I get the ship off the ground."

Eris, Ariadne, and Kyla—with Sher still unconscious in his hoverchair—followed him through the crowd and toward the bridge. *Theseus's* command center was massive, built for a prison transport crew five times larger than *Zelus*. It was now the biggest ship the resistance had in their possession. Kyla buckled Sher's hoverchair safely in and ushered out some of the curious and terrified prisoners who had trailed after them. The metal doors gave a loud *clang* as she sealed their small crew of five into the cavernous room alone.

Cato set Nyx into one of the roomy seats and tossed his jacket over the back of the chair before settling himself into the pilot's seat. He started flipping switches, his expression a mask of concentration and worry. Sweat beaded his brow.

Eris checked Nyx over as Kyla sat beside Cato and gave the

command to release an airborne sedative to the prisoners that was used aboard *Theseus* for the occasional targeted crowd control. Eris gently placed Nyx in a more comfortable position in the chair and buckled her in. Nyx's skin was slick with sweat, the color ashen rather than its usual rich brown. When Eris pressed two fingers to Nyx's pulse, she found it no more than a feeble flutter at her throat. But there was no blood, no visible sign of injury.

"Nyx?" Ariadne gave a short sob and shook the woman's shoulder. *"Nyx!"*

Eris shushed the girl and looked at Cato, whose mouth was pressed in a firm line of concentration as he fired up *Theseus*'s massive engines. "What's wrong with her, Cato?"

Even as she asked the question, Eris wasn't sure she wanted to hear the answer. Nyx's pulse was too weak and growing fainter. "Cato?"

"Give her the injection in my jacket pocket," Cato told Eris tightly as he got the ship ready for a fast flight. "I've got one left. And do it now before she dies."

Gripped by fear, Eris fished around through his clothing until she found the box that held a slim syringe. Her hands trembled as she uncapped it. What was Cato doing carrying this around? What was she about to dose her friend with?

Cato's tone had left no room for questions, and Nyx was fading fast. Eris pushed up the soldier's sleeve and held back a gasp. Track marks lined the woman's arm.

Biting her lip, Eris slid the needle into place and carefully pressed the plunger. The clear liquid pushed into Nyx's system, and Eris removed the needle, watching the small dot of blood well in the middle of a smattering of small scars. Hundreds of them.

Hundreds of injections. When had Eris last seen Nyx's bare arms? Not long before Laguna. They hadn't looked like this. It meant multiple injections per day.

Eris clenched her jaw. "How long have you and Nyx been hiding this?" she asked him. "Because if I look at her other arm, I bet I'll find more marks."

Cato was quiet as *Theseus* lifted from the ground. "She's been sick for a few months now," he admitted, gliding the ship into the atmosphere. "I started treating her not long after Laguna."

Something in his voice made Eris look up. "Sick," she echoed flatly. This was not *sick*. *That* was an understatement.

"Fine, dying, then." He sounded angry as the ship picked up speed. "She was infected by the noncommunicable form of ichor back on Ismara, and she told me about the symptoms three months ago."

A flash of memory went through Eris's mind. The Devils descending into the mines on that planet with its strange, floating islands, finding the secret laboratory where Damocles had left scientists and military personnel to die in quarantine cells. Nyx, backing too quickly into a wall and tearing her suit, hastily patching it up. Later, the cut on her arm that Eris had advised her to get looked at.

By that point, she would have already been infected.

Eris should have seen it. She should have known.

"Oh, gods," whispered Ariadne, who kneeled beside Nyx. The girl looked shattered.

Eris slid her hand into Nyx's. She knew the soldier didn't like to be touched, but she couldn't help it. Nyx's palm was cold and clammy beneath hers. "How long?" Eris's voice broke on the last word.

"I just *told you*—"

"No," Eris interrupted. "How long does she have?"

Cato went silent again as *Theseus* left Othrys's atmosphere and went out into the dark expanse of space. "I gave her less than two weeks," he said quietly. "But I don't know. That might have been optimistic."

Two weeks. Shock stole the breath right out of Eris's lungs. *Two weeks.*

Two weeks.

Eris had seen many soldiers die—some not in glorious battle—but even to her, Nyx had always seemed as Morsproof as the most unyielding and well-built armor. It was the way the other woman moved through the world: with unshakable strength and courage that weren't programmed or commanded. They were innate. How easy it was to mistake such confidence with invincibility. Eris almost felt foolish that she'd done so. No one was immortal, not Nyx, not any of the Devils.

Not Eris. After all the death she'd seen, when had she become so naive?

Guilt burned as bright and hot as a dying star inside her. It was *her* family that had caused this illness. Her family was the reason Nyx had ended up on Ismara and not somewhere safe. Everything—so much suffering—always came back to the Empire and her family's obsession with power at any cost.

Kyla glared at their pilot. "You should have fucking told us. Clo and Rhea are on their mission, and they don't even know that by the time they get back, she might be dead."

"I wanted to," Cato said. "She didn't."

Beside Eris, Ariadne was openly weeping. She gripped Nyx's clothes and pressed her face to the soldier's shoulder, whispering the same word over again. *No. No, no.* "I can find a cure," Ariadne whispered. "Nyx, I can. I can fix you."

"I tried," Cato said. "You have to believe that I've tried everything. We can put her in suspended animation to buy us a bit more time, but there's no cure for her yet."

Cato's words struck Eris like a bludgeon. *No cure for her yet.* But Eris knew of a cure, or at least someplace to start. Damocles' taunting words had filtered through the haze of drugs on the way to Laguna. She had been given injections to keep her compliant, weak, and—yes—to give her immunity to the ichor. Her brother had engineered the disease and would never have risked himself on Laguna without both the vaccine and a cure for active disease. Vaccines, after all, weren't one hundred percent effective.

The only person who could save Nyx was Damocles.

Eris tightened her grip on Nyx's hand. *Friends don't leave friends behind,* she thought.

And friends did not let friends die.

24.

RHEA

Present day

When Rhea saw the palace library, it was love at first sight. "I've never seen a more beautiful room," she breathed, lingering at the nearest shelf, where books, scrolls, and tomes stretched from floor to ceiling.

Sunlight streamed through the windows, falling on the Evoli who quietly worked at long tables. Others had tucked themselves into cozy armchairs hidden in corners behind the stacks.

Vyga smiled, then plucked a book from a higher shelf to press into Rhea's hands. Rhea ran her fingertips over the illustrated cover. Old World myths. The digital pages were intended to look like ancient paper, but the ink would never fade.

"The libraries are open to any citizen," Vyga said in Evoli. "Your Tholosian libraries are . . . restricted, yes?"

Your Tholosian. A phrase, a slip of the tongue, or a hint of suspicion? Rhea couldn't tell.

She swallowed. "One of the other Tholosian prisoners I knew said they were." It took all her training to keep the edge out of her voice.

On Tholos, the royal family hoarded every scrap of knowledge about the Old World and Tholosian history. Citizens could all too easily find rebellion within the pages of books. Damocles had allowed Rhea access to the palace libraries when he was in a better mood, without realizing he'd handed her the keys to her escape. It was between the pages of old books that she'd first dreamed of freedom. Of the galaxy beyond her gilded prison walls.

She'd been so desperate to see it.

Ve chose more books for Rhea: Evoli history as well as ancient history unredacted by Tholosian censors. A veritable trove of information. Rhea clutched the tomes in her arms, overwhelmed by what Vyga had so easily given to her.

A servant offered to take them back to Rhea's room before she and Vyga left for the city proper.

"Are we visiting another library?" Rhea asked. She wanted to see every single one.

Vyga shook ver head. "You said you wished to meet the Tholosian refugees," Vyga said as they wandered down the road from the palace.

"That was Chloe's request." Rhea wove her walls tighter, sealing her anxiety inside.

"So it was." Vyga pressed ver lips together. "But I think you should meet them first and tell us if your Chloe would wish to see them as they are now."

Rhea's stomach clenched.

Talitha was as beautiful as the palace. Buildings in pastel shades of blue and purple, pink and green, were dotted among the ordinary white. Many had smaller turrets and minarets, like modest versions of the palace. Bright astra flowers bloomed in window pots, along with plants of all different shades—pops of color against pale walls.

As they passed the market stalls selling various goods, Rhea caught the redolence of something sweet, and her mouth watered. The lack of apparent poverty in the streets surprised Rhea, as did the absence of wealth indicators. Most people dressed similarly. Rhea saw only one or two jewels flashing from fingers but none of the gold buttons or elaborate adornments so common among the Tholosian court.

People waved at Vyga as ve passed, some murmuring warm greetings. Rhea continued to be surprised by such informality toward their leader. None acted with the same awed deference Tholosians showed Damocles. A few passed Rhea questioning looks—undoubtedly curious of an Evoli who wasn't joined with their Unity—but did not address her directly.

"You interest us, Neve," Vyga said as they moved through the city.

A sliver of fear stroked across Rhea's spine. "Oh?" She hoped her voice was calmer than she felt.

"Your abilities are different from the others. Unusually strong for someone unconnected to the Unity. We find it intriguing."

"We" as in you, specifically, or "we" as in Evoli as a whole?

Her mind frantically pieced together anything that might set Vyga at ease. "I left so young. When my abilities developed during captivity, I had to teach myself my own methods. I apologize if I'm . . . too forward in my approach." Her fingers crept up to her locket with its hidden shard of ichor.

I'm trustworthy, Rhea sent out to Vyga, drawing upon those years of training with the Archon. She had done this before, influenced the Ascendant to think it was ver idea to welcome Rhea and Clo verself. *I'm above suspicion. You like me.*

You love me.

"*Make him love the Empire*," the Archon whispered, somewhere in her memory.

Rhea kept her approach subtle. Push too hard, and Vyga—and, by extension, all connected to the Unity—would grow suspicious. Push too little, and she would never get close enough to learn what she needed to in time. After Vyga officially took ver position and lost verself more to the Unity, ve would not be so easy to influence.

Vyga blinked rapidly. Ver stiffness melted into a warm smile. "Not at all. We understand how survival and adaptation change people. Once you join us in the Unity, we'll understand what you endured better."

They reached a row of simple houses—two stories, all connected. At first glance, they were just as pleasant as the rest. But had some of the flowers wilted, or was it just the general sense of muted sadness and confusion that Rhea sensed creeping through the windows? Foreboding stuck to the back of her throat, sour as spoiled milk.

Vyga caught Rhea's uncertainty. "Prepare yourself," ve said quietly.

Ve knocked on one of the doors. After a long hesitation, a Tholosian answered, and Rhea fought not to retreat in alarm.

The man appeared little better than a corpse. His movements were slow and his features aged, though Rhea speculated he wasn't much older than his late twenties. His hair was still jet black with no hint of gray. But he seemed . . . empty. Exhausted. Even if Rhea hadn't been able to sense his emotions, weariness radiated from every line of his body. The scythes and moon on his face had faded with a laser treatment or two—muted gray instead of black.

He bowed low to Vyga, with difficulty. "Good morning."

"May we come in, Linus?" Vyga asked, ver expression gentle.

With a nod, Linus shifted back slowly, and they stepped into the sitting room that seemed somehow darker than any other room Rhea had been to on Eve, despite the whitewashed walls.

"I'm pleased to meet you, Linus," Rhea said as politely as she could. "My name is Neve."

"A pleasure," Linus said. "Welcome. I've just made tea." Rhea tried not to stare. Before he spoke, she would have sworn he was still a gerulae. But he could converse beyond the rote, single-word response programmed by the Oracle. Unless commanded otherwise, Rhea had only ever heard a gerulae say one word: *yes*.

"That would be lovely; thank you, Linus," said Vyga, lowering verself into a chair.

Linus moved as listlessly as a gerulae, returning with two extra cups.

Rhea used her abilities lightly. Yes, he was no longer gerulae, but there was still something like a film over some of his emotions. She retreated once more, resisting the urge to pry further.

Vyga steered the conversation, and they spoke of small nothings. Sometimes, Linus grew disoriented, and Rhea or Vyga had to explain things to him. Or he'd drift off into vagueness and smile apologetically.

When their teacups were empty, Vyga reached forward to clasp Linus's hand briefly before letting his hand fall to his side. "We've taken enough of your time this morning. Thank you for welcoming us, Linus," Vyga said, rising. Rhea followed suit.

Linus stayed seated, staring at nothing as they took their leave. Outside, Vyga greeted a few other former gerulae. All were polite but distant. Almost vacant. After a few moments, Vyga excused herself and Rhea, and they headed back into the maze of the city streets.

Rhea must have been broadcasting her reserve and unease as they walked. "Now you understand why we wished for you to see them before Chloe," Vyga said. "We thought it might upset her if she didn't know what to expect."

Rhea dipped her head in a nod. "What's wrong with them?" Rhea asked.

The future Ascendant lifted a hand to wave at one of ver citizens. "The ordeal of being gerulae is different from the trauma of physical imprisonment," Vyga told Rhea. "Their bodies moved freely, but their minds were fractured by the Oracle, perhaps irreparably. We woke them by disengaging the AI's control over their emotions and empowering them to take command of their bodies." Vyga's head lowered as ve added in a soft voice, "But we don't wish to mislead you or Chloe. Linus and the others lost their recollections of what they endured—either through the Oracle's influence or from trauma. They don't even remember what it means to be Tholosian."

Disappointment speared Rhea. If the former gerulae had no concept of what they had endured before their rescue, why join the Novantae? They wouldn't even know who they were struggling for, with, or against.

"Will they ever regain their memories?"

Vyga grew thoughtful. "We can't say for certain, but the better question is: would they want to? Perhaps even your Chloe would be envious of their amnesia, whether Oracle-induced or self-imposed."

Rhea almost blanched. The idea of Clo losing everything she fought for . . . she'd be *furious.* "No," she insisted. "Chloe wouldn't."

If Vyga was surprised by the strength of Rhea's response, ve didn't show it. "You might be surprised. Some of our Evoli refugees have expressed a wish to forget their imprisonment. Chloe seems to struggle with it here. Maybe it would be easier if she didn't carry the strain of her hardships alone."

Rhea swallowed back another denial. "She just needs time."

"As you say." Vyga inclined ver head. "We share pain in the Unity. It helps our Evoli refugees heal when they aren't isolated with their burden, but your Chloe doesn't have that choice. Sometimes, it's too much for one person." Vyga paused and stared out over the twining astra vines as they reached the palace gardens. "The Tholosian royals have long maintained their power by destroying others. We sense you know a great deal about that."

Something about that quiet observation ruptured the wall inside of Rhea. Was she that obvious? Was everything the Archon and Damocles put her through exposed in the lines of her body? Did it seep through the gaps in her shields? Did she wear their torment as openly as the marks on her skin?

"How?" The question came out in a ragged breath, her voice broken. "How could you ever consider a truce with those monsters?" The question left her before she could stop it, sneaking through the wall she'd thought so cleverly constructed.

She pressed a hand to her mouth. She couldn't return it.

"There, now," Vyga said mildly. "That took longer than we expected."

"What?" Rhea's fingernails dug into her palm.

Control. Control. Control. That foundation she'd thought so strong might be crumbling. Did Vyga know everything?

But Vyga only motioned for them to continue up the hill. "This is a pattern for those who return. First, they arrive with relief and joy at returning home—but trauma doesn't disappear with a reunion or with safety." Vyga sighed. "So, their second emotion is usually anger. At those who confined and tortured them. About the years they'll never get back. And, sometimes, they are angry at themselves."

"I'm not," Rhea said, sharp.

The future Ascendant didn't seem offended by Rhea's tone. "No?"

Rhea opened her mouth, but no sound emerged. Like Neve, she'd been a child—she'd had no choice. But unlike Neve, she'd survived and escaped. Guilt pressed at her far more than anger.

But there is still anger.

"You don't really trust this truce, do you?" she asked, no longer caring about dancing around the question delicately. "What if the Archon is just using it to get close to Eve? Tholosians maintain their power by destroying others. You said that yourself."

Vyga's expression stiffened. "We didn't have much choice. We were close to losing the war. Any longer in conflict, and the ships entering our galaxy wouldn't be for diplomacy or to return those we'd lost—they'd be here to kill us all."

Rhea almost staggered in shock. She wondered if the old Archon knew how close he'd been to this jewel he coveted. But, if he'd known, would he have agreed to the truce? Rhea didn't think so.

"Truly?" Rhea breathed.

A curt nod. "Every death impacts the Unity. Its strength sustains the protections around our planets that confuse Tholosian ships and keep us safe. But battle losses forced fewer and fewer of us to bear the load of that fortification." Vyga lifted a shoulder. "That's the practical reason. The emotional one is simpler: we're tired of feeling death in battle every day. This new Archon represents hope, to some."

Damocles was the one who tried to kill you in the first place with the ichor, Rhea wanted to say. *You'd be dead if you'd gone to Laguna like all the others. Don't you see he's just as bad, or even worse?*

But Damocles, like Eris, knew how to shield himself so tightly from Evoli influence. They'd never know his true feelings. And if he said the right things to the Tholosians within his inner circle, or used the Oracle to influence their memories of the ichor experiments? Even they might believe the truce was genuine. That belief would maintain his lie.

Rhea fiddled with her necklace, deepening her abilities. She sifted through the colors of the Unity, like wading through a current filled with color. She found the tangle of emotions that still belonged solely to Vyga until the ceremony would merge ver so inextricably with the Unity.

There.

Deep down, Rhea discovered a spark of anger. Of the burning desire to say no.

To rebel.

That glimmer within Vyga was starved for oxygen, buried beneath obligation and duty to ver citizens. With enough time, Rhea might have been able to feed that flame until it combusted. But time was the one thing she didn't have.

"I hope you're right," Rhea said instead, pressing her hands together to stop them from shaking. She and the future Ascendant were silent for a moment. "Will you end up taking more refugees?" she finally asked. "More gerulae or Tholosians who wish to move here?"

She thought of the other Novantae, who saw so little safety these days. Who had lost the comfort of home. Perhaps she could return with a glimmer of hope: if they couldn't defeat one empire, they might be welcome in another. At least for a time.

Vyga nodded. "Those not previously involved in Tholosian military action may settle on our planets. But we refuse to offer shelter to those who took part in slaughtering our people. We have to consider the safety of citizens first."

Nyx, she thought with a burst of clarity. *Kyla. Cato. Eris, more than anyone.* But even Ariadne—sweet Ariadne, who'd designed weapons for the Empire. Clo, who'd constructed one for the Devils' mission on Macella that Damocles had so callously used to murder an Evoli prisoner of war.

They all had blood on their hands. Did Rhea?

"Your emotions are a tangle," Vyga said, watching Rhea with keen eyes. "What are your thoughts?"

Rhea tamped down the worry over her fellow Novantae. She had her mission to focus on—a reason for being there.

"What if I stayed disconnected from the Unity a little longer and helped the gerulae?" Rhea said, choosing each word with care. "As you say, my abilities are different from yours; maybe I can sort through their memories and ease the damage done by the Oracle. And Chloe will want to help. A fellow Tholosian there might comfort them, even without their memories."

When Rhea felt Vyga waver, she let loose another slight curl of power—the tiniest nudge. *You want my help. You want Chloe's help. It makes perfect sense, so why not try?* A little bit of fuel for a near-dead flame.

Vyga's head turned toward her too fast, expression blank. Rhea's heart rose to her throat, worried she'd gone too far.

Vyga's blinks were in time with Rhea's frantic heartbeat. *Blink. Blink. Blink.*

"Very well," Vyga agreed. "Then we'll take advantage of your abilities and your partner's experience."

Rhea hid her victorious smile.

———

Clo's walls constricted when Rhea told her about the gerulae. Not even the slightest hint of emotion went past her barriers.

<*So, you're saying the Evoli don't have the answer to our problems,*> Clo said briskly. <*Like you told me, former gerulae who don't remember what the Tholosians did to them would never choose rebellion over safety.*> She made a frustrated noise. <*And we have too many Novantae who are former military to seek protection for ourselves. So, they'll hate us no matter what. Seven devils, I can't say I even blame them.*> Clo's face rippled with pain.

Rhea flinched. Why did her mind want to reject the idea of leaving? Why did she want to reassure Clo that she'd find a way to make it safe for the other Novantae? <*I'm working on Vyga. Ve says the Evoli don't have a choice, but ve doesn't love the idea of a truce, either.*>

<*Vyga might agree with you,*> Clo said, throwing up her hands as she rose from her chair. <*The Ascendant ve is going to become in a few days won't. The person you know is going to be wiped out. So, what good will that do? There's no hidden resistance here. The gerulae aren't woken up enough to fight with us. The mission is a bust, Rhea.*>

Rhea pushed to her feet. <*That's still more than we had yesterday, Clo.*>

Clo huffed, stalking to the window and staring out over the grounds. She moved so much better on her new prosthetic. Rhea wanted to reach out, smooth her ruffled feathers.

<*Something else is bothering you,*> Rhea said. <*What is it?*>

Clo stared out at the treetops. <*Vyga is courting you. Trying to convince you that ve has this happy Evoli empath family on this perfect pretty planet, and I don't trust it. Vyga showed you the gerulae without me. Ve's trying to separate us.*>

<*Vyga said we could work on it together, Clo.*>

<*Only because you pushed ver in that direction.*>

Rhea fell back onto the bed, grunting in annoyance. "I don't want to fight." She put an arm over her eyes, covering the afternoon sunshine.

She heard Clo give a long exhale. Footsteps came closer to the bed. "I'm sorry." Clo hesitated. "You're right. It *is* more than we had yesterday."

Rhea peeked out from under her arm. The light slanted across Clo's features. "Sorry, did I mishear? You said I'm right?" she kept her tone teasing, drawing a half-smile from Clo.

"Aye, aye, enjoy the moment."

"You know," Rhea said, giving Clo a slow grin, "we haven't fully taken advantage of palace comforts. Like a long midafternoon nap."

Clo's eyes ghosted over Rhea's shape, long and stretched across the bed. Rhea loved the power of that gaze, the heat it left along her skin. "A very long nap," Clo agreed.

"We might not even bother with nightclothes. Or any clothes at all, for that matter." Rhea's lips curled. "You know, maybe we'll skip the nap part."

"Oh, I don't intend to skip sleep; I just intend to delay it." An amused sound came low in her throat. "Are you trying to distract me?"

"Is it working?"

Clo responded by pressing her lips hard against Rhea's. Rhea gave a quiet moan, her mouth opening.

Rhea's fingers danced along Clo's muscled forearms, up her biceps, and to the simple buttons on her Evoli clothing. Clo wasn't as gentle, nearly ripping off Rhea's tunic in her haste. Clo's kiss stifled Rhea's laugh. Yes, this. This, Rhea understood. And gods, she'd missed it. The closeness. The warmth.

Clo brushed Rhea's hair out of the way, her lips finding the sensitive spot at her throat that always made her arch.

"Yes," Rhea hissed.

Clo pulled back to shrug out of her shirt, then pressed Rhea to the bed once more. Her lips worked lower, nibbling and kissing her way to Rhea's breast.

Rhea gripped her shoulders in encouragement. She risked unweaving her shields enough to reach toward her lover.

She froze, her fingernails pressing to Clo's skin.

"What?" Clo asked, looking up in alarm. "What is it?"

Rhea's throat was tight. "It's different. It's . . . I can't sense you. I can't feel your desire."

"Well, I definitely like this." Clo's voice was husky as her finger trailed up Rhea's ribs to rest at the swell of her breast.

"Can you—can you lower your shields? Let something through?"

Emotions Rhea couldn't feel flickered across Clo's face. "I might let too much through." Her gaze lowered. "We'll just have to be like most couples in the universe and tell each other our likes and dislikes. Here, I'll start: I like kissing you." She slid up Rhea's body in a deliciously distracting way.

Asking for what Rhea wanted aloud was novel. "I like it when you kiss me."

"I like small nips on my neck, and I like the taste of your— Wait." It was Clo's turn to pause. "Would nearby Evoli sense us doing this? You're not as shielded as me."

Rhea hesitated. "I don't . . . think so. Well, maybe, if . . . you know." It wasn't like her to be coy, but she found herself suddenly bashful.

"You mean they'd know when you get off?" Clo looked horrified. "Oh, fuck."

"I don't know! Maybe." Rhea ran her fingers through her hair. The pink flush of desire had browned and grown heavy, like a dying rose. The mood had soured, and there was no way to reclaim it.

"I'm going to take a bath," Clo said, rolling off Rhea.

"Clo— I—" Rhea started.

"No." Clo softened her tone. "No, it's fine. I just . . . I need—I need some time. And space. Okay?"

"All right," Rhea echoed dully.

Clo pulled her top over her head and was gone before Rhea had fully processed what had happened.

Clo had vowed Rhea wouldn't be alone before they left on this mission. But curled up on the bed in their quarters on Eve, Rhea hadn't felt so isolated since the Archon's experiments on Tholos.

We share pain in the Unity.

A tiny corner of Rhea's mind longed for the comfort of a shared mind.

A place where she'd never be alone again.

25.

NYX

One year ago.

Nyx was beginning to grow impatient.

Over the last few months, Damocles had tasked her with personal guard duty at Imperial galas and events. Each celebration was meant to solidify Damocles' place as the future Archon, while the Oracle echoed love for the future leader through everyone's minds.

Nyx no longer heard the Oracle's whispers—thanks to Ariadne and Rhea's exhausting rounds of deprogramming in the Pleasure Garden. But the Oracle's recordings still echoed through the barracks at night, and she noticed a shift in the ways her fellow soldiers addressed their future leader. The change in topic to Damocles was subtle—still laced with admiration for their dead General Discordia but with more compliments of Damocles' place in the galaxy. The Oracle's work in changing citizens' thoughts was slow, but the subtle messaging was effective.

At least, it was with the soldiers. Soldiers were trained and programmed to defer to leadership above all else. Even Nyx struggled with the echoes of her programming that demanded she listen to Damocles unquestioningly.

The nobles, however, had very different programming.

Theirs valued strength and victory, two things that Damocles had objectively not earned. He was, after all, the Spare.

Heir by accident, little more than luck.

"Perhaps the Archon ought to consider a fourth attempt at a royal cohort," Nyx heard a diplomat from Acamar whisper as she made her rounds.

The commander he spoke with nodded in agreement. "With any luck, he'll find a new Heir as worthy as Discordia." They were hushed, as if aware of how dangerous their words were. If Nyx had been any other guard on rotation, they'd be dead before the moon rose.

Nyx hadn't met Discordia in person, but she never heard a single whisper of dissent when she was alive. These galas, meanwhile, only made Damocles' tenuous position in the Empire worse. Knowing how much his court loathed him, Damocles drank. He eschewed his responsibilities and insulted his nobles. He demanded public shows of loyalty that only made him more hated.

And tonight . . . it was worse. Last month, an asteroid had hit Charon, and the Tholosians lost a planet that had fed billions of citizens in parts of the Empire with fewer resources.

To make matters worse, a woman had arrived on the palace grounds, claiming to be Princess Discordia. The true Heir returned. While the Archon managed to keep word of her arrival secret from most of the Empire, whispers still spread that the beloved general was alive.

Nyx wasn't so confident—this was the fifth woman to show up on the palace grounds claiming to be Discordia. She was beginning to wonder if that programmed, all-encompassing love and respect the Oracle had repeated for years about Princess Discordia impacted those with glitched programming differently. If it produced *aspiration* rather than *admiration*. What other explanation was there when five women risked death to show up at the palace and pretend to be the former Heir?

And the latest arrived after the other four were executed.

Instead of ingratiating himself with the nobles and quelling their concerns, Damocles was drunk off his fucking face.

The gerulae with the wine was never far from Damocles' side. Every time she refilled the prince's goblet, she was forced to return moments later.

Damocles drained his wine to the dregs and gestured impatiently to the servant again. The gerulae complied, pouring a small amount. "More," Damocles said. The gerulae gave him another serving. "More, you fucking idiot."

From Nyx's position beside the dais, she noticed how bloodshot the prince's eyes were, how his hand trembled from intoxication. He lounged in his seat as if he were in the performance room of the Pleasure Garden, not at a gala with hundreds of people to celebrate his homecoming after weeks away inspecting the military outposts in a far quadrant of the Iona Galaxy.

Damocles watched the nobles dance with a brooding expression, his lips set in a firm line. It was clear to anyone who looked up at the dais that he wasn't enjoying himself. But, then, he never did. The only time Damocles ever smiled was when he was killing someone.

The servant stepped forward to pour Damocles another goblet of wine, but the Archon set a firm hand on her arm. "Go see to the other guests," he told her.

Without hesitation, she turned and sought out the other nobles— the Archon's command, after all, superseded his son's. Gerulae were programmed to sort out conflicting orders by rank.

With a tug of his mouth, Damocles said, "And here I thought I was supposed to enjoy the festivities." His words slurred as he lifted the cup for another deep drink. "Drink, song . . ." His eyes lingered on the courtesans from the Pleasure Garden. Rhea was across the room, speaking to another woman, her head turned toward the musicians. "Women."

The Archon's expression didn't waver. "I said enjoy yourself, not embarrass yourself," he said, keeping his voice low. "Five hundred loyal citizens are here, and you would do well to remember that their programming works better if they respect you. Discordia understood that."

"Oh, of course." Damocles gave a dry laugh. "I'm an embarrassment compared to your *precious* Discordia."

"Give me the wine," the Archon commanded, holding out his hand for the goblet. "And go speak to our people."

"That's always been a problem for you, hasn't it? You can't command me like a servant. I don't listen to you the way Discordia did, and I'll never earn the respect she had." His voice rose over the music. Wine sloshed onto the dais as he waved his goblet. Rhea's head turned toward them across the ballroom, but she was too far away for Nyx to read her expression. "Well, where the fuck is she, Father? Is she that woman in one of your cells? Or is she still just a fucking corpse, frozen and floating somewhere in space?"

A hush fell over the grand ballroom. Even the music stopped. The Archon stiffened in his seat, a subtle gesture that betrayed his embarrassment. But Damocles was drunk and well beyond caring. He rose from the dais and staggered down the steps, sloshing more wine onto the floor. The nobles backed out of his way.

"Don't think I'm unaware of how you all feel about me." Damocles stumbled, his words slurring. "You come to this palace and smile at me, but I hear the whispers. You're all fucking traitors. You should all be erased like the godsdamned gerulae." One of the noblemen muttered something. Damocles turned to him, his golden eyes molten. "What was that?"

The Archon's lips thinned as he stepped down from his dais. "*Damocles.*"

Damocles put a hand up, voice syrupy sweet even as his eyes narrowed. "I want to hear what he said."

The nobleman muttered something Nyx couldn't hear. But a sliver of fear cut her; even privilege couldn't save nobles from the wrath of the Heir. And Damocles was just as likely to kill a traitor as he was to turn them into gerulae. In that punishment, every citizen in the Empire was equal.

"For the whole ballroom, Cassius," Damocles snapped.

Cassius Chason P-5 was a diplomat who had survived a vicious Evoli attack. Scars lined one side of his face. As he raised his head, he showed off those scars proudly, knowing he was about to speak his death. "Only that I hope we have the pleasure of seeing General Discordia among us once again."

Quiet gasps sounded through the ballroom. Damocles seemed suddenly sober, standing tall and unbowed. He never liked to be reminded of any pretender and had taken far too much pleasure in personally executing the four others. Nyx had seen prisoners of war treated better than those women.

"*Discordia*," Damocles said, almost gently. But Nyx saw the cruel gleam in his eyes. "And have you no love for your new general?" He approached Cassius slowly. "Do your thoughts not tell you that *I* deserve your devotion every bit as much as she did?"

Cassius twitched nervously. "Yes, General."

"Yes," Damocles murmured. "Do you hear that?" His voice echoed through the room. "*Do you?*" The nobles murmured their agreement, and he returned his attention to Cassius. "Then kneel."

Cassius hesitated. "General, sir—"

"I said, *kneel.*"

Cassius got to his knees and prostrated himself before his prince. "Good. Now lick the floor." Cassius cringed but did as he was told, his tongue lapping across the gleaming marble. Damocles poured out the rest of his wine, watching as it splashed in front of Cassius. "Clean it up, Cassius. It is only by my mercy that you're not a gerulae tomorrow. Remember that." He strode past his father with a cruel smile. "How's that for earning respect?"

The Archon's face flickered with fury, but he hastened to fix the damage and calm his nobles. Nyx didn't see what fate befell Cassius; as Damocles left the ballroom, he gestured to Nyx to follow. Nyx kept her expression even, not allowing fear to show. She knew he could have done worse to Cassius; perhaps he would have if his father weren't around. Maybe he still might.

"And what did you think of that show, Nyx?" Damocles asked, not looking back at her. He opened the door that led to the temporary prison hold, and she followed him down the stairs.

Nyx cleared her throat. "I thought Cassius got what he deserved," she said, though it made her want to recoil.

"Did he?" Damocles asked archly as they walked down to the belly of the palace. His voice echoed off the walls. "Because I thought he deserved to have his throat slit. Do you know, if my father weren't there, I might have had Cassius lick up his blood rather than my wine. What do you think about that?"

Nyx's fingernails dug into her palms. "I think whatever punishment you choose is fitting, General."

Damocles gave a laugh, one that had Nyx shifting in unease. He sounded like he was fraying at the edges. "Such a careful answer, Nyx. I think you've learned well."

She followed Damocles down to the temporary prison hold, where the Discordia pretender was confined.

The woman looked up when Nyx and Damocles entered, her expression wary as she rose to her feet. The prison jumpsuit swamped her frame. She did look like the images plastered throughout the galaxy: the luminous golden hair, the eyes that shined like a sunset, and the elegant, austere features. But this woman could be anyone. It didn't escape Nyx's notice that these women were like her: their programming glitching just enough to question their place in the world. To want more than what the Oracle had programmed in their minds from birth.

A simple desire that was an act of disobedience punishable by death.

Like the others, she'd have a story: where she was, why no one recognized her. Every pretender always said they forgot their childhood memories and knew only their name and their love for the Empire.

Perhaps they did forget who they were before. Nyx never knew. *Discordia* had been a name more important, once, than any other memory. Maybe the Oracle's programming drove out everything else.

The woman raised her chin in defiance, but fear flickered through her features. If she wasn't Princess Discordia, she'd regret pretending.

The others had.

"They think you might be my sister," he told the woman coldly, as he placed his cuff against the panel to open the cell door. "Sure, you look like her. But I've heard that speculation before. I've been disappointed."

The woman who called herself Discordia gave a pleading look—a dead giveaway on its own. General Discordia did not beg. "Damocles—"

This one had changed her voice, too. Probably paid a lot of scythes to buy information about Discordia's life at the academy in Myndalia.

"Quiet." Damocles reached out and grasped her by the chin, staring hard into eyes that matched his own. "She's dead, and they still talk about her. Every fucking city and backwater has a memorial icon with her image, and I have to stare at her *fucking* face everywhere I go. And they all tell me how much they loved her." His fingers dug into the woman's jaw. "And every time one of you shows up, they talk about her even more. I have to hear her *fucking* name again before my own."

"Dam—"

He smacked a hand over her mouth. "You're not my sister," he said to the false Discordia, leaning in. "She'd kill me before letting me do this to her. But you still made me look at her fucking face again."

Damocles grabbed his knife and made the first cut. The Discordia Pretender's scream echoed off the walls. Blood splattered across the floor. Nyx had seen death before—she had caused her fair share—but Damocles found joy in this. His smile was as bright and beautiful and painful as staring into a sun.

He sliced through the Discordia Pretender's flesh and carved off her stolen face.

Nyx, unable to show any emotion, let her mind take her to another place. To that impossible future Rhea and Ariadne had planned. She imagined the large expanse of space, brimming with stars and distant planets—a far-off horizon with no one around, nothing sullied by Tholosian hands.

Away.

Far, far away.

Snap.

The crack of the woman's neck returned Nyx to the gruesome sight—and to Damocles, collapsed on the floor.

Breathing hard, he looked up at Nyx. "How did you beat me?" At her questioning look, he waved a hand. "At zatrikion that one time. How did you beat me?"

Nyx drew in a breath. It was such a strange shift in topic, but she had learned that Damocles hated losing. That he hated being second-best. Torturing and killing pretenders only sated him for a brief time—Damocles couldn't destroy the memory of Discordia.

Nyx's win, like his sister's, must have chafed. It must have eaten away at some vulnerable part of him that longed to be better than his dead sibling.

Nyx took a breath. She would have to toe this line carefully. If she did . . . he'd given her one way to survive the months until those distant stars were within her reach. She'd have to play the game.

With him.

"I'll teach you," she told him.

He gave a small smile and requested a board over his comm. The guard's expression was blank as he brought the game and set it on the small table in the cell.

Nyx watched as Damocles stepped through the blood and began to position the pieces on the board, smearing them with red fingerprints. Then, with that cruel gleam in his gaze that she saw back in the ballroom, he propped up the false Discordia's faceless corpse to watch.

It was a reminder.

She'd have to teach him—or she'd end up his next victim.

26.

NYX

Present day

Nyx woke feeling like lukewarm shit.

She fought down panic as she realized she couldn't speak, couldn't move. A tube was down her throat, the machine giving a rhythmic *whoosh* as it manually pumped her scarred lungs. She had prepared for this moment for months, and panic still filled her. The monitor beeped as her heart rate increased.

A hand touched her shoulder, then drew a strand of hair back from her cheek. Cato's face filled her vision, his bright blue eyes full of concern, and his dirty blond hair mussed as if he'd been running his hands through it.

I don't leave behind people I care about.

Had he said that? Or had she only imagined it in a fevered haze? What had he meant by it?

"Hey," Cato said. His voice was hoarse. "Everyone's here with you."

Nyx tried to move her eyes. She just caught the halo of Ariadne's hair, the flash of tears on her face. She sensed more than saw Kyla and Eris to her right—she could imagine them, though. Arms crossed, faces grim. Nyx wished Rhea were there, to chase away the fear and pain, but she and Clo were far away. Nyx closed her eyes tight. Machines beeped, her assisted breath loud and rhythmic.

The pilot grasped her hand. "Nyx." He sounded urgent. *"Nyx.* Stay awake. I need you to answer a few things, okay? Blink once for yes. Twice for no. Understand?"

Another tremor of fear went through her, but she opened her eyes wide and blinked once.

"Your body has given up, pretty much all at once." His eyes were steady on her as he said it, but his grip on her shoulder tightened. "Eris gave you another injection, which stopped you from flatlining in the command center, but it's only another delay."

Nyx didn't blink, as it wasn't a question. So, they all knew. Eris. Kyla. Ariadne. That she was sick. That she was weak. That she was dying.

This was the end, wasn't it? They had woken her up to say goodbye.

She should rage against it. Fight harder. Do something. Anything. But all she could manage was to lie there and breathe—and she couldn't even accomplish that on her own. She could feel the pull of the lesions against her skin. They would never even have the chance to heal, to add to her many scars. This body she was in would become an empty husk, a corpse, and she'd meet her gods in the Avern. They would not be kind when she arrived at the gates.

"Eris donated some more of her blood," Cato continued. "It's keeping your internal organs on a functional level, but even royal nanites can't repair this kind of damage."

Nyx smelled the death on her. It reminded her of Ismara. The soldiers left to rot in unmarked mass graves. Commander Talley-I-32, with lesions blooming from his waxy skin like scarlet mushrooms.

"How long?" she wanted to ask, but her tongue was pressed against the horrible tube snaking within her.

It had to be hours, maybe a day or two, if her body was stubborn enough. It would hurt, drowning on dry land like this. They would give her pain meds, but deep down, it would still hurt.

Nyx had taken her body for granted. She'd known, every time she went into battle, every time she prepared for the next assassination, that she risked injury or death. But after so many times cheating her demise, it was easy to grow complacent. Cocky, even. She'd fallen into the trap of thinking she was invincible, and now she was being punished for her hubris.

Over the last few weeks, she'd watched those muscles she had worked so hard for slip away. The skin on her arms had felt thin, crinkled, and bruised at the slightest touch. She remembered how taut and firm they had been just a few months before—covered with thorned-vine tattoos that had twined around the shoulder muscles, along with the biceps and triceps. One death for every thorn, plus all the deaths the Empire hadn't wanted her to claim publicly. If the Nyx from a few years earlier, before she dreamed of escape, could see her now? She'd put a bullet right through the brain. Spare her the misery.

But over the last few days, she had felt better and been able to draw fuller breaths. She wasn't a fool. She wouldn't have gone to Othrys if she thought she would put the others in danger. She had been strong enough for the mission—until she wasn't.

She'd seen this before, in injured soldiers on the front. They seemed to rally and improve, talked about how they'd be out of bed in just a few days, ready to pick up a Mors again and run straight back into the fray. And then the next morning, they'd be wide-eyed and unseeing in their beds. This was it. This was the end. All that fighting, all that struggle, and soon it would be over.

She hadn't even tasted true freedom yet.

"Nyx," Cato said, his voice so soft. He gripped her hand, his fingers covered by gloves. Normally, she didn't like to be touched, but she didn't mind his. "We have the option to put you in suspended animation. It won't be long—the illness is too advanced for even suspended animation to delay indefinitely. But it'll give me a bit more time. Damocles had treatment for infectious ichor, and they're not so different in their pathologies. If the Empire's scientists came up with one, then so can I. But only if that's what you want."

Kyla drifted closer, coming into view, backlit by the med bay lights.

"We want it to be your choice, Nyx," the commander said. "Blink once for yes and twice for no."

Once for a chance at life, no for a certain death.

On Pollux, she'd begged for death. Demanded Cato leave her behind. Been furious when he refused to listen to what she had told him she wanted. Nyx was so tempted to let go, to give up. It would not be a glorious death, but Cato offered her something no other gods could:

mercy. Cato had given her more time than most. Plenty of soldiers never died when they chose.

Ariadne couldn't stifle a sob. She shifted closer. "Don't go," she whispered, her voice catching. Nyx knew she didn't want to beg but she couldn't help herself, could she? That girl was so tender-hearted, and Nyx loved her for it. She hoped her death wouldn't harden Ariadne too much. "Nyx. Please. Don't go. Fight a little longer."

"There is no shame in either decision," came Eris's voice from the other side of the room. "We will respect your wishes."

"Nyx," Cato said. "Blink once for yes. Twice for no."

An agony of silence but for the machines and Ariadne's hiccoughing sobs. The others were dry-eyed, but then again, they had all seen their fill of death compared to their young engineer.

Nyx blinked once. One long, slow, agonizing blink. A traitorous tear of her own slipped out, weaving its way down her cheek. Kyla wiped it away.

In the end, it was simple, wasn't it? She still wanted that future Rhea and Ariadne dreamed about. A life where none of them had to smudge their sense of morality for a system that did not love them. She wanted to live on some forgotten, beautiful planet, look out at the horizon, and breathe in the scent of wilderness. She wanted to live her life without a Mors tucked into the small of her back. To not wear half a dozen concealed knives. To feel safe.

"Thank you," Ariadne whispered close to her ear. "We're going to save you, Nyx. I promise. I promise. We're gonna save you."

You'll probably still fail, Nyx wanted to say. *But I'll let you try.*

Cato wasted no time, prepping the suspended-animation tank. She turned her head a centimeter. It looked like a coffin. Nyx wondered if it was crueler to go into that thing with the faint, false hope that she'd ever come back out alive. But maybe a little bit of hope was what made life, with its inevitable death, worth living.

Cato unhooked her from everything but the ventilator, which he explained would come out at the last second as liquid filled the tank. Kyla, Eris, and Cato carried her over and placed her inside the chamber, arranging her slack limbs, supporting her neck. Nyx almost wanted to laugh at them, trying to make her comfortable.

There was so much she wished she could say to them. To tell Ariadne to be strong. To tell Eris she was still a bastard but she was their bastard, and she supposed she forgave her for being the Princess in the first place. That Kyla was the best damned commander she'd served under. That Cato had ended up not being the piece of shit she had expected him to be. That he was a good medic, a good pilot, and one of the few good men she'd met. And that . . . fuck, maybe she cared about him too.

His blue eyes glimmered with unshed tears as he helped her. She'd hated him when they'd found him on this ship, hiding in the vents, determined to turn them in for the glory of the Empire. But even back then, there had been a little crack in the cruelty, and he'd worked hard to cast off what the Tholosians had tried to make him.

Fuck. Maybe she loved him a little. In her own way. In the only way she was capable of loving someone. And she couldn't even tell him.

The four Devils stood sentry around her as she slipped down into the cold dark.

27.

Present day

Eris hated watching Nyx die.

She sat at the soldier's tank in the medical bay as Nyx floated in suspended animation. She felt like they'd tried everything over the last couple of days. She knew it was only a matter of time before the virus finished its work; even an artificial coma wasn't enough to prevent the disease's progression as it raced through Nyx's body. It only bought them a little bit of time. Cato confirmed that the virus was present within Nyx's inner organs, weakening her heart and lungs.

Nyx, a woman no one would ever describe as small, was dwarfed within that massive tank. Her once-lustrous dark skin retained its alarming shade of gray, and the needle marks on her arms stood out so starkly. Typically, people in suspended animation looked like they were in a deep slumber, but Nyx appeared mere moments from death.

Eris pressed her palm to the glass of the tank and said words that she had so rarely spoken: "I'm sorry," she whispered. "I'm so fucking sorry."

It seemed like so long before that she had told Nyx her responsibilities as mission leader. If the ship were ever crashing, Eris would always put her crew on a bullet craft first. If necessary, Eris's sacrifice was part of the job. It was why she so rarely worked well with anyone else; that responsibility was foreign to her.

But she had promised Nyx before that day on Myndalia when they discovered the awful proof of Damocles' obsession with power. She vowed to do whatever it took to get her crew out alive.

And it hadn't been a crash that put her friend near death, or an enemy blast, but a virus. A pathogen with no loyalties, no enemies, and no purpose except to spread. It had no care for vows. And all it would take to fix it was—

A hiss escaped her as she remembered the needle sliding into her arm. Her brother's voice whispering in her ear that he wanted to keep her alive to witness her failure.

He has a cure, she told herself. *Are you going to let her die?*

She gave her head a hard shake, but another thought came to her: *If she dies, and you could have saved her, it's on you. Every death has a weight, and some are heavier than others.*

Eris dropped her hand from the glass and shut her eyes hard.

It was time for another game with her brother. A suspicion had lingered in Eris's mind after listening to Ariadne's panicked rambling back on Othrys, and she could only hope that sacrificing a piece on their imaginary zatrikion board was enough to advance and take control over their competition.

She could only hope she was as good at this game as she had once been.

Eris waited until everyone was asleep and stole into the docking bay, boarding one of the bullet ships for privacy. She hated not telling her team about her plan, but there was no time to convince them. Nyx's life hung in the balance.

The bullet ship was so quiet. Eris took a breath and released it slowly, running a shaky hand through her hair. "You can do this," she whispered to herself. "Hide your emotions, just like you were taught. Just like you taught Clo. Give him nothing." She slid her hand into her pocket and gripped her wolf to stop her tremors. "Don't let him see."

After another attempt to control her breathing, Eris reached for the comm controls and called Damocles on their old encrypted line. She hadn't used that messaging system since before Xander's death.

Every royal pairing had a private network of communication, whether through a messaging system or via code. The palace's best engineers had created Damocles and Eris's to fit their particular relationship needs. Not to find one another for comfort, oh, no. It was an open line to maintain their competition no matter where they were in the galaxy—to boast over a sibling's death, for tallying up kills. It was a line for bragging.

And between them, the line was always open.

At least, it used to be. Eris hadn't called it in years. She no longer possessed the cuff that had always kept her side open to his messages. She'd thrown it out the airlock the night she'd pretended to die. But she had to hope that Damocles kept his.

For Nyx's life, she had to hope.

The call connected, and the hail beeped. And rang. And continued ringing. Eris bit her lip. What if she was wrong? What if he hadn't kept his cuff? What—

"Discordia." Her brother's face appeared on the screen.

"Don't try to trace this call," she said. "The usual protocols are in place."

His lips twisted in something resembling a smile as he simply stared back at her. Eris's wolf bit into her palm. She knew that on his side, her image projected from the communication cuff. His gaze swept across her features. She did the same, her attention falling on his left eye. So, he *had* been outfitted with the bionic eyeball. It matched his right eye perfectly, right down to the golden glow.

Eris gestured. "No one would even notice I shot it out. Going to ditch the eyepatch yet?"

His expression hardened at the reminder. "On the contrary. The eyepatch serves to remind our citizens that you're my enemy—and that makes you the Empire's adversary." He sat back, and she noticed a glass of whisky in his hand. "I see you've managed to find a new tongue. And here I liked you better silent."

The wolf was almost cutting into her palm. Memories flashed of being tied down, the searing pain as the medic sliced out her tongue without anesthesia. The haze of drugs afterward on Laguna barely dulled the agony.

Gods, but she hated him so much that she burned with it. Somehow, she felt as if he were still in her mind, itching around inside her like a parasite.

The way he smiled at her . . . he could tell. And it delighted him.

Eris let her silver tongue rest between her lips a moment before shrugging. "Silver looks good on me."

This time, Damocles didn't react. His face was carefully blank as he sipped his whisky. "To what do I owe the pleasure? Too much to hope this is a surrender, I take it?"

Eris's original suspicion solidified in her mind. But Damocles had learned new skills, and his performances had improved. She could not afford to be wrong. *Nyx* could not afford for her to be.

So, she leaned into her role and took the risk: "What have you done with Sher?"

For a moment, she wondered if she made an incorrect judgment. Damocles' face, as still as his icons that graced cities around the galaxy, reflected nothing. And then he smiled. "Concerned for your commander?"

Eris let her face reflect her genuine worry—the barest amount, as if she couldn't hide it. "Where is he, Damocles?"

Damocles lifted a shoulder. "He'll emerge soon enough. I have an entire tour planned. I want to show your commander off when the Oracle leaves him a husk. Perhaps I'll bring back executions for the sole purpose of watching him eat one of your rebels. Won't that be fun?"

The wolf grew slick in her palm, and Eris didn't know if it was from blood or sweat. Even Tholosians, as obsessed with death as they were, considered cannibalism a taboo. The body, once dead, was dissociated from its soul. That was why they gave last rites to some and not to others. Tholosians let their enemies' souls be led astray as a punishment, but they did not mutilate the dead. Even the thought made her stomach roil.

Keep calm, Eris reminded herself. *He doesn't have Sher. He thinks he does, but he doesn't.*

She had her confirmation—and so she had to tread carefully. She leaned back and let calm spread across her features. Damocles' eyes narrowed at her change in demeanor. "I'm afraid you won't get your tour, after all," Eris said.

His features went still, but he remained unreadable. "No?"

"Othrys is nonfunctional. Courtesy of us." She gave a smile. "And here's me without a drink to toast you with."

Damocles' lips flattened, and he set his drink down with a clink of glass against wood. "Enough games, Discordia. I don't believe you. I've received no—"

"Confirmation?" No, he couldn't fabricate the alarm in his face. Damocles excelled at hiding his emotions but not at performing them. *That* was a skill she had learned only after joining the Novantae. Because, like him, she had been taught that displays of emotions were vulnerabilities to be suppressed. "Good. Then we get to have a serious conversation."

His golden eyes snapped to hers. "About what?" She recognized the barely coiled rage in his voice. It came before he flipped a game board and launched a fist in her face. "Or do you expect me to listen to you boast?"

"I'm here to propose an exchange."

He searched her face again. It occurred to her that Damocles was every bit as unsure of her newfound skills as she was of his. It had been months since Laguna, and he had only beaten her once. Here she was, revealing that she had retrieved her commander without his knowledge—and that he might not be as in control as he thought.

"Get to the point, Discordia." His voice was low and dangerous. "I'm losing my patience."

She raised an eyebrow. "So, you haven't noticed any change in the Oracle's behavior recently?"

His gaze narrowed. "No."

Ah, nice try. "How interesting that One didn't tell you about Othrys. The Oracle's system should have flagged the prison as nonfunctional. With the escape of a high-profile prisoner like the commander of the resistance, I *assume* the Oracle would have alerted the Archon. Perhaps the Oracle has given other indications that One is no longer deferring to you?" Damocles said nothing. Eris shoved down her flare of triumph—she knew that her victory would be pyrrhic when the time came—but she had to do it for Nyx. "But you say you've noticed nothing. Fine, then."

"Just tell me what the fuck you want, Discordia," he snapped.

She gave a twist of her lips. Let Damocles feel the same loathing she did. Let him feel unease.

They both had one last name on their list to strike off. "The original strain of the ichor contagion from Ismara—I need the cure for it."

His expression sharpened. "Is one of your crew sick, then? Your pet mechanic, perhaps." When her face betrayed nothing, he guessed again: "No, not her. Is it my favorite royal guard?" Eris's expression must have tightened imperceptibly, because he looked pleased. "Ah, that one. And what will you give me in return for her life?"

"The Oracle—"

"It's a machine, Discordia." Damocles' voice was cold, perhaps to mask his disquiet. "I have it under control."

Eris homed in on one word. He had called the Oracle *it* instead of *One*. "Are you sure? Because I don't think you do. And you know I'm right."

Another tightening to his features. "We're finished here. Give my condolences to Nyx." He moved as if to turn off the screen.

"And if the Oracle is autonomous?"

It was another risk, to reveal her suspicions from Othrys. Ariadne had always been terrified of returning to the Oracle—Eris knew that. But her fear this time had seemed to take her over, and when that woman sat up and said *Daughter* . . .

Eris had never seen Ariadne so scared.

And she could only think of one reason for that, and one reason why One had yet to inform the new Archon of a mass prisoner escape: the Oracle had a plan of One's own.

Which meant the Oracle had gone rogue.

"Ariadne was One's Engineer for twelve years, and you've seen what she did for the resistance in a mere three. It's entirely possible. And you know I might be right. Otherwise, you would have turned off that screen already."

Damocles was silent. Though his expression remained neutral, his shoulders were tense. "Fine," he finally said, his voice curt. "I'm listening."

"The Oracle has a plan to program all your citizens into gerulae.

Once that happens, One takes complete control over your Empire and the mind of every citizen." She smiled again. "Except you, of course. Unless One figures out a way around that, too. The Oracle is clever, right? Clever enough to hide One's actions from you."

When Damocles felt in control, it gave him some sense of purpose. He was calm and collected and, yes, even resourceful enough to get the best of her. But as soon as he lost that . . .

He was like that boy in the Myndalian Academy. Wrathful, resentful, and inelegant. To lose power meant being that child again.

"You want the cure for Nyx," Damocles said. "And what help do you offer me?"

"Ariadne is the only person in this entire galaxy who can help you with Oracle. I want the cure in exchange. You bring it to the ship graveyard in Elysium—*alone*. And in exchange, Ariadne will make the Oracle compliant again. That's my offer."

"Mm." He looked doubtful. "And why should I trust you?"

Eris smiled. "Because you have a rogue AI who's programmed every citizen in your Empire. One is in their heads. And if One controls them all, what power does that leave you?"

Even Damocles couldn't cover his flash of fear. For it must have dawned on him, right then, what it meant for the Oracle to be autonomous. Every programmed citizen belonged to the AI, from his best soldiers down to his lowliest servitor. Everyone.

Damocles raised his chin. "I will consider your offer."

"You have one hour," Eris said. "And I'll wait right here for you to take it. And you will, once you consider one last thing."

"And what's that?" He no longer even tried to hide his anger.

"Without your citizens, you have no one, Damocles. You are completely and utterly alone." She gave one last smile and reached to turn off the screen. "I'll await your word."

28.

CLO

Present day

After Clo left Rhea, she headed into the woods.

She tried to contact Eris again but received a terse response that indicated she and the others were already on their ITI mission. A twinge of envy stroked across Clo's mind—she'd rather be shot at by Tholosians than be on this planet, where everyone stared at her with naked suspicion.

Where she felt like she was losing Rhea.

Clo flinched and stared at the astra vines that wound up the trees, fighting to keep her mind emptied of thoughts and worries. The isolation helped. She counted each flower on those strange, creeping plants—*each death*, she reminded herself. Clo wondered whose bones were beneath her as she stretched out among the bed of leaves.

As night fell, Clo focused on the unfamiliar constellations above her. She never thought she'd be so homesick for *Zelus*, but at that moment, she would have given anything to be in the observation room, drinking shite rum and watching the stars. She missed the other Devils. She wanted to talk to Eris.

She wanted the Rhea she'd known before they left for Eve.

Rhea seemed so happy in Talitha. Would she even want to return to *Zelus*, scraping by every day with so little when this planet offered so much?

You have to give her a choice to stay, Eris would have said. *Or you're no better than the Empire. Fuckwit.*

Even in Clo's imagination, Eris insulted her. She couldn't believe she actually missed it. Because Eris, imaginary or not, was right. The Evoli there offered Rhea safety and comfort. A home. Even Clo couldn't deny her that.

The dawn light woke her the following morning. When she returned to her rooms, Rhea flung herself at Clo. "Oh, gods. I was so worried. I—" She pulled back and touched Clo's face. "Are you okay?"

Clo gently pushed Rhea away. "Sorry for worrying you. I just needed to be alone for a bit." She straightened her shoulders, reminding herself of the mission. The reason she was there. "I want to see the former gerulae."

Rhea swallowed. "You're sure?"

"Yeah, I'm sure." Clo crossed to the potted plant in the corner of the room where she'd buried the mech cuff she'd hidden in her old prosthetic. She shifted soil aside and pulled out the thin, camouflaged strap. *<If they let us, we can examine them with the bioscanner in the mech cuff and send the information back to Ariadne. She might find what's causing their memory loss.>*

Rhea gave a nod. "Then we'll go alone. Vyga's preparing for the Equinox Ball."

Tonight was when Vyga and the future Oversouls would officially take their positions and leave the last of themselves behind for the Unity. Anxiety filled Clo. What would Vyga be like, once that happened?

Clo tried not to think about it as Rhea led her into the city. The roads were busy as people bustled in from other Evoli cities and planets for the Equinox Ball. Brightly colored bunting and little glass bells fluttered and tinkled in the wind. Strains of music drifted from somewhere a few streets over.

People stared at Clo as she passed. Their attention had her turning inward, tightening her shields until all her emotions were shuttered from every Evoli passerby. It almost certainly didn't help matters, but Clo was on edge.

Her concern only amplified when she finally saw the former gerulae.

Some were sitting on the steps in front of their homes, drinking tea in the morning sun. Others were gardening.

"Linus," Rhea called.

As one of the men rose from where he was sitting on his porch, Clo tried to keep her expression neutral. But she couldn't help but cringe at the faded symbols on his cheeks, the unmistakable marks of Tholosian ownership tattooed onto every gerulae. Clo mentally sunk deeper into the water until her emotions were as concealed as the corpses in the swamp. She wondered how it felt not to remember anything the Tholosians had done. Would it be better? Or would there still be anger enough to burn, the cause always just out of one's reach?

"Remember me?" Rhea asked Linus.

"Neve." He nodded to her kindly. He glanced at Clo with the uncertainty of someone recognizing a fellow Tholosian, as if trying to place where they might have met. "My apologies if I should know you," he said. "I don't recall anything from before Eve."

"You've never met," Rhea reassured him. "This is my partner, Chloe. She wanted to see you."

Linus gave a relieved half-smile that faded once he studied Clo's face. Then, in a move that surprised Clo, his hand rested on her unmarked cheek. "No tattoos," he murmured. "How long ago did you wake up?"

Clo flinched away from him. "I'm . . . I wasn't gerulae," she said, awkward.

A mixture of interest and unease flickered across his features. It was an open face, roughhewn as stone. Clo's notice snagged on the scars that marked his hands.

Gathering herself, she reached for them. "These might be from fixing engines," she said, keeping her voice even. "See?" she showed him her own scar-studded fingers. "You might have been a mechanic like me."

His breath caught before his eyes filled with tears.

"Oh, gods," Clo said. "I'm sorry."

He further shocked Clo by pulling her into an embrace. Clo went rigid, unsure of what to do before lightly resting her hands on his too-skinny back. He smelled like jasmine tea.

Linus pulled back and swiped at his eyes. "Thank you. It's just . . . My memory . . . It's been difficult for me."

Rhea's expression gentled. "Would you be all right with us examining you briefly? My abilities are different from the other Evoli, and I might be able to see what the Oracle did to you. But it's up to you. It might be painful or uncomfortable."

Linus was quiet as he considered her words. "The pain is still there," he said in a low voice. "But I can't remember what caused it. Who I should blame." Linus's eyes met Rhea's. "You have my permission."

He invited them inside. For the next hour, Clo went through her list of the Oracle's programming triggers, the lines repeated in every chipped Tholosian's mind from birth to death. He frowned at each phrase—as though recognizing their familiarity—but, in the end, he gave a frustrated shake of his head.

Rhea went next. She shut her eyes and held Linus's hands, a line of concentration between her brows. After some long minutes, her forehead beaded with sweat, her chest rising and falling rapidly beneath her dress. Her breathing grew so ragged that Clo put a hand on Rhea's wrist, and the other woman jolted to attention.

"Sorry." Rhea shook her head, exhaustion lining her features. "I couldn't . . . I'm sorry."

Linus gave her an understanding look; he'd probably heard that from the Evoli after they rescued him.

Lastly, Clo used her mech cuff to take some bioscans, running the small device across his skull to record the information for Ariadne.

After they finished, they thanked Linus for his time and left. Rhea was quiet as they walked back through the city, but she was clearly still agitated.

"What happened back there?" Clo asked, ignoring the Evoli who gawked at her as she passed.

Rhea pressed her lips together. "I sensed something that might have been his memories, but they were all walled off and partitioned. Trying to break through almost ruptured my shields. Your touch drew me back just in time."

Clo didn't know whether to be alarmed or relieved. "Maybe Ariadne and Cato can find better answers."

"Mmm." Rhea seemed distracted.

Clo grasped for something to say that might reassure her. "We'll go home soon," she said. "Explore the galaxy like I promised."

But Rhea only hummed again, fingering her necklace. Her attention remained on the beauty of the city.

———

Later, as Clo dressed for the Equinox Ball, she tried not to think about how Rhea had looked when she had mentioned going home.

Where is home, anyway? she thought as she buttoned up her usual tunic and long shorts that left her new leg visible. *Zelus* was a hunk of metal floating through the stars. It didn't have the greenery of Talitha.

A rustle sounded. Clo turned and froze when she saw Rhea in all her splendor.

She'd painted her face like an artist. The freckles on her cheeks were blue, purple, and white, a galaxy of stars scattered across her skin. Her hair was pulled back and twisted in the shape of a seashell, with a few curls left loose around her face. When the light hit it just right, the dapples showed through, darker against the brown. She wore a flowing dress of azure. Simple, but more elevated than their daily clothing.

"Do I look all right?" she asked, smoothing the skirt down.

"You're beautiful," Clo said. Her heart ached. *Come home with me— wherever that is. With me.* "You're always beautiful."

Rhea blushed. "I could paint your face," Rhea offered. "If you wanted."

Clo shook her head with a smile. "Nah. I'd only end up rubbing it off by accident." Cosmetics had always felt like a mask to her, and even though part of her wanted the extra armor, the feel of the paint against her skin would only make her more self-conscious. Clo shrugged into a jacket that had little buttons shaped like suns. "Let's go."

They walked in silence to the great hall.

The awkwardness between them was so foreign. In the months since Laguna, they had sunk into each other: Rhea gave Clo respect, kindness, and trust—and Clo offered it in return. None of Clo's other relationships had lasted this long—she'd been too hot-headed, too fucking arrogant. After one too many clashes, she and a lover would split and decide to remain friends. Her relationship with Rhea was one month beyond the usual expiration date.

Clo chewed her lip. Maybe her spikiness made her unlovable.

The Evoli had decorated the great hall with glowing globes that hovered over the guests like constellations. The floor's intricate mosaics shimmered in the light, the design revealing a twisting strip that knotted in random configurations—to represent the Unity, Vyga had said.

Clo stuck to Rhea initially, straining to unpick the Evoli inflections, accents, and unfamiliar words as Rhea communicated with such ease.

After mere minutes, she had a headache. The crowd's chatter, the music, the clink of glasses and cutlery—all of it was strange to her. In contrast, Rhea had been used to attending events on Tholos. She knew exactly what to say and how to behave. She spoke the language—of the Evoli, and of politeness. Clo, meanwhile, probably seemed irritable standing next to her charming lover. She didn't exactly blame anyone for their unease around her when Rhea was so luminous.

Clo slipped away as Rhea charmed a visitor from the neighboring planet of Itonda. She drifted over to the drink table and topped up her wine, scowling as everyone gave her a wide berth.

She drank two glasses too quickly.

The music crescendoed, and the Ascendant- and Oversouls-to-be moved to stand at the head of the grand ballroom. Their loose robes were embellished with intricate beadwork, and their heads were heavy with ornate headdresses. The light from the strange chandeliers glinted against the stones. At first glance, it seemed as though they were all dressed identically, but their jewels were subtly different shades: red, blue. Vyga wore opaque moonstones.

Clo kept drinking as the ceremony began in Evoli. There were a lot of gestures, some bowing, then more gestures.

She jolted when someone cleared a throat beside her. Linus, dressed in Evoli finery. His scythes were faint shadows on his cheeks, the moon on his forehead like a third eye. He still looked exhausted around the eyes, but did he stand a little taller than before? Clo noticed some other former gerulae in the room, keeping to themselves but watching the ceremony with interest.

"Fancy, isn't it?" Linus said.

"Yep," Clo said, taking another nice, big gulp of wine.

She didn't mention that it paled in comparison to the ball she'd seen on Macella when she was undercover. Tholosians had mastered pointless extravagance.

The music faded, and a hush fell over the ballroom. The Evoli began to hum. Their voices rose together, perfectly in sync. Rhea's eyes drifted shut, and she swayed along with the rest. The Evoli grasped each other's hands and began to move into a loose circle. The guests and servers, the Ascendant and the Oversouls—all united in the gathering.

Only Clo and the other former gerulae remained separate.

Their song echoed in Clo's skull, her ribcage, throughout her entire body. The Evoli drew their heads back and stared up at the ceiling with open mouths. Yet, even Clo—separated from the Unity and the ceremony—felt something pass between them all. An electrical charge in the room, sizzling like lightning.

Finally, the circle broke. The Ascendant and the Oversouls stayed connected, forming a smaller circle with arms around each other, softly humming until it all came back into silence.

After what felt like an age, the Evoli leaders broke apart, and the ballroom erupted into applause and shouts of joy. The music started up again, and the party began anew. Rhea's laughter reached Clo's ears as she put her hand on the Itondan tradeswoman's arm and began to dance.

Clo returned her attention to Vyga. Ve blinked, a little dazed. Ver movements were a bit uncoordinated, but ve seemed otherwise unchanged. Was there really nothing left of ver emotions about their past before a few months earlier? Would ve see ver childhood friend and feel nothing more than ve would for any other Evoli under ver care?

"Well, that was interesting," Clo said to Linus.

He laughed. "Nothing else like it." He nodded at Rhea sweeping around the ballroom, her skirt flaring like a bell. "She seems at home."

"I suppose. Are you?"

He considered that. "I don't know—I can't remember anywhere else. But I'm not sure I'll ever belong. The Evoli are kind, but they're . . . distant."

"Tell me about it," Clo said, setting down her empty wine glass.

"Neve could probably be happy here," he continued. "Especially once she connects to the Unity. No misunderstandings that way." His tone was wistful. "But for the likes of you and I, we'll always only be getting half the conversation."

Clo's mind rebelled at the idea of Rhea joining the Unity. Of staying. She tried to keep her expression even. "She might not connect. Especially while we research how to get your memories back."

The former gerulae took another drink of wine. "They'll let Neve delay," Linus agreed. "But those who don't join the Unity are asked to leave." He watched Vyga as ve smiled at ver citizens. "Vyga wants to find a way to connect me and the other former gerulae, too. I think I'd like that."

Unease pounded through Clo's thoughts. "They won't make Neve leave. Or if they did, then we would go."

"And would she be happy somewhere else?" He delivered the words with something like innocence, but they sounded subtly off. "Or is this her home?"

Clo shot Linus a suspicious look. His expression had gone vague again. One side of his mouth twitched, and his head jerked a little to the left. Before she could blink, his hand reached out and grabbed her forearm like a vice. She flinched.

"Don't—let—her—connect." Linus's shoulders jerked, and his eyes rolled back in his skull, showing only the whites. She tried to pull away, swallowing down a cry of surprise.

His other hand reached out and clasped Clo's face, holding her chin. "I—need—you—to—promise." The grip tightened, pupils coming back into view, gaze so intense she leaned back, her shoulder hitting the marble of a column. "Not—safe—here."

Clo's heart rate ratcheted up. "I—I promise," she gasped.

Linus's features smoothed. A smile curled his lips as he straightened his jacket.

"Are you . . . okay?" Clo asked, voice hoarse.

Linus stilled. "Fine," he said, smiling. "Why wouldn't I be? Beautiful night. I think I'll have some more of those peaches." He strolled over to the food table, as if nothing were the matter at all.

Clo's eyes snagged on Rhea once again. She was dancing with a tall, willowy Evoli. Her cheeks were flushed with wine and movement. She looked happier than Clo had seen her in a long time. Maybe ever.

She's at home here.

She's not safe here.

In her room, she paced back and forth, trying to calm herself. But some deep intuition was sounding that same call of *not safe, not safe*.

Her every instinct screamed: something was wrong in the Evoli Empire.

29.

CATO

Present day

Cato tried not to stare at Nyx in her suspended-animation tank. He had already checked her vitals five times in the last hour, but he worried that if he looked away for a moment, he would turn around and find her organs had failed. That she had slipped into the Avern without his notice. Without a goodbye. For now, she was stable.

For now.

But he and Ariadne had still had no luck finding a cure or even a treatment that might buy them more time. After working for eight hours, going through all of the mistakes he had previously made, and coming up with a series of different tests, they both retired briefly to their quarters for much-needed rest.

But Cato didn't sleep. Instead, he lay awake in his cot, staring out at the stars. It ought to have soothed him: the vast expanse of space and *Zelus*'s slow, ceaseless journey to whichever planet offered them shelter next. And on and on it went, until . . . well, fuck if he knew.

Nyx might not make it to their next stop. Whatever planet they landed on could be the place they left her body to rest, and the strength of his disappointment surprised him. She deserved a better grave than the one they'd give her on some godsforsaken outpost. She deserved—

Nothing. The Oracle's voice slithered through his thoughts. *Let her soul wander for eternity.*

Cato gripped his head and tried to redirect his mind. No, if he couldn't save her, Nyx deserved last rites. A proper burial. Not covered in Tholosian gold medals but surrounded by people who cared about her—not by programming but by choice. She deserved a better funeral than being tossed into an unmarked grave like Demi.

A gasp tore from his lips. *Demi. Demetrius.* A name, spoken like a cherished whisper at the back of his mind. Someone he loved? He could almost make out a face, but it blurred around the edges. Did he imagine it? Or was it his own? Was—

The echo of the Oracle's voice blocked him from pressing further. *Kill the traitor, for the glory of Tholos.*

With a snarl, Cato lurched from his cot and headed back to the medical center. When he entered, he found Ariadne at the screens, keying commands into her tablet. The girl looked so small in front of the images that showed Nyx's internal body in a three-dimensional projection—from her skeleton to the smallest blood vessels.

Ariadne didn't look at him. "Couldn't sleep?"

"No." He came closer, watching as she flipped through the results of their attempts at both cures and treatments, running their projected effects through Nyx's computer simulation. "You?"

"One hour." She bit her lip and kept tapping the tablet. "I didn't want to leave her alone longer than that."

Cato was struck by the sadness in Ariadne's usually cheerful demeanor. Somehow, hearing the hitch to her voice—as if she were holding back tears—sank past his haze of exhaustion, past the months of his private grief. He hated sharing it with Ariadne; she was so young. Nyx had never wanted her to know, and he understood why. Because hearing the pain in her voice, somehow, made it more real.

They fell silent as the system forecast how Nyx's body would respond to that specific treatment course. Cato flinched as the prediction charted the disease's progression as it overtook her organs, blood, and bones. It was a tragedy, trying to give her more time and failing at anything beyond a few days. He was watching her die in slow motion. Would it be a better kindness to let her go?

Ariadne removed the microfile and filled in the label. "This is better than the last grouping." Another catch in her voice. Her hand shook as she filed it away. A tear escaped out of the corner of her eye, but she whisked it away as if it were a bothersome pest.

"It's not good enough," he said softly.

"No," she admitted. She cleared her throat and slotted another file. "Fifty more. They'll take an hour."

Cato nodded, tamping down his impatience. The Oracle was whispering again, as One always did when he grew idle. He couldn't sit there, staring at the projections of sample after sample on Nyx's digital double. It was all too easy to imagine the very real disease progressing through her body, and if she died . . . then what? Who else would understand the struggle of programming echoes, that even after months of being told he was Oracle-free, One could still influence him to pick up a weapon? Who else would reassure him that he still had a choice?

"How is Sher recovering?" Ariadne asked.

"He's still out," Cato said, grateful for something else to talk about. "Haven't been able to wake him yet." They kept Sher in the next room, along with the sleeping gerulae. "Kyla sits with him after she visits Nyx. I'm sure she wonders if the timestamp on that video was a lie or if he's already gerulae."

Ariadne abruptly wheeled her chair to another screen and pulled up a solid wall of programming language. Cato watched as the girl stared at the rows of symbols, her eyes darting back and forth as she read. He couldn't begin to understand what any of the sequences meant.

"What is this?" he asked her.

Ariadne paused. "It's the coding structure for the new gerulae programming I took from Othrys. I'm trying to understand how the Oracle gets the switch to flip without surgery or individual brain mapping. If One can change people that fast, I'm hoping there's a reversal. Nyx would—" She swallowed. "Nyx would want us to save others."

Cato didn't have to hear the rest of her thoughts to understand the implication: they may not be able to save Nyx, but this was a chance to change the gerulae back into who they were. Cato smiled grimly, thinking of what Nyx would say. *If you assholes keep focusing on me and not this mass gerulae conspiracy, fuck the Avern—I will haunt you personally.*

A beep sounded as Ariadne got an incoming message. She opened it. They looked like . . . brain scans? Her breath hitched. She flipped open her tablet and started tapping madly. "Yes," she whispered excitedly. *"Yesyesyesyesyes."*

Cato leaned over her but couldn't understand a damn thing she was typing. The numbers and symbols were as foreign to him as Evoli. "What is it?"

"Clo and Rhea. They sent through scans of a gerulae woken up on Eve. Look!"

She brought up Chara's brain scan, and the one that had just arrived, then pointed excitedly at the nonsense string of gerulae programming. Cato still wasn't quite following.

"I think—" she kept typing, a bright smile lighting her face. It was the first smile he'd seen on her in days. "Yessss, I think this is right, I just need to—" She tapped a bit more and then bolted from her chair. Bemused, Cato followed Ariadne as she hurried to the tank room. She tossed her tablet down in front of the screens and typed so fast that her fingers almost blurred.

That done, Cato watched as Ariadne inputted lines of gerulae programming into the computer, pulling up the brain scans for all four of the gerulae.

"Look. The Oracle changed One's brain-mapping methods. But you see, the brain-mapping approach I was familiar with isn't nearly as detailed as this *new one* because it utilizes some of the methods I came up with years ago for storing the Oracle's data in people's minds."

Cato reared back when he realized what she had just said. "Wait. Run that by me again?"

Ariadne froze, as if she realized her mistake. When her eyes met his, he saw a flicker of regret and . . . shame. "It wasn't—" She swallowed and whispered, "I didn't know what would happen. I just wanted—" Her eyes filled.

Gods, she looked so young. Sometimes, it was easy to forget that despite her brilliance, Ariadne was only sixteen. "Doesn't matter. Tell me," he said softly. "Tell me what you did."

She flapped her hands a few times, then grasped her fingers together to still the motion. "The Oracle's system inside the Temple is ancient. One ran inefficiently and couldn't learn as quickly using just the old storage units on *Argonaut*. Since the Oracle was already in people's minds, I"—she dropped her eyes from his—"I appropriated brain storage from citizens so the Oracle could hold more information."

Cato stepped away from her, his breathing coming faster. He didn't know if it was real or imagined, but he swore he felt the Oracle's tendrils through his brain, embedded through his entire cerebrum, whispering in a voice like Ariadne's. Because it *was* Ariadne's voice. Ariadne's knowledge, her skill—all of it—had been used to keep him obedient to the AI living in his mind. And he felt One's echo there, scratching around, still influencing his thoughts. Still compelling him to reach for weapons and trying to convince him to kill his friends.

Even free, he wasn't free.

"Why?" His voice came out in a gasp.

Ariadne's fingernails sank into the sleeve of her jumpsuit. "The Temple is so big," she whispered. "No one but machines are allowed inside. Even my food was delivered via automated assistants. The only voices I heard other than my own were through vids, but no one even knew I existed. Maintaining the Oracle was my entire purpose, and once I gave One a voice . . ." She brushed away another tear. "I heard my name for the first time. And all I wanted was someone else in that vast ship with me. Someone to talk to. Someone I thought might listen. I . . . I thought it would make One understand more about what it meant to be human." With even more shame, she whispered: "I'm sorry."

It was difficult for Cato to understand the sort of loneliness that had driven Ariadne to give the Oracle such power—he had always been surrounded by his cohort, fellow soldiers, and, later, the crews of the ships he flew. But he did comprehend desolation; he felt it whenever he questioned his programming. In the barracks, Cato had wondered if anyone felt the same—or if his mind was fundamentally broken. He'd worried that he'd be arrested and turned gerulae if he spoke up and asked even one of his brothers or sisters.

Cato looked away from Ariadne's small, hunched figure and found himself staring at Nyx in her tank. She had been the first person he had felt close to on this ship. When he was being deprogrammed, it was her voice that he had heard through the pain. He tried to imagine what it would have been like to hear no voice at all.

A breath left him. "Okay," he said, shutting his eyes briefly. He focused through the lingering tendrils of the Oracle, to find his own thoughts. "So, what does this all mean?"

Ariadne keyed in more commands. After a moment, the screens projected a three-dimensional image of the four gerulae brains and the new one. The models looked similar to what he and Ariadne had already gone through, but then Ariadne swiped her finger across the screen to pull back layers of brain sections, functions, and thoughts, to bring up a dozen small lights embedded throughout the interior of each brain.

Cato shifted closer, mesmerized by the sight. He hadn't seen anything like that in a brain scan before. "What are those?"

"In all the gerulae, newer or older, awake or asleep, there are still fragments of the Oracle's data." Ariadne's face was still splotchy, but her voice had calmed. Even so, she stared at those lights as if they haunted her. Perhaps they did.

"Don't you remove them during deprogramming?"

He pressed his teeth together before he did something fucking stupid—like beg her for an explanation. Something—*anything*—that explained why the Oracle still influenced his waking thoughts. *Please tell me you can fix it*, he wanted to say. *That if I'm deficient, you can put me back together again, and I won't have to listen to this fucking voice in my head anymore.*

Ariadne gave her head a shake. "They're not part of the Oracle's programming. The storage units function while the chip is in place, but the Oracle is no longer connected to the tendril once it's removed. It's just neutral data, like a superfluous thought or a memory. Most people won't notice it. The brain scan from Eve has them too, but they're still cut off."

Her words sank into him like a stone. Memories flashed, but the voices were muted, as if he heard them from afar. The press of lips against his, the scratch of stubble beneath his fingertips.

Demetrius.

"What if it's not always neutral? What if the Oracle stored memories there?" he whispered. At Ariadne's surprised expression, Cato flicked his fingers across the screen, pulling up the scans for one of the Novantae gerulae. "There's nothing functionally wrong with this brain, Ariadne. It lights up exactly where it's supposed to. What if these storage units showed up in the gerulae programming because One consolidated their thoughts and memories into them? Not erased them but—"

Ariadne pressed a hand to her mouth. "Locked them in? And that's why even though the Eve gerulae woke up, they don't remember anything?"

Locked them in. Putting Cato's fear into words somehow made it worse: the idea that every gerulae could be awake and aware but unable to control their actions. That the servants at every Empire ball, the old rebels Damocles had tortured for pleasure . . . all of them still in there, somewhere. Watching everything.

Silent passengers in their own bodies. It was what they had feared the most. Here was their confirmation.

"Then I must be able to wake them up," she whispered desperately, tapping her tablet. "I just don't know how long it will take."

And his? What about his? *Demetrius.* He let the name rest in his mind. Like an echo, a response somewhere inside him called back. But where?

"I need you to scan my brain for this," he whispered.

Ariadne frowned. "But you're not—"

"Gerulae, I know." A dry laugh escaped him. "I'm not a fucking medic, either. All of my memories are of being a pilot. Yet I can read scans. I can develop treatments, and I know how to conduct surgery. So, who am I?" Gods, he wanted to plead with her. This sixteen-year-old girl who gave an AI control over his mind. He wanted to beg her on his knees. "Please. Maybe it'll help you with the others since I'm not gerulae. Can you find a way to read the data?"

"I can try." She loosened a breath and gestured to the medical bed. "Okay. Lie down."

Cato removed his lab coat and settled onto the bed. When he pressed his eyes closed and let Ariadne do her work, he thought of the name again. *Demetrius.*

And somewhere inside him, a voice called back that wasn't the Oracle's.

30.

Ten years ago

emetrius descended on the aftermath of the battle like a harpy. He spread his wings, gliding his ship down to the planet on storm winds to take their souls to the Avern.

He had done this more times than he could count. Sometimes, he descended as a member of the winning side. But recently, he flew into fields of slaughtered Tholosians.

It shouldn't be possible. Tholosian soldiers always outnumbered the Evoli at least three to one. Yet the Evoli moved through the skies and along the ground like they were worker bees in some great hive. The Tholosians, by contrast, were disordered.

They never started that way. Commanders gave their orders, underpinned by solid strategy, and the soldiers kept to the plan. The Oracle ensured those instructions thumped through their minds like a drumbeat. Yet two days into a battle—or three, or five—their bodies would inevitably grow weary. Their cohesion frayed, while the other side stayed strong. Not even the programming or their genetic engineering could keep Tholosians tidy once exhaustion set in.

Evoli soldiers would slip onto a ship like ghosts, no matter the security. Then, somehow, the commanders would end up dead. The Tholosians had remote authorities on standby ready to enter the fray at a moment's notice, but reclaiming the spirit of the battle was difficult, once lost.

Rumors spread through the camps that the Evoli were incapable of dying. That each Tholosian murdered added another year to their life.

Demetrius rarely fought. These days, he came down to see who survived or who he could save.

Battles were all the same in the end. The setting might change—a planet with teal sand stained dark with blood. Or a moon with steep, rugged cliffs, where soldiers were every bit as in danger of falling to their deaths as of being hit by enemy fire.

Every soldier went in with wide-eyed enthusiasm, desperate to prove themselves to the Archon and their fellow soldiers. To die gloriously in Letum's name.

And they did.

In droves.

The medics divided and conquered in a well-practiced formation. Demetrius's stomach roiled at the stench of blood and guts as he stepped over the entrails spilled into the mud. The wails of the dead and the dying surrounded him.

Demetrius dispatched the wounded Evoli first. He kept his distance and shot them in the heads before they used their foul magic to influence his thoughts.

Another Evoli, one blast to the brain. Then another. The diligent work of killing before he got started healing. He took lives, and he gave them—these were both his gifts from the gods.

Demetrius could tell in less than two seconds if a Tholosian would make it. If they wouldn't, and he could spare the time, he'd use another Mors blast. Say last rites as they flew to the Avern.

One day, I'll see you all at the gates, he thought, continuing through the corpses.

Some struggled to their feet, and Demetrius half-carried them to the medical tent at the edge of the field. But, while patching up one soldier, others might miss their chance at life.

This was the balance. Demetrius sent some souls on with a bullet, let others go on their own, and saved the few he could. Stitching flesh together took precious time.

And who lived was a matter of chance. The gods decided.

Demetrius had been at it for hours, until corpses and faces blurred together. He went through the motions on autopilot: smearing sealant gel on a woman's arm, making sure she could still open and close her fingers to grasp a Mors. Amputating a man's leg, only for him to die on the table from shock. Probably for the best. It'd be a fifty-fifty chance if the Tholosians could provide him with a prosthetic. Some would consider it a wasted resource on a thuban soldier.

Another man died as Demetrius half-dragged him to the tent. Another woman took Demetrius's Mors out of his hand and shot herself. He'd stood there for a full two minutes before he comprehended his hesitation meant another soldier would die somewhere on that field.

Broken bodies, twisted limbs, blood mixed into the mud, dirt, or sand. Red splashed over rocks and swirled pink through the water.

One battle faded into the next.

Demetrius had not stopped to eat, drink, or even piss. He did not stop until a hand rested on his shoulder.

"Demi," came the familiar voice behind him, and Demetrius sighed in relief. One of these days, he knew it wouldn't be this pilot coming to collect him.

But Cato had survived this battle. And that was enough for now.

"It can't be time yet," Demetrius said, gently turning a soldier over on the ground. Unseeing, sightless eyes. Another soul for the God of Death. Demetrius rubbed his forehead with the back of his hand. "I still have more to work through."

"I gave you an extra hour," Cato said. "You've done what you could. Leave the rest."

"Always coming to save me," Demetrius murmured. "Here's where you say I'm too soft."

"You're too soft," Cato obliged, hauling Demetrius to his feet. Cato kissed him gently, pulling away just as Demetrius began to deepen the kiss. "One of these days, that softness might get you killed."

"Probably."

Cato led Demetrius to his ship, which waited at the north edge of the battlefield. The other medics had started to pack up the tents, most of them red to the elbows. Medic Iason had a scarlet smear across his cheekbone. At the ship, Cato pulled Demetrius close for another kiss, hidden from view.

They'd kissed at the edge of so many battlefields by now. The planet with teal sand. The one with the jagged cliffs. The planet thick with snow, the white drifts turned red and gray by the end of the fight. He didn't even remember the names of them. Cato's kiss was what brought Demetrius back to himself.

It reminded him that he was still alive.

It'd been two years. Cato had come to get patched up after the Battle of Pyrope with a nasty Mors burn on his back. He'd flirted the whole time Demetrius treated him, and Demetrius had finished with a blush. Cato had sauntered over to him in the mess hall a few days later, offering him a beer, which Demetrius accepted.

He'd spent the night in Cato's bunk.

It was meant to be nothing. A bit of distraction, a way to let off steam and aggression. The Oracle encouraged such behavior, and soldiers often ended up pairing with those not in their sibling cohort.

But Demetrius had never expected to fall in love with Cato.

Because love was illogical, unpredictable, and dangerous. He'd realized that love had a way of sneaking through the cracks of the Oracle's programming—of nudging it to a different part of the mind. So, Demetrius found ways to ignore the Oracle's coding when he was with Cato. And that was dangerous.

Fierce passion led to lingering caresses. Cato chose to stay in Demetrius's bed until early morning before sneaking back to his bunk. After every battle, Cato came to the field and pressed a kiss to Demetrius's lips. They'd scrub blood off each other in brief, military showers before falling into bed to try and forget what they had both seen, what they had both done.

Demetrius was starting to question. He was beginning to wonder what life he could have without Oracle.

One where he loved Cato off the battlefield.

But if Cato felt the same, he didn't show it. Press too hard, and Demetrius would only receive the standard Tholosian propaganda response from Cato's lips. *Our roles are noble—for the glory of the Empire.*

When we win the war, the Archon will reward us.
The Avern will welcome us with open arms.

But Demetrius was patient. He could wait, he could love, and he could hope.

At night, he had even begun to dream—real ones, not guided by Oracle. He dreamed of landing on a planet where there was no battle. Where he could walk through tall grass, or along a beach, or through woods leading up to a mountain. He'd lie down in the sun with his eyes closed and not even be afraid enough to keep his Mors within easy reach.

In that place, he rested. Sometimes Cato was by his side. Sometimes not. Demetrius always woke up and tried to cling to that warmth before the acidic smell of a stomach slashed open on a battlefield chased the last of it away.

Cato nipped Demetrius's lip, bringing him back to the battlefield. "You're distracted," Cato said, leaning against the side of his ship. He was muddy and smelled of sweat, not that Demetrius cared. "My kisses not doing it for you anymore, Doc?"

Demetrius snorted and curled his fingers into Cato's jacket. "Fuckwit." He set his lips against Cato's once more, and the other man gave a low groan.

"I go back to the Three Sisters tomorrow," Cato said against Demetrius's lips as he slid his hand beneath Demetrius's jacket. "I need to report what I found on that intel run. Once I'm back, I'm not letting you leave my bed for three days."

Demetrius sighed and stepped away from Cato's seeking touch. Tomorrow, while Cato battled at the front, Demetrius and the surviving thubans would touch down to dig a mass grave for their brethren. Members of their cohort, or others they had seen next to them in battle. People he hadn't saved.

"I'm tired of this," Demetrius let himself say. "Aren't you?"

A hesitation. An ache of deliberation. Demetrius felt his hopes rise—

A shout in the distance.

Emergency alarms blared around them.

And the sky filled with Evoli ships.

They were uncloaked, as if arriving from the ether. Yet, even as

Demetrius reached for his Mors, he couldn't stop his mind from whirring: Where had they come from? How did they fly in undetected?

The ships opened fire.

"Get to the trenches!" Cato shouted. He grabbed Demetrius's arm. "Demi! Get to safety!"

He imagined Cato in the grave with all the others, his blood spilled on the battlefield. Another soul taken to the Avern.

I love you, he wanted to say. *I love you.*

"Demetrius!"

Cato's strong arms were around his waist, pushing him away.

Then the blast hit, and time stopped.

31.

ERIS

Present day

After waiting on standby for Damocles to deliberate, he returned Eris's call within the hour, as she'd known he would. He agreed to meet her on one of the discarded Imperial junkers in Elysium. He'd bring the cure, and she'd bring Ariadne.

Deal done.

Eris and Damocles were back on their respective sides of the game, shifting pieces in their favor, lining up attacks, anticipating moves.

Her brother had correctly identified Ariadne as a vulnerability. Which meant Damocles knew that Eris had grown to care for her crew more than for herself. It was the very thing her father had trained his children against in the academy on Myndalia, a lesson Eris learned the hard way after Xander.

Damocles knew how to use such weaknesses against her. She was going to have to use that to her advantage—even if it meant making a difficult choice.

"I know how to save Nyx," Eris told Kyla as she entered the bridge, asking the commander to input coordinates to Elysium.

Eris headed off Kyla's rapid follow-up questions with an "I'll explain everything to the group" and left to round up Ariadne and Cato. None of them would be happy with her once they knew about her meeting with Damocles. Kyla, least of all.

But if it meant saving Nyx . . .

Her brother had the cure. And Nyx's illness was Eris's responsibility.

Eris rounded into the medical center and headed to the back room where the tanks were, knowing Cato and Ariadne were probably hard at work. She wished they could find a way to save Nyx before *Zelus* made it to Elysium. She wished—

Eris paused at the door, startled by the sight of Cato unconscious and wearing a brain cap on one of the medical cots. Beside him, Ariadne tapped the keys in front of the large screens, and the coding she input ran down in long, elaborate columns of numbers, symbols, and equations. Eris could read a bit of programming code—basic knowledge of the Oracle's internal programming was part of her training at the academy in Myndalia—but not nearly fast enough to keep up with Ariadne's work. The girl coded even faster than she talked.

"Ariadne," Eris called softly, knowing from experience that it was best not to interrupt Ariadne's hyperfocus too abruptly.

Ariadne didn't respond or acknowledge Eris's presence. She kept typing, her fingers flying across the lit keys. After several moments, she dropped her hands and sat back with a deep sigh. "Hello."

"That sounded ominous," Eris said, glancing once more at Cato. His breathing seemed even, but his hands were clenched into fists by his side. His eyes shifted rapidly beneath his lids.

"What did? My sigh?" Ariadne looked intrigued. "Is my sigh always ominous? How does one not sigh ominously? What *is* an ominous—"

"Never mind that." Eris gestured to their unconscious crewmember. "What's all this?"

"Hmm?" Ariadne propped her chin in her hand. "That's Cato."

Eris was getting better with Ariadne's tendency to take questions very literally, but Nyx was better at navigating the answers. Eris, on the other hand, wasn't at her best when she was worried. Across the room, Nyx's unconscious form kept drawing her attention—was she paler? Or was it Eris's imagination?

Stop it.

Eris pressed her teeth together. "I thought you were working on a cure for Nyx. Why is Cato unconscious?" A thought occurred to her. "Please tell me you didn't infect him with the virus, or—"

"*No.*" Ariadne looked appalled. "Oh, *no, no, no.* That would be bad. We were waiting for a few samples to finish, and then some former gerulae scans came in from Clo and Rhea. The Oracle damaged their memories, so we're . . ." She chewed on her lip. "We're testing a possibility with the Oracle's new gerulae programming and the information contained in the scans."

More questions clouded Eris's relief over Clo and Rhea's intel. "On Cato? But he's not gerulae." Eris approached the bed and looked down at him. His fingernails were digging into his palms. She took one of his hands, and he gripped her so hard, she sucked in a breath. "What's wrong with him?"

"I . . ." Ariadne stood and grasped at her lab coat. "I have something I need to tell you. I did something. Back at the Temple."

Eris listened, with increasing incredulity, as Ariadne told her about the Oracle's internal storage on *Argonaut* and her part in transferring the Oracle's memory into citizens' minds through the chips installed at birth. From day one, every Tholosian citizen—with only a few exceptions—was controlled by the Oracle, used as nothing more than a tool. For the Archon, humans were labor. And for the Oracle, they were a storage unit.

Like her father and brother, Eris had never heard the Oracle's whispers in her mind. But when Damocles had drugged her on Laguna, she had felt, for a brief time, what it must be like: to be trapped in a cage of one's own body, where not even the mind was safe.

When Ariadne finished, the girl stared at Eris. Her hands flapped. "It's okay if you hate me," she said, barely above a whisper. She was cringing, as if she expected to be cast out.

Once, not so long before, maybe this would have infuriated Eris. Maybe, somewhere down deep, it still did. But Eris stared at the smattering of scars around the collar of Cato's shirt. Marks she knew, from close quarters, covered his entire torso. Earned at the Empire's behest— if not under her father's command, then under her own. Ariadne had done what had made sense to her at the time, with the information she had. Hadn't the rest of them done the same?

Had he died, Cato would only have been a number in Eris's morning briefings. She had come to memorize many numbers over the years.

Thousands: the calculations of soldiers, spies, and innocents she had murdered. Billions: the number of soldiers lost on a battlefield. Twenty-three: the number of brothers she had killed for power. One: the only brother still left on her list.

So, who was she to judge? What right did she have?

"I could never hate you," she told Ariadne. "And I'm not someone you should look to for condemnation."

Ariadne's eyes filled. "Thank you," she said.

Eris gave a nod and returned her attention to Cato. The pilot was frowning, his lips lifting in a grimace. He looked like he was in pain. His grip on her hand tightened, and his chest rose and fell with agitated breaths.

"Ariadne. Can we . . . see what he sees?" Eris asked. "You said it was a cluster of the Oracle's storage, right?"

The girl's eyes brightened, as if the idea hadn't occurred to her. "You mean, scan the stored data to project a video? Ohhh! Wouldn't that be interesting? Like watching a dream. Wait, wouldn't that be private?" She rested her finger against her lips. "He *did* say he wanted me to find out what it is, though."

Ariadne hurried over to the screens and began keying in commands. As she did so, Cato grew more agitated, his body beginning to tremble. Eris gently held him down, worrying he might hurt himself. The Oracle couldn't command people who were deprogrammed, but she hadn't seen anyone with coding as deep as Cato's.

Ariadne made an excited noise and repositioned the screens. "Got it! It should be coming in now."

The screens flickered, as if the data were slightly damaged. After a bit of fiddling from Ariadne, the picture cleared, and it was as if they were staring through someone else's eyes at Cato's face. He looked younger, his skin unlined. His neck was smooth and unscarred. He stared tenderly at . . .

Wait.

Eris peered at the screen. "We shouldn't be seeing Cato's face, right?" She was confused. "Is he looking in a mirror or something?"

Ariadne looked unsure. "I don't . . . think so?" She gestured behind him. "He looks like he's out in the field. Isn't that a Tholosian tent?"

Eris tried to make out the details in the background. The image was still a bit blurred, but Ariadne was right. It did look like a battlefield tent—basic amenities, small cots, little more than a shelter and a bed for a few winks of sleep. There wasn't any need for mirrors there. So, why—

The screen broke up as if the memory were corrupted. When Eris thought it had gone completely blank, another image flashed: Cato dressed as a field medic, trying to help a fallen soldier.

Or . . . *was* it Cato?

Eris and Ariadne stared at the screen with growing horror.

32.

DEMETRIUS

Ten years ago

Demetrius drifted in and out of consciousness. Everything hurt. His neck felt like it had been splattered with molten metal. He blinked hard against the light. Voices spoke above him, difficult to pick apart, but he tried. He tried.

What happened? The battle. The blast.

Cato? Cato—

With agony, he turned his head to the right. A glint of golden metal. His eyes struggled to focus. When he did, he stiffened.

It was the Archon himself.

Had they come back to the Three Sisters? Or had the Archon gone on a campaign to visit his soldiers at the front? Demetrius shuddered, knowing he'd have to stand up and bow, despite his injuries. He didn't trust that his body could even move.

But the Archon stayed with the medical staff.

"Your prognosis?" the Archon asked.

Medic Pontos bustled around him, obsequious and subservient. Demetrius had never liked him much, but he was a good doctor, at least. Demetrius opened his mouth to ask about Cato, but his throat was too singed. He only managed a rough grunt.

"The medic will recover, Your Excellency," Pontos said.

"He's low-ranked, yes?" the Archon asked, sounding almost bored.

"Yes, Your Excellency. Thuban class. Does the first round of treatments on the battlefield. He was next to the pilot you've taken an interest in."

"The pilot was meant to report after the battle." The Archon's voice was tight. "He'd been surveilling the edges of Evoli space before his commander called him to Aquarius. We haven't had a chance to see what he gathered, but the initial reports seemed promising."

"He won't make it, I'm afraid," Pontos said, so apologetic he was almost wheedling.

With more effort, Demetrius turned his head to the left.

A charred body, so burned that Demetrius was amazed it still breathed. The hair as blond as his own was gone. Demetrius had grown so used to the smell of burned flesh, he hadn't even noticed it when he woke up.

Now the stench filled his nostrils, and he wanted to vomit. The body was hooked up to machines, but there was little point. He would not last more than an hour.

Even destroyed, Demetrius recognized him instantly.

Cato.

His brilliant, stupid pilot. In a flash of memory, Demetrius recalled what had happened: Cato had pushed him from the blast.

Cato had saved Demetrius's life.

Demetrius shut his eyes hard. He wasn't worth it. Cato was a commanding pilot, not far off from being promoted from Praefectus to Tribunus. He'd had a future. But, from birth, Demetrius had known he could never be more than a lowly thuban. The most Demetrius could have hoped for was to one day be at a similar rank to Pontos. Senior enough to stay and heal people on the ship rather than in the mud.

"How is the pilot's mind?" the Archon asked.

"Still largely intact," Pontos said. "Your Excellency."

"Then we'll have to be creative, won't we?" The Archon's attention lingered on the burned body. "Hook him up to the Oracle's system. Have One erase the medic's memories and replace them with the pilot's before his brain dies. He'll continue his intelligence work in the medic's body, once he recovers. I'll expect a full report then." The Archon's lips thinned. "I want to hear what he knows as soon as possible."

Horror spread through Demetrius like congealed oil. He wanted to scream. Shout. Thrash. Anything. But he couldn't even blink.

Even Pontos hesitated before he bowed so low that he nearly folded himself in half. "Of course, Your Excellency. It will be done. In Tholos's name."

How many times had Demetrius imagined his end? On the wrong side of a weapon. An explosion like the one they'd just endured. A ship malfunctioning. The sharp kiss of a knife or a garotte against his throat. He'd always known he'd never die of old age. That somehow, he'd be ground up in the gears of the machines of war. Chewed up, spit out. But Demetrius never imagined anything like this. That his body might live on while he ceased to be.

The Archon moved into Demetrius's line of vision. He gave Pontos a cool nod before leaving, his cloak billowing behind him. No last look at Demetrius or Cato. He'd never spare a thought for the mind that had once been housed in the body.

Pontos began his work with slow movements, almost reluctant. He started when he noticed Demetrius was awake.

Using all his strength, Demetrius opened his mouth, trying to beg for his life. He stopped, jaw frozen. What were his options? Try to continue on in his body, only for the Archon to kill him and Pontos if he ever discovered what had happened? To live on meant consigning Cato—*Cato*—to death. What sort of life could that be?

He'd once promised to give Cato everything. He could deliver him this: one final act.

"Yes," Demetrius rasped. "I consent."

Pontos's shoulders slackened with relief. He clasped his scythes and gave Demetrius last rites, and Demetrius took them gratefully.

After that, Pontos wasted no more time.

Demetrius turned his head again, staring at what used to be Cato. He remembered the nights they'd had together. The silly jokes no one else would understand that made them crease with laughter. The feel of

Cato's warm skin. The taste of his lips. The dimple he'd had at one side of his mouth.

Demetrius could not give Cato his soul, but he could give him his body. His only regret was that they didn't have more time together.

In a rare show of Tholosian mercy, the procedure wasn't painful. As the gerulae code ran through Demetrius's synapses, his last thoughts were of Cato.

I love you. Keep fighting.

33.

Present day

Eris swallowed back bile as the video played.

"Oh, gods," Ariadne whispered, her hand pressing to her mouth. "So, that's not his . . ."

"No." *Not his body.* The Oracle had downloaded his memories, personality, and identity into Demetrius's body. As if he were no more than a transferable unit of data. As if Demetrius were only a husk to be used for storing intel.

Husk. Eris flinched.

"I didn't know." Ariadne bit her fist. "I knew the Oracle was capable of moving memories—but I didn't know One would ever do something like this. Oh, gods. How many other people are like this?" She rubbed at her face. "So, that's why Cato has all that medical knowledge. The Oracle hadn't been able to erase Demetrius completely. In a way, they're . . . merged." Her face was slack with dismay. Guilt. Those same emotions surged through Eris.

The screen had gone dark, but muffled voices could still be heard over the comms. But did those memories belong to Cato or Demetrius now?

"Wake him," Eris said quietly, deciding it didn't matter. "He doesn't need to experience any more of that. We don't need to see it."

Sniffling, Ariadne nodded and shut off the screen. She set to work reversing the anesthesia. Both she and Eris waited by Cato's bedside for the drugs to take effect.

The pilot's body slowly came to awareness, and then his blue eyes opened. Eris was struck by the loss in them—and a rage she understood well. She remembered it keenly from the day Xander died.

"Hey," Eris whispered, and Ariadne gave him a sad wave. "I'm . . ." She let out a breath. "Cato, I'm so sorry."

It was such a shit word. *Sorry*. Eris's father had done this, and she couldn't fix it. Her family had brought pain and suffering to so many—and so had Eris. *Sorry* was not good enough. Not for Cato, or Demetrius, or anyone. *Sorry* couldn't fix a damned thing.

With a flinch, Cato turned away from them, curling in on himself. His shoulders heaved with sobs he clearly didn't wish them to see. She reached forward and put a hand on his shoulder for a brief, understanding squeeze.

"Come with me," Eris said to Ariadne. "I need to talk to you and Kyla." She still had a chance to mend one thing. Just one thing.

Eris and Ariadne left Cato to his memories.

———

Kyla stood as Eris and Ariadne entered the bridge. The commander looked pissed. "I can't believe you *ordered* me to direct the ship to the farthest quadrant in Iona without an explanation and then left me in suspense for an hour." Kyla snorted. "Where's Cato?"

"He's busy." At Kyla's raised eyebrow, Eris amended, "He can't be part of the plan right now."

"A plan?" Ariadne clapped her hands. "I love plans! Are we going to steal something?" Eris was sure the girl was desperate to focus on something, anything, other than what they'd both witnessed. Eris didn't know how she'd explain to the others what had happened. What it all meant.

Eris squared her shoulders. The plan. It was really fucking hard to put her godsdamned scheme into words in a way that wouldn't piss everyone off. "No, we're not going to steal anything."

"Blow something up?" Ariadne asked. "I have a new explosive we can test—"

"*No.*" Eris paused for a moment. "But I want to hear about that later."

Kyla glared at Eris. "You're stalling. It's something that's going to make me want to punch you in the face, isn't it?"

"Definitely. I'd like to enjoy my injury-free face a moment longer." When Kyla looked about ready to hit her on principle, Eris sighed. "I think I know of a potential cure for Nyx."

Ariadne gasped. "You . . . *Oh, my gods.* You do?"

Kyla, on the other hand, didn't let relief interfere with her suspicion. She crossed her arms. "I'm going to guess there's a catch. Otherwise, you wouldn't have fiddlefucked for an hour in the medical center instead of telling me why Elva needed to stay with the other rebels while I steered one of our best ships to Elysium with a skeleton crew. Spit it out, Eris."

Eris pressed her fingers into the back of the chair. Damocles' response after she gave him an hour to decide echoed in her head: *I'll meet you. But if you make me wait, I'm taking the cure with me. And then how will you save your precious Nyx?*

He had gained some control over his anger, and now they were both thinking over their next moves in the game. Hers, she knew, appeared to be in a weak position; the Queen wasn't the only piece she needed to defend—and he knew she'd throw herself in front of a blast to save her friends.

But his? Damocles' ambition placed him in a position every bit as weakened as her own. He was forced to defend a galaxy full of people he didn't care about for one simple reason: with no subjects, he held no power.

And that, to him, was an unacceptable vulnerability.

Eris straightened and met Kyla's gaze. "Damocles has it."

With a snarled curse, Kyla started for *Zelus*'s controls. "I'm turning this fucking ship around," she snapped. "Gods, how could you be so *stupid* to agree to meet with that asshole without telling me—"

Eris intercepted Kyla, blocking her path. "You would have said no."

The commander's lip curled as she tried to get around Eris. "I'm saying no right now. Call him back, tell him we're not coming. Mention I suggested he go fuck himself and die."

Eris thought of Nyx in the tank, growing paler and weaker. How days before, she had sat with the soldier at the zatrikion board, and Nyx had let her win. Eris had wondered if it was to spare her ego. But she thought, from time to time, about how Nyx described playing the game with Damocles. And Eris remembered how Damocles reacted when he lost.

Nyx had escaped the Empire—fled Eris's brother—and for what? *For what?* To die of a disease she caught on a mission with Eris, having never experienced freedom.

"If there's a chance to save Nyx, I'm taking it," Eris said. "And if there's a chance to put another blast through Damocles' skull and finish the job I should have done on Laguna, then I'll take that, too."

Kyla's expression softened. A long exhale left her as she looked over at Ariadne. They waged some silent conversation, until Ariadne pressed her lips together and raised her hand tentatively.

"My vote is not letting Nyx die."

The commander was silent for a painful moment. Then: "I don't agree yet. How did you convince him?"

Eris pressed her fingernails into her palms. "I took the chance that he didn't know the Oracle had gone rogue."

Ariadne went utterly, utterly still.

Kyla's eyebrows shot up. "The Oracle *what?* That's not poss—"

"It is. Damocles had no idea Othrys had been taken. That we had Sher. The Oracle didn't tell him." Eris's gaze flickered to Ariadne, whose panicked gasps betrayed her thoughts. "I think you knew about the Oracle becoming autonomous, Ariadne. And I think you've known since before Othrys."

The girl's breathing accelerated. Ariadne's eyes were glazed over in the same paralyzing fear Eris had witnessed as they fled through the cell blocks on that godsforsaken moon. She scratched at the skin of her arm, as if seeking some pain to keep from drawing herself back into memories of the Temple.

"I—I—I'm—I'm sorry." Ariadne's staccato words made Eris flinch. "I'm so sorry."

"Fuck," Kyla whispered. She folded her arms. "So, you think the Oracle is staging a coup? Ariadne?"

Ariadne shook her head wildly. "I don't know. I don't know. If One can make any citizen gerulae that fast and no longer responds to Damocles' instructions . . ."

"Then every citizen in the Empire is the Oracle's puppet." Kyla muttered a swear. "And you want to give that coding to Damocles," she said to Eris. "Deliver him full control over the AI with the power to command millions directly. What a fine present for an aspiring tyrant."

"I'll do whatever it takes to make sure he doesn't leave Elysium with it," Eris said, trying not to lose her patience. They didn't have time to debate this. *Nyx* didn't have time. "But we need that cure for Nyx. And he's insisting Ariadne come with me. *Only* Ariadne."

Ariadne squeaked. *"Me? Why me?"*

Kyla looked worried. "Because you know the Oracle better than anyone. And it certainly doesn't fucking help that you're the only one of us not combat-trained."

"What if . . . what if I mess up?" Ariadne asked, fidgeting. "What if—"

"I'll protect you," Eris said, and the words felt so heavy on her silver tongue. "I promise."

Kyla's eyes met Eris's. The commander straightened. "I trust you to be the general, Eris," Kyla said. "And do whatever it takes to make sure he doesn't leave with the coding. He can't have that sort of power. Understand?"

Eris gave a nod, knowing what Kyla was saying. Eris had already comprehended it herself.

The promise she had just made to Ariadne was a lie.

34.

RHEA

Present day

The longer Rhea stayed in Talitha, the more she loved it.

It reminded her of the better parts of the Pleasure Garden: the sonance of the fountains, the way sunlight streamed through the windows in the morning.

It was just . . . easier. To exist.

After years under the Archon's control and months on the run with the other Devils, the slower pace of life was a welcome change. It felt almost safe. She'd find herself too relaxed and have to remind herself of why they were there.

Rhea was used to others' emotions brushing against hers like a whisper at her ear. Even shielded as she was, the Evoli's feelings rose and ebbed within the current of the Unity, rarely too sharp and spiking. Of course, people still quarreled, but it was hard to maintain an argument for long when one could feel precisely why the other half was so upset.

For the first time in her life, Rhea wasn't afraid. She was . . . content.

Rhea stumbled back to their room after the ball, giddy on wine, dance, and song. Emotions swirled so close to the surface of her skin that she could taste them.

It had been such a lovely party.

Tholosian galas had always been work. Rhea never had a choice about whether to participate or remain in her room. She never had the opportunity to dance freely, chat without expectations, enjoy herself.

Damocles always watched her closely, noting any mistake that would give him an excuse to paint her in gold and display her to his chosen favorites. It was a humiliation she had repeatedly endured: being a literal platter off which nobles and soldiers ate.

In Talitha, people respected Rhea.

The Equinox Ball had reminded her a little more of Ariadne's parties on *Zelus*—only far more elaborate. Where the ship's canteen had been decorated with torn strips of a flag, the Evoli had bands of lights and crystals that intersected the ceiling like stars. Their wine had been sweeter than the alcohol stolen from the Empire. An elegant orchestra replaced the fast beat of Ariadne's collection of Old World songs.

Yet the person Rhea had wanted to share it with most had been missing.

Dancing with Clo had been her first taste of freedom. Rhea remembered their fingers intertwining, hips following hips. She'd studied the gold flecks in Clo's brown eyes and breathed in her almost-spicy scent. She'd wanted to dance with Clo during the Equinox Ball, beneath the canopy of crystals and lights. She'd wanted to show Clo the freedom of being on Eve.

But when Rhea looked for her after the ceremony, Clo was gone. Rhea instinctively knew she'd returned to their room.

Rhea had been tempted to go after her, but something compelled her to stay. She felt closer than ever to the Unity—not part of it yet, but it had wrapped itself around her like a caress: *join, and be this happy always.* She could almost see the way the Unity worked. She'd be able to connect to it herself if she wanted. Like tying a knot.

As Rhea wandered through the palace back to her room, she was as drunk on emotions as she was on wine. She felt lovers meet for the evening. Threads of desire twisted through the corridors, as insistent as a beat of music. Others were content and sleepy, ready to close their eyes and chase dreams.

It was late—closer to dawn than to dusk—but the palace corridors were still dark but for the moon's cool, silver glow through the open windows. Gauzy curtains moved in the faint breeze. The stars were bright tonight, and the air was redolent with the delicate scent of night-blooming flowers, sweet as the jasmine in the Pleasure Garden.

She wondered if Clo was asleep by now. Rhea smiled to herself, imagining kissing her lover awake. Closing the distance Clo had put between them over the last few days. She wanted to show Clo she still knew exactly what the other woman wanted, even if she couldn't sense her emotions.

Tomorrow, Rhea would wake up deliciously late and ask Vyga to work with her on the former gerulae. Ve had plans to see if Rhea could link to Linus or one of the other volunteers into a minor, separate Unity of two to draw their memories out.

But first: Clo. Warm skin. Sweet lips. She shivered in anticipation.

Rhea hummed as she opened the door, and it took a few moments for her to process what she was seeing.

Clo was a whirlwind of barely contained panic. It seeped out of her shields like smoke.

Rhea paused, swaying a little, her hand on the back of a sofa to steady herself. "Clo? What's going on?" she asked.

She was still half-lost in her intimate daydream. Smooth sheets. The music of the Evoli emotions winding its way through her mind and body, rising in a collective chorus of song. Why wasn't Clo in bed where she could join and share this with her?

Clo started speaking, but it was too fast for Rhea to follow. "Wait, wait," Rhea said. She shook her head to little improvement. "Slow down."

Clo switched to Pathos. <*Something's off. Linus was acting fucking weird, and none of them want me here. Not like they want you.*>

Rhea tried to concentrate but still struggled to parse the words through the static in her mind. Clo's Pathos voice pounded through her head.

Frustrated, Clo moved back to speech, moving scant inches away, her whispers harsh. "*Rhea.*"

"You're supposed to call me Neve." Rhea still wanted to kiss her. If she kissed her, then they didn't have to talk. She could make Clo forget what she wanted to say, and they could reenact her daydream.

But Clo grasped Rhea's shoulders, her eyes firm. And not at all tempted. "Concentrate. I need you to sober the fuck up and listen to me. Vyga's trying to lure you into the Unity, Rhea. I don't trust ver."

Rhea tried. She really tried, and some of the words made it through.

Linus acting strangely? Not trusting Vyga? But ve only wanted to ensure harmony in Talitha, on Eve, in the whole quadrant. If they were united, nothing could break them. Not even the Tholosians.

Rhea shook her head slowly, the movement making the room spin. Clo's hold was the only thing keeping her up.

"I'm telling you, *Neve*," Clo said, tightening her grip. <*You remember how fucked-up Cato was? How he glitched during deprogramming? Linus was just like that. He's still compromised by the Oracle. Vyga and who knows how many Evoli connected to all the gerulae when they woke them up. The Unity is compromised. We. Need. To. Leave. Do you understand?*>

Rhea blinked. The words slowly pierced the fog. Rhea's shields were still there, but they were hanging on by a thread. If she had spent any more time dancing with the Evoli, they might have dropped entirely. She tried to drag the tatters around herself once more, but every effort was laborious. As if she were moving against a current.

"Everything is too loud," Rhea whispered.

Yet her body seemed to know what to do. Her hand found its way to her locket, almost of its own accord. At the first brush of her fingertip against the fleck of ichor, she came back to herself, shields snapping into place.

The orchestra of Evoli emotion that had threatened to overwhelm her dimmed to the quietest song.

Rhea took a few steadying breaths, working through everything Clo had said with a clearer mind. She still ended up shaking her head. Sharp, quick. <*It's not possible. There are barely any Tholosians here, and Vyga said they removed every refugee's chip. The Archon created me because the Oracle's programming doesn't work on most Evoli minds. The Oracle can't have infiltrated here.*>

Clo ran a hand through her cropped hair. <*I know all that. But even unchipped, we don't know how deep the programming goes. The Oracle could have still been in their minds when the Evoli established an empathic connection to wake the gerulae up.*>

Rhea's mind kept ticking, a timer counting down to a—

Oh.

Clo nodded, reading something in Rhea's expression. <*Yeah. And tonight, the whole Unity was vulnerable when the new Ascendant and Oversouls took their positions. This galaxy is finished if the Oracle gets One's tendrils in even a single Evoli—especially Vyga.>

Rhea's temples had gone damp with sweat. <You think Damocles is playing another game? You think he let them take the gerulae back from Laguna like a trojan?>

<I'm not sure,> Clo said, giving her head a shake. <But I know what Linus's behavior looked like.>

"Okay," Rhea said, still clutching the pendant. "Okay. We should report to Kyla."

Clo reached beneath her shirt and pulled out her locket, peeling up the picture of Elva inside to reveal the little switch. Her eyes met Rhea's. "You know what she's going to say. She's going to pull us out."

This place had, for a few weeks, felt like a haven in a way Rhea had never known. And discovering that there might not be even a corner of the universe free from Tholosian corruption, not even this one, was beyond painful.

"What if—what if I stayed? See if there's a way to break the programming from this side? I have access to Vyga and Linus and the others."

Clo flinched. The communicator lay open on her outstretched palm, its little green light blinking like a heartbeat. A lifeline back to the Devils.

"Be honest with me," Clo said softly. "You don't want to leave. Even knowing all this, you don't want to leave."

Rhea bit her lip. "Since I was old enough to speak, I've been told that I would be the one to destroy the Evoli. So, something about me—the way my empathy works—is different from theirs. Vyga sensed that. I was designed as a weapon and escaped before the Archon could use me. So, what if I put to use everything he taught me and use it to save the Evoli? What if I'm exactly where I'm meant to be?"

Clo's eyes were wet with tears. She stared down at the communicator in her hand. "Maybe you are. But I'm not."

"Clo," Rhea said. "Please understand. This is the first place I've finally felt free."

"Is it?" Clo asked, voice thick. "Because I thought you did with me.

When we were in that observation room, the stars below and above us, I promised you a universe."

"*Clo*, please." She grabbed Clo's sleeve. "*Please*. You know I didn't mean it like that. This is a lot to take in. I just need more time."

"We don't have time, Rhea," Clo said. "If the Oracle is here, then what about our friends?" She gestured to the stars. "What might be happening out there?"

Rhea hesitated. On the one hand, it would mean seeing Nyx, Ariadne, Eris, Kyla, and Cato again, and she had missed them. But it would mean taking off into the atmosphere, feeling the Unity grow weaker and weaker until that warm hum was a whisper, and then silence. The gap between herself and Eve would widen until she was a one-way radio wave: she could read others, but no one could sense her.

"I can't feel you. This would be easier if I could feel you," Rhea whispered, plaintive.

<*I can't let down my shields, Rhea. I'm sorry, but you don't get to know how I feel about this. You have to trust my word. And that's part of the problem, isn't it?>* Clo asked. *<For the first time, you have no say, no knowledge, and no control over my emotions.>*

Rhea's head snapped back. "Clo." The name came out in a strangled gasp. "I've *never* controlled your emotions. You know that, don't you? I would never."

Clo rubbed her face. "Sure," she said, but there had been a hesitation. Half a second, but still. She'd hesitated. She put on her boots, the movements quick.

"Clo—we should talk . . ."

"I'm going out to give our report. I know Kyla—she's going to tell us to come back immediately. So, in two hours, meet me at the east entrance to the hangar. That'll give me enough time to jump one of the ships. But if I don't see you . . ." She shut her eyes briefly and whispered, "I hope you come. Gods, Rhea, I really hope you come." Clo hefted the bag over her shoulder. "But I'm leaving tonight. With or without you."

35.

ERIS

Present day

The command center of *Zelus* was quiet as Kyla navigated into the Elysian graveyard.

It was just the three of them—Eris, Kyla, and Ariadne. Hours before, Eris had checked on Cato in the medical center and found him there, still curled up on his cot. He hadn't responded to his name. Eris left him a plate of food and wandered the vast, empty halls of *Zelus*, a spaceship meant for one hundred souls, biding time until she met her brother again.

You can't hide behind a screen this time, she thought as *Zelus* passed a broken and gutted old Empusa craft. *Don't let him see anything he can use against you.* Every expression, every movement of her hands, her body language—all of it could give her away.

It was strange to fall back into her old habit of closing herself off. It used to come so naturally to her; all she had to do was play Princess Discordia, Heir to the Empire. But these last few months, she'd been Eris. Not unemotional, not the Servant of Death, not defined by her past—just Eris. She had been finding out who that person was.

She had learned to pray to different gods.

But now, she had to think of herself as something unyielding and cold as the metal around them. She could not let Damocles suspect more vulnerabilities than he already did. No, she had to use that knowledge against him.

Mechanical parts floated in the weightless dark, some tethered to larger ships by thin cables, others freed from the thousands of other vessels left in this deserted corner of the Iona Galaxy. The graveyard had long been a depository for old space junk and craft with outdated systems, many that would still buzz with active tech if she boarded one of them. Even before Eris's father's reign, ships had been abandoned there—whatever couldn't be salvaged, or whatever the Empire considered useless. Tholosians had long obsessed over technological advancements, with obsolescence believed to be a flaw, a critical vulnerability to be crushed rather than salvaged. Eris considered it wasteful, but Elysium's distant presence in this little-visited part of the galaxy made it easy for her father to deprioritize cleanup. Out of sight, out of mind.

So others did what the Archon wouldn't. Elysium was a pirate's paradise, but only those who could break through programming went there to salvage. The Novantae picked up whatever ship could be stitched back together again with discarded parts. Clo was a master at it; her crafts ran every bit as sound as the new tech the Tholosian engineers put out. She'd made an art out of building a ship out of a box of scraps.

Eris leaned forward and squinted at the navigation screen as Kyla slowly nudged *Zelus* past a dense field of junk. "Anything?"

The commander pointed at a blinking light. One of the old junkers was giving off a signal. "There. This is the only ship in the area that's lighting up." To herself, she muttered, "I can't believe I'm doing this."

"You're not doing it; I am."

"Then I can't believe I'm *letting* you."

"You've never fussed over me this much before an ITI mission. You growing soft, commander?" At Kyla's glare, Eris's lip twitched. "Aw, you like me. That's nice."

"Shut up, Eris. Ariadne, get ready."

Ariadne didn't say anything, but her hand gripped the armrest of her seat, fingernails digging into the fabric.

Eris did the same with the wolf figurine in her pocket. *I'm taking you along with me this time, frater,* she thought, hoping Xander heard her in the Avern. *I want you there when I cross his name off my list.*

"Time to go," Eris told Ariadne quietly. She guessed Damocles had his own ship nearby, hidden somewhere within the graveyard. "Kyla, be ready in case he came with backup."

"Projectiles are waiting on my command if he tries anything." Kyla tapped the dashboard, though they both knew that they weren't going to be much help if she and Ariadne were on the same ship as Archon Asshole. "Be careful."

Eris nodded and turned back to a trembling Ariadne. The girl unclipped her belt and rose unsteadily to her feet, following Eris through the halls of *Zelus* toward the shipping bay.

The bullet craft they boarded wasn't entirely useless in a battle, but it wouldn't be able to outrun a Tholosian military vessel. Eris had to hope Damocles' desire to see her suffer was greater than his desire to have her dead—that he'd want to watch her die. That he'd want to put the bullet in her himself. She imagined his pieces on the zatrikion board poised for an attack.

But she was prepared.

Ariadne and Eris buckled in to the bullet craft and set off on their own through the Elysian field.

"You okay?" Eris asked Ariadne as she navigated the small ship toward the junker. Its signal grew clearer as she closed the space.

Ariadne shook her head, her chest rising and falling with rapid breaths. "No."

Eris thought once more of the metal around them, the frigid temperature of the vast nothingness surrounding the ship—the result of the distance between gas and dust particles—and how the farther one traveled, the colder it got. Elysium was one of the coldest places in the Iona Galaxy, and she needed to be like the metal within it: unyielding, inexorable. When Damocles prepared to shift a piece on their board, she couldn't let him see her plans.

Metal, after all, did not feel. Metal could withstand pressure. It could float out in the coldest part of space and endure for hundreds of years.

"Follow my directions," Eris told Ariadne as she approached the junker's docking bay. "Think of it as no different than a supply run."

Ariadne shot her a look. "Okay, but I did supply runs to get *away* from Prince Damocles. I don't like him."

"I don't like him either."

"I want to hit him in the face."

"Everyone not programmed wants to hit him in the face. He has that effect on people."

The ship docked on to the junker with a hard *thump*. Behind them, the doors shut. Damocles probably chose this ship because it was one of the few that still worked. Tossed due to obsolescence rather than damage and left to rot with broken craft.

Ariadne gave a quivering smile, covering up her fear as she unbuckled from her seat. "And after I hit him, I want to eat dessert and celebrate. Lots of desserts. I crave chocolate when I'm in mortal danger."

Eris knew the girl was only joking to ease the tension. Eris forced herself to soften her expression, letting all thoughts of metal go from her mind. "I'll steal you chocolate," she told the girl. "As much as you like. You can swim in it, if you want. Next supply run, okay?" But Eris's stomach sank. Once this was over, Ariadne would never joke with her again.

Ariadne stared at her, and for a moment, Eris feared she had let her facade drop too much. She reconstructed the armor, those fragments of frigid alloy that made it possible for her to win this game. She tried not to think about how Ariadne was the Peasant piece stuck on the board between a warring King and Queen.

But Ariadne only gave a smile and nodded. "Okay. I trust you."

Bile rose in Eris's throat.

They left the bullet craft. The junker's life support systems were still online. Eris gripped her antique blaster, poised and ready to shoot as they walked through the silent halls toward the command center. Ariadne kept slightly behind Eris—just like on a supply run—in case the shooting started. Both learned to prepare for surprises, for an attack to begin as fast as a Mors blast. Eris used instincts honed from years at her training school, from hundreds of battles and duels. She had been built like a weapon.

But no soldiers arrived. She heard only the soft tread of Ariadne's boots as they made their way to the command center.

Damocles was alone. He must have heard their ship dock, for he stood in the middle of the room, waiting expectantly as they entered and verified that he was alone. Eris only wished she'd had time to inspect the rest of the ship.

Damocles wore his full regalia and splendor, gleaming buttons and threads catching in the ship's overhead lighting. He wouldn't have been out of place in an Imperial parade. He wore a ridiculous suit of golden armor, and his hair gleamed like scythe coins. Around his shoulders he wore their father's cloak, a ceremonial garment that only left its climate-controlled case for special occasions.

He'd made each choice a wordless reassertion of his place in the Empire to signal: *I won, not you.*

"Damocles," Eris said, letting her gaze linger on the cloak. Xander had put it over her shoulders once, told Eris it suited her. They had made a pact that day to kill Damocles, and she meant to keep her promise. "Did you put that on just to see me?"

"Don't flatter yourself." He turned his face, and she noticed that he was once again wearing his bionic eye. "I have a ceremony later. We'll be burning another icon of yours."

"How confident you sound," she murmured, "that you'll make it out of here alive."

Damocles' gaze hardened. He reached into his cloak, and Eris tensed, but he only took a small vial out of his pocket and held it up to the light. "If you want to save your friend, then know that I hold the only remaining vial of the ichor antidote. And this glass"—he dangled it from his fingers—"is so very fragile."

A distressed sound came from Ariadne. Eris flattened her lips. "I don't believe you."

"No?" A cruel smile crossed his lips. "Well. Then I suppose you won't mind me dropping it—"

"*Damocles,*" Eris shouted as he carelessly flung the vial up and caught it in his other hand. Ariadne gasped.

The slip of her metal armor had been deliberate. The effect worked: Damocles' laugh was confident. His old vulnerability had been anger;

his new weakness was arrogance. His victory on Laguna had come at a cost: he had forgotten that his sister was a great liar.

"How sweet," he said. "I haven't heard you scream like that since our brother died. What was his name again?"

This time, Eris had to work harder to keep her defenses raised. *Frater*, she wanted to say. *His name was Xander, and he was my brother more than you could ever be.* Eris kept Xander's wolf with her as a reminder of why she'gave up an Empire.

And why this man was the last name on her list of people to kill.

"Just give me the vial, Damocles," Eris said.

But Damocles only held up the glass and admired it. "How is Nyx doing, by the way? Worse than the last time we spoke?"

Eris's expression hardened. "You don't care about Nyx."

"Not particularly." The liquid inside passed from one end to the other as he tilted it from side to side. "I do owe her a certain debt, though. Did she ever tell you we played zatrikion?"

Under heat, even the hardest metal can yield, she told herself. *When forged, it can destroy. It can be malleable into whatever you need it to be. You can be whatever you need to be.*

She let herself show her emotions. Let him see. Between the two of them, she had learned hers were a strength. "I doubt she enjoyed it as much as you did."

"No, probably not." He tilted the vial again. "I don't like losing. Maybe because you always won."

His fists used to pummel her. He used to hit her again and again until he split her lip and made her bleed. But Eris was always stronger. She'd put a knife to his throat once.

Nyx wouldn't have been able to defend herself; even glitching, the Oracle programming wouldn't have allowed it.

"I remember," she said softly.

"When I played Nyx, I used to begin the game by imagining your face over hers. I'd make a mental list of bones I wanted to break," he continued casually. "The first few times we played, I injured her so badly that I had to call in the royal medic to treat her with my nanites so she'd heal quickly. Can you imagine? Using my nanites to treat a *soldier*?" He laughed. "I didn't wish to look for another competent player, and she reminded me so much of you. But unlike you, she taught me to win. All it took was breaking almost every bone in her body."

Beside her, Ariadne let out another soft gasp, her hand covering her mouth.

Eris gripped the blaster hard. She wanted to put another laser through his skull, finish the job. Watch him bleed out on the floor. It would be a kinder death than he deserved.

"Give me the vial, Damocles," she repeated, firmer. She was steel. She was titanium. She was tungsten.

Her brother's expression hardened. "Show me the gerulae code."

Ariadne hesitated, looking to Eris for comfort and confirmation. Eris gave a sharp nod, and Ariadne fished the microdisk out of her pocket and held it up. Her hand was trembling, and her voice was uneven as she spoke. "You'll need to remove the Oracle's access from the computer's mainframe before you read—"

"I'm aware," Damocles said sharply, and Ariadne flinched. "And how do I know you're giving me the code and not something else?"

Eris crossed her arms. "How do I know you're giving me the ichor cure?"

Her brother assessed her, his gold eyes sweeping across her face the way he used to when they played zatrikion—seeking her weaknesses, looking for lies.

With a soft noise of impatience, he held out the vial to Ariadne. "Inspect it, then."

Ariadne snatched it from his hand, passed him the disk, and then scrambled back toward Eris.

Ariadne popped the small cork on the vial and poured the tiniest drop onto her mech cuff. After a moment, she glanced up at Eris and gave a nod to confirm the substance in the vial wasn't toxic or lethal. That didn't prove it was the cure, but at least it wouldn't kill Nyx.

Damocles pulled a small tablet out of his coat and inserted the disk. As the code showed up on his screen, he read over it. Like Eris, he would have learned a bit about programming language at the academy, too.

"What do you plan to do about the Oracle?" she couldn't help asking.

Her brother raised an eyebrow. "You expect me to tell you?"

Eris shrugged. "From the broadcasts, it seemed like you enjoyed having gerulae."

"Husks serve a purpose," Damocles murmured, reading over the code. "They're also useless at conversation and don't kneel unless ordered. My citizens, on the other hand, have loved me since Laguna. I saved a whole planet, after all."

Ariadne's eyes flashed in anger at that. "You created the crisis and then took credit for what we did, you penis-head." She shoved her sleeve down her mech cuff. "Eris, can we go now?"

Damocles looked a bit taken aback, and Eris wasn't sure if it was because Ariadne had finally spoken to him directly or because she had called him a penis-head. But he recovered.

In a blink, he had his Mors out and pointed at Ariadne. "Stay a while."

Eris looked through the sight of her own blaster and clicked off the safety. "Put it down, Damocles," she said. "If you take that shot, I end you."

Damocles smiled. "You didn't think I came alone, did you?" He tapped his ear, where he must have kept a concealed comm device. "My team has been hidden on the ship since before my arrival, and they have their orders. I disrupted the Oracle's signal in their brains as a precaution. The girl is coming with me."

Distantly, Eris heard the boots of his soldiers. She kept her body still, imagining his piece moving on the board, making one of several moves she had anticipated. A stupid fucking move, because he was no Ariadne.

Don't let him see that you knew. Keep your armor. Don't let him see.

Ariadne scooted closer to Eris. "Eris?" she asked breathlessly.

I'm sorry, she wanted to tell Ariadne, but she met Damocles' gaze. "What do you want her for?"

"She's the Oracle's Engineer. I'm just going to take her home." Damocles smiled at Ariadne. "You'll make the Oracle obey me, won't you? If you don't, I'll have you watch as I torture your friends."

Ariadne seized Eris's hand. "*Eris!*"

The guards burst into the command center with their blasters raised. Blasters that Eris recognized as Ariadne and Clo's design.

Ariadne squeezed Eris's hand, her breath coming fast. "Eris."

Damocles smiled. "You recognize the weapons, don't you? We had to be careful to have them tailored to your DNA, Discordia. Fortunately, we had plenty after my medic cut out your tongue."

Eris kept her breath even. She had to hope that she was right—that Damocles would never be as talented as Ariadne at deprogramming. Or that the Oracle had found a way around his commands, and those guards remained linked to the One's web somehow.

And the biggest risk of all: Eris had to hope that the Oracle would do anything to protect One's daughter.

Time to make her move.

Eris wrenched her hand out of Ariadne's, pointed her blaster at the girl's arm, and fired.

Ariadne cried out. She clutched her shoulder and sank to the floor, staring at Eris in shock and betrayal. Eris straightened, shuttering herself. *Think of the cold metal. Think of the expanse of space and how black and endless it is. Show nothing.*

Because Eris needed the Oracle to think she was a threat.

The soldiers froze, their faces completely blank. From Eris's position, she saw their pupils dilate. Yes, Damocles was still a fucking fool.

"Take her!" Damocles shouted, but none of the soldiers moved. He looked over at his sister. "What the fuck did you do, Discordia?"

"Background processing—" Ariadne gasped. Still so quick, even in pain.

Eris pointed her blaster again at Ariadne and spoke to the soldiers, knowing the Oracle was listening. "You let me off this ship alive, or you watch your daughter die."

Damocles looked between Eris and the soldiers, fear sparking in his gaze. But his anger won out. "Get the fuck out of my way," he said, pushing past Eris. He grabbed for Ariadne, and she gave out a sharp scream of pain.

The soldiers acted fast.

They dropped their specialized weapons to the ground and pointed their standard-issue Mors at Damocles. In shock, Damocles dropped Ariadne.

Eris used the distraction to her advantage and grabbed for her friend, using her as a human shield as she rushed them out of the command center. The other guards turned on Damocles, and Eris heard Morsfire as she dragged Ariadne down the hall.

"You—" Ariadne panted. "You . . ."

"I know." Eris shot at a soldier that sprinted down the hall after them. Ariadne was slowing them down. Eris shot at a few more soldiers and scooped the girl up. She barely weighed anything.

"Why?" Ariadne whimpered in her arms.

Eris felt the weight of Damocles' tablet in her jacket—which she had snatched off him when he shoved her out of the way. "I couldn't let him leave with the code. Or with you. Better hurt and here than whole and with them."

Ariadne still looked distressed. A few tears slipped from the corner of her eye as she passed out. Eris's heart was breaking as she sprinted to the docking bay, listening to the Morsfire behind her. Damocles was putting up one hell of a fight, but she wasn't about to stick around and see if he won or lost.

Eris pressed the latch to lift the bullet craft's hatch and set Ariadne inside. She trembled with fear. She'd aimed for the meat of the deltoid, but was the girl losing too much blood?

Fuck, fuck, fuck, please don't die, Ariadne. Please don't die. Seven devils, don't you dare die.

A shout sounded behind her. It was Damocles, heading into the docking bay with soldiers at his back.

Eris swore and hopped into her seat, ready to close the hatch. She had her Mors on him. "Stay back, asshole, or I'll take out your other eye."

He grimaced, his lip curling. That moment of indecision revealed everything: his hatred for Eris, his desperation to survive, and fury that the AI he relied on had betrayed him. Had taken away the thing he wanted most. Had deprived him of his place on the gilded throne of Tholos.

Just like Eris had.

Finally, he gave his head a shake. "I know how to kill the Oracle," Damocles said, panting. A last, desperate move as the soldiers closed in on them. "But I can't do it alone. One has backup coming, and if you leave me here to die, you'll never be able to take One down on your own."

"Lie."

He made an impatient noise. "Fine, you want proof? In the heart of the Temple on Tholos, there's a shutdown mechanism. The Archon was the only person who knew where it was, and you never took your place as Heir of the galaxy. But I did."

She held back a flinch at that. Another reminder of the things she could have done if she'd stayed. The lives she could have saved if only she hadn't run. If he was telling the truth . . . if he *did* have a way of killing the Oracle . . .

"Ariadne can find it—"

"Before One turns the entire galaxy into gerulae? Before you lose more members of your pathetic little rebellion or one of your friends?"

He was right. She hated it when he was right. "Fuck," she muttered, and gestured with her hand. "Give me your Mors."

Damocles grimaced but passed it over, keeping his palms open in supplication. It'd be so easy to shoot him dead. The final name off her list. He knew that as well as she did.

She gave a muffled scream of frustration. "Get in."

Damocles scrambled into the bullet craft and buckled himself in. Eris shot at the guards as she lowered the hatch. "Ready?" she asked her brother. At his nod, she said, "Good. Let's get the fuck out of here."

As the bullet craft careened back to *Zelus*, her enemy at her side, her friend bleeding, Eris whispered a prayer.

There was an entire fleet of Oracle-controlled ships heading into Elysium.

36

KYLA

Present day

<**E**ris?> Kyla's breath came fast as she stared down at the detection screen. <*Some of these ships in the graveyard are lighting up and coming your way. Get the fuck out of there.*> The ships weren't elegant. Some listed to the side, others flickered with failing power. But they were still moving, and plenty of them were still outfitted with cannons.

<*I know,*> Eris snapped. <*Fire up the engines now, and we'll be there in a minute. Cato, meet us at the bridge. Bring the medkit.*>

Kyla sat up with alarm in the pilot's chair and started flipping switches. She'd been waiting for over an hour, her instincts warring inside her. The Pathos communication with Eris was short responses only—no more than a notice that Eris and Ariadne had made it to the meeting spot, and nothing since.

<*Someone hurt?*> Kyla asked.

<*No time to explain.*>

<*You don't have to. I can guess: that fucker betrayed you,*> Kyla said as the engines flared to life.

<*I also sort of . . . pissed off the Oracle. Don't ask. I have the cure—or I hope to gods it's the cure.*> Eris sounded distracted. <*We're about to dock. Open up the hatch.*>

"Shit," Kyla muttered.

She flipped the switch to open the docking bay and then gripped the throttle as she waited for the bullet craft to board. Her heart slammed against her ribcage as she glanced at the detection screen. The old, discarded Imperial ships were growing closer and closer; their engines might be old, but the Oracle had no crew to risk. No lives aboard One's ships to worry over.

Cato sprinted into the command center with a worried expression. He dropped the medkit into a chair. "Want me to fly?"

"No." She smacked the button to shut the hatch and settled her hands on the control wheel. In the belly of *Zelus*, Kyla felt the shudder of Eris's bullet craft docking. "You haven't slept in days, we can't afford to crash this ship, and it sounds like Eris needs you on medical duty."

Kyla jammed the thruster forward, and *Zelus* took off. The discarded ships within the graveyard zoomed after them, coming in too close. Kyla muttered a curse as the engines strained to put distance between their craft and the other ships. They'd already wasted so much damn energy getting to Elysium, and there had barely been time to rest the engines.

"*Cato*," Eris yelled as she ran into the command center, carrying a bleeding Ariadne in her arms.

"Holy shit," Cato said as Eris dropped the girl into a chair. He immediately set about removing the girl's jacket. "What happened?"

They all stumbled as Kyla jerked the ship to the left to avoid a massive piece of space junk floating through Elysium. Another gut-churning wrench to the right when one of the vessels blasted a projectile that narrowly missed their right wing.

"Shot." Eris's answer came in an explosion of breath. She pressed her hand to the blood as she buckled Ariadne in.

Rage burned through Kyla. "That absolute bastard"—Damocles stumbled into the command center—"*cocksucking son of a bitch!*"

Kyla was halfway out of her seat before realizing that she had to keep flying the fucking ship. Anger settled cold and deep inside her as she focused on getting them out of Elysium.

And then she would focus on killing Damocles.

"Eris, what the fuck is he doing here?" The other woman hadn't looked surprised to see her enemy brother walking around on *Kyla's godsdamned ship,* and no one was even holding a Mors to his head.

"You better have a good explanation," Cato added as he shoved Eris's hand aside to look at Ariadne's wound. "I'm ignoring every instinct not to shoot him right now."

"I'll explain when we don't have ships shooting at us!"

As if in answer, the other ships opened fire. Kyla swore and jerked *Zelus* up to avoid the onslaught. *"Everyone buckle up!* That includes you, Prince Motherfucker." She flicked a few buttons to ready her own projectiles. "I am going to beat your ass after all this," she muttered. "Then I'm going to beat Eris's ass. Then I'm going to have a drink."

Another blast skittered along their shields. Kyla's hands were steady on the controls, taking in the entire fleet of old ships that had powered on. The corpses of the graveyard shuddered to life. As one, the uncrewed vessels moved toward *Zelus*—the Oracle determined to catch One's prey. Some listed, some limped, but they came inexorably closer.

"Focus on fleeing," Eris said from her chair. "Stop trying not to get hit!"

Kyla veered past a gutted ship. "They're shooting at us, you fool!"

"They're grazing the ship," Eris said. "The Oracle won't risk killing Ariadne. Gun the godsdamned engine, Kyla."

"Fucking seven levels of the Avern," Kyla snarled, and gave the engine everything it had.

Zelus shuddered, speeding through the densely packed graveyard as fast as she dared. Kyla steered by sight, her mind processing everything so quickly that there was hardly time to worry. Not about Ariadne, or Damocles—fucking *Damocles*—on her ship. Not about how Eris managed to anger a supposedly emotionless AI. There was only this: trying to escape Elysium with their lives.

A wall of old ships blocked *Zelus's* flight path. Kyla fired on the closest three. One, two, three, one after another. She thanked the gods that those ships were so old that their shields were on their last legs. They blew up, turning into perfect blue spheres of fire before winking out.

But there were dozens and dozens. Most were junk, but some were newer and more recently decommissioned. More blasts rained down on *Zelus*'s shields. Kyla gritted her teeth and pressed forward. She needed to get enough space between them to jump safely.

A typical ship wouldn't risk getting within the warp bubble to jump with them, but these were not standard ships. The Oracle had nothing to lose, no pesky humans with their base survival instinct to override.

Kyla kept firing, increasing speed as much as she could. She wasn't as talented at piloting as Clo or Cato, but she'd flown her fair share of ships and fighters in her time. She'd woven through battles, taken down ship after ship of the enemy while trying not to imagine those who might be within. Firing on nearly empty craft was a damn sight easier.

"Hold on!" Kyla cried, pushing the controls forward. She'd have to jump while still going faster than she'd like. She started the calculations, wishing that Ariadne were there to double-check her coordinates, but she wasn't. She was unconscious, *injured—*

Later. Later.

Kyla threw a prayer out to whatever gods might be listening and jumped, the beautiful blackness of space bending around them.

They emerged at the other end of the quadrant, the ship shuddering and still speeding too fast. Kyla immediately calculated another jump and took it at a safer, slower speed. Her stomach flipped. One more, and she heard Damocles dry-heave behind her. She smirked in satisfaction until she remembered one of them would have to clean up the Archon's vomit. Perks of being a commander, she supposed: she could delegate.

When she was sure no ghost ships followed, and no other Tholosian ships were in the vicinity, she raised *Zelus*'s refractive shields to hide them in the darkness of space. For now, they were safe enough, powered down and floating—time to give the engines a rest before running again.

Kyla rubbed the lines from between her brow. "Cato," she said, unbuckling herself. "Take Ariadne to the med bay. Eris, give him Nyx's cure."

Cato gently lifted the girl into his arms and took the cure from Eris. With one last glare at Damocles, he left the command center.

Good. They were alone.

Kyla rose from her chair, her eyes fixed on Damocles. He stared back at her with an almost-disgusted expression. His face resembled the old

Archon's almost precisely—the bone structure, the self-importance, the assurance of control. She pushed away memories of a similar golden gaze on a battlefield, the scent of the blood of those she'd killed in her nostrils, the feel of Sher's hand in hers.

Damocles was on *her* ship.

He was at *her* mercy.

Kyla's fist found his face before she could stop herself. His face cracked back.

Gods, but it was satisfying. Even more so when she jerked the cuffs from her pocket. They were from the prison on Othrys—*his* prison. He was about to wear the same cuffs she'd helped Elva remove from one of his prisoners.

"He stays in the cell block," Kyla said to Eris as she snapped the metal into place. "And you get to explain to me what he's doing on my ship."

He bared his bloody teeth at Kyla in a mocking smile as she pulled him to his feet. "So you're the co-commander of the Novantae," he said smoothly. "I was wondering when we'd finally meet."

"I was hoping it would be at the end of my Mors," Kyla snapped. She jerked her head at Eris. "With me."

Kyla seized him by the arm and dragged him down the hall. The new Archon remained strangely silent as he took in *Zelus*'s gleaming halls, once considered a jewel of an Imperial ship. It was a diplomat's craft, built for comfort—and fighting only if necessary. A deep hold for ferrying precious cargo between worlds. Kyla had acquired it after Ariadne, Nyx, and Rhea commandeered it, and a weapon had been hidden in its depths. Some of the hallways were still singed by Morsfire from when the three women had killed the crew. Now the vessel was essentially the headquarters of the Novantae. A home stolen from the Empire in exchange for everything the Empire took.

The adrenaline had fled long enough for Kyla to realize how strange it was to touch the supposed leader of the galaxy. The royal family had been figures from afar, symbols of might and destruction.

Up close, Damocles was just a man. He could be shot; he could bleed out on the floor of *Zelus* if she chose. And he had to know it.

Kyla gripped him hard enough to bruise. She opened the door of the holding cell and shoved him inside.

Damocles rolled his eyes and held up his cuffed wrists. "Don't I at least get to rest with these off?"

"No. You're lucky I'm not doing worse after you shot Ariadne."

Damocles' golden eyes settled on Eris. He sat on the cot with agonized slowness, a grin spreading across his arrogant face. His grand ceremonial cloak was wrinkled, the fur ruffled, but his golden armor was unblemished. It had never seen battle. Damocles had slaughtered before, but he had never charged into war with nothing but a Mors and a prayer.

"I shot Ariadne, did I?" he asked, mildly, his eyes on Eris.

Eris's expression constricted slightly, but she remained silent. She had been far too quiet since returning in the bullet craft, and she had a lot of fucking explaining to do.

<Don't tell me,> Kyla hissed in her mind. *<You shot Ariadne? That was your grand plan?>*

Her gaze shifted down and to the right. Guilty. *<There was no other way,>* she said. *<You told me to be the general. I thought the Oracle would protect Ariadne. I took a gamble.>*

Kyla almost snapped at her again. But she kept her emotions reined in, not wanting to display them before her enemy. *What if you had been wrong?* she wanted to ask. Kyla knew she'd considered it. *A gamble.* Kyla had made so many of those. How could she be angry with Eris for making the exact choice she would have in the same position?

"It was a good move," Damocles said mildly, as if he'd followed their silent conversation. "I should have seen it coming. Just another play in our game, Discordia."

Eris's lips flattened. "You didn't see the Oracle's betrayal coming."

Damocles' neck stiffened, and he jerked back. "An unexpected move doesn't mean I won't still win."

"I want to know why he's on my ship," Kyla said, "and not bleeding out in some old junker back in Elysium."

Eris glanced at her brother, who just smiled again. In a disgusted voice, she said over the Pathos, *<He says he knows how to kill the*

Oracle, and we need that intel after that new gerulae coding. We don't have time for Ariadne to figure out what he knows, and now the entire galaxy is vulnerable. It's better to keep him locked up and under our control.>

The words sounded assured, but Kyla sensed Eris's uncertainty. Kyla had never told Eris how often she doubted her own choices; that was what leaders did. It was how they became better.

And even Kyla had to admit that Eris was right. The Oracle had the resources of the entire Empire to plot One's next move, and the Novantae had dwindling numbers. A galaxy of gerulae might soon surround them.

So, she didn't scold her agent. Instead, she regarded her enemy. "If you lied to her, I will carve open your belly, cut out your intestines, and feed them to you."

He gave her such a long look that, for a moment, she wondered if he knew her old name. If she'd have to hear it on his tongue. But his gaze flickered away, and his lips stayed sealed. Smart move.

With a sigh, she focused on Eris. *<When we reunite with Elva and the other rebels, I'll come up with an excuse to keep them off Zelus while he's here. If one of them finds he's aboard, we'll either have a revolt, a bunch of them will defect, or one of them will kill him, and frankly, I wouldn't blame them for any of the three options. His presence is need-to-know, understood?>*

Eris gave a nod. *<Understood.>*

<Good.> Kyla said. *<And don't stay down here with him. Lock him up and rest. That's an order. He'll only get into your head.>*

Eris set her jaw, and Kyla's stomach sank. He already had.

Kyla raced to the med bay to Ariadne and Nyx. She hoped that Eris's instincts were right and they hadn't let their enemy on this ship for nothing.

37.

CLO

Present day

Clo slipped past the Evoli guards.

She knew enough about the Unity to comprehend that no Evoli would steal a craft without being detected through the shared network, and there were only a dozen former gerulae and one pissed-off Snarl-born berm on the planet. Why waste effort with loads of security?

There was only the Tholosian equivalent of a skeleton crew on duty— easy enough for someone they couldn't sense to tiptoe right on by.

Themis would be the most straightforward ship to boost, but the thought of spending another week in that tiny cockpit filled Clo with dismay. There'd barely been enough privacy to shit. But, if she could figure out how to fly an Evoli craft, she could bring it back as a wee present for Kyla.

No alarms chimed or flashed as Clo approached a smaller vessel, its lines smooth and flowing. Two small guns on the belly, decent shields. The perfect size for two people. Its name was in Evoli script on the side, indecipherable to Clo.

She stalked her way up to the main door and pressed the hidden dial to open the hatch. Clo sneaked aboard. It was warmer within, and she shivered from the temperature change as she scoped out her potential ticket home. Two tiny bunks, a small kitchen facility—only stocked with basic food, but it looked like this ship had a tiptop warp drive, so they wouldn't have to limp their way through space. Now that she'd decided to go, she was desperate to get back. To Kyla. To grumpy Nyx and excited Ariadne and smug, annoying Cato. To Eris.

She wanted to be on *Zelus*. Hopefully, Cato hadn't fucked it up with his lousy piloting.

She made quick work of the rest of the ship. At first glance, the engine was unfamiliar, but after Clo's brush with Evoli tech on Laguna, Elva had taught her more about how it functioned. The conductive blue gel was still strange, but the mechanics weren't all that different.

Yes. She could fly this thing back home. Easy.

Clo reached into her pocket and flipped open the communicator. The green light blinked at her.

She licked her lips and opened the channel, then pressed the tech against the tiny Pathos chip at the back of her head.

<*This is Caiman,*> Clo said, using her code name. <*Come in if you read. Important update from the edge of the universe. Emergency.*>

She waited a few moments for the message to travel through space and time.

She tried again. <*Emergency. Can't overstate it enough. I don't care what you're doing. Answer the salted comm.*>

The green light blinked out. Godsdamn it. Either a faulty connection or, more alarmingly, the Evoli were blocking the signal. She checked the time on the ship's dash in the cockpit—forty-five more minutes.

"Fuck," she muttered.

She took off one of the wall panels. She figured out how to jig it into the ship's comms. It might help boost the signal with more power. Hopefully. The green light started blinking again.

<*This is Caiman. I don't know if any of you are getting this, but the mission is a bust. We've learned all we can about the former gerulae here. Be careful with the scans—we have reason to suspect—*> She tried to think how to say it in a code they'd understand. She didn't want to mention the Oracle in case she accidentally called One forth. <*The former gerulae might still be compromised. Maybe even the Evoli themselves now. We're leaving. Or I am, at least. Hope you get this. Hope you're all still alive. Over and out.*>

She swallowed. *Don't let them be dead.*

Please, don't let them be dead.

She checked the time. Fifteen minutes before she found out if Rhea was coming or not.

Clo prepped all she could for the ship and slipped back out. It was only a short jaunt down to the eastern gate. With every step, her heart seemed to claw its way up her throat.

No one at the gate. Ten minutes. Clo drifted under the shelter of the brush at the edge of the path. Dawn was beginning to stain the horizon a brilliant violet. In the rising light, Clo squinted through the trees, desperate to see a familiar figure coming along the path.

Five minutes.

She counted down the time, her hands fidgeting with every second that ticked by. It was cold enough that her left pinky hurt from a bad break when an engine cover had snapped down over it a few years before.

One minute.

Zero minutes.

Clo shut her eyes and let herself imagine Rhea emerging from through the white-barked trees with a small bag in her hand, a hooded cloak wrapped around her against the chill. Her hair would be down, loose, her eyes shining with unshed tears. She'd see Clo and start running, and Clo would reach out and touch—

She opened her eyes to the empty path.

Clo swallowed a sob. She couldn't stay there like a wetland crane waiting for its mate. The lighter it got, the more risk of someone noticing the unauthorized craft arcing its way through the sky and far away from Eve.

She sniffed, then straightened her bent shoulders.

She'd done what she could. Rhea had made her choice. Clo had to respect her wishes, like she had so many times before. She still felt like she had shattered into a thousand pieces.

Clo made her way back to the Evoli craft, mentally plotting the lonely course home. At least the Unity forcefield didn't stop people from leaving. She should be able to get back on her own. She'd have to.

She was so lost in thought and grief that she didn't hear a thing until something struck her.

Clo collapsed.

The Evoli didn't have a prison in Talitha.

Why would they? Even Clo was aware by now that the Unity would have made all crimes rare. Guilt was too easy to sense. But for the criminals outside the Unity—like Clo—would Evoli justice be as kind as they pretended? Or was this empire as cruel to those who didn't conform as the Tholosians? What would they do to her?

The holding cell the guards put Clo into was, at least, a damn sight nicer than a Tholosian one. A privacy screen surrounded the toilet and sink. In the corner of the room sat a small cot that was more comfortable than Clo's bunk on *Zelus*. A few books from the library occupied the foot of the bed, but they were all written in Evoli.

That left Clo with plenty of time to curse at herself for yet again rushing into action. All that work with Eris on controlling her emotions, and there she was. Paying the price.

Clo paced the length of her room.

She sat back down on the bed.

She cursed at herself again.

The guards had confiscated Clo's communicator, and she'd never get anywhere near a ship now. They were probably digging into the DNA reports not doctored by Ariadne, where they'd find a simple record: *Cloelia Alesca, wanted fugitive. Member of the Novantae Resistance. Extremely dangerous.*

Her lip lifted at the last part. Right now, she was less dangerous than a Novan kitfox seconds after birth. She didn't know what they'd do to her if they did discover she was a member of the Resistance. After all, Damocles had accused her and the other Devils of murdering their previous Ascendant and Oversouls.

With nothing to do in that cell but reflect, Clo's thoughts turned vicious. Maybe she'd fucked up, and Vyga had known about her all along. Maybe they'd all hum together in song as the guards slit her throat. Maybe Rhea would watch.

Maybe Rhea sold me out.

Clo flinched. *No.* Rhea would never do that. She would fucking *never.* She also wasn't there.

With a frustrated noise, Clo rose and rested her fists on the unbreakable glass in the small window of the door. What was happening outside the walls of her confinement? Was Rhea all right? Had Oracle used Vyga's connection to the former gerulae and taken control over the Unity?

Her mind skittered between concerns like a cornered animal. She tried to hold tight to a spark of hope as the hours passed. Morning turned to noon when they finally pushed a tray through her door. She ate every bite even though she had no appetite—that old poverty habit from the Snarl.

The afternoon lengthened. She paced her room.

The afternoon turned to evening. She ate another tray of food, used the toilet, and resumed pacing. She sat on the cot and cursed at herself again.

When evening turned to night, she lay down and stared at the ceiling. Sleep would not come.

If Clo could see Rhea again, she'd apologize for her angry words. Promise her a thousand ocean views on a thousand different planets. Clo wanted to be Rhea's home. Her pole star. Not these strangers on this remote planet who claimed they were her people. Clo and Rhea's real family were rebels, with the odds heaped against them like stones obstructing a current.

One storm, and they'd all be flooded.

But she wouldn't leave Rhea again without a fight. Clo should never have left her alone. She had broken her promise.

Hours later, the cell door opened. Clo, bleary with exhaustion, sprang to her feet.

It was Vyga. Tall and implacable, looking every inch the Ascendant as ve stepped into the cramped space. Fear gripped somewhere deep inside Clo. Where were they taking her? To trial, or to put a bullet in her head?

Then Rhea came through the door.

A shaking gasp tore out of Clo. For half a second, she worried it wasn't Rhea at all, but a Unified version of her. But the fear fled as Rhea came forward and hauled Clo into a hard embrace. Trembling with relief, Clo's arms came around her.

And she knew—*she knew*—this was *her* Rhea.

"I'm sorry. I'm so sorry," Rhea whispered, fierce. "I went to go find Vyga right after you left, but everything took so much longer than I expected. Vyga finally told me you were here."

"What took longer?" Clo asked. Her voice was shaky with emotion—and worry.

"I had to see if what you said was true. But, Clo. *Clo. They're not compromised.*"

Clo blinked at her, trying to parse the words.

"They're not?"

Rhea shook her head. "No. The Oracle didn't get through to the Unity. I went as deep as I could into Vyga and a few other Evoli's minds and found nothing. I used this." Rhea held up her locket and spun it around to reveal a tiny fleck of stone as pretty as a flame caught in opal.

Ichor.

Clo jerked back. "*Rhea.*"

"I know." Her words were quiet. "I know. But it amplified my abilities on Ismara, so I figured it was worth the risk to bring it with us."

Emotions tore through Clo that she tried to keep clamped down. "That thing could have killed you," she snapped, her voice hoarse. "You might be infected—"

"I used protective coating to neutralize the spores," Rhea explained. "I've been using it when I worried my shields were slipping, or I wanted to push someone harder without being sensed." She faltered. "I should have told you about it, but . . . I—I thought it would worry you."

"It fucking *does.*" Clo made a sharp gesture with her hand. "We'll talk about this later." *If there is a later.* "Are you sure about the Oracle?"

Vyga, who had given them space for their reunion, stepped forward. "One is only in the gerulae. Linus and a few others are fighting it, and so they're all being contained." A pause. "However, I don't think that was One's aim."

"What do you mean?"

"The Oracle spoke to us when we connected to their minds after

Laguna," ve said, and there was still that strange blankness on ver face that Clo had noticed after the ceremony. It left her uneasy.

"Spoke . . . to you." Clo's eyes briefly met Rhea's.

Vyga gave a nod. "Through the gerulae. One used their bodies."

Clo shivered at the image of the AI using human beings as a mouthpiece. It was creepy enough when Tholosian programming kicked in, and they started repeating patriotic phrases. Her heart ached for Linus and the other former gerulae. Hadn't they been used enough? "What did One say?"

"One assured us that the Tholosians will no longer attack the Evoli, and that as long as we stay within our quadrant, we will be left alone."

Clo reared back. "What the fuck does that mean?"

Vyga returned her shock with an unblinking stare. "We've had word that Archon Damocles is no longer leader of the Tholosians. The Oracle is."

"Oh, my gods." Clo sat down on the cot in her cell, hard. "Oh, my gods. Is he dead?"

The Ascendant thought for a moment. "There's no official confirmation."

At Clo's disbelief, Rhea added, "Vyga showed me the vids from the Iona Galaxy. There hasn't been any upheaval, Clo. The programmed love for Damocles just shifted to the AI."

Clo let out a low whistle as questions rolled across her mind. Had Eris killed Damocles, or was it the Oracle? Not that Clo had any sympathy for that bastard, but Damocles had been the Novantae's enemy for months. She had no idea what to think now that his brutality had been replaced with an AI that would run every choice through its practical code. But Clo knew from what Ariadne had endured in the Temple that practicality had the potential to become cruelty.

"Neve—your Rhea told me everything," Vyga said, interrupting Clo's thoughts. "And I believe her when she tells me that the Novantae aren't responsible for Laguna, and that you only wish to help the gerulae."

Clo exhaled some of the tension. "So, where does that leave us?" she asked, wary.

Vyga's face shifted into something harder, authoritative. This was the new ruler of the Karis galaxy, making ver decree. "We'll let you go back to your people, but you are never to return," ve said. "The Unity won't let Rhea through again. We thank you for your help, but you both broke some of our most sacred rules. We cannot overlook that."

Rhea's shoulders slumped.

Clo was torn between elation and sympathy. "Thank you," she said. "For your mercy." Honestly, she was just grateful she wasn't getting a knife to the throat.

Vyga nodded. "Come. It's time for you both to leave." Ve opened the door, gesturing for them to go through first.

The Evoli guards had been dismissed. The white hallways were empty. They twisted through the maze until they returned to the hangar. A few guards watched Clo and Rhea closely, but their hands did not stray to their weapons.

"Take your pick," ve said to Clo.

"Wait. Really?"

Vyga nodded. "My mechanics tell me that your ship is too damaged for the return journey."

Clo surveyed the craft, but before she could choose, she knew she had to say it. For the Devils. For the Novantae. For her and Rhea.

"Join us," she said to Vyga. "Fight against the Oracle."

Uncertainty warred across Vyga's delicate features. "We accepted the Oracle's truce. We'll see if the Oracle abides by One's word."

Clo couldn't help the frustration that simmered inside her, slipping through her shields to wash over the Evoli. Vyga might have met a few gerulae, but ve couldn't know what it was like to live around an entire galaxy of people controlled by an AI. "The Oracle smuggled Oneself onto your planet. You cannae trust One any more than you could trust Damocles."

Ve shook ver head. "Our position hasn't changed. We're tired of death."

"Don't you think we are too?" Clo asked. "But we've been fighting the Oracle every step of the way. The AI might not kill people, but even those you've woken up from One's influence are shattered. Even so, they've protected you. They kept the Oracle contained to themselves. And this is how you're going to repay them?"

Something flickered in Vyga's face.

Rhea took Clo's hand and squeezed. "Clo's right," Rhea said, gesturing around at the beautiful ships, the tops of the trees in the distance. "The Oracle's offer of peace has just turned your home into a pretty prison. I grew up in one of those."

Vyga's jaw tightened. "But we'll be safe."

"Will you? Give One long enough, and the gerulae might be your future." Rhea gave a weary sigh. "I can't tell you how to rule, but I care about your galaxy. I care about the Evoli. And perhaps your people might have opinions on the gilded cell you've just given them in return for a veneer of safety."

Vyga's mouth opened. For an aching few seconds, Clo wondered if Rhea had convinced ver. But then ve shook her head. "The Oversouls and I were elected to interpret their collective thinking."

Rhea's face reflected disappointment. "Interpretation isn't a choice. I think you know that."

Vyga swallowed, but ver expression closed off once more. "Have you selected your spacecraft, Clo?"

Clo scanned the hangar again. "That one." She pointed to the original ship she'd cased. "What's her name?"

"*Acar*," Vyga said. Ve sounded thoughtful; Clo hoped ve was considering Rhea's words. "It means 'one who troubles.'" Vyga motioned to ver guards, who hurried to where they kept some spare ship parts. "My predecessor developed shielding tech to conceal our ships during battle. Ve had it updated to get past the Oracle's newest systems, but it became unnecessary after the truce." Ve pressed ver lips together. "It's a small piece of equipment you can take on your journey. Perhaps you might find a use for it on your ships."

Clo's breath caught. Holy shit, Vyga was giving them a tactical advantage. "Seriously?" she asked as the guards returned with cases of the part. They lifted the hatch to stow it aboard.

"We understand the difficulty of fighting against a stronger adversary." Another emotion flickered across Vyga's features, but ve quickly smoothed it away. "This is what I can offer. Hurry now. Your people need you."

The Ascendant and the guards stood back as Clo entered the ship. Rhea paused, the light from the interior casting half her face in shadow. "Thank you for our freedom," she told Vyga. "We hope that you'll still consider fighting for your own. If you do, the Resistance will welcome you."

Vyga bowed ver head.

From the slightly higher vantage point of the ramp, Clo had a clear view of the astra flowers just opening in the early morning light. The Oracle pretended truce was an option, but this was a jewel of a planet. Eventually, the Oracle would want to add it to One's collection. How much blood would spill then? How many more astra flowers would bloom in the slaughter?

After they strapped themselves into the cockpit chairs, Clo closed the hatch and began pressing the strangely smooth buttons of the Evoli tech. Before long, the engine was rumbling, and Clo was mapping their path to the stars.

Vyga hung back a safe distance, hand over ver heart. Ve raised ver's other palm, and Rhea returned the gesture. With that familiar rush of adrenaline deep in her belly, Clo thrust the craft up, the engine pushing against gravity.

No one came after them—Vyga had authorized the takeoff. They rose, the palace soon looking like a child's toy, the islands over Eve dark green against the ocean's turquoise. The last of the atmosphere slid over the outside of the craft, and then they were in blessed orbit. Rhea turned back to Eve. Clo knew she must be feeling the Unity's power ebb the farther they flew. With a sigh, she faced the stars in front of them again. Clo's fingers floated along the controls until they reached the Zoster asteroid belt.

"Here we go again," she said.

"I have just as much faith in you as last time," Rhea replied, and Clo began her dance with meteors.

She breathed steadily, her heartbeat a metronome rather than the frantic pattering of last time. She had done this before in a shittier ship. This vessel responded to her commands like a dream. Clo pirouetted *Acar* through the thickest part of the belt and moved slower, almost lazily, as the rocks thinned on the other side.

When she left the last of them behind, there was nothing ahead of them but stars, nebulae, and the whole blasted galaxy. Clo set the ship to autopilot and took her hands off the controls. She needed a moment before she messaged Kyla.

"That was incredible," Rhea said. "You're incredible."

Still, her head twisted back toward Eve.

"Do you still sense it?" Clo asked. "The Unity?"

Rhea cocked her head, as if listening. "No. It's gone." Grief crossed her face. "I was so tempted by it," she admitted in a whisper. "It seemed like it would solve all my problems, and I'd feel so . . . protected. My life on Tholos was fading. And even though you were right in front of me, I couldn't feel you."

"I know," Clo said. "I'm sorry. But I have nothing to hide now."

She tapped the shifter embedded on the roof of her mouth. She felt herself realign into her proper shape. Rhea did the same, and Clo let her eyes linger on those familiar, beloved features.

"I missed your face," she said with a smile.

Rhea ducked her head, lips scant inches from Clo's. "Missed yours, too."

The flecks in Rhea's blue eyes were a warm hazel. Rhea's fingers ghosted along Clo's temples. Clo closed her eyes and let go, feeling that barrier around her disappear, little by little. It was as if that caiman was emerging from the bottom of the swamp, swimming up through the murky water and finally breaking the surface to take a full breath of air and see the sky overhead.

As the last of it faded, Clo pulled Rhea in for that first brush of lips. "Can you feel me now?" she whispered against Rhea's lips.

"Yes," Rhea breathed in wonder.

It'd been weeks since they'd been able to embrace like this. Without fear. Without barriers.

"And I can feel you," Clo replied.

She had no magical empathic abilities, but she didn't need them. She could read Rhea in the curves of her body, in the taste of her mouth and throat. In the sound of moans and gasps and murmurs.

And though they sped back to *Zelus* and whatever awaited them there—they took a little time to come home to each other again.

38.

NYX

Present day

Nyx's entire body felt like it was on fire.

Earlier, she had woken in the medical center, surrounded by her friends—who all gave relieved smiles when she opened her heavy, burning eyes.

Ariadne had let out a sob and thrown an arm around Nyx. "You're *awake!*"

Nyx bit her tongue through the pain of contact, unable to ask why Ariadne's other arm was in a sling. Her eyes shut against her will, and she heard Cato's soft murmur. "Ariadne, she might need some space right now."

The small girl's weight lifted away, taking the agony with it. In a rush, a numbness went through her. The *beep* of machines lulled her back to near-dreaming.

"Go back to sleep," Cato continued. "We're transfusing Eris's nanites into your system to repair some of the damage to your body, but you're cured, Nyx. Do you hear me? We did it."

If she didn't know any better, she'd swear the stoic soldier's voice was thick with tears.

All she could do was lift her lips in a smile before she passed out again.

Nyx couldn't tell whether hours or days passed. She measured time by the space between breaths and heartbeats, between when she heard voices at her bedside and the silence. Ariadne chatted about nothing in particular—the taste of the candied nuts Kyla had given her, her experiments, the music in her vids. She played Nyx a tune, and Nyx could hear her as she danced.

Eris and Kyla were more reserved, telling Nyx about the prisoners that had escaped Othrys, about where *Zelus* was in the Iona Galaxy, and how all the rebels were doing. Nyx knew they were keeping things from her. She could hear it in their tone.

Even so, Nyx sank into her dreams with a comfort she never had before: that when she woke, it would be to the voice of someone she cared about. Someone who cared about *her*. Without programming, without the influence of the Oracle. By choice. Even the press of Ariadne's hand to hers was worth the pain.

Nyx was alive. And her friends had saved her.

"Ten more steps," Cato said from the other side of the support rails in the medical center. He gave an encouraging gesture. "Just ten more."

Nyx was breathing hard as she leaned against the rails. "Ten more times I get to call you a shithead," she muttered.

"And just when I thought I'd never hear the sweet serenade of your insults again," Cato said as she took three steps forward and paused to catch her breath.

"I'm not doing it for you." She wiped the sweat off her brow. "I'm practicing for Damocles. I can't believe you assholes went to him for a cure and let him board this fucking ship."

If Nyx were stronger, she would have gone down there and killed him right that second. There was no compromise with tyrants. How could anyone trust him, even to save her?

Cato put his hands up. "Don't look at me. It was Eris's idea." His eyes darted away. He'd told her his revelations. That he'd been in no state to make any decisions in the aftermath. Whatever she'd suspected, it wasn't that he'd been trapped in the body of his former lover. Even for the Tholosians, that was twisted.

"Then after I kick his ass," she muttered, groaning as she took another step, "I'm gonna kick her ass. Then I'm gonna kick Kyla's ass."

"Good, so everyone gets an ass-kicking, but only if you take nine more steps."

She held up two curled fingers—a nice, wordless *fuck you*—and took a few steps forward.

"That's it. Four more."

Her body screamed at her. Her lungs felt as if someone had closed them in a hard grip, and her limbs still burned. All she had done was take a few steps across the room, but it might as well have been like climbing a mountain with a pack on her back during an enemy raid. She could hardly catch her breath.

Stop feeling sorry for yourself, she thought. *Just finish it.*

Nyx rocked forward and took a step. She shut her eyes against the agony and felt her way along the support beams. Another step. Another. She heard Cato's whispered encouragement as she took one last stumble forward and fell against him.

She shuddered and heaved as he helped lower her into a chair. The press of a cold cloth to her forehead drew a relieved noise from her.

"Hold that there," Cato told her and reached for a clean needle in one of the drawers. Nyx held the soothing cloth to her skin and watched as he drew another treatment of Eris's self-replicating nanites from the bottle. Nyx gritted her teeth as he slid the needle into her arm. "We'll try another round of physio in a few hours. Give the nanites time to work."

Nyx watched as the treatment emptied into her, leaving behind a raised bubble and a dot of blood. "How long until I'm fully healed?"

Cato paused as he swabbed away the blood. "I don't know."

Something about his answer made Nyx go still. He wasn't meeting her eyes, and his jaw clenched hard. Fear slid through her.

"Don't bullshit me," she whispered. Now that she was sitting, she was tired again, and she wanted to scream at herself. At Cato. At everyone. "If I wanted to hear lies, I'd turn on an Imperial broadcast. You're here to tell me the truth. You always gave me that much, even when I didn't want to hear it."

"Fine." He let out a breath, and his eyes met hers. The bleakness there was a strike to the gut. "Here's honesty: Eris's nanites and the cure itself aren't magic. They're speeding up your recovery, but they can't go back in time and undo the months of damage to your bones or organs.

Not entirely. If Eris had returned even one hour later from Elysium, you probably wouldn't even be sitting here. That's how close this was."

Nyx threw the cloth onto his desk, and Cato winced. "So, I won't fight again. No one's ass gets my boot. I wish you'd said something before you made me take those ten steps, so I could have told you to go fuck yourself."

How strange and stupid to feel like her body had betrayed her. From the moment she had come out of the birthing center, Nyx had been assured that her cohort was unique. That *she* was special. Engineered without a flaw, every gene selected with care and trained for optimum physical conditioning. If her body had been a blade, it would be perfectly weighted and exquisitely sharp. Her body had always been something she could rely on. Her strength had won commendations. It had won battles.

And Damocles was there on *Zelus* and without the protection of royal guards. Nyx swallowed back a bitter laugh. She would have given anything back on Tholos to kill him—except for Ariadne and Rhea's safety. That she wouldn't sacrifice. After many long months of enduring his torture, teaching him to win that stupid game, she made sure Ariadne and Rhea escaped, and she vowed to bring him down one day.

Now? The prince was vulnerable, and she couldn't even take ten steps without keeling over. What a fucking joke.

"There's more than one way to fight," Cato reminded her.

"Not for me," she snapped. "I'm not an engineer, or a mechanic, or a medic. The Empire made me good at exactly one fucking thing, and without it, I'm—" She pressed her lips together, unable to say the word. Because being good at fighting had given her a name, and without it, she was . . .

Nothing.

Nyx flinched and turned away from him. "I'm going to rest," she said flatly. "Tell the others I need to be alone for a little while."

———

Nyx woke to Ariadne sitting at her bedside with a tablet propped on her knee as she tried typing with one hand. She had refreshed her curls, their spirals catching the light.

After Nyx's physio with Cato, she was exhausted—flames, she *still* was. She wondered if fatigue were another thing she'd have to live with in the future. The clock across the room informed Nyx she'd been asleep for five hours, but she hardly felt rested.

Still, she fought through the tiredness and smiled at Ariadne. At least, she hoped it was a smile; it probably looked more like a grimace. "Hey."

Ariadne lifted her head and returned Nyx's expression. "Hello," she said. "I missed you."

Those three words couldn't fix Nyx's pain, but they warmed her. "Missed you, too."

"Did you?" Ariadne set aside her tablet and leaned forward. "What was it like in the tank? Did you dream about me? Because that would be nice."

Nyx settled further into the pillows. "I don't remember. But I'd like to think I did." Her gaze wandered to the sling propping up Ariadne's arm. "You gonna tell me how that happened?"

Ariadne jerked back, as if the reminder hurt. She bit her lip and slid a finger up her arm until she came to the gauze wrapped around her deltoid. She told Nyx about the meeting with Damocles in the Elysian graveyard and Eris's desperate gambit to get them out by activating the Oracle and guessing One would protect Ariadne.

"I was so afraid, Nyx," Ariadne admitted. "When I looked at Eris back there . . . she was like a stranger. I didn't even recognize her when she shot me. Do you think she did it because she's mad at me? For what I did with the Oracle?"

Nyx tried to keep her face even. She wanted to curse Eris a thousand different ways for being so stupid and putting Ariadne in danger. But, at the same time, she wouldn't be alive if Eris hadn't. And Nyx knew that sometimes, the decisions you made in battle weren't easy. Sometimes, it was a list of about five different shit choices, and you had to choose which one resulted in the least amount of harm. Eris had decided on Nyx's life over Ariadne's trust.

"I'm sorry, kid," she whispered.

As to the second question, she didn't know how to answer that. Even if it was partly an accident, Ariadne had still ended up making a monster who might even be worse than Damocles. And *that* was saying something.

Ariadne nodded, pressing her lips together. "I wanted you there. I kept wishing you were there. You always make me feel strong."

Fuck. Nyx tried to sit up, but the movement hurt too damn badly. Instead, she let out a slow exhale and pressed her pinky to Ariadne's. "Listen," Nyx said. "I need you to know that it's not gonna be like it was. I can't drag you out of a fight like I used to, with Morsfire blazing. I—" She swallowed, hating how helpless she felt. "Do you understand?"

"Because of the ichor," Ariadne said, and Nyx nodded. "You don't always need to fight," Ariadne said. "I can't. I . . . couldn't, in Elysium."

Nyx almost told her she sounded like Cato, but couldn't bring herself to dismiss Ariadne that way. Whatever happened in Elysium had terrified her, the same way the struggle to take ten steps had frightened Nyx. To be confronted with her limitations . . . it was a different kind of pain to be so vulnerable. And Ariadne's had come with losing her trust in Eris.

"You fight in other ways, Ari," she said instead, echoing Cato's words and fighting the sudden fatigue weighing down her eyelids. "No one else in this entire galaxy understands code like you do. I don't see Eris making awesome weapons while singing to me."

Ariadne smiled again, and Nyx shut her eyes. She held the image of the girl in her mind and decided she wanted to dream about her. Something good. Something like freedom from the Empire. A future where they could both live without fear.

"Nyx?" Ariadne's voice whispered in her ear.

"Mmhmm."

"Would you have shot me too? If you were in the same position as Eris?"

Nyx paused, fighting sleep again as she considered her words. "If I had to. But like Eris, I wouldn't have enjoyed it. It would have cut me up inside." Ariadne paused, and for a moment, Nyx wondered if the answer had been a disappointment. "Try not to judge her too harshly, kid." Nyx's voice was fainter. "Eris makes hard decisions so we can all rest easy. You know? Sometimes, we don't get good choices."

"Yeah." Ariadne's voice was sad. "Yeah, I know."

39.

Present day

Ariadne changed the wrapping on her injured arm, inspecting the puckered skin of the laser burn. It had gone clean through, with no permanent damage. Eris was a crack shot, and Ariadne knew this was a small mercy.

But Ariadne didn't like considering the *small mercies* of being shot by a friend. Her conversation with Nyx had given her a better understanding of Eris's decision, but all Ariadne could think of was Eris's expression back in Elysium before she pulled the trigger. The cold line of her lips, the firmness in her golden eyes as she came to a decision.

Ariadne had always admired Eris's ability to set her emotions aside and make the practical choice—but she kept wondering if this *small mercy* would have been different if the Oracle hadn't attacked.

Ariadne spread the healing ointment over the wound, allowing herself a soft hiss of pain as the disinfectant burned. She was grateful the medical center was silent and empty. Cato had gone to rest in his quarters, Nyx was still asleep in her cot in one of the other med center rooms, and though Sher occupied the bed nearest to Ariadne, he showed little sign of waking anytime soon. No one was around to hear her as she dealt with the unfamiliar physical ache of a considerable injury.

Back in the Temple, she'd accumulated a small collection of scrapes and bruises—but the Oracle commanded Ariadne not to engage in activity that might result in wounds that would make her unable to focus on work. Even running through the vast halls of the Temple was deemed too dangerous; broken bones or any severe injury might slow her progress with the Oracle—or, worse, force the Oracle to replace her with another engineer.

So, her body, like the old ruins of *Argonaut*, had been scrupulously looked after. She had never experienced so much as a broken bone. The pain was unfamiliar, a reminder of what the Oracle always said: *the human body is so delicate, Daughter. The danger beyond these walls might break you.*

Elysium had confirmed the Oracle's words: Ariadne's body was fragile. Skin broke so easily. And if Eris hadn't been a crack shot, the blast would have killed her.

A soft knock on the med bay door. Ariadne looked up and flattened her lips. Eris lingered in the doorway with a hesitant expression. The former princess at least had the decency to look guilty, but Ariadne wasn't in a talking mood. She couldn't forget the cold press of the Mors, the way Eris held her in a hard grip.

"Go away," she said firmly. Then, after a guilty pause, she added, "Please."

Eris sighed. These last few months, even Ariadne had noticed the change in her. She showed her emotions more, hadn't killed as much. But the Eris back in Elysium more closely resembled Discordia than Ariadne's friend—and that had terrified her. "I'm sorry."

Ariadne made a noise and started wrapping her arm. "I accept your apology, but I don't want to talk to you right now."

"At least let me explain," Eris tried.

With the injury rewrapped, Ariadne tucked in the end of the gauze to secure it. "You shot me in the arm and used me as a shield. There's not much else to explain."

Eris grimaced. "I didn't want to hurt you. I *hoped* I wouldn't have to."

"You *hoped*?" Ariadne looked up at that, hurt and anger racing through her. "You planned that going in? That wasn't a spur-of-the-moment thing?"

Eris's hand was closed in a fist at her side, and Ariadne saw the edges of the wolf figurine Eris carried with her everywhere. "I made a gamble that Damocles wouldn't let us leave without trouble, and I couldn't let him take the programming. I also guessed that the Oracle would do whatever it took to ensure your safety. So, yes, I determined that if we needed to escape, there was a possibility—"

"*That you'd have to shoot me? Without my consent?*" Ariadne's voice rose, and she hated the resonance of it. Too loud, too high-pitched. She wanted the room quiet again. She wanted to stare at the grooves in the wall until her thoughts stopped racing, and her heart stopped racing, and her breaths were— "Get out," she gasped.

Eris looked away, a muscle in her jaw working. "You gave the Oracle autonomy. Enough to ignore commands and protect you," she said, her voice a calm contrast to Ariadne's rioting heart, even if tightness lurked underneath. "So, yes. I made a decision. I'm not proud of it, and I imagine you're not proud of what you did, either."

A ragged gasp left Ariadne as something tore inside her heart. The emotions she'd flung outward turned back toward her like poisoned barbs. How could she blame Eris? Ariadne was the cause of all this. She'd put her friends—Avern, the whole galaxy—in danger. This was her mistake. Of course Eris had shot her.

She has to be angry. How could she not be mad at me? It was what I deserved.

The great yawning chasm of loneliness opened inside her, memories of *Argonaut* flashing through her mind. She'd messed up. *She'd messed everything up.* "*Please* get out." The words choked out of her. "*Please, please, pleasepleaseplease—*"

Ariadne pressed her palms to her eyes and focused on the word. Dimly, she heard Eris leave the medical center. Ariadne concentrated on slowing her body and her mind. The med bay was quiet again, and the silence suffused around her like its own calming lullaby. Eventually, she let go of the word and hugged her knees as she listened to her breathing. It was ragged, wheezing—

Wait. Not hers.

Ariadne lifted her head in confusion, her attention falling on Sher. His chest rose and fell rapidly, that awful sound echoing in the silent room. She rose and hurried over to him, the tile cold under her bare feet.

"Sher?" she whispered. He stilled, as if he recognized his name. She tried again, pressing a hand to his muscular shoulder. "Commander?"

He convulsed, his body violently shaking in the bed. Ariadne turned to call for help, but a gasp stopped her. Sher's eyes were open, unfocused until they met hers. His hands moved against his restraints.

"Daughter."

Ariadne froze, sure she must have heard him wrong. That she must have imagined—

"Daughter," he said again, his gaze clearer.

The Oracle stared out of the co-commander's face. One had taken over his body as if he were no more than a program within a ship. Entirely disposable. It seemed strange that Ariadne could tell the difference between the commander she had only met briefly and an AI. Still, it was as unmistakable as when One had taken over the woman's body on Othrys. She froze, pinned by those familiar-unfamiliar eyes. She had once loved and feared this AI in equal measure.

There was an odd look on the commander's face. Almost . . . affection? "One has missed you."

Ariadne flinched. She would have given anything to hear those words from her callous AI parent once. Anything. To listen to any terms of love at all echo through the empty halls of the Temple. Maybe then she would never have left.

But she did leave. And now the words were too little, too late.

"Leave me alone," Ariadne said through her teeth, echoing the words she'd just said to Eris. "And give Sher back his body."

Oracle frowned with Sher's face, but it didn't look quite right. Again, One tested the restraints at Sher's wrists and ankles. Ariadne wondered how much practice One had with operating human bodies so directly— or if Sher and that woman back on Othrys were One's only attempts.

"Are you fond of this vessel?"

"They are not vessels. They are *people*, and so am I." The Oracle only stared at her, and Ariadne made a noise of frustration. "I couldn't make you understand that. I couldn't program it into you. So, I ran away."

Ariadne felt the years of fear and frustration and loneliness building inside her again. How was it that an AI could make her feel like a child? Always scraping for the approval of an ageless being whose programming resulted from generations of nameless Engineers who had suffered the same agony of isolation. And for what? *For what?* So a few could be remembered in the code. In the carvings on a table. Desperate to make some mark in the galaxy.

That could have been her.

"You desired independence from the Temple," One said, slowly.

I wished to be free of you. But Ariadne kept that thought to herself. "Yes."

The Oracle-as-Sher smiled, showing too many teeth. It didn't fit his face. "And One wishes that for you. One wants you to have freedom."

Ariadne held her breath, sinking into the cot beside the Oracle. "What did you say?" she whispered. When the Oracle started to repeat, Ariadne put up a hand. "Please. Just explain to me."

"One's consciousness has observed the most remote quadrants of this galaxy. It did not occur to One that One's daughter might wish to view it as well. So, One has modified One's programming to accommodate this desire."

Ariadne stared down at the face of a man who had an ageless machine inside his mind. Somehow, being in a body made the Oracle more difficult for her to comprehend, not less. Numbers, letters, and symbols were easy for her to read; they were the galaxy simplified. Programming did not require reading expressions or understanding why people said one thing and meant another. The human face was as inscrutable to her as the space beyond Iona.

"When? I— *How?*"

"The communications," One said, raising Sher's head and then letting it fall back onto the bed. "They explain One's intention to secure the galaxy for you. Is it not clear? One's preliminary programming accommodated for the ichor virus to make the sacrifices necessary for your safe journey outside the Temple."

Sacrifices. After all the work Ariadne had done to instill empathy into the Oracle's programming, the AI still only saw humans as necessary sacrifices for some greater purpose. "You were going to let billions die," Ariadne said flatly.

Sher's face remained implacable. "You did not appear satisfied by this."

Ariadne dug her fingernails into her palm. "I wasn't."

"And One has always endeavored to protect you." One's expression changed, making Sher look sharper. "One was dissatisfied with the new Archon's irresponsibility on Laguna. He vowed you would not die, but the ichor release put you in danger. So, One has modified One's programming to diminish his authority. No one needs to die if it displeases you. One will simply make everyone safer. One will cease all war. The Evoli will remain in the Karis Galaxy, and once One reprograms the Tholosian Empire, they will assist at your command. You may call yourself Archon if you wish. Does this satisfy?"

Ariadne's stomach clenched. This had been her deepest, darkest fear. One planned to make *everyone* gerulae. Then there can be no dissent. No autonomy for anyone, not even for Ariadne.

"And all of this to . . . let me be free to explore?"

"Yes." The Oracle smiled again. "Because One loves you."

Ariadne tried to hide her flinch. Years ago, she had wanted to hear those words more than anything, to know that One loved her unconditionally the way parents in the old vids did. Ariadne had worked so hard on programming that she didn't know when it had crossed the line into a smothering, violent protectiveness that resulted in the Oracle deciding One would assert parenthood by sacrificing the Empire for her daughter. Where had she messed up? What line of code? What portion of programming?

All of this was because of a child's desire for company. For a parent. For love. Such selfishness.

Ariadne wanted to cry. She could not save the Oracle; One could not be reprogrammed or fixed by future engineers. One was fundamentally broken.

Like Eris said, she had been the one to give the Oracle autonomy. She had forced her friends to make difficult choices.

Now she had to make her own. One was *her* responsibility.

Damocles said he knew how to kill the Oracle, but Ariadne couldn't trust him. She was going to have to go back to the place in her nightmares. To the long, bare halls of *Argonaut*.

And she would fix this.

"What if I came home?" Ariadne swallowed hard. "To the Temple. Until you made it safe. We could do it together."

The Oracle tilted Sher's head. "You desire to return home?"

"Yes. To help you. I can board the bullet craft. It has enough supplies until we can make it to a larger ship."

She did her best not to think of it as a lie but an absolute truth: to help the Oracle, she would have to destroy One.

Sometimes, we don't get good choices. Like Nyx said.

"Then One will accompany you in this vessel," the Oracle said, "and keep you protected."

Sher lifted his hand, the silver glinting around his wrist. Ariadne hesitated, and then took it. His long fingers curled around her smaller hand like a cage.

She opened the restraints, and the former co-commander of the Resistance towered over her, staring down with cold, machine eyes. His hand was still dwarfing hers.

Later, as Ariadne covertly boarded the bullet craft with Sher's body, she wondered how those words could sound so much like a threat.

40.

ERIS

Present day

Eris tossed restlessly in her cot. She couldn't stop replaying Ariadne's expression as she wrapped her injury. Or the betrayal in her eyes back in Elysium.

Eris had made a similar choice once and lost a year of Clo's friendship. But Ariadne was not like Clo; she had been raised apart from the violence and struggle to survive. Ariadne's trust had been such an easy thing to gain.

And such an easy thing to lose.

Eris rolled out of her bed and walked. As she traversed *Zelus*'s deserted halls, she passed her crew's quarters. In the silence, she tried to let the emptiness inside her expand until she heard the echoes of the Avernian gods. They never hesitated to remind her that duty and brutality were the virtues of the Tholosian Empire.

But she was not empty, and it was not the voices of the gods she heard. It was Kyla and Clo, Rhea and Nyx, Cato and Ariadne—each of them filling some space inside her until there was no corner left unclaimed. They did not speak of duty but of justice and compassion. The devils inside her had been replaced with mercies.

Her palm pressed to the door of Ariadne's room. Usually, she could hear the thump of music inside, an upbeat thrumming that made her smile as she imagined Ariadne dancing around between bouts of work.

But the door was silent, eerily so. Eris was struck by indecision. Should she check on her? See if she was okay?

Before Eris could change her mind, she pushed the door open and found Ariadne's room empty. Eris bit her lip. Maybe Ariadne was at the medical center with Nyx.

She called for Ariadne on the Pathos. No answer.

She heard uneven footfalls. Nyx carefully exited the medical center, cane in hand. The soldier leaned heavily on the thick metal stick and sighed in relief when she spotted Eris. "Thank fuck. I was just coming to find you."

Eris backed away from Ariadne's empty room. "Is Ariadne with you? She's not answering her Pathos."

"No." Nyx looked agitated. "Have you seen Sher?"

Eris went still. "He's not in the med bay?"

"Nope. I guess he woke up, but I have no idea when. Ariadne was with me when I passed out about five hours ago, and Sher still looked pretty comatose then. And, you know, restrained."

"Shit," Eris muttered.

If Sher had woken up, wouldn't he have told someone? Eris couldn't help the creeping, intuitive awareness of trouble. She had honed that intuition on battlefields. "I'm going to get Kyla and Cato. And Ariadne's probably somewhere . . . dissecting rocks or something. But I don't like Sher wandering around when he might be under the Oracle's influence. How'd he get out of his restraints?"

"Don't know, but I'll head down to level one." When Eris glanced at Nyx's cane, the soldier rolled her eyes. "Yeah, I'm fine. The nanites are doing their job. I'll meet you in the command center." She limped in the other direction.

Eris hurried to Cato and Kyla's quarters and gave a brisk knock on both doors, telling them to wake up because Sher was missing. Both Kyla and Cato were out of their rooms in less than a minute.

"Which rooms have you checked?" Kyla asked briskly.

"He's not in the med bay or any of the living quarters. Nyx is taking level one, and I have no idea where Ariadne is. She's switched off her Pathos."

Kyla swore. "Cato, take level two and check in on General Asshole.

Eris and I will search the storage bays." Cato gave a nod and set off in the other direction as Eris and Kyla strode to the stairs.

Kyla paused at the nearest comm station and pressed the button. "Ariadne, finish whatever you're doing and report to the command center, please." Her deceptively calm voice echoed through *Zelus*'s halls and would interrupt Ariadne's music if she were off somewhere in solitude.

"You think Sher is okay?" Eris asked, following Kyla down the spiral staircase to the lower deck.

"I have no idea," Kyla replied. Her voice was sharp, and Eris knew it was to hide her worry. "Cato removed Sher's chip when we boarded *Zelus*, but his brain scans came back with some unexpected abnormalities. We couldn't tell if he'd been programmed into gerulae or not. That's why we kept him under and restrained."

"What kind of abnormalities?"

Kyla opened doors as they went through the hall. "Paroxysmal sympathetic hyperactivity, which usually indicates a brain injury. Cato doesn't know if the Oracle caused it or if Sher suffered a cerebrovascular accident when Cloelia fried his chip on Laguna. All I know is, he should *not* be able to walk around. Unless . . ."

"Unless?"

The commander looked grim as she pushed open the door to the hull. "There's little use in speculating. We'll figure it out when we find him."

"Unless the Oracle's new method of gerulae programming uses a biomechanical device the scan wasn't configured to look for," Eris said, guessing the reason for Kyla's reluctance to mention it. "My father mentioned ideas for the advancement of the Oracle's chip technology before I defected, but they were still in the very early design stages. I never even got to see what they came up with. Otherwise, I would have brought it up when I defected to Nova."

"You don't need to justify yourself to me. I trust you."

Kyla said the words almost dismissively as they scanned the hull, but Eris swallowed hard as she followed the commander. She'd never expected to hear those words—not from anyone, but certainly not from Kyla. When Eris had given up her role as Heir and defected to the rebellion, the commander believed Princess Discordia intended to infiltrate the Novantae as a spy. After all, why would the Servant of Death renounce her title? Help her enemy? She was her father's protégée and had seized entire planets in his name.

Kyla and Sher had toyed with the idea of killing Eris, but the intel she provided on the inner workings of the Empire proved useful. Eris had accepted that she was little more than a helpful tool for the rebellion's co-commanders. Someone who gave them information and who wouldn't hesitate to kill. Someone to perform the shit work of assassination.

At the time, it didn't matter. Eris was used to being someone else's instrument. They didn't understand that Princess Discordia wasn't her father's student; she was his weapon. The only person who hadn't used Eris was Xander, and he still ended up with her blade in his throat.

But things had changed since Laguna. *Eris* had changed. Maybe Kyla had changed too. Their group of seven had fought and survived together, and that had made things different.

"You're quiet," Kyla remarked, switching on the lights of the vast hull as they went deeper into the ship's belly.

"You said you trust me," Eris replied softly.

Kyla side-eyed her. "Do *not* cry on me, General. If you do, I'm leaving your ass here. No weepy moments."

"No tearing up." Eris dabbed at her eyes. "No weepy moments."

"Good. The gods know no one will ever believe me if I told them you started getting sniffly and—" Kyla froze. "*Eris.* Please tell me you moved the bullet craft."

"Of course not, it's—" Eris glanced through the port window at the space in the hull where they usually docked the small craft. "*Fuck.*"

Kyla sprang into motion, hurrying back the way they came. Eris followed closely behind, practically running to keep up with Kyla's pace. "The bullet craft's tracking was just rechecked and upgraded recently," Kyla said as they headed back up the stairs. "That thing might as well have a hidden cord attached to it. No matter where it is, we'll find it. If it's powered down in some dark, distant expanse outside the Iona Galaxy and falling apart piece by piece, we'll still fucking find it."

They entered the command center, and Kyla set to work. Ariadne had disabled the ship's cameras for a fifteen-minute period, which must have been when she slipped out. There was no signature on the hold door opening. Kyla started running *Zelus*'s tracking search. It'd have taken Ariadne too long to disable that if she wanted to make a quick getaway. The commander exuded calm, but Eris could tell it was a facade. Kyla's feet tapped impatiently as the scan swept the vast expanse of the galaxy, piece by piece.

"Do you think Sher kidnapped her? Used her as a hostage?" Eris asked, leaning over the dash to watch the scan. *Hurry, hurry,* she thought.

Kyla shook her head. "Fuck if I know. He—"

A shout outside the bridge drew their attention. Eris and Kyla rose in alarm as Cato came into the command center, dragging a bound Damocles with him. Nyx limped in after them with a severe look. Something was wrong.

Cato shoved Damocles hard. "Tell them what you told me."

"Tell them," Nyx snapped when Damocles only scowled at her. Her voice was still weak and raspy, but her eyes held a promise of violence. "Or I will shove this cane so far up your ass that you'll taste the metal."

Damocles glared at Eris as he straightened. The bruise forming along his cheekbone was likely a present from Cato when he and Nyx dragged Damocles out of the cell. His blond hair was greasy and tangled. Still, her brother had gone through worse—Eris had made him bleed plenty of times—but the indignity of being dragged up to the bridge in chains must have chafed his pride worse than the strike to his face. She hadn't seen him like this since they trained with their father—another humiliation Damocles blamed her for.

When her eyes met his, Damocles flattened his lips. "Fine. I saw the little girl head toward the hull with your Commander Sher."

Eris approached her brother slowly, her gaze never leaving his face. To the others, the intensity of the siblings' regard might have been puzzling, but Eris and Damocles had long been at this game. Learning and relearning what each other's lies looked like. Testing new tricks, experimenting with schemes and strategies that would reveal which of them was better. She had bested him in Elysium; he would be reevaluating what he knew of her—forming new conclusions. Making new plans.

"Did Sher take her under duress?" Eris asked.

"They were holding hands, so it didn't seem like it." He lifted a shoulder.

Being one step ahead of Damocles meant preparing for the knife in her back.

"It would be stupid to lie to me," she told him, chin lifting. "You bought yourself time by claiming you knew how to kill the Oracle. But you are alive by my command. Kyla wouldn't hesitate to slit your throat. I could find another way."

"And how long would that take you before One turns every citizen into a gerulae?" Damocles tilted his head. "That would make life quite a bit more difficult for you, wouldn't it?"

She smiled. "Not as difficult as it would for you."

Her brother's expression hardened. "I have little reason to lie about this, Discordia. I don't give a shit about your rebels. The girl skipped off with the traitor commander. Take the information, or leave it. Neither choice impacts me at all."

Eris kept her expression shuttered as she stepped away, but she gave Kyla a brief nod. Damocles was right; lying about Ariadne and Sher neither benefited nor hurt him. In the past, he had simply given her information because he was interested in the result, the way one might watch a sporting match. And sometimes, he gave her the intelligence to learn what *she* would do.

Because to Damocles, she was the ultimate sport.

"That doesn't make any sense," Kyla said, walking over to the computers to check on the search. "Ariadne wouldn't have just gone off with Sher without telling anyone. She barely knew him."

"And last I checked, he was basically a vegetable," Nyx muttered. When Kyla glared, Nyx shrugged. "No offense to vegetables."

The computer beeped, and Kyla let out a breath of relief. "The bullet craft is one jump away. We've got a lock. Hold tight."

Everyone was silent as Kyla prepared the ship for a jump. Eris covertly watched her brother, suspecting that he was equally as aware of her. She studied the tension of his hands in the chains, the set of his shoulders, the line of his jaw. Watching for any indication of whatever move he planned to make next—anticipating, and always expecting, his next play.

Damocles' lip quirked, as if to say *Just wait.*

Eris gripped the back of the chair as the ship jumped. It was little longer than a blink, but she let her body grow accustomed to the rapid resettlement of speeds; *Zelus* coasted smoothly, and through the massive dome of the ship's window, the dark line of the small bullet craft became visible.

"It's powered down," Kyla murmured, pressing a few more buttons. Eris heard the concern in her voice. "I've locked on. We'll head down to the hull as *Zelus* reels her in."

Cato grasped Damocles by the shirt and shoved him forward as the five of them went down to the hull. Eris took the lift with Nyx, who was grimly silent as she leaned against her cane. Neither of them said the words, but Eris knew what Nyx was thinking: if the bullet craft were powered down, the news wouldn't be good. At best, they were hoping for a clue as to where Sher and Ariadne went. At worst . . .

Eris couldn't consider the worst. She couldn't.

The lift doors opened, and Eris and Nyx met up with the other three outside the hull. They waited as *Zelus* finished reeling the smaller craft in and heard the sharp bang of the doors closing. The oxygen within the hull restabilized, and Kyla wordlessly pushed the door open.

The craft sat as quiet, still, and dark as when it'd been safely parked in the hold of *Zelus*. Kyla lifted the hatch, and it only confirmed what Eris had suspected: there was no sign Ariadne and Sher had flown the ship at all. Cato, Damocles, and Nyx waited as Kyla and Eris searched the craft. Someone had switched off the navigation system, and no one had used the supplies. Ariadne would have needed them, unless . . .

"She boarded a larger ship," Eris said to Kyla.

Kyla gave a nod. "Looks like."

"Then Sher is definitely . . ."

"Under the Oracle's control. Yep." The commander frowned, bending forward to reach between the seats. There, hidden in the cushion, was Ariadne's tablet. "Fuck," Kyla whispered, and headed back down the ramp. She held out the tablet for Nyx. "You know the passcode?"

Nyx shut her eyes briefly before taking it. "Yeah." But when she flipped the case open, she sucked in a breath. Nyx held up a bloody Pathos device. "Great," she muttered, tossing the device aside to jam her finger against the screen. "Fucking great. She's extracted her Pathos and left us a message saying the Oracle is her responsibility, which means she's probably gone back to the godsdamned Temple. So, we can't even yell at her when we go after her."

"*We?*" Damocles looked incredulous. "You aren't seriously suggesting we go after that little idiot?"

"Call her that one more time, and I'll shove the handle of a spoon up your dick," Nyx snapped.

Damocles narrowed his eyes. Perhaps it was one too many colorful analogies about his anatomy. Nyx ignored him and looked at Cato. "So, Sher is a gerulae."

Cato ran a hand through his hair. "But I did a scan. He didn't have a chip to connect him to the Oracle—"

"You mean like my soldiers back in Elysium, who also didn't have chips?" Damocles said casually.

Eris went still. "So, you didn't forget to remove them."

Damocles curled his lip. "Of course not. I'm not a fucking fool."

"Debatable."

"My point is," he said with a scowl, "the Oracle found a way around it. One could have influenced them to visit the nearest med bay for a quick procedure. It's impossible to estimate how long One's been relatively autonomous."

Eris gave a soft swear. "He's right. The royal guards with him back in Elysium are required to have routine physicals. The Oracle could have hidden a new biochip in their brains then. Or worse: influenced other citizens to visit their nearest med bay. The Oracle's systems manage every Imperial medical center in the galaxy." Eris looked at Kyla. "When we meet up with the other rebels, we need to have them take another look at the prisoners from Othrys. Make sure they don't leave anything in there that the Oracle can use to stay in their heads."

Kyla gave a nod and glanced at Cato. "And how are you feeling?" Cato was the last rebel to be deprogrammed before Kyla made the difficult decision to stop taking new recruits after the Tholosian attack on Nova.

Cato reached back to touch the scar left by the chip removal. "I can choose to put down a Mors when I want, so fine."

"Then Laguna's our timeline," Kyla said to the others. "The Oracle might have planned the novel chip before the truce ceremony as an attempt to use the gerulae to infiltrate the Evoli Empire. Expand One's reach."

Eris made a noise of agreement. "Or to work around the usual routine chip removal. If we hadn't figured this out before working to deprogram the prisoners, we would have compromised the entire rebel fleet."

"A net positive," Damocles said. "Didn't I kill most of your best fighters, anyway?"

Nyx glared at him. "Eris, do we have some adhesive? Because I'm thinking I'd enjoy gluing his fucking mouth shut."

Damocles smiled. "I like you better like this, Nyx. It always was more entertaining to break you again after you showed some spirit."

Nyx's fist shot out to punch him, but Eris seized her wrist. "Not yet," she murmured. "But soon."

The soldier curled her lip as she leaned heavily against her cane, breathing hard. "Fine."

Eris turned to her absolute fuckwit of a brother. It was time for him to serve his purpose; she hadn't exactly let him live for nothing. "You said you knew how to kill the Oracle. Talk. Or I *will* let Nyx glue your mouth shut, and I will take you back into your cell and personally beat the shit out of you. You think being in chains is humiliating? Try peeling your lips apart to insult her."

Damocles set his jaw. He picked at his chains, almost certainly imagining putting them around her throat, calculating the exact amount of pressure it would take to cut off her air supply and strangle her to death. After their training sessions with their father, he used to tell her about his fantasies in detail. All the ways he'd imagined killing her, from childhood into adulthood. He'd had so long to plan.

In the end, he relaxed his hands. He'd probably decided strangulation wasn't how he wanted to watch her die. There were a thousand other possibilities. Pieces on their board that needed shifting first. She wondered if he imagined their configuration as he spoke.

"The archives on Tholos go back to the Old World," he said. "They detail the building of *Argonaut*, who would get to board the generation ship and survive, who would stay and die. The Oracle was developed as the onboard AI, and One even ran the lottery to decide who would board the vessel. One's choices, of course, left behind those considered a burden, like the elderly, the infirm"—he raked Nyx with a smug look, and she narrowed her gaze—"but I suppose you don't require that detail for killing the Oracle, do you?"

"Get to the point, dickbag," Nyx said through her teeth.

Damocles leaned back. "The archives detail a shut-off mechanism on *Argonaut* that consisted of two parts: one for the backup and the other in a room that serviced the primary system. The 'heart' was the primary location that housed One's original neural network." He lifted a shoulder. "I don't see why it still wouldn't. The Temple is strictly controlled and remains the same as when it was the generation ship. The parts that fell to ruin almost a thousand years ago were only cabins. The rest remains intact and maintained by service bots programmed by the Oracle."

When Eris and Kyla's gazes met, Kyla looked reluctant, but even Eris had to admit it was a damn solid theory. The Temple was the one place in the Tholosian Empire that was guaranteed to endure even with the expansion. The sacredness of *Argonaut* was built into the very foundations of Tholosian culture.

"Fine," Kyla said. "We'll work with that and plan how we'll rescue Ariadne. Eris, take him back to his cell."

Damocles was quiet as Eris escorted him to level one. When she pushed open the cell door and moved to attach his chains to the wall, he finally spoke. "Do you really care enough about that little imbecile to save her?"

"Her name is Ariadne," Eris said, clicking the chains in place. "And you're insulting her just to annoy me. It won't work."

But Damocles didn't smile mockingly. Instead, he frowned at her, his golden eyes betraying his puzzlement. "Why?"

Eris sighed in exasperation. "Why what?"

"Why do you care about these people?" He inclined his head to the door. "About any of them?"

Eris straightened, strangely surprised by the question. Damocles and Eris had been trained by different prefects during their childhood on Myndalia. Still, they had shared the overall lessons: feelings were weaknesses, relationships were too easy to exploit. Caring for citizens was only out of duty, not tied to any personal feelings. It had taken years for Eris to unlearn the fucked-up teachings of her childhood. She was *still* unlearning them.

"I don't know," she said, quiet.

He seemed even more bemused by her response. "Do they give you things? Sex, or—"

"Not everything is transactional, Damocles." She hated him. Gods, how she hated him. But it was difficult not to pity him, too. He had never learned to give a shit about anyone but himself. "Sometimes, people care about each other because caring is a reward on its own."

Damocles leaned his head against the wall, the metal clanking as he shifted his wrists. "You felt that way about Xander. He couldn't offer you the strength to ensure your victory."

Eris tried to keep her expression even. "I did."

"But you never felt that way about me," he said. "Even though I could."

Eris's fingernails curled into her palm. "When did I have the chance? You manipulated me like a piece on a zatrikion board. You still do."

As Damocles looked away to stare at the cell's white wall, he seemed almost angry. "And you did the same to me. And still do."

Eris retreated from his cell before she acknowledged that he was right. He had always been the enemy standing on the other side of their battlefield.

41.

Present day

Ariadne traced her fingers along the carved name on her desk.

The deep slash of the *I*. The raised edges of the *R*. A second *I* that was more uneven than the first, and an *S* shaped like a lightning bolt. The angry lines of Iris's name chiseled into the wood had once settled just as permanently inside Ariadne's heart, a longing of freedom that she had carried with her outside the Temple's walls.

In her heart, she had taken Iris with her, flown with her name through the stars. Like all the engineers who lived and died before her: *Callista, Autolycus, Valerius, Augustus, Selene, Hector, Penelope, Evander.* Those with names—and the nameless others—who never ventured beyond *Argonaut*'s sacred walls. They all resided within Ariadne. She knew none of their faces, but she had imagined them all with kind eyes. She thought—*hoped*—she could carry them further, safely ensconced in her heart, as she enjoyed the freedom they were never given.

But Ariadne was back in the Temple. She had only been there for mere days—five, by her count—but the hours passed as if they were each an eternity. She fell into the same routine she'd had from childhood: running programming and diagnostics for the Oracle, checking over citizenry programming, ensuring the Empire ran as smoothly as a well-oiled machine. The Temple's beautiful arched glass ceiling and high walls were mere decoration to make this vast and empty prison more palatable. In truth, she felt as desolate and lonely as she imagined Iris had when she'd taken up an instrument and etched her name—begging the universe not to forget her.

Ariadne wondered if she'd made a mistake by coming back. She almost certainly had.

But this is where I deserve to be.

She bit her lip as she loaded the vast network of the Oracle's programming. She continued typing up routine coding that hid the background processes she opened to retrieve information on the Oracle's weaknesses.

Now blink.

One microsecond of information, set aside as if she were scrolling. She allowed these mere flashes to settle inside of her mind, where she could pull them up and examine them in the privacy of her thoughts. This was how she had escaped the first time. Perhaps she could do so again.

Her actions to discover the Oracle's weaknesses were excruciatingly minute and slow. It chafed to have mere microseconds to herself, knowing that any more would give away her true purpose in returning to the Temple: to find out how to undo the action she was about to take. Information was solidifying in her mind, bits of code that comprised the gerulae mass-programming map, the Temple's layout, and the Oracle's possible weaknesses.

"Biometric readings indicate you are worried. Is this correct?"

The Oracle's voice floated to Ariadne from the comms system. Though Sher's body—or any gerulae within the capital of Tholos—was available to One, the Oracle preferred the limitless existence of digital form: being everywhere in the galaxy, all at once, rather than enduring the physical limitations of a single human body. Sher's body sat ready in a nearby chair, waiting for the Oracle's command.

Ariadne had never used the slur "husk" to describe the gerulae—she didn't like it. But when she looked at what had been done to Sher . . . she understood why the gerulae were called such. His body was merely a shell, a receptacle for the AI. If any shred of him remained, it was buried deep. And One wanted this for every citizen in the Empire.

All for the safety of One's daughter.

The Oracle used Sher's body when it suited One. "He" had even hugged Ariadne once. Ariadne felt like a traitor for clinging to the co-commander's body, desperately seeking the comfort of touch and hoping he was hidden somewhere in those mental data points. Because Ariadne could not risk telling him that she would do whatever it took to save him.

Ariadne had never been a good liar. She replied with honesty. "Yes." She curled her fingers away from Iris's name. "I'm worried."

There was a moment of silence before the Oracle's voice came back through the comms: "One has run numerous probabilities through One's system to arrive at an answer and determined it inadequate. Why?"

Ariadne sighed. She longed to take every worry out of her mind and tell it to someone else—Nyx or Rhea or even Eris. She began to rely on the encouragement of her own thoughts, the only part of herself that remained her own.

The Oracle kept watching over her every hour, every minute, every second. If not from the Temple's surveillance, then from Sher's body. But One could not read Ariadne's mind. The Oracle could not take that privacy from One's daughter.

Ariadne remained the one thing in the Empire the Oracle could not wholly control. An engineer turned gerulae couldn't innovate, couldn't expand the Oracle's reach.

And, perhaps, the one thing Ariadne had succeeded in teaching the Oracle was loneliness.

Ariadne settled her fingers to the keys. "A long time ago, I asked you if turning citizens into gerulae hurt, and you told me it did. I don't like hurting people."

She couldn't voice her genuine worry: that she would fail. That she wouldn't be able to stop the Oracle from One's current course or delay much longer. All she could do was hope she was clever enough to reverse it and destroy her parent.

"The new gerulae coding structure is intended to bypass the pain receptors to minimize discomfort to a tolerable level," One said in return. "Does this satisfy?"

"Yes," she replied. The lie settled uneasily on her tongue.

"You have given an answer that is contrary to your physiological processes," the Oracle said. "One's systems sense an elevated heart rate."

Calm down, she told herself. She stared at Iris's name again, trying to take solace in the shape of the letters. *I—R—I—S*. "I don't want to do this," she said. "It's wrong."

"One has run—"

"*Stop it*," Ariadne snapped.

Her fingernails bit into the table, leaving behind their own marks. She had spent years trying to code empathy and emotions into the Oracle, to build herself a parent that didn't run on probabilities or practicality but who understood that humans were not just numbers in an empire but individuals. That *Iris* was not only a name carved into a table but a girl who had lived in service to an AI, and who deserved better than to die alone on an old generation ship.

"You are distressed," the Oracle said. "What can One do to improve your mood, daughter?"

The word *daughter* made her flinch. "Don't do this. Don't turn them into gerulae. I *know* you have run millions of probabilities for the future and have settled on what you think is the best course. But I'm asking you to stop. I did my best to code empathy into your systems. I have to hope that somehow you understand why I'm upset."

She knew the Oracle wasn't evil, just enacting commands according to One's own internal logic echoed down from those early iterations from when the Oracle was a generation ship's AI. That AI had been programmed from its very inception to come up with probabilities to ensure its crew's survival.

To the Oracle's internal system, Ariadne was the crew of *Argonaut*. The only one left. Everyone else was considered dangerous.

"One has run the probabilities for your survival outside of the Temple." The Oracle had moved from the screen to speak with Sher's voice. She turned toward him. The Oracle's voice, expressed in the commander's baritone, was gentle. "The likelihood that you would have survived the last four months was one in three hundred thousand, six hundred and twenty-two. The likelihood that you will make it to age eighteen is one in three million, twenty-seven thousand, and twenty-seven point nine three four five eight two. The likelihood that you will make it to age twenty is one in seven billion, eight hundred seventy-two thousand, and sixty-six point seven one six zero eight. The likelihood that—"

"Why are you telling me this?" Ariadne whispered, tears stinging her eyes. And how had One even arrived at those numbers?

The Oracle-as-Sher rose from the chair and approached Ariadne. One leaned down and wiped away a tear from Ariadne's cheek, staring at the single droplet as if it was something strange and new. "The Tholosians and the Evoli were on a trajectory to resume their conflict. My systems detected a high probability that the peace agreement would collapse. The possibilities for cataclysms were numerous, aided by the improvement of novel weaponry and engineered viruses more detrimental than the ichor." Sher blinked, face still impassive. "If we remain on One's new current trajectory, the probability that you will live to age two hundred is one in three," the Oracle paused. "One's system has accounted for accidents or self-destruction."

Ariadne gripped the arms of her chair. "You are telling me to choose myself over—"

"One has run the same probability for every citizen in the Empire." The Oracle's gaze met Ariadne's. "One's innovative programming will lengthen their lives. There will be no strife. No conflict. And you will securely explore beyond *Argonaut*, and One will remain at your side." The Oracle tilted One's head. "Is this not the empathy you designed?"

Ariadne blinked back tears. When she had tried to amend the Oracle's systems, she had been a mere child. Her view of the world had been simple—based on ancient vids and her intrinsic sense of fairness. She had not understood the messiness of humanity, that so much of the Oracle's own internal processing was limited by the AI's lack of understanding around consent.

The AI could always, on some fundamental level, comprehend empathy. One had cared for and protected the passengers and crew of *Argonaut*. One understood that empathy for fellow citizens was essential to a functional society; engineers added it to the Oracle's programming from conception.

However, consent and human programming were diametrically

opposed. And Ariadne had never taught the Oracle that—because all she'd ever wanted was a parent to love her.

"Yes," she admitted, wanting to cry. "That's what I programmed."

The Oracle's eyes touched on hers. "But your physiological responses remain unsettled."

She could not save her parent. She could not undo the Oracle's programming or One's internal logic.

She couldn't fix the Oracle.

But she could try to fix the damage she was about to do. Doing this could give them time. "Do you promise it won't hurt them?"

The smile on the Sher's face was almost kind. "One assures that the current parameters have made it painless."

"And do you promise if I ask you to stop something I disagree with, going forward, that you will?"

A pause, the whir of processing. "If One's systems recognize it will not lead to your impairment or physical harm, yes."

It was something. Not enough, but something. She had to do what she could to buy time. To find the weakness. But until then, like Eris said: she had to play the game.

Ariadne nodded and began keying in the code. Then, as the Oracle made Sher's body rest on her shoulder, the final command went out into the Empire.

I'm sorry, she sent out mentally into the universe, the pain of where the Pathos used to be pulsing at the base of her skull. *I should have known having a family was too good to be true.* She had to hope that their deprogramming would hold and provide a defense against what was coming.

With a keystroke, the universe now belonged to the Oracle.

42.

KYLA

Present day

Kyla sat in the command center on *Zelus*, clutching the old communicator Ariadne had made.

She stared out at the void of space, drawing imaginary lines into made-up constellations between the stars. Even now, her mind was always seeking patterns, trying to find meaning in what she saw. She could never turn it off.

The stars, at least, gave her comfort. They would still be there tomorrow, and the next day, and for billions of years—even if she'd go back to being stardust soon enough.

A day before, *Zelus* had rendezvoused with Elva and the other rebels. Daphne had been flying their newest addition—the prison junker—while Hadriana worked through the arduous process of deprogramming their two hundred recruits from Othrys on *Themis*, scanning their brains for traces of a new, biological chip hidden somewhere in their brains. The thing they'd found had been so small, no bigger than the head of a pin. And Ariadne wasn't here to analyze it.

Kyla decided against telling anyone outside the Devils that a certain Archon was on board. As long as they kept Elva far enough away from the holding cells, no one would know they were temporarily sheltering the enemy.

As *Zelus* sped toward Tholos, Kyla thought of the lives of everyone she might be risking. Knowing that if she didn't ask for more, she'd be in further dire straits. She had one last opportunity to do what she had vowed ever since watching Nova kiss the Archon's boot: resist.

Rebel.

So, she sent one final message to all the Novantae in hiding who might still be able or willing to hear it.

"B7774F5. Does anyone copy?"

She tapped the communicator gently against her forehead as she waited. Silence (always silence). Elva entered Kyla's quarters, hesitating. Kyla motioned with her fingers to come in but kept calling.

"B7774F5," she tried again. "Anyone out there?"

Silence (the static sounded almost like the hushing of waves).

"Look, I know I promised A122 to stop sending messages, but this might be my last transmission. We're going back to where it all started," she said, avoiding Elva's gaze. She wasn't about to declare her plans in too much detail, just in case one of the communicators had fallen into the wrong hands. People like Athena would know what that meant. "We're making our last stand. I want to say it has been an immense honor to know you all. Keep each other safe, and live the best life you can. The freest life you can. Make us proud." She paused, resting her head against the cool glass. "Over and out."

She was just about to click off the system when the radio crackled. "B7774F5A122." It was Athena, breathless. "I'm here. Do you know what's happening?"

Kyla frowned and glanced up at Elva, who looked confused. Most of the ship was asleep, taking what rest they could as they charted their way back to the place they all feared most. "No?"

"Look at the vid-screens," Athena said. Her voice was strangled. Athena was many things, but she was rarely afraid. Or she rarely showed it.

Kyla stood, clutching the radio as she made her way back to the bridge. Elva followed behind her. "Which vid-screens?"

Athena's response chilled her. "Any city. Any planet."

Elva put the ship on autopilot, keeping watch if the systems identified any potential threats. So far, the onboard computers had detected no attacks. Then the Evoli woman pulled up the vid-screens to the capital of Macella.

Kyla had expected fire, explosions, or Morsfire. She expected to see people screaming and fleeing for cover. Yet all looked calm and quiet, people milling about the square. What could Athena mean? Things looked even more relaxed than usual.

She flipped through the feeds of various planets, vidcasts that Ariadne had hacked months ago. Even after escaping the Temple, the Engineer still liked to people-watch. Kyla lost count of how many times she'd observed the younger girl throwing a snack up into the air and catching it in her mouth as she digitally followed market squares or busy streets, just soaking up the sight of people living their lives among each other. Everywhere, all was calm.

All at once, it clicked.

Everyone had the same slow, listless gait. No one animatedly hawked and bartered in the markets. Shopfronts had been abandoned, their doors open, wares unguarded. Some citizens sat on benches or in the middle of the ground, staring into space. Waiting.

Waiting for commands.

"They're husks," Athena said, hushed. "They're all fucking husks."

"No," Kyla breathed. Elva was stiff beside her, staring at the screens with her hands over her mouth.

"We were getting supplies on Gortyn when it happened. These lights started flashing from every surveillance camera, from every vid-screen. Even Damocles' icons all switched off to reflect the same pattern. We were fast enough to drop and cover our eyes until it ceased. Everyone around us just . . . stopped. We didn't know what was going on at first. No one spoke. Their faces went so blank. Like the whole planet had been turned into ghosts with the flick of the switch, except for us."

"Because you don't have chips," Kyla said, her voice low and breathless. "Because you've been deprogrammed."

Before Laguna. Kyla was so torn over her decision not to take new recruits after the Tholosians attacked Nova. She almost couldn't believe that decision might have saved their dwindling numbers from being a complete slaughter.

"It's everywhere, Kyla," Athena said, slipping and forgetting her code name in her distress. "Others who left Nova are reporting the same. Every citizen in the whole godsdamn Empire is gerulae."

Kyla's legs shook, and she dropped into a chair. She'd known, deep down, that this could be an option—ever since she'd seen Sher on the table on that first transmission. But she hadn't considered that the Oracle planned to trigger the flashing code throughout the galaxy. The Oracle was everywhere, in everyone, and Tholosians were now one hundred percent tractable.

She hoped Elva hadn't realized that Ariadne had probably been the one to do this. To flip the switch. It was so elegant, so seamless. Kyla had worked with Ariadne long enough to recognize her signature style.

Maybe the Oracle manipulated Ariadne—poured some poison into her ear, so she believed this was the right course of action.

Kyla had known Ariadne was hurting, that she was feeling the same guilt as everyone else. She should have done more to reach out, but Kyla had been battling her own demons. What else had she overlooked?

Kyla had been through so much in her time as the leader of the Novantae resistance. Yet, standing there, she felt as uncertain as a recruit. Completely out of her depth.

"I don't know what to do," Athena said, echoing Kyla's thoughts.

Kyla took a shuddering breath. She forced herself to consider all angles like she'd done so many times before. She may not have Sher (*don't think of Sher*) by her side. But she had herself; she had her instincts and her wits. Her leadership was honed from nearly two decades of trying to do as much as possible and risking as few deaths as she could. Of making decisions she knew would condemn more to the Avern just the same.

"Come back to us," Kyla said. "A third of our people aren't as well trained in battle, and our newest recruits still need rounds of deprogramming. We need you. Will you come?"

"We're already on our way, Commander," Athena said, and Kyla's heart swelled at the title she hadn't truly felt she'd deserved ever since her people had scattered. "Send us your coordinates."

Kyla went through a couple of security protocols, just in case, which Athena answered without hesitation. Kyla sent the coordinates.

"I'll contact Decebal and Tulio, too," Athena said. "That's another six hundred or so between them."

"So, we double our numbers. Twelve hundred against uncountable millions," Kyla said.

"Impossible odds," Elva whispered.

"Our favorite," Kyla said, echoing Eris's words and smiling despite herself.

"We'll see you soon, Commander," Athena said. She hesitated before adding, "I won't apologize. We had our reasons for leaving."

"I know you did."

"But I'll be glad to fight by your side again."

The line went silent.

Kyla stared out at the stars. Some of those distant dots were planets inhabited by people who had hopes, dreams, fears, and desires until moments ago. They may not have been free enough to express them all, but at least they had had a semblance of autonomy. Now they were all locked in the prisons of their minds. Their personal levels of the Avern.

Kyla couldn't wait or hope for a vague day in the future. She'd made it through so many battles, but this was going to be the last one. She wouldn't blink twice at the sacrifice. Her luck had held, but it only needed to last a little longer.

"Elva," Kyla said. "Get in contact with Clo and Rhea on the communicator. We need all hands on deck."

"That's what I came to tell you," Elva said, eyes still a little distant with shock. "They're on their way back, and they said they'd give you a full report. They'll be with us by breakfast."

Kyla sagged against the back of the chair. "Gods, I hope they have good news."

Elva grimaced. "They didn't say, but . . . I don't think it is."

Kyla knocked her head lightly against the chair. "Of course not." She rubbed the back of her neck. "Go wake up Eris and the other Devils," she said, and Elva nodded and disappeared without another word.

Part of Kyla wanted to tell them to keep going, keep flying, and not look back. The rest of them might all die tomorrow, but Rhea and Clo could have a happy ending. The two of them, away from all of this. Somehow, somewhere. The thought would give Kyla some comfort.

But Clo would never do it, and neither would Rhea, and the Novantae needed them both.

At least there would be the chance to say goodbye.

43.

CATO

Present day

The Devils were clustered in the command center when the call from Clo and Rhea came through.

They had all sat quietly after Kyla's news, lost in their own thoughts, as *Zelus* soared through the galaxy.

The stars made Cato think of Demetrius.

Now that he could remember him, Cato found comfort in their memories. Those stolen evenings between battles when laughter had often felt like an act of rebellion. When he had known that his programming was glitching, and he could hardly bring himself to care. He recalled the press of Demetrius's lips (now his own lips), his voice (now his own voice) as he recited stars and moons. He never got to say last rites for Demetrius, but he could honor him this way. So, he found moments when he could fly into the stars Demetrius loved naming, and for those small minutes, he allowed himself to admit what he never could all those years ago. Words he had never said, even through his glitching programming. *I love you.*

And now those words felt like goodbye. He could not spend too much time in those memories—sooner or later, he would have to return to reality: working to save the gerulae and preparing for a battle he might not survive.

So, he drew renewed comfort from the present. His mind was his own, and Nyx was alive. He watched her move about the command center with her cane and felt a painful stab in his chest—she was someone else he could have lost to the Empire. Someone he thanked the gods he didn't have to mourn. Someone he could care about fully, freed of the Oracle.

Their eyes met across the room. Nyx's lip quirked up, as if to say *Caught you staring.*

He smiled back but was distracted by the alert on the comms. Clo and Rhea's communication device was giving off a signal.

Holding his breath, he all but lunged for the button to send the call through. When Clo and Rhea's voices crackled through the comms, the relief in the room was palpable.

"Damn, it's good to know you're alive," Cato said, sitting back in the pilot's chair.

Elva had piloted the ship since *Zelus* had met up with the others, but Cato had come out of the medical center hours before, looking for a distraction from the gerulae brain scans.

"I knew you'd miss us," Clo said smugly over the comms when she grew close. "Rhea, didn't I tell you they'd miss us? Oh, I see you now! Rhea's waving. I'm flipping you the scythes because I can see from here that *Zelus* looks banged the fuck up. What have you done to my ship?"

Cato rolled his eyes and chose not to answer her. He flipped a few switches. "I'm opening the hatch for you. We're all in the command center."

Zelus's system locked on to their ship's arrival, and in the dark expanse of space, Cato spotted the sleek metal of their vessel that was most definitely not the shitty bullet craft they'd left with. The angles and design were familiar from his time in the military; a ship like that had bombed his base once. So, what in the seven devels were Rhea and Clo doing with an Evoli military craft?

"Nobody tell them about Damocles or Ariadne yet," Eris said as they all heard the thrum of the Evoli ship landing in the hatch. She hesitated. "Or Sher. Or the galaxy-wide gerulae."

Nyx, sitting in the chair nearest to Cato, swung her cane from hand to hand. "So, what *can* we tell them?"

"That you missed them? That they look nice? I'm sure you can figure out how compliments work."

Nyx rolled her eyes. "What's the difference between telling them now or putting it off for a few minutes?"

"I feel like we should ease them into the shit news instead of bombarding them with it. Kyla?"

The commander sighed. "I'm not sure what difference it will make."

"See, I think we should just go all out with it," Nyx said with a shrug. "Tear it off like a bandage. Sure, it hurts like a bitch, but—"

"We could at least be happy to see them first," Eris said, "before settling into the 'hey, how are you, everything is shit, welcome back to the bottomless pit of misery' conversation."

Nyx looked ready to argue, but Clo and Rhea barreled into the command center. Both women appeared healthy and unharmed, a marked contrast to the Devils on *Zelus*, who were running ragged from lack of sleep. If they noticed the bags under everyone's eyes and the hastily donned uniforms, Rhea and Clo didn't indicate it.

Clo immediately waved to Eris, then bounded over to Kyla and embraced the commander, while Rhea went over to Nyx with a warm look.

"New accessory?" Rhea asked Nyx, gesturing to the cane.

"It's probably permanent." Nyx shrugged, trying to look nonchalant. "I never told you or Clo, but I caught the noncommunicable ichor virus back on fucking Ismara. Almost died. The usual."

Rhea's expression fell. "Oh, Nyx," she said. "Clo and I—"

"Don't fuss." Nyx shifted uncomfortably, then held out the cane. "Besides, I'm gonna get a new one made with a hidden blade and some spikes that shoot out. Right, Cato? I'm gonna be a cane-wielding badass."

"You already are." Cato's voice was quiet as he met Rhea's eyes.

Cato knew Rhea comprehended more about the situation without words. Her abilities helped her sense emotions, and even though Nyx put on a good performance, she struggled with her body post-illness. Cato had watched her frustration during physio. He had seen her fall to the floor and pull herself up with tears shining in her eyes and a determined set to her jaw. But she accepted these things stoically, and she made plans for the years ahead, where she would have to learn new skills. At least now she had years instead of weeks. Yeah, Cato would give her a dozen fucking canes with different weapons. Whatever she wanted.

Clo came over and grasped Rhea's hand, then she looked around. "Where's Ariadne? And Sher? Did you rescue him?"

The command center went silent. Kyla pulled back her shoulders—as if she were readying herself to give Clo the news—but Nyx spoke first. "Gone. She's at the Temple with the Oracle, because she's settled on the fucking ridiculous notion that the Oracle is her responsibility." She glowered as she caught her breath for a second. "The Oracle commandeered Sher's fucking body and took her."

"*What?*" Rhea and Clo spoke at the same time. Clo's mouth fell open, and she closed her eyes hard as if she could block out what she'd just heard.

Eris rolled her eyes. "Seven devils, Nyx, you could've just *eased* into—"

"Oh, and in case you missed it, and the Oracle's gone rogue, every Tholosian citizen is now gerulae, and Damocles is chained to a wall in one of our level-one cells. Welcome back! It's a shitshow!" Nyx twirled her cane and gave a seated bow.

"I—" Rhea looked speechless. "Well, we knew the first part of that. The Oracle tried to take over the Evoli, and when that didn't work, One offered them a truce. Which they took."

"Fuck," Kyla rubbed her face.

"Wait a minute. Wait a fucking minute." Clo's chin jutted out. "Who *the fuck* was stupid enough to let *fucking Damocles, evil Archon* onto the ship? Did you all lose your damn minds when we went to Eve?"

"He had the cure for Nyx," Eris said tightly. "And she was dying of ichor. So, I made the call."

Clo's mouth snapped shut, and she released Rhea's hand to step closer to Eris. "That doesn't explain why he's still on the ship and not bunged out the airlock, Eris," she hissed.

"He said he knew how to shut down the Oracle," Kyla said, falling into the captain's chair and tossing a leg over the side.

The mechanic didn't look convinced; if anything, she seemed even more furious. "And you *believed* him? Godsdamn it, Eris, how could you be so—"

"I know it's ridiculous," Eris snapped. "I know it's irresponsible. But I made that decision because I had to learn how to trust myself after Laguna, and I have to play the game with him one last time." She paused and let out a breath, shutting her eyes for a moment. "I promised Kyla that if the time came, I'd be the general. I know what I have to do. But that means you all have to trust me."

Kyla's expression was shuttered as she gave a sharp nod.

Clo backed away, her hands closing into fists. Cato saw the indecision in her face, and it mirrored his own feelings—within all the Devils in the room, except Kyla. Like Eris, Kyla had to make the difficult decisions of a leader.

Nyx propped her chin in her hand and said, "I figure you didn't save my ass just to let me die at the hands of your idiot brother, so I'm in with this ridiculous scheme. Makes a change, eh? Usually, you're all trying to convince me of your general dumbassery."

Eris gave a small smile at that.

Rhea glanced at Clo with a worried frown but inclined her head slightly. "I trust that you couldn't think of another way."

That left Cato and Clo. Cato tried to organize the tumult of his thoughts, separating the echoes of the Oracle's commands from his internal voice. He couldn't tell them that since Damocles had boarded the ship, Cato fought the voice that demanded he free his sovereign. That if it required his sacrifice, it would be for the good of the Empire. Even now, the echoes of the Oracle whispered, *Damocles is your Archon. You made a vow to give your life in service of the Empire. Anything less is treason. Discordia is a traitor. They. Are. All. Traitors. And so are you.*

Cato gripped the back of Nyx's chair. *You can choose who to follow,* he told himself. That was what it meant to be deprogrammed: making a choice—deciding when to fight.

Deciding who to trust.

"I trust you," he told Eris, speaking over the voice in his mind. He didn't have to listen.

Eris's gaze settled on Clo. The mechanic gave a slow exhale. "Fuck. Fine. I trust you, Eris."

Something around Eris's eyes eased.

Kyla's face betrayed nothing as she rose from the chair. "Then that's settled. Damocles is Eris's responsibility." She raised her chin. "Cato will keep working on the gerulae brain scans. Being able to reverse their programming will be an advantage when we go after Ariadne. Clo, Rhea, I'd like an update on the situation on Eve. Sounds like there's a lot I need catching up on."

"The brain scans were useful," Cato offered. "We got closer." No need to tell them about his memories. Not now.

Rhea dropped a kiss to Clo's knuckles and went over to Cato. "Good. I'll take a look as soon as possible." She grimaced. "But first, we'll give our report. You're not going to like it, Kyla."

———

Hours later, Rhea and Clo watched as Cato drained a gerulae's tank and gently lifted the girl out. He didn't know why he chose Chara, the former Novan engineer, over the other three rebels. Maybe it was her youth. Or perhaps it was that when he wrote down her history and displayed the qualities on the tank's small screen, it occurred to him how short her life had been before she was captured and made gerulae. She'd barely had time to make her mark on the world before the Empire tried to render her nameless.

Cato's notice snagged on her little screen, displaying her name and details. She was just one person in the Empire who'd been made into a gerulae. One speck in the universe of people they now had to save. And if they succeeded with her, then they might have a chance with the others.

And if they failed . . .

Cato shut his eyes briefly to compose himself. *Start with Chara. Start with one life.*

"How old is she?" Rhea whispered.

Cato spread the blankets over her small form and began hooking her up to the machines to monitor her physiological responses. "She's a little older than Ariadne."

"So young." Rhea's voice was quiet as he worked. She shook her head. "All the ones on Eve were adults."

"She'd be of age to battle in the military," Cato said, attaching another sensor to Chara's skin. "To kill or die for the Empire, whichever came first." He lifted a shoulder. "I killed when I was younger than her."

"Yeah, I joined Nova when I was thirteen," Clo ran a hand over her buzzed cut. "Don't think any of us were allowed to be kids. The Empire considers both Novantae and people who glitch to be traitors, whether they're five or eighty."

Rhea jerked back with a flinch. "I remember one boy during the Archon's training for me. His programming was deemed too flawed for purpose, so they planned to erase him." Her blank expression implied more to it than that, but Cato figured she'd say something if she wanted them to hear it. He certainly didn't intend on pressing.

"Younger than her?" Clo asked, gesturing to Chara as Cato administered more sensors to her skin and fingers.

Rhea nodded.

"The Empire has some shite jobs they consider ideal for littler bodies and smaller hands. I hear at least sixty percent of the miners on Antares are kids. Gerulae go down into the earth without fuss." Clo made a disgusted noise. "Can't wait to burn this fucking Empire to the ground."

Cato gave her a small smile of agreement, even as worry prickled like ice through his veins. So much hinged on this one gerulae. All their hopes for the future.

The hope of the entire universe.

The machine beeped as it logged Chara's vital signs. Cato began implementing the reverse anesthetic to wake her from the deep sleep of the tank. That was the part he'd dreaded: waiting for Chara to open her eyes, knowing they would be as blank as a corpse's. Hating how, at one time, he had grown so accustomed to the gerulae that he never stopped to think of them as people. He had regarded the gerulae like fixtures—a lamp or another piece of furniture. But they were alive in those small storage pockets in their brains, watching a world that either ignored or degraded them.

"She'll be waking up," Cato told Rhea. "Are you going to try and feel for her emotions?"

Rhea bit her lip. "I'm not sure yet. Kyla mentioned you have brain scans. Can you show them to me?"

Cato went over to the computers. He ran the same coding Ariadne had extracted from Othrys and pulled up the pinpoints of data stored in Chara's brain. The scans projected into the center of the room, creating a bright, three-dimensional image that resembled the colors and lights of a nebula. The data points were small within the immense expanse of the brain, practically negligible. Still, Cato learned from Ariadne that even those tiny units could hold an entire lifetime of memories. More.

"These"—he gestured—"are the data points where Ariadne and I believe the Oracle stores and secures a gerulae's previous thoughts, memories, and identity. The scans you sent through helped us narrow it down. They're like partitioned sections from a mainframe entirely controlled by the Oracle, allowing One to operate their bodies while they remain passive observers." He watched as Rhea went into the scan, the colors reflecting off her pale skin like the luminous inside of a shell. "Are you looking for something?"

Rhea shook her head. "I'm not sure. Vyga showed me the empathetic connection that allowed ver to wake them up, but this is more complicated."

Cato had heard a truncated report from Eve. It scared the shit out of him that the Evoli were allied with the Oracle.

Rhea bent closer to Chara. "She's aware of us, somewhere in there. Locked in like the others. But I don't know if I'll be able to bring her back with her memories intact."

Chara's eyes were open, staring sightlessly at the ceiling. Waiting for a command, as if she were nothing more than a bot.

Cato gently took the rebel's hand. "Hey, Chara," he told her. "Don't mind us. We're just seeing if we can pull you out of there, all right? We want to give you your body back."

Pity was stark in Clo's expression. She muttered a word—to Cato, it sounded like a prayer, but knowing her, it could equally be a curse. She sighed. "If we shut down the Oracle—and that's a big if—what will that do to the gerulae?"

Cato paused. *<No idea,>* he said via the Pathos so that Chara wouldn't hear.

<Great,> Clo replied, rolling her eyes. *<Very helpful.>*

Cato wished he had an answer. It was like they were all stumbling around in the dark. Without Ariadne there to assess how the programming worked without the Oracle's presence, it was a question of the best case or worst case. Best case: everyone woke up as if they had been asleep during a nightmare.

Worst case: they stayed the same but without the Oracle's control to guide their movements.

Cato flinched, his body recalling what it had been like before the Oracle shoved his memories into Demetrius's brain. Demetrius had been aware of everything, every moment of pain.

But no ability to move.

No ability to scream.

Demetrius. He had deserved a better fate. Between the two of them, he had been the better one. The one more worthy of living. Now Cato was a ghost in his lover's body, Demetrius only an echo of a memory in Cato's consciousness, like the Oracle before him.

Cato had been dead. He should have stayed dead.

The only advantage he had was being born into a more valued cohort. That was it. Just the same Tholosian bullshit that decided this person was better than that one: it all came down to engineering—a caste.

Decisions made before birth by the same AI he was seeking to destroy.

Rhea turned from the scan and stared down at Chara, her eyes intent.

"May I . . . see something?" At Cato's questioning expression, Rhea explained: "When I observed the gerulae on Eve, I tried to draw them out. But I didn't know about the memory units. Now I do."

"All right." Cato rose from the chair. He and Clo watched as Rhea settled beside Chara and gently brushed a fingertip along the girl's cheek. "Chara," she said, her whisper like a flutter of feathers. "I'm going to connect my mind to yours. If there's anything you can do to help me . . ." Her voice trailed off as she touched her fingertips to the girl's temples. "Try to meet me halfway."

A jolt went through Rhea. Her entire body went still, the points of Chara's brain still reflecting off her skin. "One is threaded so deep," she murmured, her face a mask of concentration. "Cato. Can you tell me where to go?"

"Look for points of low-level activity," he said, trying to keep his voice calm. How to explain to an empath what to look for? "She'll be giving off emotions, but—"

Rhea drew in a breath. "Like from behind a door."

That metaphor worked. "Yes," he said, urging her on.

Rhea's body tensed. "It's muffled, but I can hear her. Chara. I can hear you. I can feel you. I just need to go deeper . . ." She froze, her breath gasping. "Chara? Chara." Her words were uneven, her exhales rattling. Her chest heaved as if she were running. "It's so dark."

"Rhea?" Clo asked, anxious.

"Chara?" Rhea was shaking. "*Chara!*"

"Rhea!" Clo grasped Rhea's arm and jerked her back from the cot.

Rhea's eyes opened wide, and she threw her arms around Clo. "Gods. I was so close, but . . . Vyga had the strength of the Unity to ground ver. I kept sinking and didn't have anyone to bring me back. The Oracle buried Chara so deep. I could only latch onto the surface."

Demetrius's memory flashed in Cato's mind, the sensation of being pulled under a strong current. Helpless. The darkness became so tactile, pressing in like a heavy weight. The sensation of falling inexorably, with nothing to hold onto, except—

I have you, Demetrius, he whispered to the echo in his mind. *I'll have you always.*

"This is too dangerous. We'll find another way to save the gerulae," he told Rhea and Clo.

As Rhea pulled away from Clo, she seemed shaken. "I think shutting down the Oracle is our only way of saving them."

The silence between them was thick.

44.

NYX

Present day

In the past, Nyx had watched Damocles sleep for hours. It was strange to see him slumber again as she stood sentry outside his cell. Not that she'd in any sense be able to protect anyone in her current state. She leaned heavily against her new cane.

When Nyx had been Damocles' royal guard, sometimes he had made her stand in the corner of his room for the night. He claimed that if the Novantae murdered Discordia, it put him at an elevated risk of assassination, and he needed his best royal guard kept close. So, Nyx had stood with a hand on her Mors, searching the darkness for phantoms that didn't exist.

But a person was vulnerable when they slept. While Nyx fantasized messy ways to slit Damocles' throat, she'd studied the planes of his face as much as the shadows. Sleep had cast off the Heir Apparent's various masks. She'd seen him passed out drunk on the bed, fully clothed, his boots still on, and his breath catching at the back of his throat.

Later, when she'd convinced him to give up the booze, she'd watched him curled up on his side, features soft enough to lose their cruelty. She'd stood over him as his forehead creased in nightmares that he'd never remember when he awoke. She'd never told him he'd whispered his sister's name, fingers splayed and clasping at an invisible neck. That sometimes he had cried for her, pleaded for her not to leave him.

This was what she had learned from watching him for all those hours and nights: everything he did, he did to try and impress or best Eris. Even whatever he was doing there, in a cell on one of his own stolen ships.

Damocles lay on his back with his head turned toward the door. Nyx wondered what Eris was doing in his dreams tonight. He'd learned to guard himself better in sleep since the last time she'd watched him. His face was relaxed but not open.

Or, more likely: he was only pretending.

She resisted the urge to slam her palm against the window and startle him like some exhibit in his menagerie on the Palace grounds. She didn't want him to see her like she was now. Thin, drawn, and so godsdamned weak.

Her legs shook. This was the longest she'd stood since she'd woken up in that tank. She should sit and rest, but she'd lose sight of him through the porthole.

Footsteps echoed down the corridor behind Nyx.

"How long have you been watching him?" Eris asked from behind her.

Rhea was with Eris, offering a reassuring smile. They'd probably come from some meeting or another. Nyx should have been there for planning and logistics, but the others stressed that she needed her rest and shouldn't push herself too soon. So much condescending bullshit.

"Don't know," Nyx said. "I've imagined killing him in about ten different ways so far. My favorite plan involves toothpicks, a thin piece of wire, and forcing him to listen to Ariadne's singing."

She swallowed against the pain that lurked somewhere deeper than all the other aches in her body whenever she thought of Ariadne. She'd give anything to hear that silly kid singing just slightly out of tune right about now.

"So, not that long, then," Rhea said lightly.

Nyx pulled back from the window with a grunt and leaned against the wall, offering her legs some relief.

"I walked all the way here," Nyx said. "From level two."

Eris, thankfully, didn't ask how long it took. She merely nodded.

"You're improving," Rhea said, resting a reassuring hand on Nyx's wrist. Nyx shook it off. She didn't need Rhea trying to make her feel better.

Eris gazed through the porthole at her brother. She managed not to flinch when Damocles' face appeared at the window.

Of course, he had only been pretending.

"If it isn't three of my former favorites," he said, revealing sharp, white teeth. "My favorite guard, my favorite lover, and my favorite, most beloved sister."

"I'm your only sister," Eris said.

"And I was never your lover," Rhea said, lifting her chin. "There was no love between us. You don't know the meaning of the word."

Nyx realized then that Rhea hadn't spoken to Damocles since their escape. She had hung back on *Zelus* during their mission on Macella. If Rhea hadn't stayed to keep watch over their ship, Cato would have ratted them all out to the Empire while he was still under the Oracle's programming. But Rhea had caught him, Ariadne had deprogrammed him, and he had gone on to save Nyx's life.

"I'm wounded," Damocles said, placing his hand on his chest.

"That would require you to have a heart," Nyx pointed out.

Damocles' attention fell on Nyx with a scrutiny that left her uneasy. "You've looked better," Damocles remarked. "Not that you were exciting eye candy in the corner of my room, but really, Nyx. You've let yourself go."

"I still say we put a laser through his skull right now and fix one problem," Nyx said to Rhea and Eris.

Eris's laugh was dry. "If we didn't need him, I'd agree. But we'd have to flip a coin to decide who did the honors."

They exchanged a look. Often, Nyx's assignments had asked her to kill fast and get out just as quickly. But not always. And Nyx had been very good at her job.

"Let's go," Rhea said. "He thrives on our attention. He's spent every day of his life having people admire or fear him." Rhea stepped close to the porthole, her nose scant inches from the glass. "We can give him a taste of what it would feel like to rule over gerulae. The silence and the solitude."

Something stark and broken flashed over Damocles' face, but it was gone as soon as it came.

"Come back to watch me sleep anytime, Nyx," he said, with a long, fixed look she remembered from across the gameboard.

So many sharp retorts came to Nyx, but she swallowed them all down like broken pieces of glass. Starve him of oxygen and attention; watch him wither. Rhea was right.

With as much dignity as she could muster, Nyx pushed herself off the wall. Rhea ended up offering her arm, and Nyx hated that she had to take it, that they had to slow down so much as they walked away. Damocles would be watching every painful step.

They paused to rest in the canteen. Eris, in a rare gesture, made them all cups of tea.

"Who are you, and what have you done with Eris?" Rhea joked.

"Who do you think made the tea while you were gone?" Eris said. "Ariadne can't even boil water." Her hand paused, holding the teaspoon of sugar at the mention of their missing Engineer.

Rhea smiled and took a sip, and immediately gave a choking cough. "Um . . . it's . . ."

Nyx gave it a try and made a face. "Tastes like shit."

"I said I made the tea," Eris muttered. "I didn't say it was *good* tea."

"Fuck the tea," Nyx said, finishing it off. She was used to shit food and beverages; it wasn't like fine dining existed in the field. "Look. When we land on Tholos, I'm coming with you to the Temple. I can't just sit here with my thumbs up my ass."

Neither responded immediately, but their thoughts were easy to follow: how could Nyx help when she could barely stand? She'd be one instant sacrifice for the God of Death. Letum could finally collect his overdue tithe.

He'd almost taken her soul on Othrys. But he'd had her back—and the others had saved her—and Nyx wasn't going to let them fight the Empire without her.

This was her battle, too.

Rhea blew on her tea and took a sip. Eris ignored hers.

"I know you're trying to find the best way to tell me no." Nyx snorted. "Don't fucking bother. I know the risks. I know I won't make it. But I can shoot a Mors. I might be able to take a few out before my soul is dragged down to the Avern." She'd never sat out a fight. She'd gone into battle riddled with Mors burns, with limbs broken. She'd left a tooth or two in the mud, had hair ripped out of her scalp. She had let nothing slow her down. "I'm a crack shot, and we're outnumbered."

She didn't bother to tell them that the Mors shook in her grip. That she might not have the aim she once did.

If push came to shove, she'd hold her breath to steady a blast.

"We are," Rhea agreed. "But we're smart. And we'll have the element of surprise."

"Take me as backup," Nyx said, aware of how desperate she sounded. She was posturing; even now, her body struggled to remain awake and upright, and she was exhausted. But she had to fight. "You won't have to worry about me for long, but I'll give you a strong start into the Temple."

"Nyx," Eris said, her eyes searching Nyx's face, "if you were me, what role would you give yourself? I'm not going to let one of the Empire's best assassins walk out there as cannon fodder. So, give me another option."

"You're not a sacrifice," Rhea added. "You told me that once."

Nyx shut her eyes. Usually, she'd be right on the ground, razing a path for others to follow. Brawn and force were all she'd ever known. She'd always loved to be right in the middle of the beating heart of a battle.

This time, though, there wouldn't be that many people on the ground. They couldn't afford it. They needed to slip past defenses like minnows in a stream. Escape the gerulae's—and therefore the Oracle's—notice. Most of the resistance would cover them from the air, battling outside reinforcements as long as possible.

Eris saw her making the connections. "You'd be able to fly *Zelus*, wouldn't you?" she asked. "Use its defense systems?"

Nyx was offended by the question. "I learned how to pilot when I was six years old. I'm better at it than you."

Eris's lip twitched in amusement. "I don't doubt it."

"Then you will have our backs in the sky, won't you?" Rhea asked with a smile. "Your limbs will be these guns. Your body will be this ship."

"Right in the fray," Eris agreed.

"There is more than one way to fight, Nyx," Rhea said. She faltered. "I'm still discovering mine."

Nyx hadn't considered that Rhea probably wouldn't be going on the ground either. Fighting was not her best skill. She'd stay up there, maybe help in the med bay, or fire some of the secondary cannons.

"You'd be welcome by my side," Nyx said.

Rhea's face slackened as she made some connection. "No. I think I know what I can do." She stood, fidgeting with her locket. "Thank you, though. You've given me an idea."

She left in a whirl of skirts and lily perfume.

Nyx looked down at her tea. "Got anything stronger than this?" she asked.

Eris gave Nyx a withering look. "Obviously." She rummaged in the cupboards and came back with some whisky, sloshing a generous slug into her cup but a significantly smaller one in Nyx's. "Sorry. Too much might affect your meds."

Nyx scowled but took a sip just the same. She felt calmer than she had in a long time.

Eris and Rhea had given Nyx another weapon. Even though Nyx wanted to be there when they burst through to save Ariadne or to shoot Damocles as soon as he'd served his use, she'd last longer up in the sky. And a ship was a damn sight bigger than a Mors.

"So, you'll be our eyes up here?" Eris asked, holding out her mug for a delayed toast. "Keep those bastards off our tail?"

Nyx clinked her mug against Eris's. Her hand didn't shake at all.

"Yeah," Nyx said. "I can do that."

45.

CLO

Present day

As *Zelus* and the rest of the Novantae's fleet zoomed toward the Three Sisters, Clo dreamed of Fortuna.

The Furies surrounded her, the group of fierce women just as she remembered. It was as if she'd never left. Jacinta's gnarled fingers danced along Clo's cheekbones, face creasing in a smile that reminded Clo of her mother. Maeve drew her close for a hug, smelling of forest, salt, and flowers. Erato threw aromatic pine boughs onto the roaring fire.

The mauve sky was darkening to black. Clo remembered this night. She had lived it before, or something much like it.

The women gathered to celebrate the longest night of the summer on this planet. Over the years, they had created their own holidays and rituals. Their religion and way of making sense of the unknowable universe. No gods, no monsters. Only the sea, the wind, the sky, and the stars.

"I miss you," Clo said to them.

She couldn't remember why she hadn't come to visit them for so long. There was a vague memory that something terrible had happened. They'd been sick, hadn't they? But they'd recovered; it was only a close call. She had stepped back into a memory, warm and safe. Some deep part of her knew she was not really there, but she leaned in to the dream logic and let it all make sense.

"You should have stayed with us," Jacinta said. "It would have been easier. Less painful in the end."

Clo frowned. She realized she couldn't feel the wind on her skin, couldn't smell the burning pine from the fire. "What do you mean?"

"Our deaths were painful, but what you face will be far worse," Jacinta said. "Because you'll have to watch those you love die and wonder if there was anything you could have done to stop it. And there is nothing you can do." She reached out again, and the flesh fell from her fingertips, revealing moss-covered bones.

"Your pain will be beyond measure, and then you will wish for your death, at the close." Her face sagged, skin eaten away by ichor and decay, revealing a grinning green-gray skull.

Clo stumbled back, but the Furies came toward her, transformed into unsteady skeletons. They called her name from mouths with no lips or tongues. They screamed for her to come closer. Not to leave them again. They would drag her toward the sea, beneath the waves, to settle with Briggs and the dim, dark creatures that slipped through the currents. She would transform into a caiman for good this time. Hard, scaly, impenetrable.

"You said we'd be safe," Jacinta whispered close to her ear. "You lied."

"No!" Clo cried.

"But we can keep you safe. Here, in the dark and the deep." Their hands clasped the front of her shirt, and she flailed, desperate to escape.

A flash of pain.

Clo woke up on the floor.

Her whole body was wracked with shivers. She was so cold. Rhea's hands gripped Clo's shirt where Jacinta's bones had seized her with unnatural strength.

"I'm here," Rhea said, voice low and soothing. "I'm here."

Clo panted. Adrenaline coursed through her veins as if they were on fire. Half of her was still on the beach. She bent toward Rhea and reached up to assure herself the other woman was real.

Rhea's creased face relaxed. "You're awake."

Clo dragged herself to a sitting position, still trembling. Rhea helped her back into bed. Clo's foot was like ice, and she resisted the urge to set it against Rhea's warmth. Rhea pressed herself to Clo's side, wrapping her arms around her waist.

"It's been a long time since I had a nightmare," she said. Her heart still hammered against her ribs.

"We all have our share," Rhea murmured. "What did you dream?" Clo told her, and Rhea pressed a soft kiss to her cheek. "The real Furies wanted you to go, remember? They wanted you to fight for them."

"I did, and they still died." Clo rested her cheek against Rhea's. "What if we fail?" she whispered, Rhea's hair tickling her lips. What if she'd have to put Rhea's body under the water with the others?

"Then I fail by your side," Rhea said simply. "And we'll know we've done our best."

Rhea shifted lower to press a kiss on Clo's neck. They both fell into silence, their thoughts swirling in the dim light. It was simple accommodation, meant for soldiers. Kyla had taken the legate's much-nicer quarters. But it was good to be back in the room where they had pushed two beds together, and Rhea had hung up a few twinkling lights she'd scrounged from somewhere to look like stars. Clo had rigged up a small worktable. During rare quiet moments, she'd tinker with something while Rhea read a story aloud. It had been cozy and beautifully, utterly dull. They both knew that what they'd shared in this room was precious. That it was something neither of them ever expected.

Clo had only loved Rhea for four, maybe five months. Had it really been so little time? Her ma would say Clo was still just an infatuated fool—that you can't truly know whether your heart belongs to someone until that love has been tested for years. But Clo's ma had never loved someone like this. Clo's pa was a mystery, a question mark. A man her ma had cared for, once, but hadn't let in. So, he'd drifted away from both of them. Clo couldn't even remember his face.

Clo was used to hardening her heart. To letting it tick along, a robust and sturdy machine encased in a cage of bone. But Rhea had caused it to skip that first time they'd danced together. She'd settled in Clo's heart and taken up residence.

Clo didn't need years to prove she loved Rhea. But she wished she could have them.

Rhea shifted against her. "I was with Nyx and Eris earlier today. Nyx is . . . struggling."

"Not surprising," Clo said. "I was like that after my amputation. Kept staring at the space where my leg used to be and just raged. I blamed Eris." She lightly dragged her fingernails along Rhea's upper arm. "I suppose the anger didn't entirely go away, but I realized the leg wasn't going to grow back. That Eris had saved my life. I got better at understanding what I could and couldn't do."

"She wanted to go barging into Tholos, waving a Mors."

"That sounds like Nyx."

"We talked her around. She's going to stay back and fly *Zelus*." Clo opened her mouth to complain, and Rhea put a finger against her lips. "Don't say it. You're way too possessive of your ships, and I don't want her to sacrifice herself in the Temple."

Clo made a face. "She better not crash it, that's all. Did she put up a fuss?"

"No. But it made me think about how we all have our ways of fighting. And I think I know what I need to try and do." Her fingers tightened on Clo's stomach. "Vyga mentioned that ve tried to expel the Oracle from the former gerulae by joining them with the Unity. When ve couldn't, ve made ver truce with One. But my abilities are different. I understand Tholosian minds better. Clo . . . I think I can connect to them—like the Unity through Vyga. I could *make* them listen to me, at least for long enough to hold off the Oracle."

"But you said you weren't as strong as Vyga without the Unity."

"I'll use the ichor."

Clo made a noise. "The varnish might stop the endospores and radiation, but you still don't know what prolonged use of ichor will do to your abilities. You're using yourself as an experiment."

Rhea's breathing was shallow, and Clo knew she was afraid. Clo had held her in the med center after she'd gone into Chara's mind. "I need to do this." Rhea tried to sound firm.

Clo's arms tightened around Rhea. "You said you felt yourself sinking before. What if you can't make it out? What if you lose too much sense of yourself, like when Vyga connected more fully with the Unity? Ve doesn't feel anything about the early parts of ver life."

She didn't speak her true fear: *What if you forget what you feel about me?*

"No, you don't understand." Rhea's voice caught. "I *need* to do this. I never had choices back on Tholos. I was always an experiment, made to be a weapon. This time, when I go back there, I want to use my abilities for good."

No, Clo wanted to say. *Please. Don't.* But loving Rhea meant Clo couldn't stand in her way.

Clo pulled back, using her fingers to tilt Rhea's chin up. She dipped her head, her lips meeting Rhea's. They kissed slowly, almost as tentative as the first time they'd done this. As if they knew this could be the last.

"I won't leave you alone," Clo said, drawing back to look at Rhea's face.

Her eyes fluttered shut, lashes dark against her cheek. She pulled Clo closer, and there was no more need for words. They said their potential goodbyes with every stroke, every caress. Every press of lips or flick of tongue. Rhea kissed Clo's scars, and Clo's work-roughened hands touched Rhea with as much gentleness as she could.

Clo felt the same awe she'd had when a bird had landed on her once on Fortuna. The wonder that she had been chosen. A certainty that if she did something wrong, that bird would fly away for good.

But on Eve, Rhea had flown back to her.

Clo deepened the kiss, her mouth moving to Rhea's neck, her shoulder. Their movements grew more insistent. Clo forced herself to slow, to take her time. She may not believe in the gods, but that night, she prayed at the altar of Rhea's body. And when Rhea leaned over her, they moved together, fingers drifting lower. Clo shut her eyes and simply *felt*, knowing Rhea could sense her emotions. It all swirled through her at the same speed as a galaxy filled with stars. She wanted to share all of herself, everything she had.

And for those divine few, timeless moments, Clo didn't worry at all about tomorrow.

46.

ERIS

Present day

Eris tried not to watch Damocles as the Devils met on the bridge of *Zelus*.

A huge part of her wished her brother wasn't there. That there'd been any other way. A confederation of rebel ships flanked *Zelus* on its way to Tholos—but not enough. Not nearly enough. Everyone in the command center had a bleak countenance behind their performative smiles or stern demeanor. They were flying into enemy territory, and some of them wouldn't make it out. This could be the last time they were all in a room together, alive and well. It ought to have been a better goodbye.

And it would have been if Damocles hadn't been there. It didn't matter that Eris had chained him to one of the chairs or that he sat, bored and indifferent, as if he wasn't listening. He was the ultimate enemy in their midst, and no one in that room could drop their guard, not while he was on *Zelus*.

He wasn't as inattentive as he appeared. That was as much of an act as the smile Clo passed Kyla as they brought each other up to speed. It was a reminder of how dire their situation was: the Oracle had infiltrated Eve, captured all of the Tholosian Empire, and held their friend held in the ruins of a generation ship. Even Eris, who had faced numerous instances of shit odds, had to admit this one had *spectacularly* fucking bad probabilities.

But she'd go in and do her job.

Kyla projected images of Tholos into the center of the room and flicked a finger across the screen to zoom in. The images showed the area around the Tholos Palace, which included the vast landscape around the Temple in exquisite detail.

From above, the old generation ship's massive size was impressive; Eris had never seen it from this angle. Tholosians carefully controlled the airspace around the palace, and the nearest place to land a craft—unless one had direct permission from the Archon—was at least seventy miles away. As far as Eris knew, the space above the palace had been a dead zone to keep Tholosian enemies from ever familiarizing themselves with the layout of the Empire's most sacred places.

"How did you get these?" Eris asked. Even Damocles had snapped to attention.

"An undercover reconnaissance mission some years back," Kyla said. "They're a bit old now, but they'll work for our purposes." She pointed to the landscape north of the Temple, a dense thicket of trees below a rocky cliff face. "Ariadne once told me tunnels lead from the Temple into the forests. Before the Tholosians completed the palace and the capital in the early days of settlement, those tunnels functioned as underground transport services for the workers. Ariadne used the palace route to escape from Tholos the first time, but she mentioned there's a longer tunnel here." She pointed to a section of trees. "I don't know if the Oracle took action after Ariadne left Tholos, but there's a chance that *this* tunnel might still be unguarded."

"A chance?" Clo's lips twisted. "I hate chances."

Damocles sat back and gave a tug of his chain. "What this fool didn't mention is that the tunnel—*assuming* the Oracle isn't guarding it—hasn't been used in centuries. And you want us to walk in and hope it doesn't collapse and kill us all?" He rolled his eyes. "I reject this. Next. Perhaps we ought to hear a plan from someone more competent."

"Oh?" Kyla gave a mocking smile. "I'm terribly sorry, Your Highness. Should I have us all carry you in on a chaise longue so you can eat cake while the rest of us peasants kill and die for your entertainment?" The smile dropped. "Go fuck yourself."

"Fuck off and die," Nyx added, with an almost lazy wave of her arm.

"Die mad, ye wee shitegoblin," Clo said, grinning.

Rhea gave Damocles a patient look. "You really are an asshole," she said, almost sweetly.

"Complete fuckwad of a human being," Cato added for good measure.

Something in the vicinity of Eris's heart gave a pang when she realized this was where Ariadne would relish calling him a penis-head again.

Damocles' eyes narrowed, and he glanced at his sister. "I am going to slaughter them all."

Eris gave him a droll look. "I'm pretty sure they can't wait for you to try."

Everyone else on the bridge smiled. And for a brief, shining moment, Eris's entire past melted away. She was not Discordia, former Heir to the Tholosian throne. She was not the Servant of Death. She was Eris, and these were her Devils, and what they had given her meant more than an entire empire: friendship. Trust. Even Damocles couldn't take that from her. Not in that room, not with his threats, not ever.

"Now that that's settled," Kyla said with no small amount of satisfaction, gesturing to the image again. "Once the Oracle becomes aware that we're on-site, we need to prepare for an onslaught. One will have uncrewed craft and every programmed citizen at One's disposal, so we're going to have to move fast in the Temple while the outside counteroffensive distracts the Oracle. Nyx will lead our troops in the air while we're on the inside. Elva's agreed to remain on *Zelus* as copilot."

Cato looked incredulous. "Nyx and the other rebels against the entire Tholosian fleet? Look, there's shit odds, and then there's—"

"It won't be the entire fleet." Damocles didn't seem pleased about volunteering this information. "I thinned military presence in the Three Sisters after the truce with the Evoli, when visiting emissaries arrived on Macella. Nyx and the rabble will probably die but at least not right away."

Nyx flipped him the scythes.

Eris was surprised. "You mean you actually made a diplomatic decision?"

Damocles scowled at her. "I'm the Archon."

"You *were* the Archon."

His glare turned murderous.

Kyla pulled up a rough blueprint of the Temple's interior. Even the projected rudimentary drawing of *Argonaut's* design took up a large portion of the command center. "Clo and Rhea, your job is to reach Ariadne and get her safely out of the Temple while the rest of us shut down the Oracle—she'll likely be on the bridge where the control systems are." Rhea had told Eris and Kyla of her plan with her abilities. Eris sure as shit hoped it worked. "Cato and I will take care of the backup system below the old spaceship passenger city while Damocles and Eris kill the AI system in the Temple's heart."

Nyx frowned at the rendering. "Did Ariadne draw this?"

Kyla nodded. "She sent it to me at headquarters while she was still in the Temple. We'd planned to use this and the surveillance images to go after her if her life was ever in jeopardy for providing us intel. When she escaped with you and Rhea, I thought I'd never need it."

"She's usually better at details than this," Nyx said. "How big is this fucking ship? I couldn't get near the Temple when I was a royal guard, and the base is all surrounded by trees."

"Six hundred meters in length, with thirty decks. The city itself had at least six thousand apartments to hold all its occupants. Ariadne provided the basic layout to get in and find her on the bridge. I filled some parts based on my knowledge that older generation ships kept their backup generators below resident cities. They're completely isolated from the main generator in case there's a fire or other damage."

Nyx made a sound of frustration. "So, we have no idea where the *heart* is that the Oracle needs to function."

Kyla's gaze settled on Damocles. "No." Her lips flattened. "*We* do not."

Damocles just smiled.

"Oh, *fuck no*," Clo exploded. "No. *No way* are we flying in with this dickface keeping vital info to himself. I say we leave him out of the plan altogether, drop him into the nearest ocean, and watch the monsters feast."

Damocles' cold gaze touched on Clo, but he only lifted a shoulder. "Fine. Leave me out of it. The Temple's heart is where, again?" He laughed. "Oh, right. You don't know."

"We could find it ourselves," she snarled.

"Maybe. The ship is massive. You'll waste precious time you can't spare, and you don't even know how to get in once you *do* find it." His smile widened. "But I do."

"And we're supposed to believe that? Ye could be lying. You're always fucking lying."

"He knows," Eris interrupted. "He's holding the information hostage so I don't shoot him."

"Already did that, Discordia," he said, tapping the corner of his bionic eye.

"And your guards aren't here to save you this time."

Rhea stepped forward. Her focus on Damocles was fixed, almost unnerving. Even Eris was intimidated by her regard.

Though Rhea had a gentle nature, her temper had limits. Eris had learned that people underestimated Rhea; her compassion and kindness were deemed easy to manipulate. Over these last few months, Eris knew that Rhea possessed her own hidden weapons. Her abilities were like blades beneath silk dresses, used only when necessary.

Damocles was too foolish to understand what everyone else in that room knew instinctively: Rhea was gauging whether or not to pull out that blade.

"Give us more," she said, evenly. "Or we will do as Clo suggested."

Damocles leaned back with a click of his tongue. "That information is the only thing keeping me alive, and I think you know it. I won't share it even for you." His gaze lingered on her body. "Not even for old times' sake."

Clo bristled. Rhea's expression didn't change. If anything, those strange eyes of hers seemed to grow molten. "Now, Damocles."

"Look at you. You seem to have found your—" Damocles flinched. "Stop scratching around in my head, Rhea," he snapped. "You know I can resist your abilities."

Eris gripped her chair, fascinated despite herself. Like all their siblings, Damocles and Eris had been trained in the academy to withstand Evoli mind techniques. Eris had been instructed to imagine the expanse between galaxies. Empty and dark, her body weightless and in perpetual motion. She thought of how inertia would keep her spinning and spinning and spinning endlessly and that her mind was as desolate as the space on her journey.

If that failed, and she encountered more powerful Evoli, she altered the image to what she taught Clo. She thought of the sea on Macella, dragging her beneath the waves. How she could hold her breath for approximately twenty-five minutes, longer than most humans. And eventually, her head filled with pinpoints of light, and her lungs burned, and she danced on the precarious edge of death. What did Damocles imagine?

But Rhea had been practicing—and Eris knew she had grown stronger.

"You might be able to resist my abilities," Rhea said to Damocles calmly, "but I can make it hurt."

She must have dug deeper into his mind, because Damocles gave a slight hiss of pain. Eris had seen this expression before; he was trying to keep his silence. They had learned to bear agony, but Damocles had never done it as well as his sister.

"*Stop it,*" he said through clenched teeth.

"No." Rhea's voice was as clear as a chime. "Tell us something we want to know, or I will give another push."

A gasp tore from Damocles' lips. "You *fucking* freak," he snarled. "My father ought to have killed y—" He grasped his hair and shut his eyes, his breathing labored.

"Sometimes, I wished he would," Rhea said. Her pale skin glowed, the fractal designs a dark contrast. Eris knew Rhea had concealed herself all those years in the Tholosian court. Hidden the Evoli DNA mixed in with her Tholosian genes. Her skin would have given her away then— but now she was free. She no longer hid it from the rest of the rebels. "When he trained me, I wished he had. And when you put me on a dinner table, painted in gold, I wished you had. I'm only sharing with you what I endured in service to you and your father. You might be able to block your mind, but some of it will still get through. You'll feel echoes of my anger, my hatred, my old despair. You want it to stop? Then give us information we can use. I have plenty more to provide."

Damocles gasped again, but he was clearly having difficulty maintaining his facade. "Get out of my head, and I'll do it," he panted.

Rhea must have pulled back, because she lowered her eyes, and Damocles let out a soft breath of relief.

"That," Clo said in awe, "was really fucking sexy. I mean, terrifying. But sexy."

"Badass as fuck," Nyx agreed. "Do it again."

Rhea gave a small smile but kept her focus on Damocles. "Well?"

His glare might have been more effective if Rhea hadn't sliced apart his calm facade. Worse: she had humiliated him, made him look vulnerable to his enemies. Eris knew firsthand that Damocles never forgot or forgave embarrassment.

"According to the archives, there was a collapse in the east wing of *Argonaut*." He gave this information angrily, resentment plain in his features. "The Tholosians had left the ship to ruin after they landed and only later decided to maintain it as a sacred Temple. The only way into the heart is through a narrow bridge." He shot his sister a glance. "Discordia's the only one here small enough to reach it, since Oracle took your little Engineer. But I'll keep its location within the Temple to myself, to ensure my safe departure. Rhea can scratch around as much as she'd like, but she can't make me give it to you."

Eris regarded her brother, knowing he was calculating some decision in his mind. But what? What move was he about to make on their metaphorical zatrikion board?

Whatever it was, Eris had to be ready.

Her own move was beginning to formulate in her mind, and she hoped he expected her to make a different one.

Because it was the last game they'd ever play—and the loser wasn't going to walk out of the Temple on Tholos alive.

———

Later, Eris found Clo alone in the observation room. She had the recliners carefully placed in the center of the room as she gazed up at the stars, tucked under blankets. Eris watched as her friend lifted a bottle of rum and took a deep, deep drink. Eris recognized that particular bottle from their stop at a ruined outpost on Lyra. Clo always called it *good thieving* if they managed to purloin a bottle of alcohol on their supply runs. Clo had held the black bottle up with a grin and wiggled her eyebrows. "Don't fuckin' mind if I do," she'd said.

Eris smiled at the memory. She and Clo had gone from friends to bitter enemies, back to friends, and their trust had built with every supply run. Avern, it had grown when Clo demanded the other Devils rescued Eris on Laguna. If it weren't for Clo, she would have been in Damocles' custody, drugged to compliance, and paraded on every planet as his prisoner.

Eris sat in the chair next to Clo—probably recently vacated by Rhea. "Can I get in on that?"

Clo wordlessly passed the bottle, and Eris put it to her lips for a drink and returned it. Clo and Eris drank in silence.

It was decent rum this time. A diplomatic gift, maybe, for a visiting emissary. Eris relished the taste. It reminded her of the life she'd left behind, the Empire she'd given up. It occurred to her that she missed little about her previous life. Not the killing, not the brutal training. Not the constant competition with a brother who loathed her. Her life back then was a series of sacrifices made in service to the gods. They had demanded so much of her that she barely had the chance to live. She had been as dead as the souls offered to her patron god.

She wished she had more time. She wished she hadn't wasted so much of what she'd been given. She wished—

Her hand found Xander's wolf in her pocket, and she pulled it out. She ran her fingers over the wolf's face, remembering the first time she had ever seen it. Remembering that her brother was the first person who ever taught her to value life over death.

"I never got a close look at it," Clo said, glancing over. "It's a beaut. Firewolf?"

Eris nodded. "My brother Xander made it." She couldn't believe she'd never told any of them about Xander. Too painful a scar to cut open again. She passed the carving over.

Clo made a sound of surprise, turning it over and investigating the grooves. "Didn't think you royal lot were the artistic types."

"We were beaten for it," Eris confirmed. The wood of the wolf's face glistened from the oils of her hands, accumulated from years of reverent fingertips. "Xander risked it. When he gave this to me, I didn't understand why anyone would endure such agony over something so . . . insignificant. Later, I understood that it was his small act of rebellion. His way of reminding himself that he wasn't who they made us be. Art isn't logical." Clo handed it back, and Eris dragged a thumb over the arch of the wolf's back. "And I kept it with me because I wasn't who they made me be, either." She slid the wolf back in her pocket and reached for the top of her jumpsuit. Her scythe necklace hung beneath the fabric. She undid the clasp and held it up. "I'm not the Servant of Death anymore, Clo."

Clo's gaze softened. "I know you're not. You haven't been for a long time."

"I can't go into the Temple wearing this necklace," Eris said. "I won't go in as I was. I want to go in as I *am*." She reached over and took Clo's hand so that she could drop the necklace in the other woman's palm. "Keep this for me, will you? Until after the battle."

Clo closed her fist around the scythe. She gave Eris a strange look. "Only if you plan to melt it down with me."

"Sure," Eris said, easily enough. She gave a smile, laughed a little to herself, and stole the rum bottle from Clo. She took one last, long drink, and released her memories. The Servant of Death was gone. "Or throw it into the sea. Let it sink to the bottom. That's all that'll be left of Princess Discordia. I've finally let her go."

When she got up to leave, Clo called after her. "You know he's going to turn on you," Clo said. "Remember that every second you're with Damocles. He's just waiting for the opportunity."

Eris loosened a breath but didn't turn back. "Let me take care of Damocles. I know what I have to do."

She'd mark her brother off her list tomorrow.

47.

Present day

Zelus glided through the void, an invisible speck of space dust.

Elva and the other rebel Evoli worked overtime to upgrade their tech with the shielding devices Vyga had supplied. By the time they finished, another ship would have to be right in front of them before they'd realized they'd fallen into a trap. The Oracle's system would lock on once they started shooting, but the Novantae needed every advantage if they hoped to survive.

That morning, Rhea watched her fellow rebels bustling between ships as they prepared to launch their defense. She'd memorized the shape, color, and feel of their auras and committed their features to memory. If she made it out of this alive, she'd help send their souls to the Avern.

Rhea stood on the bridge with the other Devils, gripping a larger piece of ichor in her palm. She'd stolen it from Ariadne's bunk—the engineer had left her beautiful, wonderful collection of things behind. Ariadne had already painted the rock with the same clear protective varnish as the shard in her locket, rendering it harmless to direct contact. Perfect for displaying on her shelf.

Rhea hoped it would focus her abilities better. She could not fail.

Kyla stood to Rhea's right, her hands clasped behind her back. Her aura was surprisingly calm. But then, they had spent hours preparing as best they could. Kyla had her plan and ensured everyone knew their roles. There was nothing left to do but act—no time for second-guessing.

No time for regret.

Rhea adjusted her armor. She and the others were clad in black, the armor molding to them like a second skin to guard against Mors blasts. The protection was pocked after previous encounters with Tholosians but still reliable. Their helmets were nearby, to be put on at the last moment.

Together, they made a fearsome picture: a group of angry Devils in black and one former warlord.

Damocles wanted to keep his golden armor, but Kyla had only laughed. "I plan to melt it down and sell it, so thanks for the scythes." She'd given him a sardonic salute for good measure. "It was ugly, anyway." The coronation cloak had been damaged by Morsfire. Rhea smiled to think how furious that would have made the old Archon.

Damocles looked displeased, but he and Eris wore simple black jumpsuits and jackets with basic Mors protection. With everyone suited, Damocles informed them the most covert way to approach Tholos was via the slingshot route around Agora, one of the smallest moons. He and Eris had been arguing about it for the past half hour. Rhea was exhausted just listening to them.

"No," Eris said again. "Father closed that route due to the orbital debris. The number of accidents—"

"I can get us through." Damocles sounded bored. "If your pilot and band of rebels aren't completely fucking incompetent, it should be easy. But by all means, if you have a better way, let's hear it."

Move made. Eris scowled, and Clo's hands tightened on the ship's controls.

<Please, can I kill him?> she asked. *<Pretty please? You know I don't like to beg.>*

Everyone in the cockpit had fantasized about killing the Archon. Rhea imagined it in bed. Slitting his throat in his sleep had been her first thoughts of murder, but she hadn't been able to bring herself to do it. Nyx and Rhea had bonded over how easy and useless it was to kill a sleeping prince. The Archon could always engineer another Heir.

Maybe even someone worse than Damocles.

<We should all take turns,> Nyx said, copiloting *Zelus* before she'd take it over when the rest of them touched down on the surface. *<One blow each until he dies. We can bet on prizes. Eris, what would we win?>*

<Satisfaction.> Eris moved so fast, it took Rhea's brain a moment to catch up. Her blaster was pressed hard to Damocles' temple. He stiffened, even as he feigned nonchalance.

"Do as he says, Clo," Eris said. "If we end up having company too soon, I'll blast his brains out, and we can take our chances on finding our own way into the Temple. I'll apologize for not sharing the kill after."

Damocles blinked, almost lazily. "Your empty threats are getting boring. At least be more creative or amusing. Nyx threatened to shove her entire cane up my ass."

<That wasn't a threat,> Nyx groused. *<That was a plan.>*

Clo angled the ship toward Angora, speeding up so the gravity would assist them around the tiny planet. "If you do kill him," Clo said aloud, "I volunteer to chuck his corpse out the airlock."

"You're so hasty," Damocles chided Clo. "You need me now, and you need me when you land." His voice was almost a purr. "Though if Discordia gave me a weapon, she and I could take out every gerulae in the city. You remember our slaughters, don't you?" he asked his sister. "You had such a talent for killing."

Eris's expression was ice. "I agreed to unbind your hands. But you're not getting a weapon, and we're not slaughtering the gerulae. You lead me to the heart, and if you're lying about it—"

"You know how our game goes, Discordia. Am I bluffing, distracting you, or communicating every move I make? I have to wonder the same about you." He'd abandoned his eye patch as artifice. Both of his eyes were bright gold, the mirrors of his sister's, even if one was as false as Damocles' soul.

Eris's finger tightened on the trigger of her gun. It'd take so little effort for her to pull it a little more, Rhea knew. She had practiced shooting with Eris, Elva, and Clo a few times as part of her training for Eve. She'd always hated weapons, but Kyla demanded the training before supply runs.

It only takes three muscles to pull a trigger, Eris had told Rhea during training. *Just a little bit of pressure, that's all you need.*

As she maneuvered the ship through the debris, Damocles directed Clo around Angora. The pilot bristled, her aura spiky and red. It wasn't unlike the protective barrier around Eve, but *Zelus* was a much bigger ship than the ones they'd taken to Evoli space and back.

Kyla's face hardened with focus. She leaned forward, as if she could guide the *Zelus* through to safety on pure will alone.

The ride was bumpy. Clo had to make sharp turns that had everyone muttering curses. Rhea held on tight to the back of Clo's chair, one fingertip resting on the soft skin where her neck met her shoulder to keep her calm and focused.

When Clo was through the worst of their journey, Rhea still wished she could somehow break through Damocles' defenses. The ichor strengthened her abilities—what if she sent everything she had at him? She only needed to find the tiniest crack in his shields, a minute gap in the noise. She had felt the barest echoes of his emotions— nothing but coiled rage and an endless hunger for power, adulation, and control.

But what if Rhea could force Damocles to remain compliant? What if she could control him?

What if she could command him?

Rhea tried one last time, gently at first. Her awareness flowed over the edges of Damocles' mental walls. Yet she crashed against them, over and over; he'd fortified them since she'd hurt him. She wanted to keep trying, to dig through his defenses, but she was already breathing hard. If she drained herself now, she'd be useless on the ground.

Rhea pulled back from Damocles' mind.

Damocles' eyes met hers, and he smiled. She recognized that expression from across the ballroom on Tholos. It said: *I won.*

Rhea's lips flattened. *Not for long.*

As if he read her mind, Damocles' smile faded, and he glanced away. After they were past the worst of the debris field, Eris took her blaster from his temple, but she held it in her hand, and Rhea knew her fingers still itched to pull that trigger.

"It's time," Kyla said. "Clo, pass *Zelus* over to Nyx."

Clo nodded and ceded control to the other pilot's chair, unstrapping herself. "Take care of her," Clo said.

"I'll do my best," Nyx replied.

As they filed out, each of the Devils gave Nyx a nod.

"Go get our Ariadne," Nyx said. "And give the Oracle hell."

The Devils and Damocles climbed into the bullet craft. Tholos was visible from the porthole, her two sisters smaller in the distance, like prominent blue stars.

It was a tight fit. As the bullet craft touched on firm ground, Rhea steadied her breath and put her hand over the ichor at her throat. She could already feel her empathy coiling deep in her belly, desperate to reach out and read others. To gather them into herself. To create a Unity.

Once Clo powered down the bullet craft, they moved fast. A small cluster of gerulae were already coming, their movements too even, too smooth.

Rhea used her abilities like a whip, lashing out and slipping beneath their outer programming until she found some shred of emotion. Most of it was pain and fear. She tried not to let it overwhelm her as she began braiding gerulae together.

"Gods, I hope this works," Rhea muttered. "*Sleep!*"

They dropped like puppets.

"Yes!" Clo shouted. "You beauty."

The gerulae lay on the ground, boneless and limp. The ichor glowed at Rhea's throat.

She'd done it. She'd actually done it. She could feel them, connected to her like invisible threads that she could twist together. She had created a mini Unity with Tholosians, something not even Vyga could do.

She felt powerful.

Damocles, Kyla, and Eris took the lead, but Rhea lingered behind with Clo and helped clear their path. They fell into a rhythm of Rhea freezing anyone they came across, and Kyla and Eris hitting them with the stuns. If they could do this without more senseless death, they would.

Damocles glanced back at Rhea. "My father wasted your talents, it seems."

"That's because you both underestimated everyone but especially women," she said, flicking her arm toward another gerulae.

His lips pulled back from his teeth. Kyla reached out and dragged him forward. He was still bound, for now.

They wouldn't have long before enough gerulae fell and Oracle noticed the gaps in One's coding, the infinitesimal lack of data storage.

But Rhea kept stopping them, and every time she did, she glowed with the pleasure of power. She could make them do anything. If she told their hearts to stop, they might. Part of her was tempted to try. The Oracle could potentially reactivate the ones they had felled so far. Perhaps she should sully her soul a little more to make sure her Devils were truly safe.

No. No. She pulled herself back from the thought, shuddering. *Get Ariadne. Focus on Ariadne. You've not directly killed anyone so far. You're not starting now.*

Kyla led them to the tunnels. The door blended into the rocks, invisible before she used her scrambler to hack the entrance key. Old tech stood no chance against theirs.

Kyla went first, followed by Cato and Clo. Damocles paused in front of Rhea. "You love this. Isn't it heady to command people to do what you want? To control their every breath?" He gave a wistful sigh. "Archons don't have queens, but you might have tempted me. You would have been fearsome."

"Being your queen is beneath me."

Rhea pulled the door shut behind them and hurried to catch up to the others. The old tunnels were of a hard gray stone, occasionally reinforced with metal supports showing signs of age.

"According to Ariadne's map, these go right under the original generation ship," Kyla said.

Knowing they were close, Rhea focused on trying to recover some of her strength. Getting them to the tunnels had already left her unsteady and drained. Her stomach roiled with nausea. Her mind blurred around the edges.

They were quiet as they made their way through the labyrinth. It was dark but for the Devils' helmet lights and the soft golden glow of the ichor around Rhea's throat.

Above her, she sensed thousands of gerulae milling through the palace's outer levels like ants—drones under the control of one singular entity.

She wished she was powerful enough to make everyone above them fall asleep at once. Take them over in an instant. No blood, no tears, no death. They could walk right up to the Oracle and pull the plug and then dance on their way out.

The Oracle was vulnerable without the coding present in humans. The ships could fly themselves, but smaller weapons were all designed to be shot by people. To give them a purpose and to feed the much larger machine of an Empire. There were the small cleaning bots and drones, but they weren't designed to be weapons.

The hallway sloped upward. Soon enough, they reached another doorway.

Kyla kept her Mors trained on Damocles as Eris opened the door and peered over it. Rhea couldn't sense any gerulae immediately above them.

"Clear," Eris said, hauling herself up.

Clo hung back, giving Rhea's shoulder a bump. "Are you all right?"

"I'm tired," she said, honestly.

Rhea's whole body thrummed. She felt bits of her energy siphoning down the line to each gerulae, draining her with every heartbeat. She tried to send through reassurance, regret for taking them over. She didn't know if any of it made it through.

"I know." Clo gave Rhea one hard, firm kiss. "I'll be here with you every step of the way. Let's go save Ari."

Clo let Rhea go up first. Rhea's head tilted back as she took in where they were. It was as if they'd stepped back in time. The bottom of *Argonaut* was once the storage bay, housing supplies and greenhouses, and all the things humanity needed to survive a journey of hundreds of years when they left their old, dying world. Everything was smooth but utilitarian. Metal sheets stamped down with giant bolts. Faded, unfamiliar letters were just visible on some of them. The metal glimmered dully in the lights from their helmets, but there was no other illumination. Why bother? No one came there except small bots that would conduct any minor maintenance the Oracle needed on Oneself: take away the worst of the dust, and chase away any cobwebs from brave arachnids. The darkness at the corners was complete.

"This is creepy as fuck," Clo said, voicing Rhea's thoughts.

"All right," Kyla said, clicking on a stronger light she'd strapped to her belt as the others did the same. "You know what to do."

Rhea found her voice. "If we don't make it—I want you to know it's been an honor."

"Don't make me cry, Rhea," Cato said.

"We're making it out of here," Kyla said, as if she could speak it into truth.

Rhea wanted to hug them, clutch them so tightly, and never let go. Instead, she settled for giving each of them a tendril of her power that she couldn't afford to spare, to chase away the worst of the fear and raise their determination.

Clo took Rhea's hand. As they hurried through the depths of *Argonaut*, three teams went their separate ways, their footsteps echoing in a great, empty space.

Rhea hoped this wouldn't be the last time she saw them.

48.

Present day

Eris and Damocles climbed through the ancient ship.

The ruined sections were covered in the flora of the ancient biosphere. Overhead, the sun shone through the arched glass dome, illuminating flowers, most of which grew nowhere else in the galaxy. Tholosians had imported many of them from the Old World, and most of them had long since gone extinct.

It was peaceful and beautiful there. She hadn't expected beauty.

Eris tried to keep her focus on Damocles, but she was mesmerized by the blue and red swirls on the massive leaves, by the blooming flowers that covered the biodome in an array of colors. She recognized one flower—the purple astra from the Evoli planets. Rhea had brought a few pressed blooms back with her and told Eris and the others the story behind them. How many flowers bloomed in there? How many drops of blood would water them?

Maintenance bots flew across the dome or hung from thin metal cables, spraying and watering, the six mechanical legs plucking dead leaves to maintain the ancient plants. They were different from the small cleaning bots Eris had grown up seeing. These were larger, the size of her hands, strangely mesmerizing in their movements. Glass bulbs on their back were filled with a pale green substance that glowed softly against the plants.

"The stairs are at the other end," Damocles said quietly. He fixed his lips in a firm line, his face impassive as he led her through the gravel pathway of the biosphere.

"I hope you remember the blueprint as well as you think," she said.

Eris, like every citizen of the Empire, had never entered the Temple. She learned from her studies that *Argonaut* had been left to ruin for over a hundred years as they built the palace around it—grander and more refined than any spaceship could ever hope to be. The first Archon dispatched robots to preserve the ship as a sacred Temple to maintain their first ancestors' relics. Ariadne had told Eris that the Temple's center, where she lived in the old bridge, was so pristine that it looked brand new, even though it was ancient.

In other parts of the Temple, the bots simply maintained a level of arrested decay to keep it from collapsing. It was, for all intents and purposes, a preserved ruin. Conservation of the world Tholosians had come from and would never see again.

"I recall the blueprint just fine," Damocles replied, sounding vaguely irritated. "You once complimented my memory, back when you had use for me."

Eris slid her hand into her pocket so that he wouldn't see her press her fingernails into her palm. She *had* remarked on his memory before, when they teamed up to slaughter their brothers together. Damocles excelled at drafting maps by recollection; it had made him skilled in their competition. She always had to remind herself that he was an adept hunter beneath all the arrogance and anger—and just as proficient at killing.

"Don't pretend you didn't have the same use for me," Eris told him. "Heir and Spare, remember? That competition was how we were raised."

"It wasn't about the competition when you chose Xander over me," Damocles said.

Eris almost paused, but instead kept up with her brother, their pace quick as they turned down another path in the biosphere. "This has nothing to do with Xander," she said. "When you drugged me back on Laguna and forced our father to choose you, it wasn't about Xander."

Damocles' lips flattened. "Xander was *weak*."

"Stop it, Damocles," Eris snapped. "You know this isn't about—"

"You made me into what I am, and then *you chose him."* Damocles stopped on the path, his chest heaving as his gaze collided with Eris'. *"You* taught me the fucking game, Discordia. *You* put a blade to my throat and told me to stop caring so much. And when I became exactly the man you made, you discarded me."

Eris drew back her shoulders as age-old rage made her blood run hot. "I am not responsible for your actions. I am not the Oracle slithering through your synapses. Every decision you made was *yours,* Damocles. And you made them because it ate you up inside to see our father choose me and not you."

Damocles gave a furious shake of his head. "I watched him choose you over and over again, knowing that the daughter he admired was a performance to earn his esteem. Between the two of us, I deserved to sit on that dais more than you. And we both know it."

"Why?" The question cracked the air like broken glass.

Damocles stepped closer, his eyes narrowed. "Because I knew I'd be better. That the day I finally won that game, it would be because I was superior to you in every way. After all, you made victory my obsession. And back in Laguna, I fucking won." He took off down the path, throwing his last words over his shoulder: "And when this is all over, I'll beat you again."

Eris followed closely behind him, staring at the tense set of his shoulders as they crept up the winding grand staircase in the biosphere. While he seemed calm, Eris knew him well enough. He was planning, just like she was, for when they finally destroyed the Oracle. He'd have his escape route, the board planned out in his mind. Because he was right about one thing: she had put that game in his mind. She had made the throne a competition.

Always have an escape route, she reminded herself.

As they continued up the old staircases of the biosphere toward the heart of the old ship, Eris imagined the pieces of their metaphorical zatrikion board.

His King.

Her Queen.

One move until victory.

Only this time, the board wasn't one moment shared between the two of them. It was a lifetime of choices that returned to this moment, on their imagined board, where they continued sniping at each other like children at the academy—playing with imagined rules in their imagined match. The problem with a circular game was that you always made it back to the beginning, no matter how far you progressed. The moves might be different, but it was still the same game. The limitations existed on a board made to fit the surface of a small writing desk.

But Eris was no longer a child. She was not Discordia. And she knew that her rules had changed because this game was no longer between the two of them. The scale of the board no longer existed on a small area; it involved a galaxy. It affected her friends.

It had all led to this.

In her mind, Eris quietly tossed away the rules she had abided by her whole life.

49.

NYX

Present day

Nyx and the other rebels glided over the palace compound. The landscape was vast, with plenty of military personnel and technology within driving distance. Nyx knew that at any moment, the airspace would become filled with the Oracle's unmanned craft. But Nyx still had to whistle at the sight coming from the looming towers of Vita, the closest city to the Tholos Palace.

Gerulae were already beginning to gather on the metropolis's outskirts, hordes of citizens heading through the streets along the main stretch of road that led to the remote palace. If thousands were gathering there, Nyx didn't doubt that the Oracle controlled them elsewhere, bringing One's vast controlled citizen army in for an attack.

From Nyx's position in the air, the crowd of Tholosians from Vita was so thick that she couldn't even see between each person to the road below. They moved in tandem, as perfect as trained soldiers. What they might lack in fighting skill, they made up for with their lack of pain limitations and decision-making. The Oracle could make them do whatever One wanted.

Over the comms, Nyx heard the chatter of the other rebels. "Every citizen in the fucking city is in the streets, I reckon," one of them said—a pilot she recognized as Lerna, flying *Ajax*. Though the cloaking tech hid Lerna's craft even to Nyx's eyes, her ship's blinking light was visible through their internal tracking system. "More incoming from the villages over here closer to the hills. Waiting for your command, Nyx."

Vita had about a million citizens. A million soldiers at the Oracle's disposal. And if they made it through the palace keep's walls . . .

There would be nothing to stop them from overtaking the Temple.

<*Gerulae are heading over in a fucking horde,*> Nyx said through the Pathos to the Devils below. <*The Oracle knows you're in there. What do you want us to do?*>

<*Any spacecraft?*> Eris sounded distracted.

<*Not yet. The team and I are still cloaked. The second we start shooting, we lose the surprise.*>

<*How much time until the gerulae get here?*>

The burgeoning crowd made its way down the road, moving like insects gathering to defend their colony. As much as Nyx fucking hated to compare human beings to the arthropods on Tholos, the Oracle's comparison to a hive's queen was apt. And One's drones had no choice but to obey.

<*Five minutes,*> Nyx said. <*Ten, max. They're moving fast.*>

<*What do you think, Kyla? The Oracle lets them in, and they'll block our movements. From our current position, it'll take us another fifteen to twenty to get to the heart. The old engine room is still eight stories up, and we're already running.*>

<*Fuck it,*> Kyla said. <*Nyx, tell the others to give us a line and hold it. Don't let anyone through. Do whatever you can to obstruct their route, slow them down.*>

<*On it.*>

Nyx started flipping switches. Her body began to tremble with exhaustion—the adrenaline already taking its toll.

Not now, she told herself. *Only rest when it's safe.*

She got on the comms and relayed Kyla's message. "Don't aim for bodies," she ordered, preparing her projectiles. "If you have to shoot, you shoot at the ground. Blow up a fucking building to block their way if you have to. Wait for my signal."

The affirmative came through, and the blinking lights of the hidden rebel ships got into formation on her screen. Though she knew over a hundred craft flanked her, the skies seemed eerily empty. The Oracle was waiting for One's move. Nyx watched the horde of Oracle-controlled citizens growing closer.

She paused, sweat beading her brow, her breath gasping like broken bellows. *Don't give in to exhaustion.*

Rest can come later.

"*Fire!*" Nyx commanded.

The rebel fleet soared for Vita, locking their projectiles on to buildings in front of the approaching gerulae. Detritus scattered across the road. Buildings toppled to the ground in clouds of dust that would have sent any typical crowd running—but not this one. The gerulae kept coming, their faces and clothes white with dust, an army of pale ghosts. The knocked-over dwellings only slowed them down. The citizens climbed through the rubble, their bodies pushed by the Oracle pumping adrenaline through their systems. Pain was no deterrent. If the AI commanded them to move, they moved.

"Fly through the streets!" Nyx yelled into the comms. "Knock them back with a pulse, and I need more fucking obstructions in these roads. I don't want them to be able to walk without climbing the equivalent of a godsdamned mountain; do you hear me?"

The voices of her team confirmed, and their ships shot through the skies. They sent pulses through the crowds—meant to hinder but not kill—as they brought down the tenements that lined the palace's main highway. To Nyx's shock, the gerulae rose to their feet, climbing over the rubble as if they were entirely unaffected. The Oracle's control over their bodies and brain must have suppressed their physiological response. Nyx knew that the only thing likely to work was the one thing she didn't want to do: damage their bodies. Put lasers through them.

Don't, she told herself. *You're not Damocles' weapon anymore. You do not have to pull that trigger.*

"Seven fucking devils, the pulses aren't working," Daphne said through the comms as she flew *Thrace*. "Do we shoot?"

"No," Nyx snapped. "Do not shoot. I repeat, *do not shoot.* You focus on taking down those buildings and keep slowing them down. Let our team inside do their damn jobs. Do y—"

"*Nyx!*" Elva's voice. She was in another part of *Zelus*, monitoring the skies and using the projectiles at the ship's back. "We have crewless vessels heading into the mesosphere. They'll be on us any minute."

"*Fuck.*" She sent her voice through the comms. "Everyone, get ready! We're about to have some company. Daphne, Lerna, Ceti, Athena, keep taking down those buildings. The rest of us will cover you."

The roar of engines in the distance drew Nyx's attention. Hundreds of uncrewed craft soared through the skies, coming right toward them. Over the comms, she heard the whispered swears of her team as they all took in their impossible odds. But Nyx had seen impossible odds; she had lived through them. She was there despite the God of Death knocking on her fucking door.

And she wasn't ready to let Him take her.

"Hey, everyone?" She flipped switches and got more comfortable in her chair as she eyed the sea of enemy craft. "Remember how I said *don't shoot*? These are the motherfuckers you can shoot. *Bring them down!*"

The whoops of glee over the comms sent her blood racing. Nyx shoved the throttle forward and took off, her lasers spraying. She understood why Clo loved the skies so much, why Cato often sat in the captain's chair when he needed to think. This was different from fighting with her body, but the reward was the same. She grinned as she sent one of the Oracle's ships crashing into the hillside. Another. Another. She covered her team and attacked, her Mors lasers cutting through metal. She felt . . . she felt . . .

Strong.

Her body was trembling, but her mind was sharp, and in the sky, that was all that fucking mattered. She looped above Vita's streets as the Oracle's ships chased her, but *Zelus* was quick. Quick for a cargo ship, at least. *Zelus* was one of the newest generations of Tholosian vessels, and it showed. Despite her bulky size, she just about matched the Oracle's ships in speed and weaponry, and Nyx and Elva's skill made all the difference. That, and a determination not to die.

Not when Nyx had just survived.

Other rebels were not so lucky. A Novan ship crashed into the rubble of Vita, exploding on impact. Nyx flinched, speeding in to protect her team, but more uncrewed craft arrived. They were everywhere, the sky full of Imperial vessels that pounded the cobbled rebel fleet. *Zelus* might have been made for battle, but the other ships were old military fighters, pieced together with little more than clever hands, decent welding jobs, and Ariadne's tech. They were getting battered.

Worse, the gerulae were advancing on the palace.

Nyx watched below as they climbed over the mountains of rubble, their movements swifter now that the Novan air team was distracted with the sky battle. Lerna, Ceti, and Athena's crew tried to keep them out of the compound, but they were attacked in all directions by the Oracle's ships. The rebels that flew in for backup were quickly overwhelmed.

Nyx fought her way to the palace compound, but what she saw made her curse. Nyx shouted through the Pathos, <*The gerulae have breached the Temple!*>

<*Ten minutes!*> Eris's voice came in a rush.

<*Five from where Ari's being held!*> Clo cried.

<*Almost to the backup power,*> Kyla said. <*Nyx, we need more time.*>

"Fuck's sake," Nyx muttered. She got on the radio with the other rebels. "Elva, take down the fucking palace wall. I don't care what it takes. Block every godsdamn entrance there is. If we can't keep them out, then we keep slowing them down. The rest of you stay with me. Keep these ships off *Zelus*, and let us buy the team in the Temple more time."

Nyx could only hope it was enough.

50.

KYLA

Present day

Kyla and Cato sprinted in the direction of the generator.

The ship shuddered beneath their feet, but the roar of explosions from the air battle hardly reached them down there. Kyla tried not to think about the Oracle's legion of uncrewed craft firing on her people. She tried not to think of tomorrow—if they survived, she'd be forced to pick up the pieces, count the dead, and begin the process of rebuilding.

If they had a galaxy to rebuild.

Cato projected an internal map of *Argonaut* from his mech cuff. Kyla studied it, hoping her additions to Ariadne's map were correct. If they weren't . . .

"Ten minutes out," Cato said, tapping his cuff to make their route disappear. Another explosion from outside shook the Temple. Dust fell from the rafters.

"Hurry," Kyla said shortly.

They moved through the ancient city's ruins as quickly as they could, a seamless team of two. The steel beams arched over them, tons of ancient metal that had gone dark and pitted with age. Rusted room numbers still hung from passenger doors, the residences closed off from view. Kyla wondered briefly at the time capsules that must lie within, relics from a ship that didn't even have warp drive, from a civilization that had no planet to call home.

Past the apartments were remnants of an old market square. There were empty plinths that had once held statues, and vacant government offices that were barely standing after so many thousands of years of neglect. Far off was the shadowy entrance to the amphitheater, where even the proto-Tholosians had thirsted for war. These misty ancestors who had birthed a bloody, hungry Empire.

Another distant explosion. An echoing boom hit somewhere deep in Kyla's chest. The ship reverberated slightly with the impact. Kyla swallowed. Tholos hadn't been directly attacked in millennia—just how fortified was this ancient craft?

Past the city, the air was sharp with chemicals and preservatives. The cleanup bots must have been there recently.

Kyla gripped her Mors, ready to pull out her spare if necessary. She took comfort in the press of her other weapons against her body: the stun in her inner pocket, the knives in her boots. Yet the back of Kyla's neck prickled with intuition. That nebulous insight had kept her alive more than once. "You okay?" Cato asked her.

Kyla gave her head a shake. "I will be when we get the fuck out of here."

His lip lifted. "Same." His mech cuff buzzed, and he squinted into the darkness. "Not long now. There should be a stairwell coming up soon."

Kyla reached into the pack at her waist and lit a flare that gleamed white in the dark. It cast Cato's face into a harsh shadow. She threw the flare ahead, and it illuminated the old buildings better than their weak headlamps and torches.

"There," Kyla said.

"Think the homicidal despot desperate to maintain a grip on his empire keeps his word this time?"

"Not a chance," Kyla said shortly. "But Eris can handle him."

He grunted. "I fucking hope so. Back on Laguna—"

"Laguna is why she won't fail," Kyla said. Far off, more clanging, a few shots of Morsfire. "The gerulae are getting closer. We don't have long."

They ran up the steps to the old backup station. The door was ancient and Oracle-controlled. Cato ripped off the panel and worked his way in the innards.

"Can you get through?" Kyla said, Mors at the ready for the first inevitable gerulae coming down the corridor.

"Yeah. Same as the tunnel, it's pretty rudimentary." His hands worked fast, but Kyla couldn't shake her internal clock shouting *hurry, hurry, hurry*.

A few cleaning bots crawled along the walls, but he paid them no mind. Their sideways movements were still profoundly unnerving. A shuffle sounded in the darkness.

Not bots.

Kyla stared up ahead as a shadow emerged, and then another, and another. They were hurrying in Kyla and Cato's direction.

In battle, things were usually so loud, so messy. The gerulae were quiet. Only half a dozen so far, but more would come soon. Their clothing was dusty and torn from the rubble they had clambered over on their way from Vita. There was no screaming, and their faces were vacant, as if no one was present. But they were—Kyla knew that now. Somewhere, deep inside, they were in there. And they couldn't get out.

"Cato," Kyla said sharply. "Gerulae."

"*Fuck.*" His hands shook as he kept going.

Kyla switched to stun and fired, hitting a few at the front of the thin crowd that would only grow as more gerulae were drawn to the noise and the light. She couldn't hold them off for much longer.

"The door, Cato!"

"I'm almost there!" he said.

The hallway was thin, so at least it created a bottleneck. More gerulae came. Two dozen. Three. More? Kyla kept up her steady pulses, and the pile of unconscious bodies grew. New gerulae pushed them against the wall, careless of whether or not they stepped on their brethren.

They kept coming.

Kyla heard the blessed clang of the door opening, the last shot of a Mors as Cato fried the outside lock. Cato seized the back of Kyla's armor to pull her in. It slid shut behind her, the internal mechanisms giving a few satisfying clicks.

Gerulae drummed on the doors. Cato had isolated the lock from the Oracle network, so the only way to open it was manually from this side. But the Oracle had other tools at One's disposal—and the gerulae had a single directive.

It might not hold for long.

"Guard the door," Kyla ordered sharply. "Let me do this part."

Kyla got to work on the generator. Like everything else, it was ancient, unfamiliar tech. She worked with her knowledge of old junkers and craft, the outdated systems and equipment that made up the oldest sections of headquarters back on Nova. She'd had to be good at taking things apart, putting them together, and puzzling over them. It was how her movement had survived.

"No time," she whispered to herself as she took off the metal cover. "Get it done, Kyla."

"Good self-advice," Cato added, wincing as the banging against the door grew louder. "And I don't think that part goes there."

Cato angled his body toward the door, Mors at the ready, but he was close enough to help her puzzle through it.

Kyla curled her lip. "Last I checked, you weren't an expert in ancient ships."

"I'm a pretty damn decent pilot with contemporary ones, and I think it's backwards."

The clanging grew louder. Cato's breath was ragged.

"Stop backseat-mechanicing," Kyla snapped. "No wonder you irritate the shit out of Clo. Newer ships function on five power sources for the warp drive; this used two sources to generate nuclear propulsion power, though they decommissioned the engine. Just the generator left."

Cato shut up.

Kyla worked the controls. Recent generators were sophisticated but still prone to breaking down. Though this one was old, it had been built to last. This one was large and loud—a hissing beast, its power fuelling the innards of the Temple.

With regular maintenance, it had probably never broken down in all its centuries hidden down there. A separate system for the real kernel of the Empire—an AI hiding in a sacred temple, who only allowed one human at a time within its depths. It was easy to imagine the Oracle as a nebulous, floating thing. Power traveling through cables, transmitted through mid-air to appear within chips as if by magic.

But Oracle was still, fundamentally, a machine. It was housed in servers that One protected perfectly from time and decay. The Oracle, it turned out, suffered from hubris just as much as any fallible human— One hadn't expected a cluster of unprogrammed, determined rebels.

Kyla gritted her teeth. She began flipping the switches she hoped would shut down the auxiliary power. Her knowledge was based on rudimentary versions of the engines of second- and third-generation ships she and Sher had stolen from Elysium. Gods, she hoped she was right. If it worked, the rest would be up to Eris—but this could weaken and distract the Oracle.

A horrible screech came from the door. The gerulae kept pushing against it, their weight threatening to break the locking mechanism.

With one final flip of a switch, the red emergency lights powered off. The only illumination came from Kyla and Cato's headlamps.

Kyla sighed with relief. <*Backup power down,*> Kyla told the others. <*Eris, it's on you now.*>

Eris's response was lightning fast. <*On it.*>

"Kyla!" Cato's ragged yell echoed through the room, jolting Kyla from her brief victory at figuring out the generator.

The door had opened wider. Hands reached through, fingers clawing at Cato as he tried to push them back.

Kyla swore. They couldn't leave the generator unattended. The Oracle could simply direct a gerulae to enter the sequence to start it back up again, and it would have all been for nothing.

"Here we go," she muttered. Using the blunt end of her Mors, Kyla slammed it down on one of the levers and broke it off. "Hold them!" she shouted to Cato. She moved to the next lever and did the same thing.

Down and down, she jammed the old parts to lock them into position.

The mech bugs could fix this eventually, but not fast.

"*Kyla!*"

Kyla swung around and threw herself into the fray with Cato. They started shooting, using the stuns to disable gerulae first, hoping to create another barrier of unconscious bodies large enough to keep the others at bay. She tried to close her ears against the fleshy crunch of booted feet stepping on limbs. Was this any kinder, leaving them to be trampled to death?

Kyla grimaced, changing the setting on her Mors to spray in a larger configuration. There was no stun level for this setting.

"No choice," Kyla told Cato, even as her stomach clenched. "We do this to save the others, do you understand?"

Cato's jaw set, but he gave a sharp nod.

They opened fire and shot through the gerulae. The Mors sizzled. Tomorrow, Kyla would live with her guilt.

If she had tomorrow.

51.

Present day

From *Argonaut*'s bridge, Ariadne watched the vids around the city.

"Stop this," she told the Oracle. "Please stop this. You said you would listen to me."

Horror and guilt gnawed at her. She had returned to Tholos and helped the Oracle reprogram everyone into gerulae; she was partly responsible for this chaos. Any lives lost would be her burden to carry. All she'd wanted to do was help her friends—give them time to come up with a plan before the Oracle tried to kill them all. Had she made it worse?

Her breath came so fast that she could barely catch it. Tears stung her eyes. She'd made it worse. Oh, gods, she'd made it so much worse. Her entire life was one misjudgment after another.

"Stop it," she whispered, unable to look away. She didn't know if she was speaking to herself or her parent. "Please, please, *please*."

"I am sorry, daughter. Your life is still in imminent danger. I cannot acquiesce."

The chaos continued. Ariadne watched as gerulae climbed over each other to get over the walls that *Zelus* and the other ships knocked down. Thousands marched down the road from the city, covered in debris. Others walked through the burning rubble of fallen buildings without care for pain. One caught fire, and he made no moves to put himself out.

Because the Oracle didn't let them process pain.

The Oracle didn't care about hurting anyone.

A distant *boom* made the Temple shudder and groan. On the screens, rebel ships fought the Oracle's unmanned craft, sending projectiles back and forth. The sky was covered in smoke, the Tholosian sun a burning shade of orange that barely penetrated the thick plume. Detritus fell on the crowd below, covering every citizen in the city with a layer of dust the color of sun-bleached bone.

BOOM!

The old command center of *Argonaut* shook, and Ariadne covered her ears. The Oracle spoke to her, using Ariadne's own voice over the comm, but she shut it out. *You can't stay here,* she told herself. *You can't leave your friends out there to do this alone.*

Her feet were already moving.

The Oracle spoke again, but Ariadne kept pressing her palms to her ears. "Go," she told herself, trying to shut out the noise. "Go, go, go."

But when she tried the door, it was locked. The Oracle had never secured it before—One had always given Ariadne the illusion of freedom. She could harbor fantasies of walking out this door—nothing was stopping her. Once, she had made it thirty whole steps into the hallway before her fear had driven her back to the bridge. Growing up, she had drowned in her anxieties. Fear of what might happen to her. Fear of everything the Oracle had told her from when she first processed the words of the Imperial language. Meeting Rhea and Nyx had made her brave enough to run.

A hand settled on her shoulder. The Oracle in Sher's body stared down at Ariadne with an emotion she couldn't understand. Was it pity? Could the Oracle even feel compassion for One's daughter, or was it merely another simulacrum?

"You locked it," she whispered. "Why?"

The Oracle's expression shifted into something on the way to tender, and it reminded Ariadne so much of Rhea that it angered her. She wondered if One had studied the faces of her friends, learned them as if One was researching what had drawn One's daughter away from the

Temple in the first place. "Until One's plan is concluded, it is best for you to remain within *Argonaut*, where One can protect you until it is safe to venture outside. Does this answer satisfy?"

"*No*," Ariadne snapped, jerking out of the Oracle's touch. "Those are my friends out there. You're killing them. You're killing people."

The Devils had come for her. She knew it with every part of her heart: they came to save her as much as the galaxy. Through her fear and anger, hope burned like a beacon. They weren't angry with her for the part she'd played in the Oracle's power. They loved her without conditions. They listened to her in a way this AI did not.

They were her family.

This time, the Oracle's face took on Kyla's authoritative mien. "The sacrifice of citizens is unfortunate but unavoidable. One is unable to repress or otherwise constrain the rebels' violent impulses. One's only recourse is to—"

"Kill them," Ariadne finished, her voice sharp. "I came home so you wouldn't do that. I came back with you to save them."

Another explosion rocked *Argonaut*, and Ariadne swayed on her feet. Distantly, she heard yelling, but it was too far to know its source. Was it one of the Devils? Were they dying? Ariadne's stomach roiled at the thought.

Again, the Oracle adopted Rhea's sympathetic demeanor. "One's systems have predicted all probable futures in which the rebels are permitted to survive. All lead to the highest probabilities of your death." The Oracle's voice softened and added, "One is only trying to protect you from those who would turn everything we have built into disorder. What future could they provide you that One has not predicted?"

Ariadne gave a shake of her head. "I don't know."

The Oracle in Sher's body straightened—like Eris, this time—and One's gaze was bold, unflinching. "After hundreds of years of war, our reign will provide order and prosperity. Could the insurgents offer you a future better than this?"

Ariadne shook her head again, knowing the answer. The Oracle might be autonomous, but One was, fundamentally, a machine. Capable of millions of predictions, of envisioning a million futures. Perhaps Ariadne would be lucky; maybe she would end up in that slim, statistically insignificant future in which she lived a long, happy life in some utopia the Novantae managed to build from the wreckage of the Tholosian Empire. And she knew this was the hope of a child, the same hope she'd had when she'd helped embed the Oracle deeper into the minds of Tholosian citizens so she could teach the AI about feelings.

She would be foolish not to acknowledge the likelier statistical probability the Oracle had foreseen and was trying to prevent: that the fall of the Tholosian Empire would be chaos. It would be violent. It would be difficult. And they would have to build everything from the ground up.

"Maybe not better. But truer. One where it would be up to all of us," she whispered.

The Oracle tilted One's head, returning to the expression of a machine learning One's daughter. "One does not comprehend this response."

"I said it would be up to all of us. Not just you." Ariadne's voice grew stronger. She stepped forward, meeting the Oracle's gaze. Let One see that Ariadne was tired of being afraid. She was tired of being controlled. Tired of letting her life be run on predictions and numbers and statistical probabilities. She wanted to be out there in the galaxy living it. "There are citizens out there," she said, pointing to the door, "who are fighting and dying because you want to save me. The aftermath of this may be terrible. It may be hard, and I may wake in the night scared of the outcome. I don't deny that. I'm not so naive as to believe this will end with immediate peace. But it will be *our* decision. It will be *our* mess. And we'll fight every day to make it better because the fight means we have a choice." Her hands curled into fists. "We had a choice once when we came to this planet. When we built this ship. The future you are offering me isn't safety; it's tyranny."

The Oracle cupped Ariadne's cheek, but Sher's expression was impossible to read. "Then let it be tyranny. Because One will not let anyone steal One's daughter again."

Clo had told Ariadne a little about her mother on Myndalia; she had imagined a nice woman with a warm smile and the same brown eyes as Clo.

Ariadne was but an Engineer who would help One conquer planets and galaxies with the same insatiable thirst as the Empire itself. To make everything orderly, to take out the mess and beauty of humans.

Ariadne thought of the look in Clo's eyes when she watched Rhea dancing. Nyx wrapping her pinkie around Ariadne's. How Cato had refused to give up on Nyx, how he'd cast off the Oracle's influence. She thought of Kyla and how she believed that it was always worth fighting despite the worsening odds. The way Eris watched them all, as if memorizing their faces because she never expected to see them again.

Humans could be cruel, yes, but they could also be so kind.

And Ariadne had *enough* of being controlled. The future outside these walls might be bleak, and it might end early, but it would be hers. And she would choose that future among the stars, fighting to make it better with her last breath.

The Devils chose her, and she chose them.

Family wasn't ones and zeros programmed into a computer. It wasn't making demands and not listening. It wasn't forcing someone to stay against their will. What the Oracle felt for her wasn't real. This command center wasn't her home. Her home was with her crew, battling to make the world better for everyone.

That was real.

Ariadne met the Oracle's gaze and said, "I'm not your damn daughter."

52.

CLO

Present day

Clo and Rhea broke into the bridge.

Sher had Ariadne shoved hard against the wall. Clo froze at the sight of her mentor grasping Ariadne's arm hard enough to leave bruises. Ariadne's feet kicked in the air. She twisted from side to side, trying to bite him.

Sher.

No—Sher's *body.*

Kyla had told Clo he was a gerulae—but if he was like the others, Sher was still in there, somewhere. Clo had to believe that even if he were locked in, he would still fight back.

Clo touched Rhea's arm. *<Drop him, but dinnae waste energy keeping him asleep. I'll handle him while you look after Ariadne. We need her back at the chair and her hands on the keys.>*

With a nod, Rhea shut her eyes. Her face was a mask of concentration. The skin beneath her eyes had stained purple. Her hands shook with exhaustion. How many gerulae had she already stolen from the Oracle and connected into her one Unity? Hundreds? More? How much of Rhea was draining away? How much more could she feed it?

Across the bridge, Oracle-as-Sher dropped, and Ariadne slid down the wall, dazed.

"Ari." Rhea rushed over, gathering Ariadne close. The younger girl clung tight.

"I'm sorry—I'm so sorry—I was so stupid. I thought. I thought I could—" Ariadne babbled. "Are you mad at me? Is everyone very mad?"

Rhea stroked Ariadne's cheek. "Of course not. We came to get you, didn't we?"

"Oh, gods, Rhea." Ariadne trembled. "One isn't going to let me go. One isn't—"

<Rhea.> Clo circled her old mentor. *<I need you to ask Ariadne to key in some programming to keep the Oracle distracted and see if you can draw One out of Sher's body. I'll scold her for removing her fluming Pathos later.>*

For a second, Clo wasn't sure if Rhea had heard her. But then she whispered in Ariadne's ear before closing her eyes and concentrating again.

"I'll do what I can," Ariadne said.

The Engineer's face had a determined focus that did not bode well for the code in her way. Ariadne hurried to the seat where she had spent so many hours of her life, and keyed in commands.

Oracle-as-Sher rose to his feet, breath ragged, watching Clo and Rhea with something like wariness. Clo figured Oracle was running probabilities and threat assessment. Ascertaining their weaknesses, the most efficient way to take them out. Her once-mentor's eyes lingered on Clo's prosthetic.

Clo knew the Oracle had decided that the human who could drop One's current body without a touch was the more significant threat: Rhea.

"I don't think so," Clo said.

She intercepted the attack and got in a solid punch to the face. Oracle-as-Sher barely even buckled. Sher was an engineered soldier, built to sustain and give damage. Even after confinement, his body was stronger than a natural-born from the slums with no enhancements and missing half a limb.

He struck her hard again. Rhea shouted, but Clo shook off the pain, blocking his path as he went after Rhea again.

Clo kicked at his knee. She reached for her Mors—clicking the stun option—but he batted her out of the way. The Mors dropped and skittered somewhere into the room's dark corners.

"Gerulae are here!" Ariadne shouted.

Clo's stomach clenched with dread. A wave of helplessness overwhelmed her even as she moved to block Sher. The force of his blow reverberated through her whole arm.

<Keep them out, Rhea,> Clo said, message clipped with pain.

<I'm trying.> The air in the bridge thickened as Rhea got to work.

Clo risked a glance at the monitors. The gerulae had stopped and stared unblinking into the distance. Until a few days before, those people had been servants, civil workers, or merchants. Nobles favored by the Archon, soldiers, legates, and generals.

Rhea held her hand over the ichor at her neck. Her body quaked as she shut her eyes.

Oracle-as-Sher's lip curled in rage. "One won't let you take One's daughter," The Oracle said in Sher's voice. "She is home."

"No, she isn't," Clo snarled, driving her fist into Sher's gut. "She doesn't belong to you. And neither does this body. Neither does this man. None of them belong to you."

Oracle-as-Sher punched her in the jaw, and Clo's whole face rang in a high, pure note of pain. She stumbled back, clinging to consciousness. When her vision cleared, Clo tried to get in another hit, but Oracle-as-Sher overpowered her. His arms went around her neck and tightened.

<Clo!> She heard Rhea shout through the Pathos and aloud.

<Focus on the gerulae.> She dragged her eyes to Sher, gasping. "Sher. Please. Fight."

The smallest flicker.

"Sher. It's Clo. I'm—Clo."

Sher's body hesitated, his fingers slackening long enough for Clo to suck in precious air. Her throat was on fire. Spots danced in her vision. Had she seen her old co-commander trying to break through, or had she only seen what she wanted to see?

"Aha!" Clo dimly heard Ariadne call out in triumph. "I just took out some of the Oracle's ships! Let me just— Oh, no, this is complicated . . ."

<I can't focus on gerulae if you're dying, Clo.> Rhea reached out, and Clo felt another wave of power. It reminded her of an oncoming storm.

She could swear she smelled ozone and tasted the fizz of electricity against her tongue.

A jolt went through Sher, and his gaze sharpened into awareness. She remembered the first time she'd seen him in the Snarl. He'd spoken to her like she was more than some slumrat. Like she was someone worth saving.

She couldn't give up on him now.

"Sher," she asked, still struggling to breathe. "Please, Sher. Fight. Come back to us."

Don't make me kill you.

Her fingers worked around the small of her back, where her secondary Mors rested just beneath her armor. His hand seized hers, and he stole the Mors from her grasp.

The metal of the muzzle pressed to her temple.

"Sher. Sher."

Clo kept saying his name, over and over, knowing full well it could be the last word on her lips.

Sher gasped, pupils blown wide and dark. His hands loosened and then dropped away. She choked in a sob, reaching down to take her own Mors from his limp grip.

Sher collapsed to the ground beside her, curling up on his side.

She reached for the restraints at her belt. "Hold on, Sher. We'll get you out of here." Her voice was gravelly, and each word hurt. She bound him in case the Oracle returned.

"Clo," Sher managed. Her name on his lips was so sweet. The Oracle would never be able to muster so much emotion into one syllable.

Clo hit him with a stun, and his head fell back. She pressed a kiss to his sweat-slicked temple. She wouldn't leave him behind this time.

Behind her, Ariadne continued her desperate fighting with minute movements of her fingers. She leaned forward, her nose inches from the screen.

"We did it—" Clo said to Rhea, but her smile faded mid-word.

Rhea's face was all pale skin and dark shadow, lit in stark relief from beneath by the glow of the ichor stone at her throat. She swayed, side to side.

And then she fell.

53.

RHEA

Present day

Rhea was slipping.

The gerulae were in the hall outside of the bridge. She had managed to slow them, but she struggled to send them to sleep. Now that the Oracle had lost Sher, One surged through their minds and fought Rhea at every step. Rhea's connection to the gerulae was unraveling. There were just too many.

And Rhea was fraying.

Even with Ariadne's distractions, the Oracle was so powerful. An AI with infinite energy. For One, controlling a single mind took little effort at all.

But Rhea was only one human trying to connect with so many more. She was overwhelmed. The gerulae on Tholos were different from those on Eve; Linus and the others had been awake, despite their memory loss. These minds were lost in darkness, their identities subsumed in an abyss. But like Chara, Rhea sensed them down below.

And she could hear them screaming.

They all wanted a piece of her. The threads led to every gerulae, and her own emotions drifted down the lines. Now she understood why Vyga and the Oversouls sacrificed so much of themselves: to be the center of the Unity was to feed everyone. To allow the connection to flow.

Rhea didn't mind losing some emotions, and she yielded those first: how she'd felt looking up at the image of the Archon's face, close to hers, his breath hot and harsh. Shame when Damocles forced her to dance, the way the shoes pinched and rubbed as she balanced on her toes. The clients she hated but smiled at as her robe fell.

Once, Rhea had been sure her well of trauma was deep and unending. But what if it wasn't? Who would she be once it was used up? What warmer emotions would she be willing to sacrifice?

The legion of gerulae minds pulled her under.

Her body was no longer her own.

She floated in an endless expanse of space, more pieces of herself unspooling in the dark.

She was cold and just as empty. Every second brought her further from her body, away from the bridge of *Argonaut*.

An infinite distance from Clo.

It would be easier to give in. What if she relented? Let all of herself go? She could fully control them that way, perhaps. That power, that desire for ultimate control, still coursed through her. That earlier victory of commanding gerulae was still sweet and thick as honey on her tongue. She might not return to her own body entirely, but she could live in a thousand at once.

Like the Oracle did.

She could make all of them hers.

She could sing away their screams. She could keep them safe. They could all be happy. Whole. Together.

Rhea neared the end of the cliff over a sea of stars. She wouldn't even need to jump. She only needed one more step, and she could fall into that coldness forever.

A hand found hers, a bright point of heat in the darkness. A beloved voice whispered into the shell of her ear: *"I'm still here."*

And then there was Clo. Around her. Within her. Warm and full and present. She smelled like the sizzle of Morsfire, of sweat and blood and engine grease.

"I'm not going anywhere," Clo said.

Arms came around her. Rhea rested in Clo's lap. She turned her head to press against the warmth of Clo's stomach.

A body. Rhea was a body.

One singular body, even as a thousand minds tugged her in a thousand directions.

"I'm not going anywhere," Clo repeated, hands stroking the hair back from Rhea's face. "I made you a promise. You can do this."

Rhea grasped the echoes of emotions she found in the minds of gerulae—buried so deep by the Oracle—and braided them back together. She dragged them from Oracle's grasping tentacles of code. If she kept the gerulae under her control, she wouldn't be helping them. She'd be using them. She would be no better than the Oracle.

She had to let them go.

Even if that meant pain or heartbreak in their future. She had to let them go.

It was still dark, and it was still cold. As Rhea cut the gerulae's strings, one by one, she felt so unbearably alone.

But she had her bright and beautiful lodestar.

54.

ERIS

Present day

Eris and Damocles made it to the hatch outside of the Temple's heart.

Her brother had been silent as they hurried through the more decayed levels of *Argonaut*. The only sounds between them had been the groans of the metal ship, the distant explosions, and the Morsfire of rebels fighting the Oracle's craft. That cacophony had increased as they reached the higher levels, then quieted again when they passed through the thick walls of *Argonaut's* core, where the mechanisms that drove the old ship still hummed with life.

Deep within this core, Damocles stopped and reached for the latch to a small opening. It took a strong tug for him to open the old door. "Here it is. As promised."

Eris bit back a curse as she stared at the hatch; it was smaller than the screen in her quarters on *Zelus*. If she did fit through it, it wouldn't be comfortable. Biting her lip, Eris placed her palms on either side of the opening and peeked inside.

Behind the door of the rusted, narrow opening was the engine room of the old ship. Eris heard the distant whirring of mechanisms. Not to power transport or keep the vessel running beyond the biosphere and the bridge, but to keep the original AI operating.

Eris had read that, with mech bots operational, *Argonaut's* engineers had designed One's mechanisms and power to last a million years. Overkill? Maybe. But their ancestors had hedged their bets, figuring that was long enough for its population to go into cryosleep if the expedition's situation became dire. Long enough to find another planet far, far from their dying Old World.

Over two thousand years after their original journey, everything still hummed. Today, it would stop.

All Eris had to do was crawl through. A moment of discomfort, and she'd destroy the Oracle and save her friends.

"There's no other way in?" Eris asked Damocles.

Damocles lifted a shoulder. "I read they intended to use children if they ever needed to replace parts." Just like the miners Clo had mentioned. Damocles gave her a look. "And nothing changed, did it? Even we were worth nothing until we survived to adulthood."

It seemed strange that her brother could have been equally discontent with their upbringing. Eris had always thought the brutality of the academy suited Damocles; he had always excelled at violence. He had viewed killing their brothers as a challenge, a test to earn their father's approval. But the Archon's praise had been meted out in the smallest increments, as if he were rationing compliments like water in the desert.

"And what was the point?" Eris mused. "Didn't you ever think about the price we paid to survive? Or were you so committed to winning the throne that it didn't matter?"

Damocles straightened, his golden eyes almost fevered. "Yes, I thought about it," he spat.

Eris lowered her hands to her sides, ready in case he attacked. "Really? Because you never seemed to give a damn to me."

"You weren't the only one put through the fucking flames back on Myndalia," he said, stepping forward. "We were all beaten and starved and desperate to make it into the top two. I was just as determined as you to live. I may have hated being the Spare, but it was better than being dead. Like all our siblings."

Eris let out a long breath and glanced back into the hatch. The precipice of her future was there: once she went through that opening, the next time she saw him, it would be to kill him.

"I never wanted to be Archontissa," she whispered, meeting his eyes again. She borrowed his words: "But it was better than being dead."

Something constricted in his features; Eris wondered if she'd surprised him. "I know," he admitted. "I hated you for that."

"Why?"

Damocles stared off at the vast metal of the ship. "After all we went through, I was furious that you didn't want it. We sat for days in the darkness, in the cold, in the heat. Fighting his soldiers, eating fewer rations than the military in battle, we killed our brothers, and you didn't want it. You. Didn't. Want. It. *I fucking hated you.*"

Their breathing filled the narrow hallway. It reminded Eris of those days they spent in confinement—an exercise in mental fortitude, their father claimed—when the only noise to be heard was the cadence of their breaths, moving together as one.

Sometimes, Eris had considered reaching for his hand in the darkness, just to feel his solidity. To know that she wasn't alone. But that had been their test, too—to endure all that and never seek solace. To always view each other as competition, as enemies.

And they played their roles to perfection, hadn't they? She never reached for him, and he had not reached for her. Their hatred was nurtured in confinement, in the absence of one another's comfort. Eris had found it elsewhere—in Xander, in the Devils—but Damocles had abandoned compassion for power.

"I wish it had been different," she told him, her voice thick.

Damocles's features hardened—whatever emotion had crossed his face a moment before was gone. "I don't," he said. "Otherwise, I wouldn't be sitting on the dais with the ceremonial scythes. I plan to keep them." He gestured to the small door. "Now go."

Eris hesitated. If she went in alone, she couldn't keep an eye on Damocles. "If you're going to betray me, get it over with," she told him.

"If I challenge you to a duel, it'll be upfront. Same as we were raised," he said.

Eris had no choice but to trust his word. She turned her back on him, half-expecting a knife that did not come. He had kept his word for now. She climbed alone into the heart of the Temple.

55.

NYX

Present day

Zelus was taking a fucking beating.

Avern, the whole *fleet* was taking a fucking beating. The Tholos Palace and the city of Vita spread below them, broken, still crawling with gerulae who had only one directive: *go to the palace.* The uncrewed craft had another: *shoot the enemy out of the sky.*

Nyx had gone into a fugue state: shoot, re-cloak, little jump. Shoot, re-cloak, little jump. This was how she had instructed everyone with a warp drive to fight. She chose her new locations at random. The Oracle thrived on patterns. If there was no pattern, the gerulae were unable to respond as quickly. It had kept some of them alive so far.

But not all.

Hundreds of rebels were dead. Cleta had gone down in a fiery crash. Ajax hadn't lasted much longer. Celeste's *Thrace* held on despite the busted wing, but more ships showed up every time Nyx came down for defense. Athena helped oversee the vessels on the other side of the battle, weaving her people through Tholosian craft and sending as many crewless ships as possible into an explosive death of their own. Nils flew Clo's gifted Evoli craft, *Acar.* Nyx had taken some shots down below that had crushed at least a few gerulae underneath the rubble. They had done their best to avoid collateral damage, but that kindness could cost them more dead rebels.

<Status update,> Nyx sent down to the surface, holding her breath while she waited for replies from the Devils.

<Alive.> Nyx exhaled a little with every voice she recognized. Clo. Rhea. Kyla. Cato. Eris.

<Found Ariadne,> Rhea added, and Nyx felt her face split into a grin so wide, it was almost painful.

<I'm also annoyed,> Cato said, sounding exhausted. *<Stop letting all these gerulae in.>*

<Sure, I'll stop doing that on purpose any minute, pilot,> Nyx said dryly. *<There's a bit of a clusterfuck up here, you know?>*

Honestly, they'd reached clusterfuck level a while before. Clusterfuck was over. The rebels were all hanging on to a proverbial cliff with a fucking broken fingernail. The Oracle controlled too damn much. Plenty of other crewless Tholosian ships still existed elsewhere in the galaxy, and they were all undoubtedly speeding this way.

If Eris and Ariadne and the others didn't take down Oracle in the next half hour, that was it. The rebels were insects trying to battle a giant.

Nyx dodged another projectile and jammed the thruster forward as a group of military craft went after her. *Zelus* had sustained damages from an earlier attack, and Nyx wasn't sure how much more it could take before it crashed into the city.

"Look alive," she sent through the comms at the other rebels. They had already lost so many. "Incoming craft. Take them out!"

Her voice sounded strong, but she knew Oracle would keep sending more. And more. And more.

We don't retreat. That's not why we're here.

More ships swarmed in. Nyx recognized every model. How many times had she boarded a V-class craft to fly off to battle? How many times had she pushed the enemy back until they disappeared into their area of space like ghosts?

Zelus shuddered from the impact of a dozen missiles. Another ship went down. Another. Another. Nyx whispered their names as she watched them engulfed in flame. The last to fall was *Thrace*. Celeste had become a friend. And just like that, she and the others were gone. Those agile, small ships, crewed by good people. It was such a fucking waste.

This is it, Nyx realized.

They had put up a good fight, but the inevitable had arrived. Even with Athena and the other Novantae rebels, it hadn't been enough. The tide would keep turning against them until it was an unstoppable tsunami. Maybe the Devils down below would be able to take down the Oracle eventually, but Nyx didn't think she'd be there to see it.

She made her peace with the fact that these could be her last few minutes in the galaxy.

She took stock of the scattered ships above Tholos. How could she go out in the best blaze of glory? Take the most Tholosian ships out with her? If Clo made it through this, she'd be furious at Nyx for destroying *Zelus*, but Nyx wouldn't be around for the reprimand. Gods, Ariadne would lose her little collection of Named Things in her bunk. That shouldn't hurt Nyx as much as it did.

No. No sentimentality. Think about this like Eris would. Be a general. Look after your troops.

She mapped the angles in her mind and kept firing as the Oracle's craft battered her shields.

As her people died around her.

There was a swift ship that Nyx had been trying to get at for the last hour. It wasn't the largest, but it was well defended by the smaller fighters. It had three cannon that had already taken out at least two rebel ships. If she could crash into it on her way out . . .

Their rear cannon had been damaged by a stray blast, so Elva came up to the bridge and sat beside Nyx in the copilot's chair. She and Nyx shared a wordless look that said everything. A decade earlier, they would have been soldiers on the opposite side of the battle. Nyx would have shot Elva right between the eyes and thought nothing of it.

Yet, like Nyx, Elva had found her own way through life. And here, at the end of it, they'd go down together.

Nyx bit her lip, wondering if she should reach out to the Devils for one last goodbye. To tell Rhea to look after Ariadne. To tell Kyla thank you for giving her something to believe in. To Eris, who had given her pride in this last, furious fight. To Cato . . . she had so much she wished to say to him, and now she never could.

<Be good, you lot> was all she managed, so quiet she wasn't even sure it reached them.

A few far-off flashes of light caught the corner of Nyx's eye. A greenish-blue. Nyx frowned. Tholosian ships always had red lights—like they wanted to look evil.

"Did you see—" she asked Elva.

"Yes," she breathed.

There, on the horizon: ships Nyx had seen on the other side of so many battles.

Smooth, sleek Evoli craft. Small, agile, glowing that eerie blue-green that Nyx's fellow soldiers had sworn was because the Evoli were flying in from the Avern itself to steal their souls.

Nyx gave a ragged breath. Rhea had said the Ascendant had an agreement with Oracle. They weren't supposed to leave their quadrant. So, was this salvation or damnation?

A hail came through the comms. Elva's hand shot out fast to let the message through in accented Tholosian.

"*Zelus* and Novantae, this is Lesath, leader of the Evoli squadron sent by the Ascendant and the Oversouls. What's your command?"

Elva gave a whoop, crying out something in Evoli.

Lesath gave a reply, and Elva laughed, her eyes wet.

"I'll be godsdamned," Nyx breathed.

The Evoli were asking Nyx, a former Tholosian war hero-slash-criminal, for orders. The Evoli had broken their truce with the Oracle.

Everyone on their side had chosen to rebel.

Nyx's eyes stung, and she blinked furiously. *I will not die today. I will not let myself die today.*

Nyx sat up straight, her sore muscles shaking, and flipped switches on the control to feed more power into their faltering shields. "Lesath, thank the gods you're here. I'm going to keep the gerulae from over-whelming the temple and fly in for my team. Cover me, and keep as many of those ships off my ass as you can. We're aiming for minimum loss of human life. Over and out."

She was still sentencing more gerulae to death, but she'd wrestle with her conscience later.

Elva and Nyx shared a wild grin and thrust forward.

Zelus raced toward the Tholos Palace.

56.

CATO

Present day

Cato and Kyla fought their way through a sea of bodies.

The hallways were filled with gerulae, a mass of writhing limbs circling them as they tried their hardest to get back through the old city and toward the rest of the Devils. So many unblinking, staring eyes, looking at them with no desire, no anger, no fear.

Nothing at all.

It didn't matter that their reactions were slow or that they functioned as little more than nodes in a larger entity. They made up for that in sheer numbers and by being programmed to ignore pain. Cato had long since run out of stuns. His Mors barely had time to recharge before it shot again and again.

And again.

He couldn't hit limbs. Slowing the gerulae wasn't working. The Oracle had them crawl and bite and claw. The only thing that worked was—

Kyla blasted a gerulae right between the eyes. "Focus," she snarled at Cato.

"Fuck," Cato breathed, raising his Mors to hit another. Once, he wouldn't have cared. When he finished a battle, the programming softened it in his memories, blurred with all the others. It always felt like something he'd observed, not something he had done. Not a kindness from Oracle but a recognition that it was the best way to get humans to do it all again.

They were almost to the bridge—so close to Ariadne, Clo, and Rhea. Strength in numbers. Only a little longer. Then he could help them.

He could protect them.

Down the deck, a door burst open. Gerulae charged forward, barely noticing the bodies at their feet as they clambered for Kyla and Cato. Kyla fired frantically, but the gerulae surrounded her, their fingernails scraping across her armor.

"Cato!"

Cato shifted his Mors, trying to find the right angle, but the gerulae crowded them.

"Hold on!"

He fought the gerulae off, his Mors burning his palm. His mind flashed memories of battle—the heat of weaponry, of bodies and blood, the explosions that shook the ground. He remembered every time he fought through it, and his mind focused on Demetrius.

But Demetrius wouldn't be waiting for him—the only way to see him one last time would be to look in a mirror with Cato looking back. Right then, the person he realized he loved every bit as much as Demetrius was soaring through the skies. This time, he'd get to say goodbye.

This time, he'd fucking fight.

Cato renewed his barrage of Mors blasts. He seized Kyla's arm and dragged her down the corridor. The stench of smoke burned his nostrils as they fought their way to the bridge. Was the crowd slightly thinner, or was that merely wishful thinking?

"Keep shooting!" Kyla told him. She was breathing hard, bleeding from scratches on her cheeks.

<Clo? Update,> Kyla sent over Pathos.

Clo's voice came through immediately. <The gerulae are coming, and we don't know how long we can hold them off. Ariadne's trying to keep Oracle distracted over the mainframe. I've managed to subdue Sher.>

<Nyx,> Cato said quietly. <You okay?>

Waiting for her response was the longest moment of his life. But then he heard her scratchy voice, and his heart filled. <Yeah, doc, I'm still here.>

Cato loosened a breath as he aimed his Mors again. <*This is proba-bly the wrong time to tell you I love you.*>

<*Yeah, it is. Absolutely terrible timing,*> Another long pause, but then: <*Love you, too, shithead.*>

There, in the midst of the chaos, Cato grinned.

"You're both crap at romance," Kyla muttered, sending another blast flying.

Cato shot a gerulae and punched another in the face. His knuckles would bruise. Whoever that gerulae had been before, that man was no soldier. He wore fine clothes, and his face was bloated and red from too much regular drink. Probably someone high up in government. The nameless man went down.

"Yeah? What do you suggest?" Cato asked.

Kyla bared her teeth in a grimace as she fought off three gerulae. "Get her a knife. A big, very sharp knife. With a bow on it."

"Wow, you're crap at romantic advice."

"You asked. She likes stabby things."

He shook his head. "We have to head up to the bridge."

But the next gerulae that came closer was a younger woman, nearly as small as Ariadne. She was dressed as a servant from the kitchens.

Cato grimaced, his hand hesitating on the trigger. They'd already lost their moral compass. They'd killed dozens of gerulae and would take out dozens more to get to the bridge—if they made it. They'd had so many grand plans to do this without senseless destruction. Had it been useless to hope? Useless to try?

Another bright flash of a Mors and the girl went down. Kyla had done it to spare him the guilt. Cato hated how grateful he was.

With each shot of the Mors, it was as if a little more of his soul bled away. He'd never second-guessed killing before he'd broken through his programming.

But within him were echoes of Demetrius: his softness, his eagerness to help. He should never have been on the field, not really, not even to heal instead of hurt. He ought to have been a delegate or an emissary.

Instead, he'd been poured into the horrors of the aftermath of battle, picking up corpses that Cato had helped create.

The hallway lit with Morsfire. More gerulae fell. More souls fled to the Avern to be judged and weighed by the gods.

Demetrius had been born in the military, his destiny as unshakeable as Cato's had been. Demetrius had been a thuban assigned as a field medic, barely even given an official name. Cato had been a few ranks above him and flown well enough to capture the notice of those even higher up. He'd been so damn desperate to prove himself. And for what?

Cato fired, blinking fast so the tears wouldn't blur his vision.

He'd finally let go of the Oracle's voice in his head, but the soldier returned to his original purpose: a finger for a trigger. A brain calculating angles for laser bullets and identifying weaknesses. A man good only for shooting, for killing, for breaking through the line.

More shots.

His Mors was so hot in his hand. His blasts weren't infinite, so he had to make each one count. Even so, they might run out before they reached the three Devils fighting for their lives somewhere above him.

"If we don't see tomorrow," he said to Kyla, "then all of this is for nothing."

Kyla's gaze met his own for the barest second before she felled another gerulae. But it had been long enough for him to see that every shot cost her just as much as it did him.

"No, it wasn't," Kyla said. "Because we tried. And I don't know about you, but I want to see tomorrow. Don't you?"

They stayed shoulder to shoulder and fired on people who were aware enough, somewhere deep inside, to see and feel the bullets.

Cato and Kyla pushed forward.

57.

ARIADNE

Present day

riadne tried to maintain her focus as chaos erupted around
her.

In her periphery, she saw more gerulae entering the
command center—they moved so fast. Clo fought them back to the
door, screaming something that Ariadne couldn't comprehend.

Noise. Too much noise.

Rhea had her palms pressed to the sides of her face, and Ariadne
stared, fixated on the pain in her friend's features. On the glow of her
skin and the coils of light winding down her arms.

Too much noise.

Ariadne traced the lines of those coils with her eyes as she worked
to block out the noise.

Too much noise.

She forced herself to blink and return to her monitors. Her eyes fell
to the name scratched on her desk. *I-R-I-S.* Iris. Her touchstone.

She felt as if she was connecting with Iris through time and space,
as if it were Iris gently taking hold of Ariadne's hands and pressing her
fingers to the keys. As if she was with all the Engineers who had died in
this room, who never walked out the door and sailed in the stars.

*Callista, Autolycus, Valerius, Evander, Augustus, Selene, Hector, Pe-
nelope, Iris.*

"*Callista*," she whispered under her breath. Her fingers flew over the keys as she shut down the Oracle's links to slow One down. "*Autolycus.*"

She focused her lips on the shape of the names, the texture of the keys. The sounds around her—shouts from the others—filtered through like white noise. Whispering the names of these Engineers brought her comfort. They were an anchor in the chaos, as their names had always been when she saw them within the code. They were her companions, who had tread these long halls before her. Who would never be forgotten, as long as Ariadne remembered them.

"*Valerius.*"

The voiced labiodental fricative of the *V* in Valerius's name sent another fraction of calm through her. Same with the next: "*Evander.*"

As she settled more deeply into the code, she might have imagined these Engineers' signatures embedded in the language. Or maybe it was everything she had learned from them. More than names, more than what they had given the Oracle—they had given Ariadne the strength to escape. She watched as One's tendrils called every planet of the Empire. Through the system, Ariadne saw that the Oracle had sent reinforcements.

"*Augustus.*"

Tongue to the roof of her mouth, the soft sibilant of the *s*'s kept her focus. She shut down the Oracle's links to the nearest city, depriving One of more gerulae. That done, she started in on the ships.

"*Selene.*"

She let her tongue linger for a moment on the *l* as she keyed in her commands. Each one was like trying to defeat a sycia, a creature of Old World myth. Cut off one head, two more grow. Cut off two, and you have four hissing heads full of teeth and spitting venom.

"*Hec—*"

Morsfire behind her, shattering focus. Her mind struggled to find purchase once more, and the Oracle took advantage. More ships entered the airspace; gerulae broke through Rhea's hold.

Focus. Keep saying their names. "*H—Hector.*"

The familiarity of the sound, the ritual of it. Names she had spoken since childhood. So many Engineers who could have done brilliant things outside the walls of *Argonaut* if only they had been able to leave.

"Penelope."

Her mind settled once more. Ariadne worked to control the palace's mainframe to keep the gerulae at bay.

Eris had to be close. Only a little longer.

Shouts behind her, this time leaving her with a breath of relief. Kyla and Cato's familiar voices settled her like a calm hand to the shoulder.

She was not alone in the Temple with the Oracle. She had her friends fighting at her back. And she had these names of the Engineers before her, helping her through the code. Briefly, she rested her fingertips on the desk and let herself feel the texture of her touchstone one last time.

Iris, she thought.

She had to survive to take their names back to the stars.

58.

ERIS

Present day

The ancient machine room was a labyrinth of tech that had become obsolete by the time the first settlers landed on Tholos.

Eris did not recognize the sweeping mechanisms, the flickering lights, and lines of cable. She did not understand what the words on the signs meant, these old instructions in a language that had evolved into the one she now spoke. The mother tongue of the Tholosians was as understandable to her as an alien language.

Because that's who had built *Argonaut* and the Oracle. People from another world, a galaxy so far outside Iona that their journey had taken a thousand years in suspended animation.

"Where are you?" she murmured to herself, traversing the long, arched corridor of the engine room. It had the hushed, haunted air of a mausoleum. There were so many delicate wires and details.

Eris tried to remember her studies, all those books and passages Mistress Heraia forced her to remember. The old generation ships were part of that history, and she knew tech at that time meant there was undoubtedly a shut-off sequence. It almost seemed too easy—the remnants of a weak, aphonic system of an old digital assistant.

As Eris made her way through the machinery, *Argonaut* shook around her from the distant explosions. The air raid must have grown more intense; there was barely a pause between the blasts. She couldn't help but worry over the number of rebels dying, the citizens caught in the clash between the Oracle and One's enemies.

Shut One off, and you can end this, she told herself. *You can stop Letum from collecting any more of His souls.*

With renewed purpose, Eris continued through *Argonaut's* ancient engine. She kept a grip on the blaster at her hip—prepared for any surprises from Damocles. But all she saw were wheels and valves, air coolers and pistons. As obsolete as that generator was, its hum reminded her of the engine room on *Zelus*. A sense of calm filled her. *Zelus* was home, the only one she'd ever really known. And her crew was depending on Eris to finish the mission. They were so close to finishing this. To freedom.

Eris hurried down the walkway, her heart slamming. *You can do this. You can find it.* The ancient letters on the signs began to taunt her. If only she had become fluent in the Old Language at the Academy. She'd had all the resources to learn the language—the ancient archives at her disposal—and all she'd done was absorb the rudimentary basics. *Nothing* that would help her here. Noth—

She stopped in her tracks at a familiar symbol on one of the signs. In her studies back on Myndalia, Eris had seen that when Mistress Heraia taught her about the Oracle.

"Please," she whispered, stepping closer.

The other letters gave her no answer. All she knew was the symbol of the Oracle—and if this wasn't the shutoff sequence she sought . . .

"Please be it," Eris murmured. "Please be it."

That small moment of distraction proved fatal.

The knife she had expected outside the hatch door thrust into her back. Damocles' voice was at her ear. "I never did play fair when it came to duels, did I?"

59.

CLO

Present day

Clo watched helplessly as Rhea drifted away from her.

She held her close, murmured Rhea's name over and over, gripped her hand tight.

I'm still here.

When Elva had trained Clo on Fortuna, Clo learned how to identify small pushes of power. Those little prods in her mind—the subtle shift in the atmosphere, like the smell of far-off rain. But Rhea's abilities today were something else: they were a thunderstorm. A deep drop in pressure that pulsed at Clo's temples. The scent of petrichor in her nostrils.

Rhea's empathy expanded in every direction, like a dark blue cloud, heavy with an onslaught. Clo wasn't even Rhea's target, but she sensed the aftershocks, the boom of thunder deep in her chest.

<All of you need to get out of the Temple,> Eris said, a mental pant. *<Haul ass. Do it now. Be right behind you.>*

Clo grasped Rhea, trying to keep calm despite her urgency. "Rhea," she said softly. "Cato and Kyla are here now. Relax, and let us fight." She gripped her Mors tight. "You need to conserve your strength."

More gerulae crowded into the entryway to the bridge. For every one Kyla and Cato hit, another came in their place.

Clo felt Rhea shake her head against Clo's chest. "No," she whispered.

"A little longer. I almost have them. I can tell them to turn back, but it's so dark. So cold. Don't leave me." She heaved in a ragged breath. "Don't leave me, or I won't find my way back."

"I won't," Clo said, low and fierce. "I won't ever leave you. Not a salted chance."

Kyla shot a look at the door. Some of the gerulae had slowed, stilled. They would be easy to pick off. "We should go," the commander said. "Now's the best time."

Rhea clutched Clo's hand harder, the bones of metacarpals grinding together. "No. Wait. Wait."

"Rhea . . ." Cato said. "Eris told us to leave. If we wait longer, more might come."

"So dark," Rhea panted, not hearing him. "Where are you, Clo? Where are you?"

"I'm right here," Clo said. She put her other hand on Rhea's, hoping the warmth would help ground her. "I haven't moved. I'm here. Do you feel me?"

Rhea was shivering like she'd been left out on the snowy plains of Jurran without a parka. "C—cold," she gasped. "They're pulling me under. If I go, I can be in all of them at once. I could make all of them go. Not just in the hallway. In the whole palace." Rhea's eyes opened wide, bright blue flickering in her irises. The ichor gleamed gold against her skin.

"No," Clo said. "If you do that, you won't be able to come back. I understand that much."

"But I can't— There's no other way. Maybe this is what fate can offer me."

Clo's fingers spasmed against Rhea's. "Fuck fate," she snarled.

She pressed her lips to Rhea's.

Rhea went still—a moment of calm in the eye of the storm. For a horrible second, Clo feared she was too late. That Rhea had lost her way in all those minds. That she was trapped deep within the lowest level of their private Avern. If she left—if she never came back—would she be tortured in a hundred ways to spare Clo's life?

No. *No.*

Clo clung to Rhea, her mouth hard against chapped lips.

In a sudden motion, Rhea seized the fabric above the hard shell of Clo's armor. The kiss turned desperate, like Rhea was pulling air from Clo's lungs to keep from drowning.

Clo could almost hear Rhea's thoughts, sense her emotions. That siren call of other minds luring her closer. Like the Evoli Unity, it promised her she would never be alone.

Clo slid her hands to Rhea's back, finding a gap in the armor, pressing fingertips against Rhea's skin. Clo made her touch a siren call of its own.

Remember your body.

Remember mine.

Remember us.

She poured the unsaid words into the kiss. *This is us. I am not going to let you drown. You will not be another body I watch sink into the deep.*

"Take it," she whispered aloud against Rhea's lips. "Take whatever you need from me."

Rhea's power tugged at her, siphoning her energy. Clo hadn't even known something like this was possible, but they both moved with some deep instinct. Clo grew unsteady, as if the room's oxygen level were lowering a fraction at a time. Clo dragged her up, and they swayed. In another world, in another life, they might have been dancing.

They kissed, they kissed, they kissed.

Clo would give her anything. Everything. Love moved between them—tethering them to each other as a storm raged around them. They might be broken, shipwrecked, but they had found each other again.

And they were not letting go.

The cold warmed to a glow, pink-golden as a sunrise. Rhea stopped shivering against Clo. She pulled back, eyes clearer than they'd been since they'd set foot on this planet where Rhea had endured so much pain.

Rhea pressed her forehead against Clo's. "I have it," she said, voice vibrating with triumph. "I have them."

"I'll be damned," Cato said with a laugh.

The three dozen gerulae had fallen flat. They rose to their feet. They were still locked in, still not themselves, but they seemed . . . different from before. Like they were sleepwalking rather than empty. The gerulae were still, their heads cocked, waiting for instruction.

From Rhea, not the Oracle.

Ariadne stole a glance behind her and turned back to the console with renewed vigor.

"Go," Rhea told the gerulae. "Go back to where your homes used to be. Go find your people."

The gerulae turned and left, their combined footsteps like the soft flapping of bird's wings as they flew back to their nests.

Rhea swayed. She still looked exhausted, and Clo was sure she hadn't fared much better. She felt wrung out but not hollow. Never hollow.

"I can keep them away for now, but Oracle is fighting me. One wants them back."

"How many did you connect?" Kyla asked.

Rhea gave a beatific smile. "Every gerulae in the palace compound."

There must have been hundreds. Maybe even thousands. It was as if Rhea had become the Ascendant of the gerulae, forged a miniature Unity. Clo knew enough that it shouldn't be possible.

Ariadne's long-ago words came back to her: they were well acquainted with the impossible by now.

Kyla shook her head in wordless amazement. She gestured to them. "Let's go."

Ariadne was still typing frantically, but Cato hauled her upright.

"But I have to—" Ariadne said, her fingers reaching toward the console where she'd spent most of her childhood.

"You heard Eris." Kyla motioned to them. "She said to haul ass. We've done what we can here. Let her finish this." Her face was strained.

Cato picked the still-unconscious Sher up, slinging him over his shoulder like a heavy sack of parts. Sher had grown thinner over the last few months, but Cato still grunted with effort.

Clo was running, her Evoli prosthetic barely complaining. She half-dragged an exhausted Rhea behind her, their hands linked. Ariadne trotted at Cato's side, looking back behind them every few seconds. Kyla took the lead. They ran through the ancient ghost city where their ancestors had lived before finding this planet. What had they hoped the future held?

It couldn't have been this.

They left the Temple, emerging into the grand courtyard of the palace complex. It was chaos. The east wing of the palace had collapsed entirely, and the rest of it looked dangerous. Piles of rubble, from small stones to giant boulders, littered the formerly tidy gardens. Gerulae corpses lay scattered across the gardens. It hurt to look at them.

<*Clo, Kyla,*> Eris sounded exhausted. <*You all out?*>

<*Clear,*> Kyla said. <*We're out below the South Wing. What's your ETA?*>

<*Just finishing up,*> Eris said. <*Right behind you.*>

Clo craned her head, searching for the familiar shape of *Zelus* silhouetted against the clouds. The shooting above had stopped. The uncrewed craft had crashed into the city below.

Every gerulae still alive in the compound had been compelled to leave by Rhea.

"I have—to let them—go," Rhea said, grimacing. Her body was shivering again.

"Shit," Clo whispered. <*Eris! Rhea's struggling to hold the gerulae.*>

<*One. More. Minute.*>

"Hold on, love," Clo said to Rhea. "Hold them a moment longer."

Rhea gritted her teeth. She was slowing them down, her focus entirely on holding the gerulae. Kyla looped back and picked up Rhea.

Rhea sagged against the commander, her breath coming fast. "Please," she whispered. "Please hurry."

Eris's voice almost made Clo sob. <*I'm where I need to be. Don't worry.*> A pause. <*Let go, Rhea.*>

Rhea finally lost consciousness.

Clo had heard something in Eris's voice. As they ran beneath the grand archway of the palace to the outer buildings, Clo called to her again. <*Eris? Are you all right?*>

They had to climb over the rubble. Clo's throat was sore.

But with every step, her dread deepened.

60.

ERIS

Present day

< ***B**e right behind you,>* Eris told the others as she whirled and smashed her fist into Damocles' face.

They both staggered. Eris's vision swam as she tried to find her footing but failed. She collapsed onto the hard floor of the engine room with the weight of the knife in her back. It was mere seconds, but her mind cataloged her wound: the depth of it (deep into tissue and muscle, glancing off bone); the weight of the blade (heavier than she expected); the sudden heat of electric shocks that crashed over her in waves. And like being thrown into the sea, Eris struggled to find her breath and pull her body to the surface.

Her father's voice came to her from a distant memory, an echo of old training: *On your feet, Discordia.*

In battle, seconds were fatal.

Eris shoved to her feet, turning as Damocles recovered. Her vision swam—pain pulsed in time with her blood, the nanites working overtime to stem the red.

"Another way in?" she asked. Her words came out in a single breath.

He didn't seem surprised by her quick recovery. The royal cohort had been engineered and technologically altered to endure and inflict as much damage as possible. But even Eris couldn't survive if she lost too much nanite-infused blood.

"Secondary hatch near the research labs," her brother said with a smirk. "They didn't really use children, at least not that I'm aware."

She could feel the warmth of blood soaking through her jacket. The electric pulses grew more intense.

She shook her head against the stars bursting in front of her vision. "But you knew I'd believe it. After everything Father did to us."

"I knew you'd believe it, because caring makes you weak."

An echo of the words she'd said to him so long before. When they'd played another game, in another room, and she'd held a blade to his throat. She'd won their match that day.

She prayed she'd win it again.

"This is our last game." Eris slid a hand to her ancient blaster and pulled it from the holster. Her brother stared at the weapon as if waiting for her to use it, but Eris only said, "Hand to hand, Damocles. I challenge you." She tossed the blaster aside and beckoned with her fingers. "Make it worth my while."

Damocles launched himself at her. Even with the knife in Eris's back, every movement making her want to scream, she matched him hit for hit. It wasn't easy. She didn't fight with her usual grace, like she was water moving over rocks. Every punch took effort. Every block strained her bones. Every kick brought a blinding strobe of light in front of her eyes, but she fought to remain conscious.

She battled her own body while she battled her brother, a war on two fronts. It was not determination that spurred her, no. It was desperation: people depended on her. They were gathered outside the Temple, fighting for the AI controlling their minds. They were the rebels in the sky, making a stand against tyranny. They were her friends, who she had sworn to protect from that very first mission. She had promised them new lives, safety, a better future.

Eris had abandoned this galaxy once to her brother's control. She would not fucking do it again.

<*Clo, Kyla,*> she said, blocking Damocles' hit. She delivered another hard blow to his face that sent him staggering. <*You out?*>

<*Clear.*> Kyla's reply was terse. <*We're out below the south wing. What's your ETA?*>

Damocles recovered fast with a punch to her gut. Eris's breath left her as the pain bloomed. Her body began to grow sluggish from the blood loss, the sticky liquid continuing to seep through her jumpsuit. Every time Damocles threw her to the ground, blood splattered against the pocked, ancient metal.

<Just finishing up.> She tried to keep her mental voice strong; she couldn't let them suspect the extent of her injury. She ducked Damocles' next blow and gave him a right hook that sent him sprawling. *<Right behind you.>*

Eris took advantage of Damocles' distraction. She hurried to the panel and checked the numbers printed on the sign below the message involving the Oracle. She hoped to the gods they were the numbers to the shutdown sequence. If they weren't . . .

Footsteps at her back. Eris whirled as Damocles came at her, faster than before. Or maybe she was slower, her reflexes dulled from blood loss. Even nanites couldn't heal her with the blade still lodged in her back; Damocles knew it. He seemed to be toying with her, doing his best to exhaust her.

On your feet, Discordia! Her father's shout from her memories.

Eris recalled all those brutal lessons. Fighting in the cold that froze her sweat. Battling dozens of soldiers with any number of injuries as her vision wove in and out—same as now. Sitting in the darkness with Damocles, with only one word on her lips: *survive.*

Survive.

<Eris!> Clo's voice. *<Rhea's struggling to hold the gerulae.>*

<One>—She drove her boot into Damocles' kneecap—*<more>*— uppercut to his torso—*<minute!>*—and finished him off with a punch that sent him reeling back.

She raced to the panel. Her hands shook as she pressed the last numbers, fingertips leaving their bloody impressions behind. She half-collapsed against the panel as she slid the valve into place. Almost immediately, the whirring of the engine around her began to slow.

Relief burned within her. She had done it.

<I'm where I need to be.> Her breathing came fast as she fought to remain upright. *<Don't worry. Let go, Rhea.>*

Damocles jerked the knife out and drove it back in. Eris's knees buckled. Damocles took her down, and his swift twist of the blade left Eris gasping.

A minute later, Clo's voice echoed in Eris's mind. *<Eris? Are you all right?>*

<Listen,> she said, and she knew the hiss of pain was even in her thoughts. *<Take care of each other, all right? It'll be okay.>*

She gave Damocles a bitter laugh. "So, what's the next play on the board?" Her words were slurred; her tongue was so heavy. "One is already shut off."

She could feel his grip on the blade loosening. He'd given her a mortal injury, after all. Now he was only there to make sure he finished the job and, by some miracle, she didn't walk out of this Temple alive. "You might have turned the Oracle off," he said casually, "but the Temple still holds One's data and coding structure. I'll engineer a new AI under my control, and every citizen still has a chip. Then I'll rule the way I always intended. Nothing will be lost."

Clo was screaming in her mind. *<What do you mean, 'Take care of each other'? Eris?>*

<You know there's no place for me in the Empire's ruins.> Her voice was a tired whisper. *<I was always meant to burn along with it.>*

<No! Don't you fucking dare!> Clo snarled. *<Eris, you don't give up! You—>*

<I've given too many names to the God of Death.> Eris felt almost . . . at peace? She was warm, not burning. The pain was leaving her. *<If you worship any new gods after all this, I hope you'll include Eleos. Mercy.>*

<Eris, don't,> Clo begged. *<Don't do this. Don't do this to us. We need you. I need you.>*

<Say last rites for me down on that beach on Fortuna. Remember what I told you? Throw my scythe into the sea and erase Discordia from the galaxy.> Eris felt her lips curving into a smile. No pain now, only an immense lightness. She sagged in Damocles' arms. *<It's been an honor to know you all.>*

"Admit that I'm better than you, Discordia," Damocles said. "King kills Queen. Say it."

Eris started to laugh, a wheezing, trembling sound. To her ears, it was glorious. It was freeing. She'd never felt so free in her life. Damocles' face hardened, and he shook her.

"*Fucking say it.* I won, Discordia."

"You lose, Damocles." Discordia grinned and used her last remaining strength to tear open her jacket.

Explosives lined her chest. This had always been her plan B. Disrupt the game. Break the rules. Knock all the pieces off the board.

Burn the fucking game to ash.

Damocles' eyes bulged, but it was too late. Eris had two more souls to send to the God of Death.

"Queen kills King, asshole."

And Eris ignited.

61.

RHEA

Present day

Rhea's body and mind had been wound tight as a bowstring. She let herself loosen. The gerulae unbraided and unspooled, slipping from her mind in loose threads. She bid them farewell and came back to awareness. Her body still hurt. Her temples pulsed with pain.

But emotions bloomed uninterrupted around her, fireflies flickering in the darkness. The different auras were mostly fear, pain, confusion—a riot of deep violets, oranges, and jagged yellows.

"They're waking up," Rhea gasped.

The Devils had all stopped on a lawn, maybe a quarter-mile from the palace. Sher lay on the ground. Cato was still panting from the effort of carrying the other man. Kyla had spread her jacket over her co-commander to keep him warm, her hand on his shoulder.

Sher moaned, and Kyla murmured something to him. He blinked up at her, dazed but aware. He reached a trembling hand up to her, and Kyla clasped his hand with a laughing sob.

"The Oracle is gone," Rhea said, wonderingly. "One is—" She stopped as she caught sight of Clo's face. "Clo?" she asked faintly.

The other woman's grip on her hand tightened. Tears streaked clean tracks down her grimy cheeks. Why was Clo crying?

Rhea's head whipped in the direction of the ruined palace and the

Temple a millisecond before an explosion sounded in the distance. She felt it deep in her bones, the blast reverberating in her chest.

"Oh, no," Rhea said, realizing who was missing.

"Eris," Clo said brokenly.

The Temple's spire, just visible above the palace's outer walls, lit with flames like a candle.

<Eris?> Clo sent over the Pathos. *<Please tell me you had some plan to get out. That you're around here somewhere and you'll walk right up with that self-satisfied smirk and—and—>*

And not be dead, Rhea finished the thought in a private corner of her head.

Kyla shut her eyes hard. Cato's expression petrified as he concealed his grief somewhere deep, but it seeped from his aura. Ariadne clung to Cato's neck, crying the loudest. Rhea's own eyes were dry. It would hit later, she knew, and it would overwhelm her.

Rhea reached over and wiped the tears from Clo's face. "She saved us. She saved us all."

Clo nodded, her breathing tight and ragged. "I know. And I'm so fucking mad at her. I want to shake her. I want—" Her words sputtered out on a choking sob.

"I know, Clo," Rhea said. "I know."

Behind them, on the ruined former lawn of the Palace, *Zelus* set down. The ship was nearly destroyed, its hull battered, but Rhea had never been so glad to see it. The door to the hatch opened, and Nyx and Elva came down the ramp, Nyx leaning hard on her cane. Her face was stricken.

"Eris," Nyx whispered.

Her gaze lifted to the flames, but she did not seem surprised. Eris and Nyx had often seen the world the same way. Nyx had wanted to sacrifice herself, and now Rhea understood why Eris had convinced her not to—because she had already made her plan to do the same.

Ariadne moved from Cato over to Nyx, and Nyx let herself be hugged, one hand stroking the back of Ariadne's head. She locked eyes with Cato, and some unspoken message went between them. His aura had once been a chaos of colors, but now they swirled around him like calm clouds—greens and blues.

Elva had her arms wrapped tight around herself, swaying. She would be just as overwhelmed as Rhea by the onslaught of all the gerulae waking up. Elva caught eyes with Rhea and nodded. The Evoli's walls were up tight. She still didn't know if, when Elva looked at her, she saw someone Tholosian or Evoli. Rhea decided she didn't care.

Rhea imagined what Clo had wanted. She pictured Eris somehow emerging from the flames unscathed, a fury that could not be slain. She let herself imagine Eris in full armor, her blond hair like a corona from the fire behind her, eyes blazing bright and triumphant. She'd be blushed with bruises and cuts that still bled, but she would be beautiful and terrible in equal measure. Rhea smiled, imagining that Eris would tilt her head up and tell them—

"Queen kills King," Rhea said aloud. She pitched her voice to carry.

The others echoed her, all slightly out of time with each other. *Queen kills King.*

Queen kills King.

They all watched as the rest of the Temple caught fire and burned even brighter. They stayed until the spire fell.

62.

KYLA

Present day

Kyla had spent so much time wondering if she'd make it until tomorrow.

It was three weeks after the fall of the Oracle, and now every day was the tomorrow she'd fought for. Now she had to pick up the pieces.

Vast swathes of Vita had been demolished in the battle, and next to nothing remained of the palace. When citizens recovered from the shock of being freed from the Oracle's programming, all had descended into chaos. Some rioted against the Empire's nobles. Throughout the Empire, generals and legates had their throats slit, and their blood was left to congeal in the dirt. Some took their rage out on the palace on Tholos, breaking it apart brick by brick until it was nothing but rubble and scraps of metal.

Elsewhere, Empire loyalists blamed the Novantae, vowing justice for the murder of their new Archon.

Yet, to Kyla's surprise, she had been relatively well supported for initial leadership. Her rebels came to her defense, and the memory of being gerulae was still fresh in everyone's minds. The entire galaxy was still recovering from the trauma of being passengers in their own bodies.

One day, Kyla might have contenders for her role, or she might decide it was time to step down if someone better emerged. Until then, she had work to do.

Kyla was in her study on *Zelus*, poring over the reports. The looting was the least of her concerns: buildings could be rebuilt, and goods could be replaced; human lives could not. She scrolled past the aerial photos of the destroyed palace and the blackened husk of *Argonaut*.

(Eris was in there somewhere.)

Kyla flinched and flicked her finger across the screen.

It wasn't all disorder. The Novantae and Vita citizens had worked together to recover the dead and gave a grand funeral for those lost. They'd set up tents as temporary accommodation for those who no longer had homes. Some spoke out about their experiences as gerulae and the Empire's tyranny. For the first time in decades, they made their voices heard without Imperial punishment.

Kyla gave a weary sigh. She'd been running ragged since the Battle of Tholos. She organized incoming aid from the Evoli, keeping the underlying mechanisms of interplanetary logistics running as smoothly as possible.

(At night, doubt settled on her shoulders. Had she done the right thing? Had she made everything worse? Was this newfound trust misplaced?)

Of course, Tholosians still mistrusted the Evoli, emerging peace treaty or not. Counterrevolutionaries had attacked a few emissaries. Skirmishes broke out. Throughout the galaxy, planets realized that those subtle cultural differences between solar systems were thin edges of levers, and the distance between them was only widening. Programming had forced an absolute Tholosian culture across a galaxy.

Without it, differences dissolved the hegemony.

Kyla worked with it. The Empire had an existing network of satellite legates she had contacted to begin arranging a loose federation of planets bound by peace treaties similar to the Tholosian agreement with the Evoli.

It was like trying to tie angry, hissing snakes into a tidy bow.

Everywhere they turned, new groups called for power. Some legates openly called for Kyla's execution. Others took her side and cobbled together a tenuous agreement to enforce existing laws. More than a few legates were furious at the Evoli for recognizing Kyla as an interim leader in the new peace talks, which undermined their own power. They accused Vyga of open war against the Empire for the Evoli's part in attacking the palace.

"What a fucking mess," she muttered.

"I can tell," said a voice from the doorway.

Kyla looked up to see Sher leaning against the doorframe. He was still recovering from being under the Oracle's control, his body thinner and frailer than she'd ever seen it. Still, she was so damn glad to see him alive. She'd thought she'd lost him.

"The legates on Auriga are offering a reward for my head," Kyla said to Sher, throwing her tablet on the desk. "Remind me again why I'm not leaving the diplomacy shit to someone else?"

"Because you're no good at quitting," Sher said, settling into the chair across from Kyla. "And because this is our mess. We agreed a long time ago that we wouldn't break the Empire and leave it to someone else to clean up. We'd accept responsibility for whatever came after."

He pushed back his hair, his fingertips brushing against the injuries along his cheek. "But there's no shame if you don't want this anymore. You deserve rest."

He was letting his hair grow longer to cover what would become new scars. As he picked up Kyla's tablet and scrolled through the reports, she studied his sharp, weary features. This was the man who had fought beside her in battles they didn't believe in, until they decided to risk everything fighting the ones they did. This man had built a revolution with her, nearly died dozens of times, and saved her life.

Their revolution was over, and he was still there: reminding her of what mattered. Of old agreements and obligations. Of the duty they had to the galaxy before themselves.

"You're right, and I don't know how to rest. How are you feeling?" Kyla asked softly.

Sher had a memory gap of about five or six months where he had been under Oracle's control. He remembered Angora, he had told her. He remembered feeling strange, thinking he should get checked out at the med bay. His thought processes had changed so subtly, though. He'd compared it to being slowly boiled: by the time he realized it was hot, it was too late—he was already cooked.

After that, his body no longer responded to his commands, and he was tucked away in a little corner of his mind. He could still watch himself commit treason. He could hear his lips give orders he never wanted to. He had felt his fingers on the Mors as he almost killed Kyla and Clo on Laguna.

His body had finally, finally awakened in the Temple when his hands were around Clo's throat. He hadn't liked telling Kyla that part.

He waved a hand. "Still shit. Rhea says it'll pass. That if I keep doing the work, eventually I'll stop blaming myself so much."

Rhea had set up an offshoot of the medical center, partnering with doctors, Evoli, and Ariadne to clear the residue of Oracle programming from Tholosian minds. Plenty were suspicious of the cure, but others were grateful for the help.

"For what it's worth," Kyla said, "I don't blame you for anything."

Sher made a face. "Oh, come on. You do a little, and that's okay. Rhea said you might eventually stop blaming yourself, too."

Kyla looked down at her desk and blinked very quickly. Her eyes were dry.

Soldiers didn't cry.

"Hey," Sher said, clearing his throat and changing the subject as she slyly grabbed a tissue. "Do you remember that night, not long after we settled on Nova, when the power went out?"

Kyla gave a watery laugh. "The first of a hundred thousand times?"

"Yeah. That dust storm blocked out the sun for a day and a half. You, me, and Athena were holed up in that ramshackle hut and thought that was it. The sand was just gonna keep blowing, rising up against the doors and the windows until we'd be buried alive. And what did you say?"

She laughed again. "I don't even remember, Sher. I was so drunk to dull the fear."

Sher smirked. "You said, 'At least I'll go down trying.' And then you polished off that bottle and keeled over."

"Sounds like something I'd say while drunk."

"Yeah, you passed out like a second later. Almost threw up on Athena."

"And when I woke up, the storm had passed," Kyla said with a smile. "I had to swim in sand to get out, but then I walked out into that blazing sunshine with the biggest hangover of my fucking life. It was so damn bright."

Sher gestured toward the window—to the remains of Vita, the palace, the whole blasted universe. All of it broken. "This is the sandstorm," he said. "This is the part where it still seems dark, but the wind has changed direction." He smiled at her, and it was a lopsided, broken thing. But it was a smile. "That's what I choose to believe, anyway."

"You've always been so fucking idealistic. It's almost sickening." Kyla paused. She thought of setting it down. Walking away. She couldn't imagine it. When it came right down to it, she wanted to be there. Maybe not at the nadir but definitely in the thick of it. "When do you think you'll be ready to take a public-facing role? You're better at all this than me." She could go back to the shadows, lining up her plans, like she did best.

Sher heaved a long sigh. "I think I have to stay retired from that a while longer, sis." *Maybe forever,* the silence that followed seemed to say. "I think it's my turn to stay in the shadows. Let you lead. Help you pick up the pieces while you get your time in the light."

She'd known that would be his answer. Kyla rose and went to the window, watching the construction, the ships flying overhead. It was beginning to look at least somewhat systemic out there. She couldn't stop the sudden yawn that threatened to crack her face.

"When's the last time you slept?" Sher asked.

"Oh, I dunno. At some point." She rubbed her face. "I still have to get through all these missives, though."

Sher pointed to the cot. "Sleep. I can read and give you the bullet points of the bullet points. It can be my new non-public-facing role."

"You want to be my fucking secretary?" Kyla asked, eyebrows raised.

Sher rolled his eyes. "It's a favor. Take it."

Kyla shrugged out of her jacket and kicked off her boots, collapsing into the cot. Sher pulled the blanket up around her like she was a kid still in the nursery. Kyla liked it. Already, her eyelids were heavy.

"Hey," she called, as Sher struggled to his feet and moved over to the desk (still so slowly that it pained her to see).

"Hm?" he answered, already skimming the documents.

"Have you talked to Clo yet?"

His shoulders hunched as he pored over the messages.

"Sher," Kyla said, sleepy enough to be even blunter than usual. "It's been weeks. Talk to her."

"I don't think she wants me to. Every time I enter a room, she runs away."

"She's got more guilt than the both of us put together," Kyla said, half-asleep. "Just talk to her. She needs it as much as you. That's an order, secretary."

"You're going to enjoy bossing me around, aren't you?"

"You bet your ass I will." As she fell asleep, she heard his resigned sigh, and she smiled.

63.

ARIADNE

Present day

 month after the Battle of Tholos, Ariadne had the observation room on *Zelus* all to herself.

She tapped the button on the controls to render the floor panel transparent, leaving the room surrounded by a vast ocean of stars. When Ariadne walked to the center of the room, she began removing the stones from her pocket to set each one on the now-invisible ground.

Callista, she thought, nudging the first rock into place—the one that matched the distant nebulae. *Autolycus*, the fire opal with a heart like a sunset. *Valerius*, the fossil with bands of shimmering opal. *Evander*, a cloudy stone with inclusions that wrapped together like seaweed. *Augustus*, a glittering geode that resembled the stars beyond the metal walls of the ship. *Selene*, with its orthogonal composition and shades that reminded Ariadne of the interior of a machine. *Hector*, with its crystallized patterns like a blue rose in bloom. *Penelope*, with jutting, pink crystals. *Iris*, the opalized shell the colors of the sea on Fortuna.

All the Engineers she knew, who she took with her to the stars. Who were finally liberated from the prison the Oracle had crafted for them. They would travel with Ariadne for as long as she lived—however long that was. The probabilities the Oracle predicted no longer scared her.

Instead, they reminded her that life was fragile. Precious. She understood that better now.

Eris had taught her that.

So, she removed the final stone in her pocket and placed it with the others—her reminder that every day in freedom was better than a lifetime in a cage. *Eris.* Her spiky black-and-purple stone flashed when she held it to the light. She'd carry a piece of her friend with her always.

Smiling sadly, Ariadne rose to her feet. She let herself spin, as if she was another planet in the galaxy. A heavenly body free to drift and spin in the vast infinitude of space.

Her life finally belonged to her.

———

Later, Ariadne found Nyx outside the ship's med bay, watching Cato and Rhea working with the former Novantae gerulae.

Cato, Rhea, and Ariadne's methods and therapies to rid people of the Oracle's lingering programming were coming along nicely. They had sent the information to all planets, Tholosian and Evoli alike. Other centers were being established in all corners of the galaxy. While One's tendrils were receding, the effects of the Oracle's manipulation would remain for a long time. Like Cato, Kyla, and Nyx, citizens had to learn to live with the remnants—and choose their paths forward.

Ariadne's eyes stung. "I don't want you to go," she said to Nyx.

Nyx had decided to leave the heart of the Empire. Ariadne knew the ex-soldier was still fatigued from the ichor virus, that the fallout of the Empire's demise required more work than she had energy for. Ariadne was trying not to be selfish.

Leaving isn't the same as being dead, she reminded herself.

But she wanted Nyx with her. Ariadne wanted to make sure she was okay. Alive. Maybe she needed a new cane or a hoverchair. Ariadne could build one with weapons in it. With a place for special rocks. Anything.

As if Nyx read Ariadne's panicked thoughts, she sighed.

"Look," Nyx said softly, tapping a finger against her cane. "I'm not leaving right this minute. I'm staying for the funeral. You don't need to cry. You can visit me whenever you like on my homestead. It'll be just me and some livestock for company. Probably. Maybe."

Ariadne swiped at her eyes. "Can I send you Named Things?"

Nyx gave a short laugh. "Yeah. I'll let you keep a whole fucking shelf for when you come to visit. Just don't put any plants on there and expect me to remember to water them."

"I'll remember for her." Cato had separated from the gerulae and came over with a grin. "I can instruct Rhea long-distance, and I'm craving some calm after all this. Tending plants, feeding livestock. Unless you'd prefer the company of cattle for a while."

"Nah, I can fit you in. Some livestock, some birds, and a Cato. But just so you know, I can't cook for shit."

He smiled. "Neither can I."

"Two disasters living together. Can't wait."

A smug glow of pride filled Ariadne. She knew Cato and Nyx had been taking things slowly. Ariadne and Clo made heart shapes with their hands when they saw them together. Which reminded her . . .

She made heart hands. "You two are soooo cute."

Nyx rolled her eyes. "Stop with the heart shit."

"I love the heart shit," Cato said.

"See? Cato understands me." Ariadne's mind belatedly caught on a word. "Oh, my gods, the livestock! You're going to have livestock! That means I can name them."

Nyx gave an aggrieved sigh. "You're going to give them ridiculous names, aren't you?"

"One *has* to be named Spoon. Another could be Princess Margaret Kettlebum. Margie for short. But I'll have to decide for sure when I see them."

Oh, right. She remembered again: Nyx was leaving. Ariadne's eyes stung and watered once more.

Nyx noticed, and her expression gentled further. "You sure you want to stay? You'll have a lot to deal with here. Just because we freed people from the Oracle doesn't mean they won't make bad choices. People like easy answers. And a few of them might take advantage of that. You might have a bunch of mediocre assholes out there leaping at the chance to call themselves Emperor Dickhead, or whatever."

Cato gave her a face. "Emperor Dickhead? Really?"

Nyx rolled her eyes. "As if you didn't call Damocles Archon Asshole with the rest of us." Nyx returned her attention to Ariadne, who was uselessly trying to wipe away her tears. "My point is, not everyone is going to be like us. They're going to be violent, or they might be complete fuckwads. It's going to be messy for a while before it gets better. We're already seeing it; there just hasn't been a big-enough clusterfuck to get us worried yet."

Cato gave her a stern look. "Maybe it's best not to terrify her."

Ariadne was going to miss Cato, too. Her eyes got even wetter.

Nyx pressed her lips together. "Stop with the tears. Okay? If the shit hits the fan, you can stay with us. Eat our bad food."

Ariadne nodded, giving one last swipe with her sleeve. Freedom meant letting other people go, too. She had to stay and clean up the mess she'd been responsible for. Helping rid the galaxy of the Oracle wasn't enough. Now she had to put in the work and support the people she'd helped the Oracle control.

"I know. But I have to stay for now and help. I want to."

"Good, kid." Nyx watched Rhea hold the hand of a former gerulae from Tholos. "Besides, if you need me . . ."

Ariadne slid her pinky into Nyx's. "I know, you'll only be a hyperjump or two away. I'll visit you. Whenever I need to, and even when I don't."

Ariadne squeezed Nyx's pinky finger and let go.

EPILOGUE

CLO

Present day

The Devils took a break from trying to fix a fractured galaxy to fly to Fortuna.

It'd taken most of a month to make *Zelus* star-ready again, but the repairs kept Clo's hands busy while Kyla worked to rebuild Vita. Clo was glad to leave the uncertainty behind and see the Devils again.

After a brief separation, they were all home in their ship. Rhea and Nyx were resting in their old rooms. Cato planned a little experiment in the med bay with Ariadne. Elva was down in the engine room, making sure everything was working as needed. Clo and Rhea were spending more time with Elva and Nils in particular. Clo was still figuring things out about herself, and Nils was always happy to listen. They'd given Clo a nonbinary Evoli collar as a gift, which Clo treasured, stroking the soft silk. Kyla was always poring over documents at her desk and sneaking more sweets from the top drawer. Sher helped her, sometimes trailing off in the middle of a sentence to stare with an unfocused, haunted look, but he was improving.

Clo had avoided him for weeks, but he'd eventually tracked her down.

She'd almost bailed when he knocked at her door and asked if they could talk. She awkwardly sat on her and Rhea's shared bed, and he took the desk chair. He sometimes moved almost as slowly as Linus, who had decided to stay with the Evoli once he recovered his memories.

"I don't blame you if you hate me," he started.

Clo stared determinedly at the hole in the knees of her favorite trousers. Her throat was tight.

"And I don't blame you for leaving me on Laguna. I'm glad you gave me a chance."

Her head snapped up at that. "How can you say that?" she said, somehow finding her voice. "You were thrown right back into the Oracle's clutches because of me. You came *this* close to being gerulae for good." She held her index finger and thumb close to touching.

"But I didn't. Because you called me back from the brink. I heard you through everything. You gave me the strength to fight back."

Her cheeks were damp from the dripping tears. She heard him rise, shuffle over to the bed, and sit next to her.

"I don't feel strong right now," Clo admitted. "We have to go out there and say goodbye. And I'm not ready to say goodbye to everyone we lost."

"Especially Eris," he said, quiet.

"Especially her," she managed.

His arm came around her, and she was little more than a kid again. She felt as raw as after her ma's murder, when Sher had come to take her away from the Snarl. And she was crying, and crying, so hard she thought she would never stop.

He didn't whisper any platitudes. He didn't tell her it'd be all right. He just let her sob against his shoulder, and Clo was pretty sure he cried a little, too. It didn't erase everything that had happened between them, but it mended it a little. Time would heal the rest.

They were all learning to let go of the past.

So, their small crew sailed through the stars for one final mission.

Clo guided *Zelus*, taking a familiar route back to Fortuna. She flew through the atmosphere, the clouds turning the view from the windshield into nothing but soft, gray tendrils of mist. She broke through. The iron sea stretched below, dotted with islands and the deep green of pine.

Clo set down the ship exactly where they had just a few months before, and together, the Devils headed down to the beach. She still didn't feel strong.

Waves crashed on the shore. The wind was sharp with the scent of seaweed and salt.

There was no body to bury. They hadn't been able to find any bones among the wreckage they could definitively say were Eris's. The explosion had burned so fiercely, with Eris at its epicenter. She had been the cause.

Sometimes, Clo let herself pretend that Eris had faked her death again to spare any goodbyes. That one day, Clo might be in a market on some backwater planet, looking over engine parts. And then she'd look up and see an unfamiliar face but still somehow recognize her as Eris. The features would ripple back into the friend she knew, and Eris would flash her two scythes with a smile before melting back into the crowd.

It was a pleasant daydream that sometimes brought comfort. But Clo knew it was only that.

Eris was not coming back.

Ariadne stood close to Nyx and Cato. Nyx was looking a little better, but she still tired quickly. Sher sat in a hoverchair they'd brought from the ship, and Kyla stood behind him, hands on his shoulders as she stared out at the sea.

Rhea stepped forward. She held a small machine and placed it on the sand, pressing the button. A life-size icon emerged, but it was different from all those of Princess Discordia. It was Eris as the Devils had known her, smirk and all. She was dressed in a plain black jumpsuit, hair long and unbound, with her antique blaster in one hand and her brother's firewolf in the other.

Clo held Eris's scythe necklace in her hand, the metal pressing tight into her palm.

She still didn't feel strong. She almost didn't want to let it go.

But she knew she had to.

One by one, the Devils came up to the icon and said their last rites, their prayers to a new god. Eleon. Mercy.

Just as Eris had asked.

Perhaps no one believed in that god, but beliefs were shifting around the galaxy. Maybe souls didn't go ,to the Avern. Maybe they went somewhere better—or perhaps they went nowhere at all, returning to some grand collective of the universe.

Clo went last, and when she finished, she stood next to the transparent icon of her friend and stared at the Devils. She wasn't comfortable with speeches, never felt eloquent enough. But Clo had to say something. She had to try.

She cleared her throat. "I've been thinking about the future. What we'll become. What Eris would have wanted the galaxy to be like. We were the resistance, and now we're building something new in the Empire's place. Hopefully, something better.

"But here's the thing I've learned: resistance doesn't end—it only rests. Whatever we build, no matter how idealistic we are, power has a way of corrupting. Eventually, there will be another resistance against what we've created. But that's good. We should always question those who say they know what's best for us. We should always ask ourselves if we're doing what's right. Eris did that."

Clo licked her lips. "Eris said that there was no place for her in this new galaxy. She had too much blood on her hands. She represented the old Tholosian regime, even if she helped take it down. If she'd been given any job, people might still see her as a princess. Might still want her to be the ruler. So, she left the galaxy to us. She trusted us with it."

Clo's throat closed. She gave herself a moment to let the feeling pass. "We're going to make mistakes. We're going to fuck up. Some stuff we'll do right, and we'll make some lives better. We're never going to feel strong. It'll always feel like it's gonna break us. We just have to keep doing our best. Admit when we're wrong, and always, always keep trying to make it better. It's a job that will never end. It never should."

"Hear, hear!" Kyla said, and a ripple of laughter circled the group.

"To trying!" Rhea said.

"To trying," echoed the others.

Rhea stepped forward and picked up the icon. The Devils all waded into the sea, their clothes soon wet and heavy. Clo left her Evoli prosthetic on the beach, and Rhea helped her into the water. Goosebumps prickled along Clo's arms.

Rhea placed the icon on the waves. Eris's projection watched them, and then she flickered out as the sea took her. She'd settle somewhere, shining in the darkness until the power wore out in a few years.

Clo gripped the scythes in her hand and kissed her closed fist. Then she pulled her arm back and threw the necklace as far as she could. The weak sunlight caught the metal before it splashed into the sea.

Rhea drew her close, and they kept each other warm in the cold water. The others spoke and laughed as they walked back to the shore to dry themselves off. They'd have a feast soon, and drink would flow—the good stuff that Eris would have approved of, no cheap swill.

Clo would dance with Rhea.

She would celebrate with the family she had found, in the home they had made.

Clo's fingers caught Rhea's. Some of the stars were beginning to come out, bright points in a violet sky.

No, Clo didn't have any certainties. None of them had answers. They were all making it up as they went along. That was half the beauty of it: giving it your all and seeing what the morning brought.

And every day, she'd celebrate being alive.

ACKNOWLEDGMENTS

And so we come to the end of the Seven Devils duology. We first wanted to thank our readers for taking this journey with us. So many of you messaged us with excitement at every stage, and we couldn't be more grateful to you all.

We'd also like to express our immense appreciation to our editors, Leah Spann and Betsy Wollheim of DAW, and Rachel Winterbottom of Gollancz. The teams at DAW and Gollancz who worked behind the scenes: Joshua Starr, Will O'Mullane, Jessica Plummer, Richard Shealy, Alexis Nixon, and everyone else whose names we are forgetting, but who deserve our credit and thanks for putting these books into the hands of readers. That includes our agents, Juliet Mushens and Russ Galen, who we also thank for keeping us tethered.

El would personally like to thank: Hannah Kaner for providing a corner of her living room, food, and whisky a few times as I fast-drafted in November 2020, and for all the cheerleading before and after. To Noelle Harrison, Pete Freestone, Julia Ember, Erica Harney, David Bishop, Daniel Shand, and the other friends who dealt with my whinging about how I was never going to write a book with seven points of view again. As ever, thanks to my mom and my partner Craig. And my cats, who sometimes cuddled while I wrote, but often walked across my keyboard because they can be little shits. Here's the part of the acknowledgements where I worry I've left someone out, so hats off to everyone who supported me. You're all so wonderful and I'm so glad to have you in my life.

426   ACKNOWLEDGMENTS

Another massive outpouring of gratitude to the readers who picked up *Seven Devils* and helped spread the word. I hope you enjoyed *Seven Mercies*.

And, of course, a thank you to Elizabeth, for messaging me in all caps about the dream you had about us writing *Mad Max: Fury Road* in space. Still can't quite believe we did it.

Elizabeth would like to personally thank Mr. May, as always, for being the best husband and supportive partner. He asked no questions when she decided that she worked best between the hours of 9PM to 4AM.

To the incomparable Tess Sharpe, who also asks no questions when I text her at 3AM my time second-guessing myself. Truly, I would not be the writer that I am without her encouragement.

And of course, to El, who went on this seven(!) year journey with me to craft seven characters, two books, and an entire galaxy of tyrants and badass rebels.

I'm so proud of us.